CAT IN A YELLOW SPOTLIGHT
A MIDNIGHT LOUIE MYSTERY

Wishlist Publishing
PO Box 331555
Fort Worth TX 76133-1555

Visit our website at www.wishlistpublishing.com

ALSO BY CAROLE NELSON DOUGLAS

Midnight Louie Mysteries

CAT in a
YELLOW SPOTLIGHT

The Twenty-sixth Midnight Louie Mystery

by Carole Nelson Douglas

"Snaps and glitters like the town that inspired it."
—*NORA ROBERTS*

WISHLIST BOOKS

For visionary WMG Publishing founders
Kristine Kathryn Rusch and Dean Wesley Smith,
with a special bouquet to Renaissance woman Allyson
Longueira,
thanks for all the support

Cat in a Yellow Spotlight: A Midnight Louie Mystery
A Wishlist Book

This is a work of fiction. Names, characters, places, and incidents
are either the product of the author's imagination or are used
fictitiously. Any resemblance to actual persons, living or dead,
events, or locales is entirely coincidental.

The copying, reproduction, and distribution of this eBook via any
means without permission of the author is illegal and punishable
by law. Please purchase only authorized electronic editions and
refuse to participate in or encourage the electronic piracy of copy-
righted materials. Your support of the author's intellectual rights
are appreciated.

All rights reserved
Copyright ©August 2014 by Carole Nelson Douglas

Copy Editor: Mary Moran
Formatter: Diane Tarbuck
Images Copyright © iStock.com
Cover and interior book design and images Copyright © Carole
Nelson Douglas

Library of Congress Cataloging-in-Publication Data

Printed in the United States of America

ISBN: 978-1500926205

9/29/14 Amazon 13.74

CAT IN A
YELLOW
SPOTLIGHT

CONTENTS

Previously in
Midnight Louie's
Lives & Times...

By the hair of my chinny-chin-chin (and other tender places), have I just undergone a proper perp-battling moment! Picture a crazed sociopath gone ballistic, picture knife-and-claw play. Shots fired. Shivs slashing. Blood shed.

O Holy Guacamole mayhem, Midnight Louie has been present in person at what resembles a season-ender episode of *CSI: Las Vegas*.

This very moment at police headquarters—relocated from its classic "downtown" address to a brand-new "campus" on Vegas' MLK Boulevard—the local forensic geeks have me by the jet-black short hairs. They are even now examining my long white whiskers and my shredded translucent nail sheaths for crucial DNA evidence from the scene of the crime.

My posse, both human and feline members, had their lives on the line, but the new Las Vegas Cat Pack came through the confrontation with snaggle-tooth and ragged nail mostly intact. The outcome is that we are all under suspicion of whatever went down, and, like the Cat Pack, the offending psycho is nowhere to be found.

I am not the only one among the wounded—if you count broken nails as a wound, and I do. Mr. Matt Devine was shot in the side, not seriously only because I launched my twenty fully-packed pounds at the perp's weapon as the gun fired. He is recovering nicely under the ministrations of my doughty roommate, Miss Temple Barr.

Mr. Max Kinsella received another blow to his already banged-up head. Who knows what setbacks his recovering AWOL memory may encounter?

The Cat Pack acted only as intimidating muscle, under my direction. However, their usual leader and my esteemed streetwise mother, Ma Barker, performed a banshee howl as I jumped the gun and then administered a four-shiv slash to the perp's face as a coup de gras.

This "coup de gras" is a classic ending move. I turned to the art of sword fighting and finished the assailant with a swipe across the face. Since our opponent is a female of the species, she will always see my handsome white-whiskered kisser and razor-sharp stilettos every time she looks in a mirror.

Perhaps I should formally introduce myself as founder and CEO of Midnight Investigations, Inc. I plied the mean streets of Las Vegas for many years as a bachelor about town, and then moved into PI work. I now have my own condo with my snazzy, red-gold-haired, live-in PR woman and amateur detective (thanks to me), Miss Temple Barr.

She may not be a Miss much longer if she weds Mr. Matt Devine as planned, alas. Our cozy condo does not need interlopers, especially on the king-size bed, which is perfect for the two of us right now, with my curl-upable twenty pounds and her one hundred.

Yes, she is a tiny thing as humans go, but she has the heart of a mountain lion and the relentless investigative instincts of a bloodhound. Actually, she is much more attractive than this characterization sounds.

So back to me again. Yes, Las Vegas is my beat.

For a Las Vegas institution, I have always kept a low profile. I like my nightlife shaken, not stirred. Being short, dark, and handsome... really short...gets me overlooked and underestimated, which is what the savvy operative wants anyway. I am your perfect undercover guy. Miss Temple Barr and I make ideal roomies. I like to hunker down under the covers with my little doll, but she also tolerates my wandering ways.

I play bodyguard without getting in her way. Call me Muscle in Midnight Black. We share a well-honed sense of justice and long, sharp fingernails and have cracked some cases too tough for the local fuzz. She is, after all, a freelance public relations specialist, and Las Vegas is full of public and private relations of all stripes and legalities.

So, there is much private investigative work left for me to do, as usual.

Then you get into the area of private lives. I say you get into that area. I do not. I remain aloof from these alien matters among humans. I will not give away the more intimate details of my roomie's life. Let me just say that everything it seemed you could bet on is now up for grabs and my Miss Temple may be in the lose-lose situation of her life and times.

Since Las Vegas is littered with guidebooks as well as bodies, I here provide a rundown of the local landmarks on my particular map of the world. A cast of characters, so to speak:

Here is the current status of who we are and where we are all at:

MIDNIGHT LOUIE, PI

None can deny that the Las Vegas crime scene is big time, and I have been treading these mean neon streets for twenty-six books now. I am an "alpha cat". Since my foundation volume, *Cat in an Alphabet Soup* (formerly *Catnap*) debuted, the title sequence features an alphabetical "color" word from A to Z, so *Cat in an Aqua Storm* (formerly *Pussyfoot*) is next, and followed by *Cat on a Blue Monday* and *Cat in a Crimson Haze,* etc. until we reach the, ahem, current volume, *Cat in a Yellow Spotlight.*

MISS TEMPLE BARR, PR

A freelance public relations ace, my lovely roommate is Miss Nancy Drew all grown up and in killer spikes. She had come to Las Vegas with her soon-to-be elusive ex-significant other...

MR. MAX KINSELLA, aka The Mystifying Max

He disappeared without a word to Miss Temple shortly after the Vegas move. This sometimes missing-in-action magician has good reason for invisibility. After his cousin Sean died in an Irish Republican Army bomb attack during a post high school jaunt to Ireland, Mr. Max joined the man who became his mentor, Garry Randolph, aka magician Gandolph the Great, in undercover counterterrorism work all over Europe.

Miss Temple's elusive ex-significant other has also been sought—on suspicion of murder, no less—by a hard-nosed dame...

LIEUTENANT C. R. MOLINA

This Las Vegas homicide detective and single mother of teenage Mariah is also the good friend of Miss Temple's freshly minted fiancé...

MR. MATT DEVINE

Mr. Matt, aka Mr. Midnight, is a radio talk show shrink on *The Midnight Hour*. The former Roman Catholic priest came to Vegas to track down his abusive stepfather and ended up a syndicated celebrity now in line for a national talk show.

MR. RAFI NADIR

After blowing his career at the LAPD when Miss Lt. C. R. Molina mysteriously left him, and for years the unsuspecting father of Mariah, he is moving up in Vegas hotel security jobs. Miss Lieutenant Carmen Regina Molina is not thrilled that her former flame now knows what is what and who is whose...

MISS KATHLEEN O'CONNOR

Deservedly nicknamed "Kitty the Cutter" by my Miss Temple, the local lass that Max and his cousin Sean boyishly competed for in that long-ago Northern Ireland has become an embittered stalker. Finding Mr. Max as impossible to trace as Lieutenant Molina has, Kitty the C settled for harassing with tooth and claw the nearest innocent bystander, primarily Mr. Matt Devine.

Now that Miss Kathleen O'Connor's popped up again like Jill the Ripper, things are shaking up again for we who reside at a vintage round apartment building called the Circle Ritz. Someone arranged for Mr. Max Kinsella to hit the wall of the Neon Nightmare club with lethal impact while in the guise of a bungee-jumping magician, the Phantom Mage.

A secret stay in a Swiss clinic repaired his broken legs, but not his traumatic memory loss. Mr. Max's recent miraculous resurrection involved going on the run with a blonde European psychiatrist babe, Revienne Schneider. I fear more than escape transpired during that adventure, since he had no memory of his serious love affair with my roommate. He now knows he and my Miss Temple were a committed couple, but has no memories of the emotional and spicy details. So far.

That is how things stand today, full of danger, angst, and confusion.

However, things are seldom what they seem, and almost never that in Las Vegas. A magician may have as many lives as a cat, in my humble estimation, and events may bear me out.

All this human sex and violence makes me glad that I have a

simpler social life, such as just trying to get along with my unacknowledged daughter...

MISS MIDNIGHT LOUISE
This streetwise minx insinuated herself into my cases until I was forced to set up shop with her as Midnight Investigations, Inc.

Meanwhile, any surprising developments do not surprise me. Everything is always up for grabs in Las Vegas 24/7: guilt, innocence, money, power, love, loss, death, and significant others.

Like Las Vegas, the City That Never Sleeps, Midnight Louie, private eye, also has a sobriquet: the Kitty That Never Sleeps.

With this crew, who could?

1
TLC to Go

For Temple nowadays, coming home after work to the Circle Ritz meant stopping by her condo to freshen up and grab a special tote bag. Today's was banana-yellow patent leather. As a PR woman, Temple cultivated a visible signature. Her colorful array of large tote bags and high heels did the job. So did her endless energy and optimism, now sorely tried.

Midnight Louie wound in and out of her ankles, black velvet in fluid motion, as she loaded the tote bag in the unit's kitchenette.

"I'm happy to see you too," she told him, "but for once I've got someone hungrier than you to tend."

Temple fluffed her vibrant red-gold hair in the living room mirror and reapplied her Peachy Going Nude lip gloss.

She had paused to download a lot of classic soft rock music to her iPod, then glanced around to ensure the French doors to the balcony were locked, and Midnight Louie's narrow horizontal window in the tiny second bathroom was still perpetually open.

If Kathleen O'Connor could slither through that space, she was welcome to come in and find Midnight Louie's claws at their most territorial again.

Louie seemed to understand Temple's mission and his guard dog role, and retreated to the living room sofa.

Temple shut the hall door behind her, testing the automatic deadbolt. She headed down the short hall to the central elevator. Since the Circle Ritz was round, every unit had a private hall like a spoke on a wheel, and they all intersected at the small elevator.

When the elevator came, she hit the third floor button. She could have walked up one floor, but her heels made a lot of clatter on the concrete service stairs. She wanted to sneak up on the object of her mission.

She retraced her steps in reverse (and still in high heels, like Ginger Rogers) on the floor above because this unit was right above hers, and then used a key to enter.

"Honey, I'm home," she sang out, delivering the sinister catch phrase from *The Shining*.

"If you are a psychotic witch from Ireland, you're not welcome," Matt Devine's voice answered her.

She followed it to the bedroom, where he reclined, fully dressed, on the queen-size comforter. Matt was an impatient patient, but a slight frown couldn't overpower the natural blond good looks the Chicago TV producers loved. Being from a big Polish family on his mother's side didn't hurt in that city, either.

Temple put the tote bag down on the bed and her hands on her hips. "Hospitals today! You could have yellow fever and they'd give you a lollipop and a thermometer and send you home within one hour flat. Gunshot wound? Overnight. You'd think you were *only* having a baby."

"Don't make me laugh, Temple. It will hurt."

"Anyway, I've brought our five o'clock picnic." She came to the bed's head to adjust the pillows holding him half upright. "I don't know why you insist on going to work every night."

"Work? I sit at a mic and talk for two hours."

"But you have to drive to get there and that doesn't help your torso muscles. You could recline at home and make out with me," she whispered against his ear.

Matt shut his eyes, obviously willing to sit back and enjoy the imaginary ride, mumbling, "I'm to avoid as much movement as possible, remember?"

"Everywhere? Oh, phooey!" She sat back, being careful not to shake the bed, though at a hundred pounds that wasn't too hard. "How do you feel, really?"

"It's the stitches, inner and outer, that cause the pain. Once I can get up and down, or sit up and down without feeling I'm tearing my muscles up, I'll be fine."

"What a martyr." She rose carefully and pulled a hospital table up to the bedside. From the yellow tote bag beside her she withdrew a red-checkered dish towel and started laying out deli sandwiches and side dishes. The silverware was real, her grandmother's sterling silver, granted to the only girl grandchild.

"You are so unexpectedly domestic," Matt said, watching her with amusement.

"I don't often get a hero at my mercy."

He shook his head. "I don't remember doing anything."

"You drew her fire long enough for Max to recover and topple her."

"I think the cat distracted her."

"Louie did go for her gun and then her eyes. I've never seen him so fierce. And that scraggly other cat screamed like a banshee. That had to have unnerved even Kitty the Cutter."

"She's Irish, Temple. I'm sure the banshee cat yowl would not keep her from committing murder. I don't think Kathleen intended to kill anyone. She's hooked on inflicting hurt, not ending it."

"She's a monster, then."

"The product of one, or several. Twisted people are made, not born."

Temple spread a white linen napkin on his chest and handed him half of a roast beef sandwich. "You think everyone is redeemable. You'd give Judas a second chance."

"One way to look at Judas is that he was needed to complete the redemption story arc. Betrayers usually have a sense of having *been* betrayed."

"That paradox is too contradictory for my simple sense of good and evil. Kitty the Cutter is a bad, bad mean girl. And that's that. You were right that her hatred for Max is so toxic it spills over onto everyone around him."

"How's he doing? No concussion backlash?"

"I don't know," Temple said. "I suspect he's out hunting Kathleen."

"How can he do that?"

"Make a target of himself, as usual."

Matt shook his head. "I wish we hadn't been there when they finally saw each other again after all those years."

Temple could only nibble on her half sandwich. She'd had a knot in her stomach ever since both Matt and Max ended up in Kathleen O'Connor's kill zone. "You think it wouldn't have been so violent?" She handed him the cole slaw.

Matt made a face. "I have a confession to make. When she forced me to 'reach out' and interact with her in some travesty of counseling, I manipulated Kathleen. I told her what you suspected was true...teenage Max had really been in love with her when they met in Northern Ireland."

Temple gave a sigh so deep it almost made her choke on a fragment of bread. She quickly downed some of the Starbuck's coffee she'd picked up for Matt, nodding her head that she was all right.

When she could talk again, she said, "You're forced to parlay with a psychopath on threat of harm to me, and *you* feel *guilty* about manipulating her? You *are* a saint."

"No. I meant I might have manipulated her in exactly the wrong way. You know what 'Bill the Bard' Shakespeare said about 'when love to hatred turned.'"

"That quote is from Congreve," Temple said. "And, yes, the rest of the line about 'hell hath no fury like a woman scorned' is right on too. Or man. But Kathleen knowing that Max maybe didn't scorn her at first, that would make her more dangerous?"

"That would make her more unpredictable, and that's always dangerous. Do *you* believe her? That his cousin, who stayed at the pub because Max went off with Kathleen, wasn't mortally wounded like everybody thought?"

"Do you believe her? You're the one who's been secretly sitting up nights with her."

"Temple..." Matt struggled to raise himself.

"No, don't hurt yourself. Ignore me. I was just being snarky. I gotta admit it's nerve-racking to know the past and future men in my life have the same whacko female persecuting them from afar. Pretty soon a demented female feline will be on Midnight Louie's tail."

Matt eased back after her joke.

"Actually," Temple added, "Shangri-La's performing Siamese,

Hyacinth, did seem to have a strange attraction-repulsion thing going about Louie."

"Shangri-La is dead," Matt said.

"Is she? That magician's act was built on Asian robes, filmic martial arts leaps, and full-face exotic paint. Could have been anyone under there at any time."

"It had to be someone your size and acrobatic enough to perform in Cirque du Soleil. And, when Shangri-La fell to her death, she was revealed to really be Asian."

Temple nodded first, and then shook her head. "Maybe not. Max was declared 'dead' when he wasn't. That saved his life. When you're dealing with magic and magicians—and you always are in Las Vegas, whether you know it or not—there's always an illusion beneath the illusion, there's always an underlying theme of death and resurrection. That's what the University of Nevada professor told me when I interviewed him a while back."

Matt put the plastic container of cole slaw back on the checkered "tablecloth" of their picnic. "I hate you nursing me like this. I should be out like Kinsella, walking the mean streets looking for Kitty the Cutter."

"You'll be out there with Max soon enough." Temple shuddered for effect as she got up to repack the food and turn his television on, the volume on a soft droning level. "I'll be up here at eleven to get you up and down to the car for the drive to WCOO. I wish you didn't insist on doing your midnight show without missing a day. Or night, actually."

"I hate," Matt said, "leaving you alone at the Circle Ritz."

"I hate," she said, "that this attack has diverted us from solving the Big Picture puzzle, all those Vegas locations that might conceal a huge cache of IRA money and guns and all the usual suspects that are involved in wanting to find it first."

"Don't worry," Matt said. "Your map based on the principal stars in the thirteenth Zodiac sign, Ophiuchus, is so complex even Stephen Hawking couldn't decipher it. Most people don't even know about that constellation or how to even pronounce 'Ophiuchus.'"

"Simple," Temple said. PR people like to be informational. "It starts with 'oh fee' and the last part rhymes with 'mucus.' "

"Whatever," Matt said. "I'm betting the stash is so hidden that it will be safe until we find it and get there."

"Once you regain easy mobility, we can return to the trail. Meanwhile, I'll be waiting here to tuck you in at three a.m. every night, fiancé-boy. Electra will keep an eye on me and my unit, and Midnight Louie will too."

"That woman is more of a threat than ever, now that she's been defaced and has gone to ground."

"Electra?" Temple quipped. Their seventy-something landlady, while brimming with post-menopausal zest, was hardly a threat.

"Don't joke. And don't underestimate Kathleen. I sleep with a jackknife in the nightstand drawer now."

"Good." Temple pecked him goodbye on the lips. She silently resolved to somehow find out where the O'Connor woman had been hiding all these months and where she was now.

None of them would have any peace of mind until Kitty the Cutter was found and imprisoned by somebody, even if it was a secret and illegal Northern Ireland IRA group.

Or killed by her cohorts.

2
Sweet Home Á La Mama

I am waiting outside Mr. Matt Devine's door to escort my Miss Temple down in the elevator.

She is so distracted by Mr. Matt's condition that I am forced to perform a silent leap to press the button for floor two.

My motion catches her eye without registering on her mind, so she leans to press the button just as The World's Slowest Elevator creaks into life. Miss Temple blinks and returns into what they call a brown study.

There is no room called a "study" in this building, so it cannot be brown. Perhaps the phrase refers to a portion of the human brain, which they boast of being so much larger than all the rest of us mammals' brains.

I will need to see more than a few hat-size measurements to buy that claim. I am not unfamiliar with hats. Once I was forced to have a flamingo-pink fedora affixed to my brain box. That was during my brief career moonlighting as a TV ad spokescat. I was able to combine the stunt with a murder investigation, so it all worked out and I met She Who Demands Obeisance, the Divine Yvette. That is one platinum-silver babe, but she lives in Hollywood and ours is a long-distance relationship.

By now I am following Miss Temple down the short hallway to her front door and into our unit.

She finally takes notice of me. "Oh, Louie, I am so worried about Matt driving back and forth from the radio station at night, with Kathleen O'Connor at a large."

I give her calves a comforting massage, tickling her thigh with the tip of my sixth member and purring in soothing full basso.

"Louie," she says, giggling. "You must be lobbying for some fresh Free-to-Be-Feline," she adds, turning into the tiny black-and-white kitchen.

Does she have no color sense? Does she not know that camouflage-green nuggets destroy the simple chic of her kitchen? Especially when they later reappear, like a magician's assistant, in a gooey warm little pile with the inelegant name of hairball?

No matter. I de-escalate the purr and hunker over the elegant footed-crystal, banana-split bowl to gag down a mittful of nuggets. Four is all I can tolerate, and then I look up for approval. Miss Temple recognizes her cue, sighs, and opens a can of sardines, head and nose averted. She stoops to spoon the savory pieces over the Free-to-Be Feline. My purr is at max range now and evokes a fond smile.

"I know you love this odious stuff, Louie, but it is too rich for every day."

I devote myself to gustatory glee. Let her cherish her little illusions. She also thinks I exit the condo to climb trees, sun myself, and spar with rival males. I have no time for these stereotypical activities.

My thriving private-eye business would be a sole proprietorship if my purported daughter, Miss Midnight Louise, had not muscled her way in. Frankly, my wild younger days are over since I was whisked off the street by a vengeful B-movie actress who took me to her plastic surgeon to be "fixed". She falsely accused me of fathering the Divine Yvette's alley-cat litter. This high-end doc gave me the human version of a fixing, which left me with a license to thrill all the ladies without the aftermath of illegal "littering". I also appreciated the tummy tuck he threw in, once I had fully recovered.

However, we mean-street walkers do not have time for a lot of relationships.

And right now I have to rustle up my freelance operatives so we can cover all three of my current or former Circle Ritz clients.

While Miss Temple settles down with her laptop to do mysterious things involving her PR business, I must be out and about doing my business, and not in a doggy way.

I eel through the window over the commode in the second bathroom and loft down onto the narrow balcony. *Oof.* A few too many sardines inhabit my interior ecology.

Then I must jump up to the railing, then to the leaning palm tree trunk (my personal ladder to all five floors of the Circle Ritz).

Off I spring again onto the balcony a floor up, where I land beside a suspected eavesdropper lingering on Mr. Matt's balcony.

"You could have come down to Miss Temple's balcony," I tell Louise.

She is the only female of my acquaintance to whom I extend the honorific "Miss" less than full time, except for Ma Barker. My long-lost mama runs a street gang and would smack me upside the head if I attempted to identify her in public by a courtesy title like "Miss". In private, she would knock me out.

Louise has her nose pressed to the glass of the French doors. "Poor Mr. Matt. That she-cat could have killed him when she tricked our favorite humans to Mr. Max's house. She was no match for our clowder, though."

A clowder is what humans call an outdoor community of felines. I just call them homeless, never being one to sugarcoat anything.

"You can take the job of tailing Mr. Matt tonight, Louise. I will stick to my Miss Temple, as usual. Also you should try to keep an eye on Mr. Max, but we need backup for a 24/7 detail."

"Ma Barker is not always agreeable to putting the Black Cat Pack under our orders," Louise notes. "She knows that Kitty the Cutter is involved in international politics as well as probable mob activity."

"I get it," I tell her. "But those schemes could tear up the Strip and disturb the peace at the police substation where the clowder has found security on a scratch-my-back, I-will-scratch-yours basis."

"Unfortunately, Louie, you are eager to believe that humans can communicate with us and have the intelligence to follow our directions. You even assume they know what is really going on most of the time, thanks to their primitive instincts to strive only for food, shelter, and reproduction. All this, with no night vision, pathetic marking abilities, flimsy fingernails, and zip for instincts? What a faulty evolution system! They should complain to Bast."

"I have done so on their behalf, but our goddess is not talking. So we must convince Ma Barker to loan us her best and brightest."

Miss Louise does a somersault over the balcony and lands like a burr on the rough palm tree trunk. "We should get on the road. I need to get back here in plenty of time before the midnight hour to escort Mr. Matt to the radio station, Daddy-o."

Louise has vanished from the tree like the Cheshire cat...if he or she had been black.

It is still daylight, so we must do the bush-to-bush slink to reach the substation, and that takes time. The little minx has fixed it so I will be bringing up the rear and thus put the CEO of Midnight Investigations, Inc., in an inferior position. Louise is still miffed about my leaving her mama with a six-pack of kittens, including her, after a one-night stand.

I am not sure I did that crime in her specific instance, but I am sure I am doing the time for it now.

So I limp into the oleander bushes surrounding the substation last to find the whole gang gathered around Louise.

Ma Barker breaks from the pack to confront me with a hiss. In case you did not know, our mamas are strict disciplinarians, all for our survival's sake.

There is no doubt that she *is* my mama, even though we separated when I was young and dumb and still playful in a dangerous world. That is the way it works among any species. Survival of the fittest. Right now, ahem, I am not feeling my most fit after the runaround Miss Midnight Louise has given me.

"So," Ma says, sitting down for a capo-to-capo chat.

She is a rangy old gal. Her thin and shabby coat has seen better years, and her face is a roadmap of the defensive wounds suffered in protecting her kits and clowder. As far as I know, no female of our species has run such a large gang. She has defended them against predators like coyotes and raccoons and other fierce-fighting wildlife driven into the city by over-construction, and now the drought threatening every urban area.

If I used to only answer to Bast (who is an ancient goddess adept at keeping her pronouncements few and far between these days), now that I have reunited with Ma Barker I have yet another imperious female on my tail.

Family reunions are not the happy, dancing affair they are purported to be...

It is while I muse on this common fact of life for felines and humans that I notice that my well-traveled mama has a shadow.

It is large, brown, and medium-haired with a black mask about the eyes.

I leap and land in battle stance. A ravaging raccoon recently engaged Ma Barker in battle. Her win had her holed up with nasty wounds for quite a while. Raccoons are normally a peaceable breed, but hunger is driving them into neighborhoods occupied by homeless domesticated animals.

"Back off, condo boy," the brown dude's low voice growls.

Those are fighting words, so I do the opposite. "You and how many rabid raccoons will manage to do that?" I reply.

"Now, Louie," I hear Ma Barker say in conciliatory tones. Ma Barker, conciliatory? Never would happen, but it has...

The shadow dude pads into the full light, a hefty bruiser wearing what looks like a raccoon coat, but is only the usual boring brown tiger stripe. Although he is big. Must be going on twenty-six pounds. Maybe some Maine Coon in him, all right, but also a lot of back-lot bully.

"I do not like outside contractors moving in on clowder business," he growls.

"Ma—?" I start to ask as his whiskers push into my face.

"Louie, be good!" she snaps. "Catso Ratso is a new member of the gang."

Me be good? I am not the one throwing slurs and my weight around. I spit out any lingering taste from his foreign-scented whiskers and prepare to ratchet those barbs out of Catso Ratso at the roots... one by one.

"Louie," Ma snarls.

"Psst, Pops." Only I can hear Louise's discreet hiss. "This is the new person of interest for your mama. Submit and slink away."

Shock freezes my powerful right cross before I can extend my shivs.

"That is better, boys," Ma murmurs. "Settle down and get along, Louie, while I consider your request for freelance muscle for your detective agency."

I exchange a long look with Catso Ratso. Apparently he is quite the rodent killer, but I regularly take out the serial human kind that weigh one-eighty. I back off only for my long-lost mama's sake, and my sanity. Ma Barker with a boyfriend? At her age and condition?

I do not need to worry for long. Miss Midnight Louise buffets me on the shoulder blades and demands a private conference under the ring of oleander bushes sheltering Cat Central.

"Who is this new bozo?" I ask when we are alone. "What is Ma thinking?"

"That is just it," Louise explains with a demeaning roll of her old-gold-colored eyes. "Ma is in heat and not thinking. This is the new stud on the block."

"Ma is too old for that!"

Louise rolls her eyes again. "I am freed from the demands of nature by a simple procedure that was given to me, but I would have wanted it anyway. You see how relentless nature is to our breed."

"Ma cannot possibly have new kits?" I am horrified. I am not sure whether it is the idea of new half-siblings or of an old mother undergoing more relentless responsibility and physical danger.

Miss Midnight Louise shrugs. "Many clowder members have been, er, retrieved for the fixing procedure. Apparently, Ma Barker and Catso Ratso escaped capture."

Just then, the dude in question sidles up and rubs against Miss Midnight Louise's soft, fluffy side. "So," he purrs in an oily way, "you are the old condo cat's smarter, younger daughter."

Outrage leaves me sputtering, but, in truth, I will be most pleased to stand by and see what I expect to happen next.

I watch Miss Midnight Louise purr back to the amorous interloper this way, every nuance reported: "You are so big and strong, Catso Ratso, oh my."

If you have ever seen a feline dude with a satisfied expression on his mug, it is this guy right now.

Wait for it.

"But I am not a slave to my hormones and your gender. The only way I deal with dudes on the make like you, is to take teeth and claws to whatever handy parts I can bite off. It may be your big, hairy ears, clown. Or it may be that delicacy that some humans consume in crude but fancy restaurants, known on the menus as 'prairie oysters'."

By the time she punctuates her remark with a full paw swipe, he has ducked behind Ma Barker for protection.

"Nicely done," I say.

"I hope Ma Barker is soon caught by the fixing people," Louise says with a furrowed furry brow.

I admit I am touched to see Louise's concern for her grandmamma. "Not likely, Ma thinks they are extraterrestrials and their cages are UFOs that land amongst the clowder to take us away for alien experimentation. She is too canny to be trapped," I say, "but she does not cotton to cowards. I would say Catso Ratso has fudged his chances."

And, indeed, Ma Barker stalks back to us with a list of concessions in hand, or mitt.

"I am convinced you need the full services of the Black Ninja Brigade with this rabid human killer on the loose. Kitty the Cutter, huh! I saw her at work at the magician's house. I am not predisposed to like the human race for all its disservice to the four-foot world, but we took her down then and we can do it again."

I give her a high four with my mitt. "Solidarity forever, Ma."

"Well, for a week or two. You will owe me a whole truckload of that free food you leave out by the Circle Ritz. It is highly nutritious and my gang cannot subsist on cop food alone. *Doughnuts!*"

I nod nervously, watching Miss Midnight Louise, who keeps her trap shut for once. In fact, she is making tiny mews of mirth as we walk away from the encampment.

"What a racket," Miss Midnight Louise finally says. "You are conveying the contents of *bags* of Free-to-Be-Feline to the Circle Ritz parking lot for Ma's clowder to dine on, Pops?"

"Feed the homeless," I say with a virtuous air. "Among the Nine Commandments of Bast Herself."

"Whatever," she says in her dismissive post-teenage way. "I will take Mr. Matt for surveillance. I do not like him traveling back and forth from WCOO-FM in the deepest dark of every night."

"He is a big boy and can take of himself."

"Not the way I can take care of Miss Kitty the Cutter."

3
Now! Live on WKTY

"Hi, Leticia," Matt said when he peeked into the radio station control booth at 11:30 p.m., well ahead of his midnight airtime.

Leticia Brown was Matt's boss, but her key role at the radio station was the on-air personality, "Ambrosia".

He had listened to her on the Jaguar's superb sound system on the way over. That was the expensive car's feature he liked most. Listeners everywhere loved Ambrosia's cooing, comforting voice massaging the air waves with sympathy and a touch of seduction. Her voice was her instrument—soft, soothing, understanding, a cello for the airways. When she'd lulled her audience's late-night anxieties, she played a classic soft rock song appropriate for each troubled caller's relationship problems.

Ambrosia was all about the words and melody. Matt's *The Midnight Hour* stint, now upped to two hours from midnight to 2:00 a.m., was all about the talk behind the emotions and the music.

Together, they blanketed most of the country in syndication.

It was weird for an ex-priest, whose counsel had been given privately one-on-one for years in what was now called the Sacrament of Reconciliation, to do it publicly. The old name, Confession, invoked whispers in dark cubicles bracketing a central priest who was heard but not seen. That made for dramatic movies and TV shows, and was depicted that way even today, but it was dead and gone. Passé. Everything was face-to-face nowadays. In the Church and in the wider, Internet- and Skype-driven world.

Newly an ex-priest, Matt had taken a job as an anonymous, unpaid hotline counselor when he came to Las Vegas a couple years ago. He had really come here to track his abusive stepfather for his mother's sake, the ultimate act of hypocrisy. He had wanted to find Effinger for revenge.

Instead of vengeance, he'd found a whole new vocation, and a new first, and final, love, Temple. Media reviewers praised him for being intuitive, compassionate, helpful, and handsome on top of that. The always bitter cranks out there dissed him as naïve, ineffective, and greedy.

As a kid, he'd always hoped that the truth would out, and life would be simple.

It never happens that way. It never happens that way.

What song was he channeling? Something dark. Oh, yeah, one of Bertolt Brecht's cynical, biting, and world-weary songs of the depressive thirties. Only those lyrics had been "It *always* happens that way".

"Always" and "never" are words you can't ever count on.

Matt had simply been good at his job, and understood what living a lie was like, what children who had to protect a parent's inability to cope felt like, what looking normal and happy and even blessed was like when life was anything but. He always winced to see the school photos of horribly abused kids after they were dead and headline news. Always that bright, hopeful smile while undergoing terminal hell at home.

He'd never undergone abuse like that, but anything a kid has to "undergo" was an unnecessary evil. And as maltreated kids went, Kathleen O'Connor was world-class, sadly.

Call it religious Mary Sunshine-ism, but as Matt recovered from what he considered an accidental bullet wound, he found the pain slight when compared to Kathleen's upbringing behind the harsh, merciless walls of a Magdalene convent.

"Hey, Matt!" Leticia had spotted him and was smiling her twelve-thousand-watt grin. "Put on a happy face. You're live in three minutes."

Commercials were unreeling, so he popped into the broadcast booth to embrace her. He winced when she returned his gingerly gesture with a 300-pound, decorative-stud-enhanced bear hug. She was all about living large and dressing loud.

"*Oooh*, Matt honey, sorry. I don't know my own strength."

"It's me. An extra-tough martial arts workout."

"You? Mr. Intervention? Martial arts? Excuse my giggle."

"Yeah. I have a secret life. What was that song you closed on?" he asked, setting into the cushy swivel chair and placing the water bottle and mic for a two-hour set.

"'Walkin' in the Rain, Talkin' Through the Pain.' Perfect intro for your *Midnight Hour*, come to think of it."

"I'm not familiar with it."

"Matt! Sometimes I think you grew up in a cave. It's by Black & White, the finest band to come out of the Eighties. Multi-cultural, multi-genre. Solid gold. French Vanilla hits so many high notes you'd swear you'd gone to heaven, and Chocolatte has that old black magic, devilish growl that makes you *wanta* go to hell."

Matt was already donning the headset. "Can't prove it by me." His introductory music was coming up, heavy on the film noir sax. "Mr. Midnight" was as corny an on-air handle as "Ambrosia", but on radio, that hokey stuff worked magic…if you had something to say.

Matt normally looked forward to stressed voices he could send away with a new point of view or some vague resolution, transient as the change might be. Oddly, he didn't have regulars. Well, except for "Elvis" a while back. That caller had been an uncanny evocation of The King. His ex-priest friend in the FBI had said the voice analysis was spot on, but this was Las Vegas and tribute performers were as common as blackjack dealers. So some were uncommonly, and uncannily, good.

Then there were the surprise call-ins from…the ever-faithful Kathleen O'Connor. Thinking of the violent set-to at Kinsella's house, Matt's stomach muscles tightened painfully. Would she call to taunt him as she had before, live and on-air? Kitty the Cutter loved to make her victims sweat.

And, in his case, did.

4
Uneasy Listening

My name may be Midnight Louise, but that reflects my coat color more than my sleeping druthers. These all-night stakeouts sure put a crimp in a girl's grooming routine.

And they are dull.

I suspect the Old Dude gives me Mr. Matt Devine to tail so he can be at the Circle Ritz in the lap of luxury "guarding" his Miss Temple Barr.

Radio station parking lots late at night host only two or three cars—whoever is on the air and the technician. Miss Leticia Brown left two hours ago in her Blue Suede Shoes special-edition PT Cruiser Mr. Matt won and gave her.

I have managed to master the sound system on this fancy English car whose name I wholly approve of. *Jag-ooo-are,* as the Brits say. Only one step down from *Bara-coo-dah.* After growing up on the streets, I am not afraid of big cats or big bad fish, even though people name their car models after them.

Anyway, I agree with Mr. Matt's many fans. He sounds dreamy over the air, caring and sympathetic, as they say on the greeting cards. I cohabited with him briefly after my days as an unofficial house detective at the Crystal Phoenix, where I was known initially as a "stray" called "Caviar".

Revolting, what people will name us. Caviar is an expensive delicacy, but while I may look as sweet and fluffy as the old song goes—"every little breeze seems to whisper Louise"—take that as a warning, not a tribute. I am more the tsunami and Nine Inch Nails type, which is why I am now the *official* Crystal Phoenix house detective of the four-footed sort.

I had it no better in the renaming sweepstakes when the Phoenix management crowd (including all ten Fontana brothers) decided to give me the feminine version of what my Old Dude was called before he traded policing the Phoenix for a life of disgusting ease and ear rubs with Miss Temple Barr at the Circle Ritz.

At least it must chap his chestnuts that even the humans think he is my papa.

I settle into two hours of uneasy listening. In my opinion, these late-night callers are a sorry and sorry-for-themselves lot. Hearing them hem and haw while pulling their dirty laundry into the light of day and the whole listening world, I want to tell them that the best way to deal with life throwing you a hairball is to gack it up, move on, and leave it for somebody else to clean up. Works for me.

While Mr. Matt is inside offering aid and comfort, I have curled up on the ivory leather front passenger seat, which is most flattering to my coloring. Black and white are a simple but stunning combination, and I particularly applaud that the Jag-ooo-are has black interior carpet so I can travel undetected on the backseat floor.

Of course I do not use any pointed parts of my person to check the interior leather for signs of life. I am not domesticated, but I do know my manners with my certain favored humans. Now, if this were the interior of a vehicle belonging to, say, a kitten mill operator, I would tattoo my initials on every surface, including his or her face as the car was entered.

But this is not the case, so I return to my pleasant thoughts of the future. I decide that I might actually miss the residents of the Circle Ritz when Miss Temple becomes Mrs. Matt and they move to Chicago, as rumored, where he will headline a big-time TV talk show. No doubt the old dude would accompany them.

Of course, I would become the sole proprietor and senior partner of Midnight Investigations, Inc., so would be too busy to miss him.

I am contemplating the ramifications of such a promotion, when my keen ears perk unbidden at a noise. I realize that while I was dreaming of a sole proprietorship the radio has gone off the air... Oh, no! Has Miss Kitty broken in?

I punch off the radio station now broadcasting prerecorded music, brace my forelegs on the leather-wrapped steering wheel, and raise my head just high enough to see out, with ears flattened.

Someone is leaving the radio station.

A parking lot light makes an instant spotlight for the sheen of a cream Persian's coat. Mr. Matt himself. Too bad he was born with those creepy brown dog-eyes. It is his only flaw. He is whistling, so I know all is well. No evil person has called the station.

I slink over the central control unit into my undercover backseat position on the floor. Even the few people who are cautious and glance into backseats on entering their cars—and Mr. Matt is one of them since his shooting—neglect to look way down on the usually dark carpeting. The dark carpet is meant not to show dirt, but also does not show a black coat, something that makes Midnight Investigations, Inc. born to go undercover, make tracks, and nail evildoers.

A silent keyless entry has Mr. Matt's weight sinking into the driver's seat and starting the car with the coolest purr ever, quiet but powerful, like a lioness. *Vrrrrm.*

I crouch down and close my eyes as the car glides under the parking lot light. The reflective quality of our eyes is our only giveaway on a case.

Then I settle back as an easy-listening station fills the interior. In this case, boring is good. I look forward to a refreshing catnap at the Circle Ritz. Mr. Matt has recently had his no-frills apartment redecorated and I have not had a chance to reclaim it by marking every nook and cranny.

Radio stations are situated away from competing signals. In Las Vegas that means we are driving through a semi-industrial area, populated only by the occasional night watchman or guard dog.

The ride is so smooth I am already catching up on my beauty sleep when a tiny distant whine ruffles my ear hairs. I suspect a mosquito and slap at my ear. No West Nile flu for this feline!

The whine gets louder.

Mr. Matt mutters a word I am sure an ex-priest should not.

Low-profile begone! I turn to brace myself on the backseat and scan the view out the back window. Manx! I spot a horsefly of buzz and speed coming after us.

I glimpse Mr. Matt's worried face in the side-view mirrors. This car—I guess we are well enough acquainted for me to call it "Jag"—was built to run cheetah-fast. I eye the back seat belts. Too hardware-heavy for me to deal with. A slip of a girl like me will get shaken, rattled, and rolled in a chase scene, unless I hunker on the floor like a set of sixteen carpet tacks.

Yet then I cannot see the action. I decide it is better if I remain conscious later, so I jump down to sink my shivs sheath-deep into the thick pile.

Mr. Matt makes the opposite decision. The Jag surges forward without an untoward jerk, greased lightning, the perfect road runner.

Meanwhile, the pursuing whine is reaching shriek level. I twist my sensitive ears from side to side, unable to free my mitts to box the evil sound into submission. If our vehicle is lightning, what follows is the howl of a tsunami.

Suddenly, Mr. Matt brakes the Jag like a rear parachute has deployed. My nails twist painfully. The scream rushes past us. We are stopped by the side of the deserted road, under an all-too-revealing street light. Before I can de-snag my shivs, Mr. Matt has put the car into park and is getting out.

Getting out? Oh, no. Beneath me the Jag purrs its contentment at having had a bit of a race.

By the time I manage to struggle back onto the center console, the screaming sound has quieted back to the drone of a buzz. A motorcycle cop has overshot us because of Mr. Matt's sprint and now comes back to issue a speeding ticket.

Why, oh, why did Mr. Matt run like that? *Males!* Even he cannot resist the urge to surge when on the road. I am most disappointed.

Right now he is leaning against the Jag's fender, arms crossed, a sitting duck.

As the noisy motorcycle idles back to the car, I depress the car window button. *Oops!* It has gone down on the passenger side, and I need access through the driver's side. The window operation is quiet, but I do not want to alert anyone to my presence, so I depress the adjacent button and cross my mitts.

Down. Done.

A figure with the spaceman head of a black motorcycle helmet approaches, full body leathers creaking in the dry air. That stuff I could tear into with no misgivings, but it is tough to penetrate.

Meanwhile, I must survey the scene through eyes at a sleepy slit. One careless reflective gleam and I am made.

I could never live that down with ML Senior.

"Back in the saddle again?" Mr. Matt asks the advancing long arm of the law, the epitome of cool, his cream-colored hair silver in the moonlight.

Something is wrong here.

He gets no answer, but the figure starts removing the black shiny bubble-head (not to be confused with a bobble-head). It turns to place the helmet on the Jag's *front* fender.

What nerve! What bad manners, abusing a racy Big Cat that way, using it as a table.

"Breaking and entering again, too," Mr. Matt says. "Or should I say broken and entering?"

That is when the figure turns, sans helmet, and I look into the heart-shaped face of the heartless and homicidally hazardous Miss Kathleen O'Connor.

5
Fast and Furryous

Matt's heart was beating overtime from the violent shifts in the car's speed and the decision that the only way to stop Kathleen O'Connor was to confront her. His short-sleeved golf shirt was hardly Kevlar.

"Come to see the damage?" he asked. "Or show it?"

"I didn't intend to shoot you just then," she said, "but it was satisfying."

"I know. You like to play with your prey, not terminate it. So…I see you 'liberated' Max's vintage Hesketh Vampire motorcycle from the Circle Ritz's storage building. I'd never used it, or heard it, at full scream. Thanks for the demonstration."

"You proved unexpectedly fast yourself. You're a shrink. Why did Max acquire a vintage motorcycle so noted for its shriek on acceleration it was nicknamed a vampire?"

"I'm a counselor, licensed. That's all. He's a stage magician, first and foremost. Hooked on the unexpected."

"You aren't surprised to see me."

"Seeing you is always enlightening, Kitty."

"Kitty? Why call me that?"

"It's a diminutive of 'Kathleen'. The full version is 'Kitty the Cutter.'"

"Huh." She pushed her hands in the front pockets of her black leather motorcycle jacket. "Who came up with that?"

Matt shrugged. "You've been using me as a crash-test dummy to harass, a stand-in for the priest, or priests, who abused you as a child. First came the razor cut, now a bullet."

She brought the back of one hand to her left cheek with its awkward patch of gauze, a home-made fix-up job. "Who would have thought an alley cat would dole out your revenge? Those slashes were deep and instantly infected."

"Your beautiful face has been your misfortune. Still, it's too bad to have it marred. Maybe you can pass the injury off as a Heidelberg dueling scar."

"What can you pass your bullet wound off as?"

"Nothing serious. Although my female physician suggested I could have a minor plastic surgery. Maybe you can too."

"Are you doing it?"

"No," he said with a weary laugh.

She pulled her other hand out of the jacket pocket. The folded razor she favored as a weapon was in her fist. "I could give you a matching slash to mine. Bad for the media career."

"You could. But it's time to face reality. You don't want to hurt me anymore. You know now I'm more like you than the rogue priests who taught you to hate everyone, even yourself. They're in hell, Kathleen."

"You believe in hell?"

"If people can create a hell on Earth, I believe they can go to one after death."

"How are we alike?"

"Let me name the ways. We're both bastards with rain and pain all through our young lives, whose unwed mothers paid for having us over and over. We went opposite ways. You into using sex as a weapon of revenge, me into dodging it entirely in the celibate priesthood because I was the unhappy result of it. Look. I can't say my physically abusive stepfather was as bad as your institutionalized nightmare in the Magdalene convent laundries, but he did enough to make me want to find and kill him."

"Effinger." Her lovely face produced a sneer. "Unreliable, stupid petty thief." She smiled. "He died a horrible death by slow drowning."

"I heard. I could have killed him with my bare hands before that. I hadn't seen him in fifteen years. And then I saw the pitiful, worthless, powerless creature he really was, and that was enough."

"For me, nothing can ever be 'enough.'"

"I think it already has been, Kathleen. You just don't know it yet. You've lost your career of seducing men for money for the IRA as a kind of international slut-heroine. The Troubles in Ireland are finally history, despite street outbreaks at parades. Whatever related scheme you're pursuing in Las Vegas, with whomever—vengeful magicians, aging mobsters, the likes of Cliff Effinger—that's not working out. Face it, you can hardly be any more of a bad girl. You've proven that. What to do with yourself for the next thirty or forty years?"

"What has your mother done?"

"Oh, punished herself for a couple decades and, with persuasion, married a nice guy recently."

"What took her so long?"

Matt considered his answer. He'd told her a dangerous amount of personal info. She could use it to expand her circle of torment. Or...

"I'm told that the one-night stand that produced me was...'incandescent'. They were teenagers. Met in a church. He was going off to war. She was in love at first sight. It took her a long time to get over him. Meanwhile, she had to rear a bastard son in a strict Catholic community. So she married the first creep who would have her, and did penance for years, even after I had left home."

He waited for Kathleen to spit like a wildcat on that scenario, for the story being sad and then romantic and redemptive when it was only true.

She backed up a step. "Incandescent. That's not a usual word."

Matt narrowed his eyes. "Maybe you had your 'incandescent' moment too."

She turned her back, made a tight little circle back to face him. "Do you know Irish men?"

"Yes, and women. Charm incarnate but some eccentricities. In my parish, there was a family of thirteen children, then quite old. Five of the sisters had never married and lived together. The land is bare and harsh, and so is the brand of Catholicism practiced there. Irish men tend to be as linked to their mothers as gay men. Many are shy, lifelong bachelors who like the drink. The others go rogue and womanize and like the drink. It's a stereotype, but was true for previous generations. I don't know what it's like now."

"Hopelessly repressed, you counselors would say, or sex-addicted dogs. Or priests. Lust at first sight."

"I know you can't believe in love at first sight," Matt said. "It isn't even *who* the other person is. It's where you are, what you feel, what you need. So a one-night stand can be a revelation of love not destined to last."

"It wasn't night. It was daylight. It was his first time."

Matt raised his hands. "Too much information."

"So you claim you were a faithful priest. Then you'd never had sex until…her."

"Too much speculation," he said.

She stepped nearer, the scent of leather stronger. Predator. "I wonder what it would be like to have sex with you."

"Not good for you. Never good for you until you heal. Besides, you don't want to sleep with priests or ex-priests anymore."

"You think I can heal?"

"Sure. Yes. You've faced the worst, and survived. You can survive fixing yourself. We all have to do quite a bit of that."

She reached out a bare hand, not the one holding the straight razor, stroked his cheek.

A banshee yowl from inside the Jag made her jump back. *"Jesus!* You travel with those wildcats now?"

Matt turned to see a small, dark shape vanishing around the rear of the car. "Must be a stray."

He realized only now that his right cheek and eye had been exposed…but Kathleen was walking back to the parked Vampire, maybe thinking about something he'd said. Maybe just spooked now.

While the motorcycle roared off, Matt got back into the Jag, both of them undamaged, surprisingly. Kathleen's injury might have taken the edge off her will and anger.

He'd seen that happen to narcissistic and manipulative personalities. They push others into noticing them, being obsessed with them, even likely to retaliate on them.

As Matt put the driver's side window up, he felt a flicker of motion on his right, and found that window needed closing too.

He didn't remember lowering it, but thinking about Kathleen

O'Connor on your tail made for inattention.

She was just a vanishing red taillight now.

Matt sighed and eased the Jag into a stately parade speed to avoid catching up with her. That was one role reversal he didn't want.

6
Maybe Baby

"Babysitting?"

Temple was too surprised to do anything but echo that word into her cell phone. This was not a word she expected to use at the start of a work-related conversation.

What did a single career woman (hoping to be married by the time thirty-one kicked her in the rear this very year) know about babies? Of course, she lived in a city built on the surprise factor and was a free-lance public relations specialist. What did she expect…except wacky assignments?

Especially when she was sitting in her living room at the fifties-vintage Circle Ritz, whose name reminded her of a ranch in a 1940s singing cowboy movie. Las Vegas was actually part of the Old West, though few people thought of ultramodern Sin City that way nowadays.

Temple loved working from home, her bare feet up on her newspaper-draped glass coffee table, and her cat, Midnight Louie, drowsing beside her, as warm and plush as black velvet. He wasn't technically "her" cat, but rather one that had chosen her for a roommate. She had discovered cohabiting with a cat involved giving the cat a lot of choices and adapting to same.

Louie had been a big, fully adult streetwise boy when she found him. Okay. He had found her, apparently in attempt to draw her attention to a dead body on her watch…a corpse murdered at a convention of 17,000 book-industry people. Temple had heard that getting published was murder, but hadn't expected having to solve one to counteract the bad publicity.

Anyway, Louie had proven to be Sam Spade with hairballs. He came and went as he pleased and never got a scratch. Instead, he doled them out to malefactors. Thanks to a rather crazy and dangerous episode involving a confused plastic surgeon, he was unable to reproduce, so the streets were safe from homeless little Louies. And Louie himself seemed to take pride in keeping the streets safe from all sorts of human vermin. Temple had even read that stray cats benefited more from vasectomies and hysterectomies than the old gonad-removal and gut-cut treatment called "fixing".

So here Temple was, decidedly "with cat" for the duration. That had been enough of an adjustment. Now the word "babysitting" was catching her unawares. It had her sitting up, dislodging the newspapers and—worse—Midnight Louie, who complained in a cranky under-his-breath growl. It was the presence of a baby at the Crystal Phoenix that had driven Louie from his position as house cat there to Temple's place. Louie was an adults-only kind of cat.

"Babysitting," Temple repeated to the woman on the cell phone, the manager of the Crystal Phoenix hotel and Temple's biggest client. "Van, your little Cinnamon is adorable, but toddlers take a lot of looking after and she's inherited the unstoppable Fontana family energy—"

A laugh came over cellular network. "I'm not calling about my daughter. Although babysitting might be good practice for you."

Temple found herself blushing over the phone, which was a wasted response. "I'm just getting married, not signing up for New Mom of the Year. So…what am I to babysit? An animal act or something?"

Van von Rhine's voice had turned brisk. The boss lady of the Crystal Phoenix, Vegas' first and classiest boutique hotel, was now all business.

"'Animal act' would be a good description," she said. "This is a mondo delicate and potentially…er, potent situation. Could you come over to discuss it? I've got a lunch date I can't break and—"

Temple consulted the large-face analog watch that obscured her tiny wrist. Yes, everything was digital nowadays, but she liked to look time in the kisser. A PR person lives or dies by the clock. "I'll kick-start the Miata and be there in fifteen minutes."

"Thank you."

Van's tone had expressed relief. Temple had never heard the Hitch-cock-cool blonde wife of dynamic hotelier Nicky Fontana display any sort of distress.

Temple headed for the bedroom to jump into her business clothes and heels. Tourists could go casual, but Vegas was a dress-up town for women serious about their work. Thank goodness hose were not required in this hothouse climate. Temple put on seriously red Stuart Weitzman heels to underline her understated lilac linen suit.

When she raced back through the main room for the front door, Midnight Louie had left the sofa spot. He was in a huff about her dash-ing off, she supposed, and playing hide-and-seek to annoy her.

"I'm not jilting you, Louie," Temple shouted to the empty rooms as she scooped up her wrist wallet and car keys. She grabbed her sunhat and one of her signature tote bags, the Revlon lipstick-red one, from a new Lucite coat tree near the door. "There's fresh Free-to-Be-Feline and water in your bowls, Louie. You'd better stay indoors for a while. You need to rest after raking off half your claws."

She concentrated on tying on her straw sunhat with the built-in scarf as the elevator made its one-story run to ground level. She left the building, trotting toward the little red convertible parked under the sunshade portion of the lot. Why not? She was a little redhead. A nat-ural redhead shouldn't have a convertible, Temple knew, but she used sunscreen and the hat, and sometimes a girl just wants to have fun.

As she drove toward the Strip, her mind started working on what the heck was going on at the Phoenix. What kind of crisis required "babysitting" as a solution?

A PR person had to be up to any eventuality, and Temple knew from previous experience that some challenges could be murder.

7
One Unhappy Return

The peace of Van von Rhine's ultramodern office felt like an oasis. Temple sank into a white-leather swivel bucket chair as if coming home. The chair was a new interpretation of the 1950s mid-century modern furniture style now reviving. After recent events of a criminal nature in her life, Temple felt like she'd been born in the fifties.

"What's up?" she asked her always formal boss.

"Besides your current fiancé and your former one supposedly developing a show together for the Phoenix?" Van's smile was knowing. "Nothing gets in the local gossip columns unless you want it in, Ms. Public Relations personified. So, what is up indeed?"

"Oh, Van, I had to do it." Temple swiveled back and forth in the chair, trying to figure how much she should tell Van, and how little. "We were all caught during an attempted commission of a crime, a crime that turned out involve blood and bullets. I had to provide a cover story for the Who and the Why of the situation, something the police would swallow. That combined act story will blow over and away as fast as a private dancer flyer on the Strip, and be forgotten."

"Most crime attempts are unexpected." Van tapped her pen on the glass desktop. "Actually, I'm pleased the Phoenix was mentioned as a venue with big ambitions. Nicky and I are planning to up our entertainment attractions. We're even now redesigning our main theater with Danny Dove consulting."

"Danny? That's fabulous news. He's the hottest choreographer in town, and, besides, he needs a big new project to distract him from the recent tragic loss of his partner."

"Temple." Van shook her head. "You not only jump on a publicity lead, but can always link it with personal therapeutic issues. No wonder you're marrying a soon-to-be-famous on-air counselor. I don't know if the 'PR' on your business card stands for public or personal relations."

"Whatever. Somehow I don't think 'The Compassionate Flack' will ever catch on. Anyway, I can't wait to prepare the world for the next coup at the Crystal Phoenix. What's the new act, and is this going to be a full frontal Fontana Family effort?"

"No. Decidedly not." Van was an only child of a European hotel manager and had grown up in hotel rooms and fancy boarding schools. She was still flummoxed by Nicky's eight madly attractive, gad-about-town brothers and the slight cologne of "mob" surrounding the Fontana Family's shady Vegas history. At least Aldo, the tenth and eldest, was settled down and married…to Temple's aunt of all people.

"But, Van, you *are* considering Max resuming his magician career here? That was the real rumor I heard and it inspired my fib." Temple sat forward, hanging on the answer.

"Would it be too awkward? Max working at the Crystal Phoenix too?"

"*Nooo*," Temple said, yet it did.

Not even she was quite ready to mingle the personal and professional. And did Nicky and Van know about Max's memory issues since that fall from a sabotaged bungee cord? Temple doubted he'd confess his weaknesses to a possible employer, or to anyone. Him being at the Phoenix would be no problem once Matt's deal as a daytime TV talk show host in Chicago went through. Temple and Matt would be married by then, and she'd be looking for work up in Cold Country.

"You don't sound sure about Max as our house magician," Van said.

"I think it's a great idea," Temple said. "Max is a terrific magician. He was too classy for his former venue at the Goliath Hotel. A boutique hotel like the Phoenix is made for him."

"We thought so too." Van smiled with obvious relief. "And isn't the rumor also going around that the soon-to-be *Mr.* Barr will be getting his own place in the spotlight in Chicago?"

"Exactly. I'm the only working schlub in the picture."

"I know that feeling. Nicky is the front man here, all glamour-boy charm. It suits me to run things in the background."

"Just kidding. I keep ending up with guys who perform and need publicity, I guess."

"Even Midnight Louie has made a TV newscast or two," Van agreed.

"See? So this makeover of the big theater is to debut Max's new show?"

"Goodness, no! It takes months to design an entire new magic show. That is a work in progress. This act is ready to go and is going to be a huge surprise. Every hotel on the Strip will be lit-up green with envy."

"Van! You've tortured me long enough. Who or what is on our menu for this huge step into major Vegas performance art?"

Van paused, then absently reseated a hairpin in her smooth French twist hairdo. She cleared her throat. And then confessed. "Black & White."

"You're kidding."

"Am I the type?"

"No. But…Black & White. It was a legend, yes. And that legend died…what? More than twenty or so years ago," she told Van. "I was just a little kid, but even I remember the headlines. The biggest post-folk, pre-metal singing group shattered apart like automobile wind-shield glass into a dozen ugly, rancorous pieces. It was a massive collision of sex, drugs, and rock 'n' roll, with a murder inquiry and a gazillion law suits."

"We know that." Van's white-tipped French-style fingernails beat a tattoo on her glass-topped desk as she leaned forward from her cra-dling executive chair. "That's why we arranged a secret reunion show with the whole group, including the two lead female singers. It took a lot of effort and money to engineer, but it's something no one would expect."

"That would be epic, but a reunion? The split was messier than a gangster hit, a bad-press free-for-all."

"It's been twenty-five years."

"You're saying the main actors are all too old to have bad feelings? What about the divas? Are they an anti-aging-abetted Madonna, or female Methuselahs? Are their voices holding up?"

"I could say your questions are slightly sexist."

"That's hard-headed PR-think. The women were the stars. That's hardly sexist."

Van spread some artsy photos—black-and-white, of course—over her desk. "Contemporary shots."

Temple was impressed. "Foxy ladies still," she agreed. Both women had jaw lines sharp enough for a shark to envy, and good bones. Their faces were commanding, instead of pouty like a lot of current young singers.

"You can do so much with promo in black-and-white now," she told Van, hyped by the possibilities. "It stands out against all the color, like that silent French film that won the Oscar a couple years back, *The Artist.* Only these recording artists are far from silent, I take it."

Van leaned forward to press a key on her desktop tablet. "A really great thing they're so photogenic, because their voices are still remarkable."

The Black & White anthem, "Walkin' in the Rain", cranked up on the office's surround-sound system. Temple recognized the jazzy-rock beat, then the woman singer's raw arena-big voice gathering strength like Tina Turner on "Proud Mary", with that "Rollin' on the River" chorus. That was Chocolatte going solo on raw rhythm and blues, offering no whipped cream, just all-out black espresso for the ears and soul.

Temple had heard the Muzak version as elevator music, but this was sound you couldn't drowse to during a few passing floors. She couldn't help nodding to the underlying drumbeat, or keeping her shoulders from joining in as the tempo and woman's husky, driving voice amped up…to meet a soaring operatic blues soprano. While the instruments and the backup singers kept a throbbing backbeat sobbing its heart out, the divas' voices wove an electric duet, like swirling smoky brandy circling in the finest French crystal.

"It's uncanny," Temple said, getting goose bumps. "I've heard *of* them, but I've never heard *much* of them. French Vanilla's soprano. It's a perfect aural evocation of the Crystal Phoenix. I can envision a video of these women in closeup, dueling voices, against a montage of the hotel's most elegant, bright crystal sculptures and the dramatic darkness of the clubs and theaters."

Van stopped the music. "They are still spectacular. Nicky and I met with the group at a recording studio when we were…wooing the women."

"So they're the key. Kinda nice to see women driving the deal for a change."

"I thought so too." Van bit her lightly glossed bottom lip.

"What?"

"That was then. Everything was fine until the deal was inked," Van said. "Now we're stuck. French Vanilla is…simply…acting psychotic, paranoid, and probably on something powerfully dangerous. At one point the quack doctor in their outfit injected French Vanilla with something right before my eyes. I'm afraid they're trying to break the contract for some reason. You should have seen the two of them during discussions, cooing doves. Now, with French Vanilla so unstable, I'm afraid Chocolatte will freak and we'll end up with the contending vultures of tabloid fodder from years ago. Even worse, we adapted all our top floor suites to accommodate the entire entourage and can't split them up without getting all the wrong headlines. I need a Crystal Phoenix insider in there."

"Possible drug use? It's a rock band, Van. They come with issues. You expect me to join the crowd of enablers in the celebrity suites to keep French Vanilla off the strong stuff?"

"I won't have Whitney Houston dying in the bathtub in *my* hotel." Van's pale blue eyes flashed steel. "'Babysitting' isn't what I want it to look like. More like white-glove service. The band has its own publicist. And I've indentified a reliable source, as reporters would put it, among the group you could interview."

Van got up to pace. "You're PR for the hotel. That's a great cover. You have a reason to keep tabs on the situation. You worked PR for the Guthrie repertory theater in Minneapolis, so you know the ins and outs of performance. I'm really hoping you'll be able to find out who is supplying what to French Vanilla, or anybody else."

Van sat again, no less agitated. "Our security and well-hidden cameras all over the hotel and grounds don't reveal any obvious source. Believe it or not, when French Vanilla is 'sober', if that's what the problem is, she's a dream to deal with. Apologizes all over the place."

"Bipolar maybe?"

"I hadn't thought of that." Van sat taller in her chair, almost relieved by the unpleasant suggestion. "They have meds for the condition, don't they?"

"Yes," a voice from the door behind Temple said, "but like all psychotropic drugs, they only work if the patient takes them, and such patients are med-phobic."

Temple hoped it wasn't too obvious how the sound of that slightly accented female voice made her spine stretch her tall-girl high. She spun in the swivel chair to confirm that the tall blonde form of Revienne Schneider did indeed command the doorway like a supermodel. She was half-French, half-German and, from what Temple had seen, all over and into her ex, Max.

"Revi." Van leaned across the desk to air-kiss her former schoolmate. "I'll be a bit late for lunch. We're just finishing up here."

"No difficulty." Revienne smiled down at Temple, standing so close she trapped Temple in the large chair. "How good to see you again, Miss Barr. That was an apt diagnosis, although I don't know what case you're discussing."

Temple felt encompassed by a cloud of ravishing scent.

So had Van. "That's a remarkable fragrance, Revi."

"Je Reviens by the House of Worth. In English it means, 'I shall return.'"

"And so you have," Van said with a dazzling smile.

Temple wrinkled her nose. She wasn't much for perfumes, or Revienne "returning" into Max's life here in Vegas after their brief adventure in Switzerland. Still, she had to admit Frenchwomen wore scents as well as they did scarves, with just the right amount of oomph and obviousness.

Van gestured to the other bucket chair, which Revienne took, her long bare legs crossing almost Brazilian-wax-job high.

Show-off, Temple thought.

Her own feet rarely touched the floor in most chairs, and wouldn't in this one until she pushed herself off to stand. She knew disliking Revienne was childish, but she'd had a hard couple of months and deserved to do some sulking about an old boyfriend's new woman. And

Revienne might prove helpful with this situation. After all, the woman was a successful psychiatrist on two continents. She must be very busy getting into Max's mashed-up head...and other things.

So Temple quit being insecure and donned her inquiring reporter hat. "Are you aware, Dr. Schneider, of any designer drugs that would produce violent acting out, and paranoia?"

"Many. And please call me Revienne."

"Temple." She managed a matching smile, both women socially circling like sharks and knowing it. Temple spun toward Van. "What did the, um, doctor on board likely use in the hypo to calm the, er, patient?" She wasn't giving away the dramatis personnel to Dr. Revienne.

"Probably just a common sedative," Revienne said. "It wouldn't be harmful, but I only prescribe sedatives as a last resort."

"This is a 'last resort' case." Van exchanged looks with Temple. The Crystal Phoenix might be the literal "last resort" people would want to go to on the Strip if this Black & White reunion mess wasn't straightened out.

"Well." Temple pushed herself upright, holding the swivel chair still with all her might to avoid a high-heel teeter. Mission accomplished. "I'll look into those matters," she told Van. "Have a wonderful lunch," she wished Revienne goodbye. "I'll finish up here."

8
Band in the Running

While Van Von Rhine sashayed off with Revienne Schneider for lunch—everyone seemed to be doing that nowadays, by which Temple meant Max Kinsella—she pulled her laptop out of her trusty tote bag to begin a thorough search for everything Black & White online.

She found oodles of entries on everything from Wikipedia to *TMZ*. First, she searched photos, scrolling through rows of dazzling images extending further back in time the deeper she delved.

The group had formed long after the nineteen-sixties turbulence on such social fronts as civil and women's rights. B&W had dominated the post-disco eighties, its urban contemporary beat blending with R&B, pop music and soulful female vocals, putting the performers around age fifty now. They were, as advertised by their name, black or white, or variations of black-and-white in one.

The "people love one another" vibe of earlier eras seemed to have melded in their music as well as their personas. Yet their dramatic blending of that vividly colorless theme seemed a sharp contrast with any lingering of the rainbow LSD trips from the psychedelic seventies.

The two female lead singers offered an extraordinary vocal range. French Vanilla and Chocolatte were the center and soul of the group. French Vanilla, tall, lanky and white, had bleached white hair. Chocolatte, tall, lanky and black, wore black dreadlocks.

Temple, a pipsqueak not a hairline over five feet, was tiring of being surrounded by showgirl-tall women. It made her feel like a truant fourth-grader. She'd even helped out the police with an undercover gig, posing as an obnoxious teen wannabe performer, Zoe Chloe Ozone. She still looked at best twenty and still got carded at just past thirty. Seeing the Black & White divas in their prime only reinforced her inferiority complex, but that didn't get her assignment done.

Growing up, Temple had been vaguely aware of Black & White as one of several hallowed "old acts" that might someday have a reunion gig on a *PBS* fund drive. She'd been surprised Van and Nicky were backing a Las Vegas reunion of such an old-fogy attraction, but the photos showcased the concept's elegance. The band members looked like they'd escaped a nineteen-forties black-and-white film, shot on the silver nitrate that created those luminous, crisp shades of black, white, and gray. Color films never came close to matching that impact.

The same thing had happened to black-and-white newspaper photos when *USA Today* introduced color in its popular "MacPaper" format in 1982. Traditional presses, no matter how new, couldn't do justice to color photos on cheap newsprint, so major newspapers sacrificed black-and-white drama to off-register mush to this day.

Black & White, the group, had been ethnically and musically variegated, but it had never been mush. The lead singers were vastly different divas. Temple imagined Tina Turner and Madonna onstage together. The group blended folk-rock, R&B, jazz, soul, arena metal, and a couple genres Temple didn't recognize. They apparently had existed to defy categorization.

She e-mailed complex histories of the group to Van's assistant in the outer office to print. Her ex-newsie history meant that her mind worked best when it had hard copy to study. Meanwhile, she swung gently to and fro in Van's white channeled-leather chair you saw on TV dramas, enjoying the executive point of view.

Tommy Foy came in with a pile of paper.

"Thanks, Tommy."

She fished a plastic case of colored highlighters out of her bag while Tommy raised one eyebrow, then the other. "You can do that online in Adobe Acrobat, you know," he said.

"My little gray cells work better dealing with hard evidence."

"Little gray cells? Is that something to contain mice?"

"Funny. You obviously haven't read Agatha Christie's Hercule Poirot mysteries."

"Hercule Poirot? It sounds like a French cheese. Something new and trendy I haven't heard of?" He looked hopeful.

Alas, Temple would never know something new and trendy Tommy Foy had not yet heard of, only things old and fading fast. She actually still read paper books.

She explained. "The brain is composed of little gray cells."

"How quaint. I must have missed that episode of *CSI: Las Vegas.*" Tommy shrugged, then left.

Temple remained, like a kid at mommy's office desk, her feet swinging free of the floor, drawing thick yellow lines through pertinent phrases.

Like...*drug addiction...personal antagonism. Explosive arguments onstage...never found. No trace...no body...multi-million-dollar suit.*

Wow. Temple leaned back in the chair. Black & White hadn't faded away. It had imploded in a blaze of tabloid headlines. A reunion would be, at the least, unforeseen and, at the most...headline news. Maybe Van and Nicky weren't the old fogies she thought they were.

She tapped the printout into a neat pile, then used Van's portable phone to dial the number Van had given her.

"Mr. Bixby, please," she requested. "Temple Barr calling."

A long pause, with conversation bubbling in the background, ensued before anyone came to the phone.

"Yeah, babe." The guy had a Barry White baritone, black, full-bodied, and purring.

She needed to establish herself right now. "*Mr.* Bixby? This is *Ms.* Temple Barr, P.R. That has a ring to it a vocalist would appreciate. Let's keep that vibe going."

A laugh that could have come off a jazz record unrolled like a lazy magic carpet of sound. "Yes, ma'am, Miz. I'm appreciating you already. You and me are supposed to do a remastering of the ballad of the band, right?"

"An interview in ordinary terms," she responded dryly.

"I don't know what two nice white ladies are going to do to unscramble all the rain and pain Black & White has always had going for it."

"'Nice' doesn't keep either Van von Rhine or me from doing our jobs."

He got her point. "And your job is—?"

"To get the show debuting on time and in good order."

That "Ole Man River" laugh came again. "Where you wanta hook up?"

This was rock 'n' roll, Temple reminded herself, it was all sex and drugs.

Unfortunately, all the Black & White performers and retinue stayed in bedrooms adjoining the main suite. She needed to talk to this guy privately, not near the other B&W people, and not in the hotel restaurants where they could be overheard by anyone.

"Yeah," his voice broke into the pause left by her mind search, "we are all one big happy family up here."

"Room seven-eleven," Temple said, committing to a wild idea. "We can have a room-service lunch in private. Ninety minutes?"

"That'll be an eternity to me, Madam Miz."

Temple expected that this lunch would be an eternity to her too. After she disconnected, she buzzed Tommy to check that what she had in mind was doable.

"Are you sure, Miss Barr? Miss Von Rhine has strong ideas about that. She will be gobsmacked," he said.

"Van is too much of a nice lady to gobsmack or *be* gobsmacked," she said of the British expression. "Make it so."

"Aye, captain."

Temple spun in Van's yummy chair, and considered that power was as addictive as any drug.

9
Killable Hours

Temple did some of her best thinking while walking. She had over an hour to kill.

And her mind, presented with an unthinkable, immense, crazy-cool project was an agitated hen house of ideas flying hither and yon, shedding spin-off notions like feathers.

She moved on autopilot through the always moving river of tourists flooding into, and out of, the Crystal Phoenix's main concourse.

"Temple."

Where, was the question. Not to be or *not* to be, but *where* to put the most PR power.

"Temple."

And how to play it? Quiet with tease ads until the pressure of everyone wanting to know was unbearable? Breaking news with an appearance on a big West Coast TV talk show? Internet and Twitter building to a crescendo?

"Temple!" A man had appeared directly in front of her, and stopped her brisk high heels in their tracks, his hands around her upper arms.

Temple might be petite, but she was not accost-able. "Hey." She braced her feet and fisted her hands.

Then the voice and face penetrated her mental backup cloud account.

"Danny!" She hugged him as people parted like the Red Sea around them. "I heard you're doing great things here. I'm—"

"We're blocking the paying customers," Danny Dove said, giving her a quick waist-lift to the side and out of the foot traffic, like she was a Broadway dancing partner.

Danny wasn't tall, but he was wiry-strong in the way of production number dancers, and his curly blond hair made him look no more than twenty-six until you looked closely and could count ladders of laugh lines.

Temple was glad to see them on a face that had recently weathered a tragedy. "Danny, we're going to be working together. I'm so jazzed. I just heard about the show and was thinking…"

"Hush, hush, Sweet Charlotte," he said, using the name of an old horror movie and looking around for eavesdroppers. "We're on strict 'need to know' here. You were in another world, that's for sure." Danny took her elbow. "Want to slip backstage and get a preview?"

Before she could answer, they were ducking back to the hotel's theater area through doors tourists never noticed. Behind the first of the doors, Danny paused. "I've been so busy, and then this came up and I had to do it. I mean, Black & White. I'm actually nervous."

"Me too. Van obviously wants it to be a surprise, but publicity should have been planned and in place long ago."

"I hear the green light was slow in coming, then it was now or never." Danny shook his head. "Crisis makes for creativity. Anyway, how are you? How is Matt?"

She filled him in on Matt's exciting offer to host a TV daytime talk show.

"Chicago! You'd leave Vegas? I'll miss you, kid."

"I know, but it's the opportunity of a lifetime."

Danny nodded. "Matt's perfect for the job. His radio audience, no matter how big, was missing out on seeing his telegenic face. He's a great counselor." Danny sobered for a moment. "I know. I almost lost it when Simon was killed. Matt helped a lot."

Temple decided not to mention Matt's bullet wound. The fewer people who knew what had gone down at Max's house a few nights back, the better.

"Okay." Danny summoned his usual upbeat self. "I hope you're cool with this, but I brought in a special consultant. We are kicking around some kickass ideas for the B&W set. More than the usual dancing and costume changes."

By then Danny was hustling Temple through the dimly lit backstage area and onto the performance area, the stage. It was a 3-D Mondrian maze of connected pipes and wood scaffolding, the functional metal and wood bones of a huge set that was bracketed at the back by two high curving staircases, one shiny black and one blazing mirror-white.

Temple stopped to scan the raked rows of empty seats, the many aisles radiating out from the thrust stage. Amateur acting in college had helped in her first career as a TV news reporter in Minneapolis and then she'd snagged the PR position for the Guthrie repertory theater.

She knew no more uplifting feeling like the shock and awe of soaking in the ambiance of a huge theater, empty and waiting for sound, music, action! It made people want to declaim some memorized Shakespeare snippet, like "To be, or not to be" from *Hamlet*.

Temple was more likely to burst into Portia's quality of mercy speech from *The Merchant of Venice*. Maybe Van was right that she was a frustrated therapist. On the other hand, she could also tear into Lady Macbeth's bloody "Out, out damned spot" speech. She grinned at her own range of sweet and sour.

A small sound made her look up, up, up…to an elaborate circle of gilded wood and plaster that in olden days would have supported a huge one-story-high chandelier. Chandeliers were only used onstage now to crash to the stage floor at the end Act I of *The Phantom of the Opera*.

Temple was getting dizzy from staring upward, the decoration seemed to be getting larger…and closer… It was falling!

Just as Temple screamed and jumped aside, Danny finished swooping her out of the way.

"Sorry," he said, breathless. "I didn't know he had it rigged to move already."

Temple eyed the huge black construction, looming larger by the second as it slowly descended on a thick metal rod, like a giant's upside-down umbrella opening from above. Temple thought of a sunshade turned nightshade.

Once it touched the stage floor, she saw it spanned ten feet, and was just able to peer over an edge that came up to her breastbone.

Midnight Louie was balanced on one interior strut.

Midnight Louie was rigging the special effects? Now that was ridiculous. *How on Earth—?*

A man rose up from the curve on the other side. It took another second to recognize Max Kinsella wearing his trademark black. He was kneeling, running one hand through his dark hair as the other tested another interior strut. Temple recognized that concentration so intense it resembled distraction.

"Max," Danny said. "I wasn't expecting the mechanism to work so soon. You nearly ran us down. And where'd you pick up the hitchhiker?"

"What hitchhiker?" Max spotted Louie washing his forepaw and face as if he rode on upside-down umbrellas every day. "That cat, then—" Max looked around. "Temple. Don't tell me you were standing under the ceiling medallion, gawking?"

"Of course, I was. That's what I do in big theaters. That's what we all three do in big theaters."

Danny laughed. "She's right. I was gawking too, only I knew what you were up to. I just didn't realize that you were coming down to our level right now."

Temple gawked at the ceiling some more. "The descending ceiling ornament is like the floating umbrellas at the Wynn's Parasol Up, Parasol Down bar. It's a grand idea, but there should be more."

"There will be." Max leaped over the unit's edge onto the stage floor. "I'm thinking of how to engineer the stage for my new magic act as well as this current project."

"No wonder you look so tired," Temple said.

"Do I?" Max smiled. "It's just the rotten lighting in here."

Even his words came a trifle slower. Temple watched Danny, inspired by her suggestion, climbing the scaffolding like a gymnast, gauging where other ceiling "umbrellas" were poised to descend.

"How's the fiancé?" came the question, closer than she'd anticipated. She'd jumped a little. "Who's tired now?" Max said.

"He's recovering, but impatient."

"Bullet wounds are no joke. Is he going to have a problem with this?" Max's glance indicated the entire hotel…with him and her in it, together.

"Not normally."

"So what's not normal now?"

"Kathleen O'Connor going berserk, trying to lure us all into a trap, is normal?"

"He must be getting annoyed that I keep showing up in his fiancée's life."

"Maybe. At least you're showing up lately with another woman."

Max's smile was self-mocking. "Smooth move on my part."

"Is that all it is?"

"And you have a need to know that...why?"

"I'm your ex. I have certain privileges."

"So you *want* to know that, why?"

Temple took a deep breath. "I'm not sure you can trust her."

"Thanks for the warning."

"I mean, it's so convenient, her being in that Swiss sanitarium when you came out of your coma."

"I took her hostage because my legs were still in casts. I needed help."

"Okay. She had no choice, apparently. She still could be working for your enemies in Ireland."

"I'm here, aren't I?"

"So's she. Why *did* she turn up here?"

"She has a professional reason, a guest-teaching assignment for a former psychology mentor at the local U."

"*Hmm.* And she's wormed her way into the Crystal Phoenix, being Van's 'old friend'. I bet Revienne barely bothered with Van at the school."

"There may be other reasons she's here," he conceded.

"You mean like sleeping with you?"

"You think so?"

"I know so. I'm all for you moving on, but not with some blonde Mata Hari who's as cold-blooded as Kitty the Cutter is hot-blooded."

Max's laughter rang out from everywhere, thanks to the theater's excellent acoustics. "Nice diagnosis."

"Everybody keeps acting like I'm some amateur therapist today."

"Everybody?"

"Van."

"Well, Temple, might as well accept it. You are. So what are you doing here?"

"Van wants me to move in upstairs temporarily as PR consultant to B&W." Using that abbreviation would help keep the band's presence a secret, Temple thought. She also decided not to tell Max how volatile the situation on the celebrity floor was.

"Is that necessary, or safe," he asked, "with Kitty on the loose?"

"At least I'm not going out nights trying to lure Kathleen O'Connor into attacking me. You're doing that, aren't you? Isn't *that* out-of-the-ballpark obsessive?"

"Probably, dear Dr. Barr. Your defection would leave the Divine Mr. D home alone at the Circle Ritz. Not ideal."

"Like I'm a bodyguard? And I wish, Max, you guys would get around to using first names with each other. Honestly, you're like a couple of high school basketball team rivals."

"In high school, it was always hard to be friends and compete for the same girl." A flash of regret rippled across Max's features.

Temple bit her lip. That was exactly what had happened when Max and his best-friend cousin took a post high school graduation trip to Ireland to look for their family roots. They'd found Kathleen, twenty-three and dedicated to the Irish cause. So Sean had encountered an IRA Belfast pub-bombing while Max had won the girl and was off making time with her. His first girl.

"I'm not in competition with Matt Devine, although he has a hard time accepting that," Max said. "I'm suspecting you and I were over long before the fall and coma impaired my memory."

"And if I said we weren't?" Temple hated having people telling her how she felt, or should feel.

"I'd tell you that you can't wish lost memories back. I've come to like you, admire your heart and endurance. But..."

"You're right." She paused to bask a little in his praise. "Your habit of disappearing on me was hard to take, even if it was to lead international thugs away from my doorstep. Still, you're a hard act to follow, Max Kinsella, and that's why Matt is edgy about you. He's not used to the mating game."

"He's doing all right," Max said, smiling. "You deserve an honest man, and my life apparently became based on lies the moment I became a counterterrorist."

"If only Kathleen O'Connor hadn't crossed paths with you and Sean. Now she tells you Sean didn't die in that attack. Can you believe anything she says, Max?" Temple asked.

"I seem to be surrounded by untrustworthy women you can ask me about."

"You were seventeen when Kathleen seduced you. That's a free pass. She was manipulative and twisted even then, so can you believe her when she says Sean didn't die in that bombing?"

"That's a possibility I'll have to look into."

"Probably in Ireland. So why are you playing with stage shows here?"

"Dreaming of a life after Kitty the Cutter?" His grin was rueful. "I just helped Danny out for a day or two in the concept stage. And, what's done with this space will influence my new stage show, but that's months off. Plenty of time before that to track Kitty the Cutter, now the cut-ee. You do have a way with a phrase, Madam PR queen. I'm thinking she's got to turn up around one of us three after she's licked her wounds."

Temple shivered in the huge air-conditioned space. She glanced around for Midnight Louie and found him tailing Danny around the set, leaping from level to level with Big Cat grace.

"Max, that slash to the face will make a beauty like her even crazier."

"*Hmm*, I wonder," he murmured. "Maybe it'll lift a burden."

"I'd be devastated, and I'm not a beauty."

"Anyone would be, man or woman, don't kid yourself. Guys have vanity too. I think Matt"—he glanced at her for emphasis and approval that he was using the first name—"was right that there's a strong self-punishing streak in Kathleen. We three knights of the round table—your Table of Crime Elements—should meet and do a post-mortem on Kathleen O'Connor's latest tricks."

"Only if you guys promise to use first names."

Max made a face. "You can't teach the world to sing in perfect harmony, Temple."

"I can darn sure make my little corner of it less tone-deaf."

10
Defying Gravity

I am taking what they call "a postprandial nap" on *PBS* shows set in Old Blighty, where the most unimpressive human digit—aka a "pinkie finger"—is always upraised, like the British flag, or my terminal member.

(I thought our side of the Atlantic beat the kippers out of those folks more than two hundred years ago, which is but an eye blink to the endurance of the Feline Nation.)

Anyway, I am dozing high up on the scaffolding, musing on what a roadshow company of *CATS!* or even Ma Barker's clowder could do with a high, wide, and handsome playground like this set, when the hairs on the back of my neck stand up and salute.

I am not alone.

Since all of the work crew and my favorite people, Miss Temple Barr, Mr. Max Kinsella, and Mr. Danny Dove, have departed the scene, I get an unpleasant feeling in my gut. I must admit it might be the illegal fish product I grabbed out by the pool area, which created my postprandial moments.

What can I do? I am away from home at the noon hour and cannot take my usual lumps, i. e., accidentally choke down a few of the Free-to-Be-Feline health nuggets under the gourmet trimmings.

(My Miss Temple cannot cook and would be the first to admit it, but she is a champ at presentation. *Oooh, baby!* Baby shrimp, that is. *Oooh,* clams! *Oooh,* oysters, which supercharge my alpha male hormones.)

Right now I feel a piranha clasp on the very tip of my second most-valuable member, which I have allowed to droop down over the edge of my perch. *Yowl!*

I somersault down to the lower level and find the fangs now in my face are known to me.

"Midnight Louise! That is no way to greet a business partner."

"You looked like you were going to nod off and fall off. An old dude like you should avoid heights."

Miss Midnight Louise is a dainty little thing, an elegant semi-long-hair with a tail so luxuriant she could claim designer genes if she ever did the Red Carpet walk. Sadly, her temperament is considerably less on the fluffy side, especially when she is claiming that I am her dead-beat dad.

I have always had a weakness for the female of the species, any species, so I allow her more leeway than I would if I could.

"You know, Louise, that I do some of my best work at Cirque du Soleil height."

"Then you will love hearing what is happening on the top, twelfth floor of the Crystal Phoenix," she says sourly.

"I know my Miss Temple left our condo at a rapid hop this morning. I barely had time to install myself in the rumble seat of the Miata so she would not see me against the black carpet. Then I saw your favorite ex-magician, Mr. Max Kinsella, slip in here as quietly as a silent meow and decided to see what was up." I stand and stretch. "As you can see, I am."

"Up to no good you mean," she sniffs. In fact, she leans even closer and sniffs even more. "Chef Song left me a nice bowl of firecracker shrimp out by the koi pond, but, alas, some interloper slunk through and left nothing but the scent."

I heroically fight off a burp. "I missed out on lunch at home myself. We can see the Phoenix is readying a big show."

"What a nose for news! In the meantime, over the past two weeks I have seen one guest after another escorted to the private elevator to the celebrity suites. And I have never seen them leave." Louise's gold eyes grow even rounder.

"You are saying they are being offed?"

"I am saying they are taking over, a strange assortment of what I would call purebreds and alley cats that would never afford a room at the Phoenix, much less several suites. And they are being showered with food and flowers. And they make an unBastly amount of noise at all hours."

"So, it is Occupy Vegas?"

"And look how that turned out." Louise jumps down to a lower pipe, just to show off. "I actually am glad you are here, because this gang has many members. I cannot follow all of them at once, even though they try to hide away up top."

"You did not know a thing about this whole theater area renovation, though," I say. "I bet you do not know how I anticipated you on that."

"Does it matter?"

"Only that you usually follow your favorite, Mr. Max Kinsella. This time *I* did."

"He is not my favorite!" She is getting hissing mad. "He is the one most likely to encounter what the police call 'bad actors'. When I am not tailing Mr. Matt, I have run my pads down to nubs keeping up with Mr. Max. It is very tiresome that your Miss Temple has had two fiancés."

"Any sightings of the appropriately named Kitty the Cutter?"

"She waylaid Mr. Matt near the radio station, but he handled her well and I was there to staple her other cheek to her gums if he had any trouble. And Mr. Max is making a target of himself in major Strip venues with a new player sometimes on his tail. The foot traffic is jammed, but I got a whiff of high-end brandy on the guy's leather sole. Not a Skid Row inhabitant."

"Hmm. More to keep up with. Our best bet is to investigate the gang that has taken over the twelfth floor. It looks like my Miss Temple is going to be up to her ankle straps in that shortly."

"Your Miss Temple is always in anything shortly," Miss Louise says with a full dose of snide ladled on like Free-to-Be-Feline toppings.

Dames! They are so competitive.

Of course, the male of the species is worth it. Sometimes.

11
Black & White All Over

Temple hunched over her laptop in the Crystal Phoenix bar, nursing a sparkling water, then reminded herself to sit upright.

She'd grown up when you still researched high school papers at libraries.

Now, everything you wanted to find was out there at the touch of a key, and also a lot that nobody should want to find. Now *everybody* was out there at the touch of a computer key or a phone app...blogging, YouTubing, Googling or, lately, twerking. She Googled her own name for the first time, suddenly curious.

Oh, God. That national essay contest she'd won in high school was online. And...some stand-up tapes from TV news reporter Barr in Minneapolis, including the gruesome shooting in a mobile home. That was her first encounter with murder. Golly, she been young and a bit breathless seven years ago.

Scrolling way down the mass of photos, the links degenerated (in her opinion) to Temple Bar with one *r*. It kept coming up...Temple Bar landing at Lake Mead.

And...in London near the Inns of Courts. She was multi-national!

Uh-oh. A picture of the Temple Bar pub in Belfast. Had Max stumbled across this impossible-to-miss, quaint, red-painted landmark with the flower boxes dripping blooms like rainbow blood over the ground-floor facade?

Omigod, a street she'd never heard of, Temple Bar in the Summerlin development in Vegas, right here in Sin City. That land was the last of

Howard Hughes' estate, still haunted by hundreds of distantly related heirs quarreling over the diminished spoils.

Temple Bar Avenue.

She was glad she was an avenue, which was classier than a street. Hey, the avenue was very short, like her, and surrounded by Figaro, Tosca, and Rigaletto Streets. Funny, she didn't care for opera.

Temple smiled. For all the Temple Bars in the world, there was not one Temple *Barr* landmark in the lot.

Born to be mild. And *not to* make headline news.

That was not true of the members of Black & White, she discovered after she had stopped checking herself out and resumed searching for "Black & White band".

Today, scandal never died, and cold cases never ended up in the ice locker of national memory.

Black & White had been over long before her day as a hot tune-listening teen. If the Internet had not given the hits and misses of every era eternal easy reruns, Temple wouldn't have even the vague impression of the band and its music she did.

And scandals now recycled, the way Las Vegas had recycled its once hush-hush mob-founded and dominated early decades. Now, Vegas hotel channels ran endless loops of mob history documentaries. The Strip featured mob museums and lore. The Fontana family's white-sheep descendants were marketing Gangster chic. Not all of this was just good, laundered fun. Gambling, prostitution, racketeering the old-fashioned way seemed "colorful" now that foreign crime families, gangs, and human trafficking had gone global.

At least Nevada's legal hookers were still enterprising freelancers these days, just like Temple. She shook her head. As Louis "Satchmo" Armstrong had sung in his irresistibly raspy way, "What a wonderful world".

The Black & White world had undergone its major quake in the nineties. Cale "Watchdog" Watson had been a hot-tempered, brash singer who mixed the iconic blues tradition of Muddy Waters with manic rock of "Lizard King" Jim Morrison and now, rapper Kanye West—a blazing talent, with a blazing, ego-driven temper.

From the photos, he was a black man with a capital B. The bones and muscles and undiluted ebony of the Dark Continent sang in his face and frame as well as his voice and music. Temple recalled the scouring prejudice Vegas dealt to Sammy Davis Jr., Frank Sinatra Rat-Packer or no, Nat King Cole, and Lena Horne, and cringed. Black performers couldn't sleep in the hotels where they entertained until Lena put her foot down. And then they burned her bed linens.

In the fifties, Vegas was known as the "Mississippi of the West". An integrated off-Strip club called the Moulin Rouge attracted both white and black Strip performers, but closed in six months. Blacks weren't allowed as guests in Strip hotels until 1960.

Now the Strip would host a major reunion of a band that had made a point of being Black & White. She couldn't ignore the fact that racial issues still existed.

It didn't take a sociologist to see that "Watchdog" Watson would have a chip on his shoulder, because in his era other folks would be sure to put it there.

So there were two bands, French Vanilla and Chocolatte, unique for their blend of black and white music and musicians. French Vanilla was singing under her down-home birth name, Selma Sue French. That sounded more country than soul, but her four-octave soprano won the Kentucky Derby of blues.

Watson had "found" and christened Chocolatte. Her "black velvet" beauty and muscular blues voice could compete with his growling baritone and iconic blackness. They were a team, more Ike and Tina Turner than Sonny and Cher. The men ran the bands and the business. Lionel Bixby had been French Vanilla's guiding spirit.

So, two divas, playing off their looks and sound. And one ring to rule them all...no, that phrase was from *The Lord of the Rings* fantasy world. In the real unreal world of bands and recording contracts, Cale Watson had the vision to unite what played on the small black club circuit with what went platinum in the mostly white-run recording industry.

Blended, the bands found redoubled success. So, of course, a messy, public, and possibly murderous romantic triangle was brewing. Sleeping around inside the bands and with groupies was not unusual. No wonder Temple's mother never wanted her to go to rock concerts, no matter how many teen girls made up the pack.

Watson and French Vanilla eloped. Or escaped. Or left separately. Nobody knew which, only that they were suddenly gone. Black & White struggled on, Bixby, the multi-instrumentalist sideman, becoming the manager and the force that kept them going.

Chocolatte went into semi-hiding during those years, only appearing onstage.

Record companies and venues had mutual nervous breakdowns. The music press speculated about lurid scenarios…the missing pair were holding out for better contracts…had gone into drug rehabilitation…had been in a kidnapping that went mortally wrong so no ransom could be asked.

Temple's mind was reeling. She'd thought she'd had a head for crime, but the possibilities here were amazing.

French Vanilla was finally found, singing under a pseudonym in a New Orleans club. "Snow", she called herself. Cocaine addiction was presumed.

And Watchdog Watson, the Great Black Hope?

He was never seen or heard of again.

French Vanilla made the most of her discovery in obscurity and got a record deal all by her lonesome.

Temple figured the Black & White band members must have been frosted about that.

Chocolatte went unplugged and made a comeback too.

What never got a second act was Black & White, as it had been when at the top of the charts, as a model for diversity, creativity and a certain amount of admirable bad-assery, based on musical chops, not X-rated videos.

Temple found a lot of pod casts of the performers, not so many of the band. Both French Vanilla and Chocolatte were powerhouse singers of the old school, born with talented tonsils, as the music press and their agents put it so cornily.

Their fans and the music press mourned the breakup for years. No one mourned Cale Watson because he'd never been sighted again, dead or alive. He became a cold case in such a deep freeze that any inquiring journalist who tried to revive it, found nothing.

Black & White, though, was also formally pronounced dead and buried.

Until now. Soon to be performing nightly at the Crystal Phoenix, Black & White was back, sponsored by Temple's dear friends, Nicky and Van.

And now the band and its members were Temple's clients, for better or worse, 'til the truth would out, or death did them part.

12
Ghost of a Romance

When a knock came on the door of Room 711, Temple's watch showed that Lionel Bixby was punctual.

She opened the door to admit a man of size who wore it well. He also wore huge diamond solitaire earrings well. Was Lionel Bixby a football linebacker or a sensitive singer-songwriter?

He had a question about Temple too. "Miz Temple Barr. A pleasure. I wasn't sure whether you were the blonde or the redhead I glimpsed around the hotel earlier," he said, then looked past her. "Well, hi-de-ho, what do we have here?"

Temple basked in the effect her great idea had on her soon-to-be prey for information.

Room 711 had belonged to the hotel's 1940s founder, Jersey Joe Jackson, and had been kept untouched decades after his death. The small, two-room suite was a symphony in the era's favored color scheme: gray, chartreuse, and forest green, with accents of maroon. It had wide-slatted wooden blinds a Sam Spade could peer through, satin drapes a Rita Hayworth could put curves in, and a room service table set up for two dead center in the living room.

"What we have here," Temple said, "is authentic nineteen-forties decor. I thought it suited the film noir look of Black & White."

"Yeah, sweet. But I am not talking about the sweet suite." He frowned at something behind Temple. "The scenery is hip and I do appreciate it, but look at *that*. Another black cat is already here. I don't know if I can take the competition."

Temple, alarmed, turned to view the chartreuse slipper chair next to the sofa. A reclining black cat hadn't even bothered to unslit its sleepy eyes to acknowledge them.

Louie? Up here? She blinked. "Oh. That's Midnight Louise, the hotel cat."

"Midnight Louise." Bixby nodded approval. "One classy cat lady. Now I could write a song about Miz Midnight Louise."

"What say we have lunch—not just from the room service menu, Mr. Bixby, but from any restaurant in the house—and talk about the songs Black & White have sung."

"I know this menu all too well," Bixby said after he'd sat, shutting the padded book and placing it on the table. "And you can call me Bix. Big Bix, I'm called. You, you tell me, are called Miz."

Temple didn't comment, since that was much preferable to "babe", and didn't have to, as a waiter had materialized from the hall. Crystal Phoenix service was immediate, yet discreet.

Bixby waited for Temple to order. She sighed over the conundrum. No salad, too much fork work for her to take notes. Anything pasta was off the table for the same reason. Also steak. Twelve stories of temptation lay in front of her and she ordered…hash with a soft-boiled egg. Baby food.

"The Reuben sandwich," Bixby told the waiter. "Two of them. Sea-salted fries. Ice tea. And the triple-chocolate sundae."

"We almost called ourselves Chocolate and Vanilla," Big Bix said after the waiter had filled their water glasses and left.

"Too many calories for prime time?" Temple asked with a smile.

"Exactly it. French Vanilla and Chocolatte both had their own bands when we decided to unite, and neither diva wanted her name to come second."

"French Vanilla is a white woman."

"Right. She didn't have a fancy performing name, but Cale Watson gave her that one. She went along because she won first place in band-naming derby since the rhythm was better. Chocolatte consoled herself that 'Vanilla' was a vanilla word for a gutless church-choir singer. Tem-per-a-ment. Both of 'em have it in truckloads." He grinned as he unrolled the utensils from the intricately wrapped linen napkin.

"Any reason you wanted to talk to me first, Miz Barr?"

"You're the oldest band member."

"So you're thinking I remember the most? Being oldest, not a sure bet. What exactly are you going for? What's your aim and what's your game?"

"Obviously, the hotel needs the group to be stable. Why did you all agree to this demanding Vegas performance schedule if French Vanilla was so fragile?"

"That's just it." He rapped his fists on the linen tablecloth. The room service table quaked at the frustrated gesture.

Temple jumped some herself, feeling foolish.

"Sorry. I've put on some weight lately and don't know my own strength. I would swear on a stack of Bibles high enough to make *you* reach six feet that Nilla was all right. Just fine. Dandy. Feelin' groovy."

"This behavior didn't show up until—?"

"Now. Here. Yeah, there was some tension between our main girls when we first met to discuss this reunion offer. They'd been soloing and doing fine. It was the rest of us who were semiretired and hankering for one last gunfight, so to speak."

"So when did you all actually start rooming together?"

"The hotel made it so our separate suites are interconnected, but not all one big happy. All the doors have locks. We'd committed to the show months ago, and had been figuring out the musicians, songs, look, theme by e-mail and video. Two weeks ago we moved in to start rehearsals."

"All that preparation was sure kept on the down low. I've done PR for the Crystal Phoenix for the past two years and didn't have a clue."

"It's not like the paparazzi follow me and the others in the group. Nilla and Latty have had solo careers for twenty years now. The rest of us are history."

"Then you'd all have a stake in this reunion gig going well."

Big Bix nodded solemnly.

Temple pulled a file folder from her tote and handed him a printed-out graphic. "Give me a rundown on who's who in this photo, if you would."

He squinted at the image, nodding.

"Maybe you can start by telling me which one is you."

His laugh was as hearty a roar as you'd expect from a man with the first name of Lionel. "Why, girl, are you blind? I'm that licorice-stick skinny dude just off-center in the first row."

Temple, recalling that a licorice stick was the nickname for a clarinet, twisted her neck around to see well. "Yeah, that Afro is wider than you are in this photo."

"Point well taken. This was when we'd just started. Oh my, oh my. Micky O'Hara on keyboards." He pointed to a white guy with busy black hair almost as skinny as his younger self. "Spider, we called him for those Daddy Longlegs fingers. Faster than a dose of salts through the cleaning girl. I was the main man of all work. Drums to start. Guitarist. Clarinet. Some sax." Bixby gave a double-entendre wink. "And manager until we could afford to pay one."

He smiled wide enough to flash the gold tooth. "And someone had to keep this boy in line, Beau Weevil there." He pointed to chunky black guy in dreadlocks. "Last name was Wilson but Weevil suited him. Odd little guy burrowing into things you'd never think of. That was our main backup duo. We'd fill in with extra girls or guys through the years, depending on the sound."

Temple felt a headache coming on. Black & White was a large group to begin with, and now she learned that everybody had nicknames. And there had been floater members really hard to track down. What did Van expect from her? Miracles?

A soft knock on the ajar door announced the lunch cart. Shortly after, their table was afloat with the flying saucer shapes of stainless steel plate covers, reminding Temple of the headline-making UFO fiasco she'd dealt with recently.

Midnight Louise bestirred herself from the chair and moved to the desk to gaze down upon the repast with round gold eyes.

"Looks like kitty likes to dine Irish." Big Bix pulled out some corned beef, put it on a saucer, and leaned back to present it to Louise on her perch, singing "Every little breeze seems to whisper Louise" in a French accent.

The fluffy little black cat looked smitten.

Temple turned off her PR and amateur detective brain to sit back to enjoy her food and conversing with Big Bix, who was quite a raconteur.

She'd never known that Michael Jackson wrote songs on his bed-sheets. Not a bad idea. She often got her best ideas when she woke up in the morning and a bedside table notepad was essential.

By then Midnight Louise had disposed of the beef with a few dainty bites. She left the desk to loft atop the blond early TV console and sat so her pert profile was expertly limned against the slatted blinds.

"What a posing little prima donna!" Bixby's easy chuckle came again, as he produced a gold toothpick to pry some corned beef from a gold tooth. Temple couldn't help but think of well-fed Victorian millionaire "Diamond" Jim Brady. Bix was bigger than life too. "I'm used to some long, tall divas, but that little cat has stage presence enough for both of them."

By then he was consuming the tall compote glass of vanilla ice cream slathered in chocolate sauce with all the delicacy of Miss Louise.

"Is that dessert in honor of the band?" Temple asked.

"That is in honor of *good*, Miz Barr."

"May we do some more photo IDs?" Temple asked.

"Sadly, yes, Miz Temple."

The band member and sometime clarinetist Temple now thought of as "Big Bix on the licorice sticks" patted his lips with the generous napkin, and then picked up his water goblet. He reminded Temple of a genie pushing himself back into his bottle, a move that was lonely and confining for all his jovial nature. "You want to talk more about our lead ladies on vocal."

"It's unusual, almost unique," Temple said, "for a music group to have two leading ladies, as you put it. How did that happen?"

"How do these things always happen in music business? The ladies both slept with the manager."

"But...at the beginning, that was you."

"Not so sadly, yes." She looked into eyes as deep as dark matter, and then they twinkled. "We were all twenty-somethings and thought we were liberated and could go on doing a lot of things forever. Turned out we were wrong."

"You're not exactly an unbiased source." Temple couldn't help sounding disappointed. It had been too easy, finding a confidential source so expansive.

"Who is, Miz Temple?"

"Miz Barr."

"See here. We're performers. We have personas. Show me who in the photo you want the dirt on, and I will oblige."

"That's just it. I don't want dirt. I was a TV news reporter when news wasn't just celebrity gossip and sports—sex and violence, if you boil it down."

"*Tsk, tsk.* Who bein' cynical now?"

"I have to protect the reputation of the Crystal Phoenix. Not just because it's my job. Nicky and Van gave me my first, and only, permanent floating freelance PR job on the Strip."

"And now it's a crap game."

"You know the song."

"I know every song. And dance. This girl." His forefinger tapped the photographed woman in the heart. "We were just the equivalent of some guys who'd drifted into a garage band when I found her. We were just some Sonnys lookin' for a Cher. And presto. We ran into her and her manager, who'd come up with her performance name. Selma Sue French. French Vanilla."

"Why 'French Vanilla'? Because she was white?" Temple was confused. That Black & White name was tripping her up, as it had been meant to. This group had been ground-breaking in every way, she saw, shattering expectations.

"Music ain't nothing without contrast. And jazz didn't get really hot globally until black musicians left the states and went to Paris."

"Because black musicians couldn't expand their careers in the U.S. back in the twenties."

"And the thirties and forties and fifties," he said.

"So Selma Sue was named 'French Vanilla' after that whole ex-patriot black Diaspora."

"Diaspora? Fancy word for taking the A-train to the next continent. Yup. In case you had forgotten, you're talking to me because I'm the oldest."

Temple accepted that she was a lot younger and had a lot to learn about this group, but she had the suspicions of a forty-five-year-old street shamus. "Just what were *you* doing before you were contacted for this reunion engagement?"

"Ah, musician-in-residence at Alvin College. It's a small performing arts institution in the Catskills."

"You're not just an ex-group member, you're an actual music professor."

"With a PhD…in life."

"I see where you come by the long view. So how did the second diva come to join Black & White? Oh, wait. She was a horizontal conquest of yours."

"For a young person nowadays you sure are strict."

"More like sane. The whole mess resulted in disappearances, suspected death, and dissolution of the group."

"We weren't a happenin' group until this bass-ass young contralto came along. Yup, I'm a self-educated music professor. She gave the highs in our repertoire the guts of the lows. The group was way more than its breaking up and all that mess. People fix on sensational headlines, not the cool, smooth years. For a long while it worked."

"So Chocolatte was the gutsy, lower voice, kinda like Cher or Lady Gaga. I can hardly tell Cher from Sonny on 'I've Got You, Babe.'"

"You've got an ear, kid." He leaned forward, selling the dream of yesterday. "So we had this ethereal white soul singer, which is a contradiction in terms, and then we have this git-down, nitty-gritty black diva, the most authentic, raw voice since Janis freaking Joplin. Velveedah Hooker outa Ill-in-nois, would you believe it? She had a band and manager, but they were eager to hook up with French Vanilla and her band." He grinned at the pun.

"So Chocolatte was a fancy stage name for Velveedah. I can see how that came about."

"The chicks played off each other like ebony and ivory. We guys just hadda hit the groove and go."

"Ebony and Ivory. That's the name of a Paul McCartney hit with Stevie Wonder."

"You are one right-on, PR maven woman. We were there first. Black & White inspired it. In 1982 we were already coming up the charts."

"Really?"

"Well, maybe. They say that comic, Spike Milligan, inspired McCartney to write the song and sing it with Stevie Wonder, by sayin' that 'black notes, white notes, and you need to play the two to make harmony, folks!' But he was a white Brit guy, so I'm guessing some forgotten black guy said it first."

Temple laughed. "Are you sure the guy who got between the divas wasn't you?"

"Naw. Everything was over between us but the music. Cale Watson was that guy. The best and worst thing that happened to us. After he and I united our divas, he was the manager. I was just a songwriter-singer and back to 'sometime' guy. Mostly guitarist, sometime sax. Cale and the girls, they had the paparazzi. It became all about the divas competing."

Temple leaned back. She shuffled the photo printouts into their folder and then into her ever-present tote bag. For an hour, she'd been visiting in another era, touching base with a past culture, trying to understand the free-wheeling morality of a past time.

"All about the divas. Maybe it still is."

She escorted Bixby out and shut the door, knowing it would lock behind her. The Ghost Suite was off-limits to regular guests...except for the spirit of hotel founder Jersey Joe Jackson.

Midnight Louise had been back sitting on the chartreuse satin chair, looking beguiling and probably thinking about...Black & White.

The door locked automatically, but somehow that barrier had never applied to the hotel cats.

"Mission accomplished," Temple told Van when she reported to her office. "Did you have a nice lunch?"

"Wonderful! Revienne has done such amazing things all over the world."

Especially on the run with Max in Switzerland, Temple wanted to mumble.

Van sighed. "I'm just a paperless-office pencil-pusher."

Temple disagreed. "You are a visionary entrepreneur."

"Thanks, Temple. We'll see about that soon. Did Lionel Bixby provide good information on the band?"

"I'm happy to report I had a good lunch too, and learned a lot of amazing history about Black & White, even the juicy scandal that broke them up."

"Lunch?" Van sounded alarmed. "Not in the hotel, I hope. The coffee stirrers have ears and eyes these days."

"Ah…in the hotel, but private."

"No place in a Las Vegas hotel is private."

"It was the perfect venue for a member of Black & White. Charmed the heck out of him and…gave me a lot of information without resorting to liquor, or worse."

Van shut her eyes revealing the soft aqua eye shadow that emphasized her eye color. Temple mused that her "Civil War" eyes, blue-gray, weren't half as beguiling.

"You *didn't,* Temple," Van said.

"Just for an hour or so."

"You *know* how superstitious I am."

"Yes."

"You *know* I don't want strangers in Room 711."

"It was just me and Big Bix."

"Big— Never mind. And if it was just two people, who served you? Jersey Joe Jackson?"

"Not noticeably. Midnight Louise was there."

"A black cat. In a Ghost Suite." Van stood at her desk. "Worse! This project is doomed, mark my words. Well…"

Van straightened the three objects already well ordered on her immaculate glass desktop. Her superstitions were the quirk that made her perfectionism charming rather than annoying.

"We might as well visit the late, great Black & White band in their lavishly redecorated just-for-them suites because I was expecting the year's engagement to reposition the Crystal Phoenix forever. It looks like getting them to stay together just for the opening will be a miracle."

"Not to worry," Temple said. "I'm not afraid of the Big Bad Divas."

13
Migraine in Black & White

"Out," Van von Rhine ordered. "Out, out, damn spot."

Midnight Louie, who'd been trotting after Van and Temple from the door of her office and now into the private elevator to the twelfth floor, drew back with a hiss.

Maybe it was because the elevator doors were already closing, but Temple suspected it was really because Van had used a word associated with a dog's name—"Spot" from the Dick and Jane early reader books.

"Sorry, boy," Temple told him, realizing that phrase was also a doggy manner of address only as the doors closed on the last glimpse of ruffled fur. She was surprised Louie was hanging around the Crystal Phoenix. Perhaps Midnight Louise was still napping on the job.

It was almost as if the two cats traded off assignments…

Anyway, Temple had to think ahead to how she'd be received by the entire Black & White entourage they were visiting. She studied Van Von Rhine's reflection in the aluminum-silver inside of the private elevator doors as they floated up three floors.

Even with Temple perched on her favorite Stuart Weitzman patent-leather pumps with the inch-high platforms, she felt like Van's younger sister, Van's Raggedy Ann-haired little sister. Temple's tumultuous red waves of hair would never be subdued into the sleek blonde French twist Van wore.

Thinking of sleek blondes, Temple wondered how the great and powerful Revienne would be received here. Like an authority figure, Temple concluded. The graduates of Van's exclusive convent school were apparently all sophisticated blondes who had a habit of attracting attractive, dark-haired men, Nicky for Van. And now this Revienne for Max Kinsella.

Somehow, Vegas didn't seem a natural match for either sophisticated lady. Van's father had managed continental hotels, so she'd easily done the same here when she and Nicky had met and married during the Crystal Phoenix's redo. She'd disliked Vegas, and owner Nicky, at first sight, but that soon changed.

Oh, that Nicky. Dark and darling, sort of a Boy Scout huckster. He was the "white sheep" of the Fontana family with its mob-tinged past, and had built the Phoenix into a squeaky-clean success. There were ten Fontana boys always around and about in their Dreamsicle ice-cream-color summer suits—tall, dark, handsome, and terrific public relations for the hotel—and only two of them married. Thinking of the Fontana brothers made Temple smile. She was sure that thinking of Van's slick lunch partner made her blue-gray eyes turn much bluer, like her mood.

Revienne hailed from abroad, like the psychopathic Kathleen O'Connor, and Temple harbored suspicions of foreign women.

"Look, Temple," Van said abruptly. She hated discussing anything but business. "I know Revienne is somehow acquainted with your ex-boyfriend Max, but, to be honest—"

"Max and I are over. I know that. You should believe that." Temple decided she wanted answers anyway. "Still, why is Revienne sticking around Vegas? It's hardly her kind of place."

Van lifted her eyebrows and rolled her eyes, an expression she'd only do in a private elevator.

"Yes, Van. No kidding. I know Max is attractive and fancy free. In fact, I'm sure it'd please Matt mightily if Max had a new girlfriend. It didn't please him to have heard that Nicky is talking about Max performing again, right here at the Phoenix."

"But, Temple, with Matt being courted by network TV execs for a talk-show hosting job in Chicago, you could both fly the coop any day now. Now that his mother has remarried, it's even more convenient for Matt to live in Chicago. He's made *The Midnight Hour* big time in talk radio, but a daytime TV talk show would allow you to have regular hours, instead of living with a man who works principally at night."

"*Hmm.*" Matt had been more than vague about that deal lately. Nobody seemed to be pouring his or her heart out to Temple lately about...anything.

"Meanwhile," Van said as the elevator doors opened, their mirror images sliding into the walls. "We've got a public relations situation to deal with."

Temple trotted out after Van. She was used to keeping up with longer strides. She stopped almost immediately.

"Van! What is that racket?"

Van listened for a second, and then folded her lips tight. "Our problem at work." Van strode onward and Temple trotted to keep up.

A wall-banging sound echoed down the plush-carpeted hallway.

"Is it a drunk?" Temple wondered.

"You tell me."

The crashing sound was punctuated by a gut-torn stream of profanity that revved Temple's heartbeat. "Why hasn't Security removed this yahoo from the premises? Is it some celebrity whale who can't take losing, someone you don't want to expose?"

"Don't I wish." Van paused at the door to the commotion, then slipped a pass key-card from the discreet side pocket of her Nina Ricci suit.

"Locked in?" Temple said.

Fists pounded the door, causing both women to lean away.

"*Getoutahere. Getoutahere. I'lltearyourfilthyheartout.*"

Temple could hear someone inside trying to wrestle this maniac away from the door.

During the brief lull, Van swiped the card and slipped inside a narrow opening, Temple making like her Siamese twin right behind her.

The hall door was slammed shut and used as a frame for a linebacker in a Crystal Phoenix security guard uniform who blocked all egress.

Temple turned from eyeing the muscleman to the ruckus still ongoing.

Several people were already in the disheveled living suite, trying to calm a struggling figure. One did a Vulcan neck pinch and got the standard sag you saw on retro TV in response.

A hypodermic needle held high caught the light as the subdued person was caught and lowered onto the long suede sectional sofa.

"This looks like a kidnapping in progress," Temple murmured.

The bald and bearded man who held the hypo frowned at her. "This is an intervention, ma'am. And who are you? You shouldn't be here." He was hard to take seriously, with his trendy soul patch and the intricate goatee at the tip of his chinny-chin-chin.

"Yes, she *should*." Van stepped into the room's center, barely glancing at the considerable mess. "You're the doctor," she told the man, "but I'm the hotel manager, and this can't go on."

Temple had come closer on little cat feet, since the carpet was thick enough to muffle the sound of a piano composition titled "Baby Elephant Walk".

"My God," Temple whispered as she stood beside Van and recognized one person in the suite, the unconscious one. "That's French Vanilla of Black & White."

Then a door to a bedroom opened. A striking black woman with black dreadlocks, wearing a Mondrian color-block dress in, yes, black and white, entered the room. "Doc, are you sedating Nilla again?" she asked. "The last thing she needs is more drugs."

"And that's," Temple softly told herself and Van, "Chocolatte of Black & White."

"And the two of them add up," Van whispered back, "to our major migraine in black and white."

"Who do you want me to 'babysit'?" Temple was appalled. "The maniac or her keepers?"

"Whom." Van knew her grammar from that exclusive prep school, by golly.

"I knew that." Temple did too, but not in a crisis.

"I'm hoping," Van said, "you can corral the whole kit and caboodle."

14
Scotch and Soda
on the Roof

I repeat as my associate, Miss Midnight Louise, darts with me back behind the ajar suite door into the small hallway niche that houses ice and soft drink machines. Hotels are hotels are hotels. "Did you hear that? Miss Van von Rhine is obviously calling on us for help."

When I had been snubbed at the elevator doors by the two little dolls I had most assumed I had a close association with, I had rounded up my resident partner, and we had hitched a ride on a maid's cart headed up to Celebrity Hell here.

"You are obviously inserting yourself into business that is not yours," Miss Louise says, pawing an ice chip. She then runs a damp paw through her spidery eyebrow hairs. "And neither of us is a kitten."

"But we *were*," I argue. "You are the house detective at the Phoenix now, Louise. It is your duty to know what is going on. What have you heard of these raucous folks who are making a hash of the Baccarat Suite and environs?"

"It has all been hush-hush."

"So you have nothing to offer. *Hmmffft.* I had better concentrate on trailing my Miss Temple to get the real skinny."

"You could not get skinny to save your soul." She eyes my heavily muscled twenty-pound frame clad in one of the colors under discussion in the suite, solid black. The younger generation is so critical. It comes from being able express their opinions endlessly on social media. *Social, hah!*

In examining Miss Midnight Louise's disrespect of her elder, it is important for the casual observer to understand that she has delusions of being my daughter, and thus is keen to sass her older but wiser associate. Teenage rebellion.

I have been a dude-about-town on the Strip for many years, so the odds of her being my offspring are fifty-fifty. But…I do not wish to face a paternity suit or being called out as a deadbeat dad, so I have to use credible deniability like the politicians, and put up with her. We old-time free spirits are in a tough spot when it comes to political correctness these days.

"Louise, I am on my own if you have nothing solid to contribute," I warn her. "I am thinking this maze of suites could provide a lot of answers for the adventuresome individual."

"I work for Miss Van and Mr. Nicky first, and she clearly does not want you involved."

The suite door opens. I recognize the two shapely sets of calves departing the suite. They pause to wait for the elevator without their owners even looking around to see that I have faithfully dogged their footsteps.

I am about to announce my nearby presence, when Miss Louise stuffs a mitt in my yap.

Mmmffffk.

The elevator swallows the two Misses, and that is that.

Miss Temple Barr and Miss Van von Rhine, career women both, have left Miss Midnight Louise and me alone by the ice machine, also abandoned and forlornly hiccupping ice chips down on us.

Does the able investigator lose heart because an invitation to the party is not forthcoming? No.

"I," Louise says, "would not be out of place accompanying the boss lady and your roommate to the offices below…were I not burdened with the senior member of the firm hanging about the vicinity and refusing to go it alone."

"There is more to be learned up here."

"How so, Pops?" Her voice goes snarky with disdain.

"Pups," I answer.

Louise's yellow eyes enlarge like a spotlight. "Pups? Are you calling me a denigrating pet name?"

"You sling around 'Pop' often enough to be Charlie Chan's number one son."

"That is different. You need taking down a peg."

"Maybe. So I guess I will not share any insights I might have gleaned when the suite door opened to admit our respective main significant others."

"There was nothing to 'glean'." But Midnight Louise looks a bit uncertain.

I sit to preen a white whisker or two. For a black dude like me to have white whiskers is rare among my kind, and a most distinguished feature, I believe. I am the one who "matches" the band in question.

"Run along," I say. "Join the Feminazis in their exclusive gossip girl confab."

Louise's gaze has narrowed. "When you start mashing up Rush Limbaugh with Joan Rivers I *know* you are trying to throw me off the scent."

"You could be righter than you know," I tell her with a Cheshire cat grin.

With that, I turn and amble farther down the hall to where the hotel's major mechanical annexes are housed.

When I glance back, I see Louise's fluffy black tail held straight up and high-flagging down the hall toward the elevators and the service stairs. She will have to encounter some major good luck to find a convenient door-opening human heading up to this sequestered floor of security suites for high rollers and celebrities.

What happens in Vegas happens here…and stays here.

I knew this hotel from rooftop sign to underground tunnel when I cut my teeth as an unofficial house detective here a couple years back, before Louise showed up and filled the vacancy when I moved in with my little doll at the Circle Ritz. All Vegas hotels are constantly "evolving", but I at last find what I am hankering for—an opening into a blind alley with six feet of chain-link fencing stretching above four feet of concrete.

Even farther above me, the unclouded blue of the Las Vegas sky yawns wide enough to swallow the Strip and the valley's surrounding mountains and maybe the whole darn Pacific Standard Time zone.

Most people visiting the Vegas Strip only look up at night to see the neon light show outshining the stars. People who live here do not even bother looking up anymore.

A mistake. Especially here and now.

I crouch on my haunches to gather my mind and muscles into one calculating, leaping force. I am not as young and rail-thin as I used to be. A five-foot bound in order to cling like Velcro to chain link is not a cakewalk anymore. Especially with my topmost shivs weakened from my last set-to with the villainous Kitty the Cutter. In which instance, *I* was the cutter.

I close my eyes and hurl myself upward like the hotel is Cape Canaveral and I am an unmanned rocket.

Oof! I am pasted to the sun-hot wire like one of those suction-cup-pawed stuffed cats in the rear windows of cars.

I know the full view of my undercarriage is not flattering, but hopefully nothing human is up on the roof right now to spot me. I claw my way upward, literally.

Thank Bast this chain-link fence sports no razor-wire crown. I spin my agile torso into a corkscrew as I hurl over the top and down the other side. My abused mitts touch sun-heated...sod.

This is a surprise. The roof had not been carpeted previously, but covered in gravel. I sniff the air and sneeze. Plain grass is not the only greenery beneath my Strip-scorched feet. I wander through plots of mondo grass and tall pampas grass and the showy canna lilies, past blooming oleander bushes and other shrubbery sporting blossoms.

This is some kind of Wonderland, shooting up like Alice on a Drink Me high.

I cannot say I care for perfume, in the flower or in the bottle. The cloying scents mess up my olfactory operations and that amounts to sniffer abuse.

This is precisely why, when I amble from the cool, tall grasses into the full sun of what looks like a putting green, I realize where I am and why it is bordered with multitudes of potted plants.

A new set of window walls backs up the celebrity suites so the visiting performers have their own private park. Pretty cushy!

I edge into the open. The carpet of grass is welcome to my weary pads, but the waft of the soil under it is not. With the stinky flowers behind me, I cannot help inhaling deeply because of my exertions. *Oh, no!* Oh, yes. This is the best of outcomes and the worst of outcomes. Or should I say "outgo"?

Two tumbleweeds are sprung from one set of sliding doors by an unknown hand. They come barreling straight for me, blurs of motion and scratchy yappy sound.

"Whodooyahthinkyouarrrgh?"

I am suddenly nose to black nose with the type of critter I find most obnoxious. Immediately, I am transported to my first case at the American Booksellers Association convention, an event title that is now only a fond memory, replaced by a new name, BookExpo America. At least publishers are now no longer confused with lawyers.

With dismay, I recall Baker and Taylor, the book distributor mascot cats from the publisher's convention. Scottish Folds they were, a foreign breed with origami ears folded down over their heads.

Unnatural.

I like my ears pricked and pointed at all times.

"Whodooyahthinkyouarrrgh?" comes from behind me now, as well as a cold nose trying to get personal with the base of my second-most valuable member.

I leap, spin, and land to confront another black nose.

Two. I had not anticipated *two* of them.

With an agile back-step, I bow out, so my confronters are now gazing into each other's beady, jet-black eyes, and they look like soul brothers.

They face me, recalling the label on a liquor bottle, not that I indulge in anything more than a little catnip now and then. Hey, it *is* legal.

I eye what is known in canine circles as a black Scottish terrier and a West Highland White terrier. "Scottie" and "Westie" are the diminutives, but I do not care to be on such close terms. For me, they are a lot better placed on the label of Black & White scotch whiskey than in my investigative backyard, or roof.

Why? Because terrier not only rhymes with, but means, "harrier".

"Scottie" and "Highland" also means I am in for a lot of dialogue out of a Classic *Star Trek* episode featuring Chief Engineer Scott. That would be more tolerable only if I can get these Highland escapees to call me "Captain".

"Who am I? I am the guy," I tell them, "who is going figure out and fix what is going on in the celebrity suites."

I extend a friendly mitt with just the tips of my built-in shivs showing. "Midnight Louie, formerly house detective at the Crystal Phoenix, now with my own agency, Midnight Investigations, Inc., at your service."

Their long faces, bristling with beards and overgrown eyebrows, tilt.

"Scotch and Soda," says the Scottie, identifying his handsome black self and his pale almost-twin image.

The Scottie has a longer more dour—dignified, I would say—aspect.

The Westie with its shorter nose and pixie cut is more on the "cute" side.

Either way, they are the pair pictured on their namesake liquor bottles since the Naughty 1890s. The brand they rep is not too bad, although vintage, and has been seen in the grasp of an old Vegas hand, singer Dean Martin, as well as cosseted by Cary Grant and James Bond in films.

Like those slick dudes in evening dress, they even wear bow ties. White on the black Scottie and black on Soda, the West Highland White. I am beginning to overdose on black and white.

"Midnight Investigations, Inc., ye say?" Scotch tilts his head at Soda. "We canna be sure, but we may have heerd a wee bit about you around the hotel."

"How long have you two been with the Black & White outfit?"

"Not verra long a-tall," Soda says. He looks the younger and peppier of the twain…uh, two. "Adopted, we were, adopted by the lovely lass herself. When a performer purrson is always on the high and low roads from town to town, she fancies a wee bit of companionship."

"And you two are the 'wee bit'."

"Not so 'wee'," Scottie growls. "We 'twa maun outweigh ye by one stone."

"Stone." That is Brit speak for fourteen pounds and requires me to do a bit of math on my toes. Bast, give me patience! You would think such long-established immigrants would deign to learn the English language. Each wee laddie is seven pounds heavier than I am or around twenty-seven pounds apiece.

"And I will get to thirty pounds afore ye," I remark. "Can we move off the sward here, lads? It smells like an outhouse."

"'Tis an ouwthouwse indeed, Mr. Midnight, specially installed for our use. And we dinna like to contemplate your kind ruffling up the fine lay of the blades fit for golfing at St. Andrew's wi' yer Wolverine paws."

Well. I have never been compared to *the* Wolverine of film fame before, and must admit to being a bit flattered. *Zfft, zfft, zfft.* See my shivs etch an invisible "M L" on the air. Call me Son of Zorro, or Antonio Banderas' Puss in Boots. As for grass "fit for golfing", I "dinna" think much of the sport. If an object is worth chasing, it should be live.

"Aye," I say modestly, "my trrrusty shivs prevented a fatal shooting just last week."

"That is nae what we do. We are nae guard dogs," Scotch says. "It is not in our contract. We are companion-only."

"You have a contract?" I am impressed.

"Miss French Vanilla has a contract with whosoever engages her services," Soda explains. "It specifies our arrangements and accommodations down to the wee details pertaining to our care and feeding."

"I wish I had one of those. I would contractually ditch the Free-to-Be-Feline kibble."

"No! Ach, my puir laddie." Scotch's jaw drops to his hairy black chest. "You dinna mean to say you are fed that terrible pile of wee mousie droppings? We are forced to spill it frequently for the roadies to clean up."

"They make it for dogs? No wonder it stinks."

"Surrre. Free-to-Be-Canine. We would nae sloch that stuff to save oor hides. That is the most awful stuff ever to roll doon a supermarket aisle in a cart."

I raise a paw for a shiv-free high five. "You have said it, brother."

Now that fear and loathing of the Free-to-Be brand has united us, I have my inside team.

Still, all the "wees" I hear from the Hibernian duo are disconcerting. Reminds me to watch where I walk on the suites' indoor carpeting in future.

15
Mass Confusion

Matt woke up, thinking, as he did every morning, of Temple, sleeping in her condo directly below his.

A Catholic conscience was a quirky thing. He'd never stay the night there until they were officially married, and not only merely married, but really most sincerely married.

Temple wouldn't be in residence here for long right now. She was soon to decamp to the Crystal Phoenix to sleep in a cluster of luxury suites while working up an intense public relations campaign for the hotel's secret new tourist draw, the reunion of some band Matt had never heard of. He hadn't heard much of anything trendy during his fifteen years as a Catholic parish priest.

Now his head was throbbing along with the healing bullet wound in his side, a particularly apt site for the wrath of Kathleen O'Connor, a fanatic anti-Catholic and ex-IRA agent.

Temple, Matt, and Max might have escaped her trap with minor damage, including "Kitty the Cutter" herself, but she remained at large, a vague and potent threat.

If Temple was safe at the Phoenix, with its myriad security systems, Matt was deemed capable of survival and he planned to do a lot more than just that.

He had spent years getting up to celebrate six o'clock mass for working people and any elderly faithful who couldn't sleep sometimes. Today was Sunday and the first mass wasn't until seven thirty. Matt needed to be there before that started.

He dressed quickly and slipped out of the Circle Ritz with a guilty conscience for walking out on Temple, although she didn't know it.

He had to idle the Jaguar out of the parking lot so the motor wouldn't wake anyone, but soon its flashy wheels were spinning him toward an older part of town.

Our Lady of Guadalupe's single spire soared only thirty feet above a neighborhood of seventy-year-old, one-story bungalows, some of them ready for gentrification.

The church was always open. Sometimes the Poor Box was robbed. Matt knew Father Hernandez considered that a small price to pay for a troubled soul to visit any time, especially in the dark-night-of-the-soul hours.

He found the priest in the sacristy, preparing the communion items.

"Matt!" The priest's high-arched nose and eyebrows and thick head of black hair gave him an autocratic air that Matt knew to be a certain stiffness of personality and spine. "Would you care to assist today?"

"I'd love to play altar boy again some time, but not today. I need to observe."

"About time." Father Hernandez smiled as stiffly as he stood. "I haven't seen you at mass here lately, nor that clever red-haired friend of yours."

"I've been sampling other Las Vegas parishes. And Temple's family is UU, so I'd like to bring her again, when time allows."

"Unitarian Universalist? That is like having no religion at all."

"Now, Father Hernandez, we all worship in our own way, as best we can. Besides," Matt added in full wicked humor, "Temple tells me she's a fallen-away UU, so perhaps there's hope of a conversion."

The priest's jaw dropped, in actuality. "How can you fall away from such a nothing creed? They don't even admit the existence of a God."

"But they're for social justice, which is a tenet of our church."

"So it is. How about this new Pope, eh?"

"Francis of Assisi is my favorite saint," Matt said. "He was totally inclusive. Like the UUs."

Father Hernandez chose to ignore the gentle prod. "Yes, he was welcoming to all of God's kingdom, including brother wolf and sister bird."

"Remarkable for a twelfth-century sensibility. Saint Francis was green before green was fashionable."

"Well." Father Hernandez had done with chit-chat. "If you can't assist me, I can play detective like your Miss Barr and guess why you're here, and why you've *not* been coming here—a certain prominent parishioner of mine who comes to mass on Sunday. Why didn't you call to find out what time was likely?"

"Is it that consistent?"

"Not always." Father Hernandez shrugged. "I imagine if you went to confession with me, I might find it necessary to assign you one, or two, or three Sunday masses in penance, so you will perhaps do that on your own today. Go in peace."

Matt bowed his head in a way that could be interpreted as agreement or concession. "Go in peace," was how the confessor dismissed the penitent. Trouble was, Matt didn't feel properly penitent about his improper ways at the moment. He could always join the UUs.

Smiling at the impossibility of that, he went out, genuflected at the red vigil light signaling the presence of a consecrated communion host, and took a side aisle seat. The ancients of the neighborhood were gathering already, men and women with snowy heads, some of the old women wearing the small black lace doilies that had been required headwear for all women entering a church decades ago.

Temple, with her love for vintage clothing drama, had liked the silly things, especially in their shoulder-brushing mantilla form. Yet, with her modern liberated sensibility, she'd say that making women cover their hair for religious reasons was a controlling rule designed to blame female beauty and sexuality for men's desire turned to criminal assault.

If Matt had been sequestered from worldliness in the church for many years, Temple had sure raised his gender social consciousness.

Matt sat through the seven thirty mass and agonized whether living in sin would disqualify him from communion. Not in Europe, where the clergy were inclined to wink at sins of the flesh. Trouble was, loving Temple didn't seem like a weakness. It was a strength, and on that strength he was going to find Kathleen O'Connor and make some final disposition of her. He didn't know quite what.

He took communion, refusing to cut God out of his relationship with Temple, who was an honest and compassionate person, the best he'd ever known.

Then he had to sit through the hour until the nine thirty mass, with no sighting of his quarry.

About nine fifteen, he heard the main aisle's terra cotta tiles echo with a stronger step than the shuffles of the many elderly people coming and going.

Yes, there. Big as life, but definitely no doily or anything on her thick dark hair, and wearing a royal blue suit and shoes with actual, if stubby, dress heels—Temple would know what to call them—was the very homicide lieutenant he'd been tracking. C.R. Molina, aka Carmen. And, surprisingly, she was not with child.

16
Taken for a Ride

"**So I get** ambushed at church on Sunday morning." Molina eyed Matt with displeasure, maybe mock. She could be hard to read. "I'm lucky you weren't acting the altar boy for communion. I might have bitten the host in half, and that's a grievous error."

They stood outside the church in the still pleasantly warm sunshine. Nearby, Father Hernandez greeted parishioners as they left.

"When's the next mass?" Matt asked.

"Not until eleven thirty. You lucked out."

"Where's Mariah?"

Molina rolled her eyes. "Teenager. Five thirty mass Saturday evening so she can go to the latest movie with her friends and have Sunday free too. So. Now that you've made the proper family inquiries, why are you here?"

"I want to consult with you in a pseudo-professional capacity."

"That's me, the pseudo-professional."

"I was referring to me—"

"I suppose you wanted to avoid police headquarters. Luckily, *mi casa es su casa* at the moment."

"Perfect," Matt said, meaning it.

"Then we have a date." She shot a look at the church parking lot. "That ultra-costly silver Candy Crush, carjacker's dream bomb is yours, I take it."

She was a cop. The silver Jag was a huge giveaway. In fact, it *was* a giveaway. "I didn't buy it. It was a gift and is a pain." He turned to head for her nearby house on foot.

"Wait." Her hand rested on his forearm. She had quite a reach, being six feet tall in heels, and was indeed the embodiment of the long arm of the law. "You don't want to leave that unattended in this lot."

"We're in easy walking distance of your house, and people keep coming and going at the church."

"Not for another forty-five minutes. Besides, I want a ride in that thing."

Matt sighed. "Come to think of it, I have something in there you should see. I forgot about that for a moment."

"I've heard that story before, from many a suspect. Something illegal, I hope. Let's roll."

Once they were in the car, there was no "rolling". Molina settled into the cushy leather passenger seat and demanded a tour of the luxury features.

"What you do want to know?"

"Everything."

Matt thumped his hands on the leather-wrapped steering wheel. "The Gospel according to Edmunds. Five hundred and fifty horses. Supercharged V8. All-aluminum body, but more than two tons. Sixty miles per hour in 3.7 seconds. Stunning acceleration, but always within legal limits, of course. Sumptuous interior, that is cozy yet gigantic. As you see, gobs of leather, carbon steel, and chrome. Temple tells me chrome can do no wrong. Quiet cruising. Not a squeak or a rock, rattle and roll. Any questions?"

"Price?" Molina asked.

"Not confided to me by the donors."

"More than the parish would raise to give Father a new car after twelve years?"

"That amount might *just* underwrite this sound system."

Molina settled her tall frame in her ivory leather passenger seat. "Cozy but lethal. Kinda describes your fiancée. How did you deserve either?"

"Luck," Matt said, revving the car into a quick, smooth start, and a breathtakingly tight right turn around the corner. Molina was in her driveway in less than fifteen seconds.

"Beats walking," was her only comment.

In no time, they were ensconced in Molina's living room and the Jag gleamed in her driveway. She went to the kitchen that lurked behind an island eating area.

"That *car* is good enough to eat," she commented, "but I usually break fast on Sunday with caramel rolls and espresso. Game?"

"Oh, God. Yes. You forget sometimes where the word 'breakfast' came from."

"That's what I love about my religion," she said, kicking off her shoes to the far side of the kitchen. "It asks for small sacrifices that make you think. Like some of the Vegas Catholic churches accept casino chips in the basket passed at mass."

"Not Father Hernandez?"

"Not Father Old-school, no. This is a working-class neighborhood. Chips around here are on shoulders, Hispanic shoulders, and often rightly so."

Matt took the mug of strong coffee she offered as she settled down with her own. "You could afford to live in Henderson or one of the more upscale suburbs."

"Probably, but it would be a stretch with college money. And I want Mariah to have the Latino neighborhood and a parochial education. Such things are really valued now. OLG's school is bringing up the price of the houses around here now that Nevada is finally coming out of the Great Repression slump."

"That's what I've always admired about you," Matt said.

"You have? Coulda fooled me."

"You're centered. You take being a parent seriously. You *don't* take any guff in your career in a male-dominated field. One thing. You could let your Carmen persona out to play a little more."

"Being a single parent isn't a playful occupation."

She rose to go into the kitchen, and he heard a microwave in action. A minute later she brought a plate of warm caramel rolls and linen napkins to the sofa table.

"I've overdone all those things, maybe," she said. "I'm at the point where I have to start letting go. When did your mother reach that point?"

"When I made her," he said with a laugh. "No. I ran away. I went into the priesthood out of high school, took the burden that was me off her shoulders after all those years."

"Oh, Matt, that's my biggest fear. That Mariah will run away, like I've always done."

"You?"

Molina looked at her watch. "She's off this morning for YouTube recording day. She wants to sing."

"So?"

"So nowadays you can be a teen who wants to sing and you don't have to be in the church choir, or the school chorus or play. You can put yourself on YouTube and become that total mess of a tattooed, animal-abandoning, ego-bustin' kid phenom and too-rich teen loser, Justin Bieber."

Matt sat for a while, sipping coffee and nibbling a caramel roll. She did the same.

Finally he asked, "So what did you think a daughter of yours was going to do? I suspect wanting to be a singing cop is a pretty good prediction, maybe with the singing out front at the moment."

"Oh, God." Molina put a hand to her forehead, like every harried parent.

"Let her work it out. You say she's practicing her singing this morning and she went to mass at five thirty last night. There are a lot worse things a teenage girl could do."

"You're right." She slapped her knees. "All right. What do *you* need? I owe you for the reality session. And the unreal ride in the Jaguar."

Matt produced his plain manila folder. "This woman." He drew out the sketch sometime police artist Janice Flanders had drawn to his description. "Five-three, hair black, eyes blue—actually a contacts-abetted aquamarine—maybe a hundred-and-twenty pounds."

"This is the bad actor from that fracas at Max Kinsella's house a few nights back. There was no robber breaking in. This is Stalker Kitty.

Janice did a good job?"

"Great. She's so talented. The first time Kitty accosted me, I was lucky to have a police artist available for a freelance job."

"Weren't you seeing Janice for a while? As I remember—"

"No, not really."

"Too bad this one's a whacko," Molina said, musing over the sketch. "Pretty woman."

"Not so much anymore. Temple's cat left his three-inch calling card on her cheek in quadruplicate the other night."

Molina glanced at the two tiger cats sleeping together on an armchair. "I got a three-incher once when they were careening together around the house as kittens. On my calf, right through my corduroy pants."

"Cat claws can be deeply effective, and septic. Anyway, I'm hoping you can circulate her image and description among the street cops, not the public."

"If I find her, I get her. At that point, it's official police business, not this private vendetta you all have been living through."

"We're still living, that's the important part. Others are not. So, Lieutenant, I'd be happy with whatever it takes to get her off the street and not a threat to Temple."

"And you and Kinsella."

Matt shrugged. "That's a secondary byproduct."

"I must admit I'm curious as heck to see this hellcat in person. I couldn't charge her with any major felony from the other night, only breaking and entering, and variations of assault."

"Speaking of major crimes, is anything still cooking on the murder of my stepfather at the Goliath and that dead man with his ID on him who fell from the ceiling over the gaming area of the Crystal Phoenix?"

"Clifford Effinger is dead, Matt. Your poor mother is remarried, I hear. Let it go."

"So those cases are cold."

"We're always alert to any new leads? Got some?"

"I'm afraid not."

"You don't need to be poking around town on your lonesome like Kinsella. You'll make yourself an easier target for O'Connor. And where's the terror of criminals everywhere?"

"You mean Midnight Louie?"

"I mean your bride-to-be. You shouldn't be here drinking my hot coffee and talking about cold cases."

"She's handling a big new publicity campaign for the Phoenix, so she's going to move in for a couple of weeks. And at the Phoenix—"

"Don't say it. Fontana, Inc. is all over the place. A hangnail couldn't happen to her." She laughed.

"I wouldn't write the brothers off, I'm telling you. You did enjoy the ride in my Jaguar. They drive Tesla roadsters."

She cocked an eyebrow. "Really? Beats my politically correct family Prius."

"I think you'd look good in a Tesla," Matt said with his own cocked eyebrow.

Her vivid blue eyes were shining with amusement. "You do? What else would I look good in?"

"*Umm,* how about arm in arm with a Fontana brother?"

"Now that's an unlikely scenario unless I'm the arresting officer."

Matt warmed to his theme. "Hey, tall, handsome, sophisticated. In your age range. And eight still left to choose from."

"Mariah would go insane. She's nuts about you already."

Matt made a face. "I know...and dread my looming escort service for the junior high Dad-Daughter dance. At least it's a couple months away. She'll change her mind by fall, girls that age always do. Say, what about drafting a Fontana brother for that?"

"With my daughter? No way I'd let those gigolos near her. You haven't seen her for a while, she's gone totally teen, and not in a good way. Curse Miley Cyrus."

Matt was about to ask what that was about when a bustle at the front door had Molina bolting for the small entry hall. Matt remained seated, hearing a young voice that was deeper than it had been. Mariah, and a man's voice.

He rose as the newcomers preceded Molina into the room. Holy Molina Junior! Mariah had shot up to five foot six and her baby fat was now just a touch of teenage pudge. Her skirt was full and short, her sox were high and so were her heels. She reminded him of a singer named

Katy Perry. A man of Middle Eastern looks hesitated behind her.

"Matt's here!" Mariah produced an excited childish squeal. "Why didn't you tell me?" she asked her mother accusingly.

Matt suspected Molina the cop was getting more accusations at home these days than she was giving out on the job. Teen daughters thought their mothers did everything wrong. Matt had seen that when he was a parish priest and was thankful his lifestyle was celibate and child-free.

"I didn't know he was coming," Molina said, her manner as fatalistic as the "facing a firing squad" tone.

Matt was more interested in the man. Who was this guy who'd gotten past the Iron Maiden of the Las Vegas Metro PD, and was out and about with her precious daughter?

Molina's sigh was almost undetectable as she said, "Matt Devine, you know my irrepressible daughter, but not our…family friend, Rafi Nadir."

By then Matt was leaning past the daughter and over an inconvenient side chair to shake Nadir's hand.

They grunted each other's surnames in acknowledgement. Matt didn't know about Nadir, but he felt like he'd just been hit by a stun gun.

Molina was infamous as a fiercely professional cop and single mom who kept her personal background and business locked tighter than a home gun safe. She'd been so successful at it that Matt had begun to believe a virgin birth might be a reasonable supposition.

"I can't believe you're here!" Mariah pulled Matt down to sit beside her on the sofa, the Sunday morning tranquility busted. "Look." She waved her smart phone in front of his face. "We just made this. Listen."

Mama Carmen was forgotten and forced to lean over the back of the couch and look over Matt's shoulder.

On the phone a tiny video broadcast a pretty big sound, Mariah animated and belting out a song like that "Call Me Maybe" thing that had been a pop hit a while back. The tune was bouncy, Mariah was bouncy, Matt's composure was still uncertain.

"Terrific," he said, sincerely. Mariah had a Voice, like her mom. The kid didn't have the range and breath control, but she wasn't mature yet. Matt eyed the new guy. Nadir had a cop-like look. He was solid and muscular, even verging on beefy. Mostly what tipped off Matt was that impassive, nonjudgmental expression, as if nothing in the world would faze it.

Except, Matt detected a glimmer of dislike in his eyes as he watched the trio gathered around what passed for the Neanderthal family campfire these days—cell phone that could call, text, take dictation and pictures, record movies and sound, and dominate everyone's attention and free time.

The dislike, Matt realized with a tiny surge of adrenaline, was for him.

What did he do to this guy he didn't know and had never suspected existed?

Mariah was literally bouncing on the couch now. "I'm gonna get a couple of girlfriends to back me up and we can do this song at the Father-Daughter dance. If they don't let us, we'll do it anyway, before they can stop us. You'd like that, wouldn't you, Matt? Hey, since you'll be there, maybe you can join us. Do you sing?"

"Only on solemn occasions," he said, thinking of the mass.

"Oh. Like Mom. All that slow, mournful stuff."

"Hey." Nadir's voice was admonishing. "What your mom does is an art form. You're just warming up, kid, and you've got a long way to go."

"I know. I know that, Rafi." The kid's tone implied she'd heard this plenty from her...singing coach?

"I need to move along," Matt said, standing.

"Already?" Mariah pleaded. "I have more song videos on here." She was swiping frantically for sites to show him.

"Mr. Devine has other things to do this morning," Molina told her daughter, formalizing his presence for Nadir's benefit, not Mariah's. Interesting. "I'll take care of what you were asking about," she assured Matt.

Nadir flashed them a frankly suspicious look.

Matt moved on with nods of goodbye all around.

He took a deep, relieved breath when he stood alone on the front steps. What had he walked into? Families were often hard to psych out. Why was Nadir coaching Mariah on her singing? Maybe he was a school choir director. He didn't act like a suitor for her mother.

Strange, but Matt was pleased overall. This part of his mission was accomplished. Kathleen O'Connor's unmarred likeness was in the hands of the authorities, who'd be on the lookout.

17
Sunday Night Fights

Max Kinsella walked through the crowds packing the shops at Caesars Palace, meditating on mortality. People brushed by him, presumably unnoticed. Each brush recalled his every pas-de-deux with death in the past year. He'd had several too many.

He was hoping for another one in the worst way.

Right here. Right now.

He'd never felt so naked. All his houses of cards had crumbled, including the residence in Las Vegas he'd kept hidden from everyone but his one-time girlfriend for so long.

Now it had been violated. His worst enemy knew where he lived. She'd knocked him out like he was a rookie and had almost murdered a man there right in front of him and Temple.

Max's recently abused head had survived the gun-butt blow, not too much more addled than before. Matt Devine was nursing a bullet wound just an inch enough to the left rather than to the right.

Call it crazy, but Max felt that *not* protecting Temple's new love from getting shot was more humiliating than getting shot himself. Although getting knocked out by a gun butt was plenty humiliating.

Kathleen O'Connor had gotten her cupful of blood, but at least she hadn't fled that fracas without a wound, one matching the scar on her soul cut so deep decades ago. He couldn't picture her with a deep slash like a ritual dueling scar across one cheek, her beauty now as cracked as her psyche.

Max wouldn't have been able to deal her a wound like that, even though she'd stalked him and his for years. Who would think Temple's feisty black alley cat might have actually understood the best way to both distract and punish such a woman? Twenty pounds of snarling alley cat could inflict a lot of damage. Was that why envious women with cruel tongues were called "catty"?

Max would grant the beast his uncanny watch-dog ways, but he'd never believe Midnight Louie had that much savvy. Max forced the obsessive rerun of that night from his mind for the third time on this stroll. He was trolling for trouble. After all, his shambling progress was just a ruse, wasn't it?

Crowding tourists spun him slightly right and then left as they pushed past.

Max lifted his head like a scent hound. Kathleen could be stalking him now. Yet, even at his most morose and distracted, Max's instincts from years of undercover work rarely let him down. Especially with Kathleen O'Connor, who'd been tracking *him* for seventeen years. Any hint of her presence was as hard to ignore now as a drug addiction.

Max imagined how he'd feel if Devine had been killed. That would have been the third life lost on his watch and conscience, but no... apparently the first death didn't count.

His semi-broken brain reeled again. If Kitty *hadn't* lied, his cousin Sean had *not* died in the IRA pub bombing seventeen years ago in Belfast. Maybe Sean was still out there, maybe known to Kathleen, maybe not. His DNA had been found in the shattered wood and stone ruins, but an injured Sean might have staggered away, or been maimed but rescued.

Max chewed his lower lip, feeling his every moving limb as a rebuke. His broken legs had finally healed. And so might have Sean's injuries. Max stopped, letting people bump into him and mutter. One of them could be Sean, more brother than cousin, and Max might never know it. His current mood was dangerous. It was undoing years of calculated caution.

But...Sean alive. The reason for all he'd ever done since that violent day was not a dead end anymore. Maybe Sean had suffered a blow to the head too. Never knew who he really was. Lived a different life from that moment. The IRA would have smuggled him to safety as a wounded Irishman or a sympathizer, just as Max turned against them and hunted down the bombers to avenge Sean.

And Kathleen O'Connor was ever capable of lying, to manipulate the situation that brought Temple into danger, to bring him the parting gift of false hope... She'd gone after Matt Devine when she couldn't find him, and she'd threatened to harm Temple. Max knew there was only one target for her hatred, though. Him.

He had to find Kathleen, lure her, before she'd had time to recover from the showdown a few days ago...

Max knew the moment he'd been made.

The realization was an ice pick in his back, one, tiny, sharp perception drilling in and spreading through all his physical and mental systems.

This time it was real, not some out-of-left-field guy who may even have mistaken him for someone else. Max concentrated on not changing his posture or pace, not letting his perception show.

Someone really jostled him hard and grunted. Max was about to turn and protest. Then that Someone kicked hard at the back of his left knee. The perfect weak point. Max flailed out an arm that was swiftly bent behind him, his wrist circled by a handcuff simultaneously. Expertly. His attacker was shorter but solid, and strong.

Max fought giving up the second wrist, and won, but found himself being perp-walked into the nearest doorway, the dark, tunnel-like entrance to the Jailhouse Rock Café. The silently struggling pair would resemble a couple more jostling tourists.

By now Max was more interested in *who* this was and *what* it was about than eluding the guy. Kathleen wouldn't have hired muscle. So who had? Or was this law enforcement of some kind?

He was jammed against a wall that smelled faintly of burger grease and piss, between the crowds thronging the entrance for gumming down food and those waiting in line for the johns to send the current occupiers on their way. Conversation was at the shouting level, cranked-up rock music vibrated the walls and his spine along with them. His left knee still hurt like hell gone platinum.

A shadow of the blinking strobe lighting from inside the restaurant made the man's profile shape-shift every quarter second when Max twisted to ID him. Nobody he knew, for sure.

"I could kill you." The voice was guttural and angry. His face was close enough to kiss, but the features weren't coming any clearer. "You know I could kill you, right now."

Yes, he could try, but a talkative hit man has other priorities.

"What'd I do to you?" Max's low growl carried the twelve inches it was meant to.

"I don't know. What *have* you done? What are you thinking of doing now?"

"Why should I tell you? I don't know you."

"Don't you? No, you don't. And that's why I could run a knife into your belly and leave you to bleed out before anyone even noticed."

Max hadn't tried any moves. He wanted the man to feel in control. Besides, Max was curious. And...how had the guy known to bang him in the legs, a hidden weakness that had happened recently enough to make him vulnerable, but had been dealt a continent away?

The man's voice held no hint of an Irish accent. He could still be an enemy from the New IRA or the old IRA. Trust Max Kinsella to alienate both sides of a fight.

"So," Max said, "it's something I *might* do you'd kill me for? Meager grounds."

"Are you the kind to rat out friends? Are you that kind of rat?"

"Not on your life."

"It's your life. Buddy." The last word was spat out.

Then, with a parting kick to the other knee, the pressure and the presence was gone before the john line closed in and kept Max upright and immobile. Max cursed to his heart's content under his breath.

When he got his knees in joint again and left the wall position, it filled. He put the wrist dangling the handcuff in his blazer pocket, fighting against the current of the crowd to the reach huge, artificially lighted concourse.

No one suspicious was hanging around just outside the restaurant. Of course.

This had been a warning, and it felt personal.

What else was new?

Max headed back toward the casino area, limping slightly. Now he had a problem to solve. He felt a lot better. He couldn't wait to try his collection of cuff keys on this model. Magicians had loved beating locks since before Harry Houdini. Was it American-made, or foreign? From an arsenal or a sex-toy shop?

In Vegas you never knew.

Max grimaced as he realized this was a side issue he couldn't afford to pursue. Whether this was an IRA or anti-IRA tough from his operations in Ireland recently, or local muscle with a license to intimidate, it was clear he needed to vanish, and fast.

And whatever this incident was about, he'd bet it had something to do with Kathleen—Kitty the Cutter—O'Connor.

18
Big Wheels

Matt would put having your fiancée pick you up from the doctor's where you had a nasty but non-life-threatening bullet wound examined as perhaps the most unromantic moment he could imagine.

Having your fiancée in one chipper mental and physical piece after an unexpected set-to with a psychopath, priceless.

An incoming rider bumped Matt as he exited the elevator on the ground floor. He winced has he headed down the hall. Having a bullet wound was painful as well as somehow embarrassing.

Matt smiled, though, as he heard Temple coming. Energy was her calling card. And…the usual high heels that came tapping over the granite-floored lobby. She was a blur of vivid blue and red-gold hair.

They met with a feeling of mutual relief. Ever since that night Temple always embraced him gingerly and kissed him hard.

"How did it go with the doctor?" she asked as she took his arm like he, or she, was a senior citizen, and slowed her pace to a walk rather than a trot.

"It's healing well. She wanted to know if I wanted some light plastic surgery for the scar."

"And you said…?"

"No. I don't care."

"Well, I might."

Matt shook his head. "Dream on. What I don't get is TV cops and detectives brush off the stray bullet wound and go on twenty-four-vengeance jags, punching and kicking their way through gangs of bad guys. I don't think I could punch a time clock at the moment."

Temple's light, ringing laugh did the heart good. "That's all I care about. That you're here to punch time clocks for a lotta decades, brother."

Outside the huge medical building, they stopped. Temple scanned the sea of parked cars. "Sorry I was late. I knew my Miata would be hard for you to get in and out of—face it, it's a metal catsuit for anybody but me. But I freak out driving your gift Jaguar. It's so big in comparison and...foreign and fancy. I didn't want anybody denting it so I parked it..." Temple waved vaguely. "By the empty spaces beyond that old Volkswagen bus."

"I guess the psychedelic paint job is appropriate," Matt said, bracing himself for a long walk with stitches stretching.

As they started down the front row of parked cars to find an aisle to the parking lot's rear, Temple slowed, jerked her head around, and frowned. "I thought I felt someone following us."

Matt jerked his head around. "Kathleen?"

Temple had stopped to ID the guilty. "It's somebody rich in a stretch limo. Maybe a celebrity. Must be nice."

They turned and resumed walking, but she kept glancing backward. "The limo has cruised beyond the passenger drop-off area and is still behind us."

"Maybe it's a pickup," Matt said. "It can't hog the crosswalk for every peon going in and out, so it's driving a circle, like at the airport."

"Imaging Kitty the Cutter taking a limo is a stretch," Temple agreed, and then laughed. "Stretch. *Stretch* limo."

Now Matt felt uneasy. "Something totally unexpected. That's her M.O., all right." His arm through Temple's swung her in a quick do-si-do, so they were near a parked minivan and out of the driving path.

Sure enough, the limo slowed to a stop. They ducked behind the lurking Odyssey and watched the driver get out. He wore no cap, no uniform. Well, it *was* a uniform, if you considered high design Ermenegildo Zegna suits the color of cigar ashes a uniform, and it was for the many and meticulously dressed Fontana brothers.

"Emilio?" Temple tried. The ten brothers looked alike, dressed alike, drove alike and all owned Gangsters luxury rental stretch-limo business.

"Ralph," he corrected her with good grace. "And Ernesto." A nod of his head indicated his sibling in the limo's front passenger seat. "I'm making an offer you can't refuse, a ride home."

"We have a car parked here," Matt said.

"Toss the keys. Ernesto will drive it home to the Circle Ritz for you. On a circuitous route impossible to follow. Meanwhile, enter."

By then Ralph had strolled around the obscenely stretched car to open the very last door.

"I don't know," Matt said, consulting Temple. "I do know you think these guys are the cat's meow, but driving my car—"

"Miss Daisy?" Ralph invited with a bow in Temple's direction.

"Well," she said, "it sure won't cramp your healing bullet wound." She walked into the back, back, backseat standing up, and Matt followed, only having to bend a bit—*ouch*—at the waist.

The darkness inside was blinding after the undiluted Las Vegas sunshine.

Matt first saw a hand holding a Baccarat glass, which in turn held a whiskey dark as liquid smoky topaz.

"To soothe the savage stitches," Max Kinsella's stage baritone came from the dark.

Temple had plunked herself down in the back-facing seat, leaning forward to accept her own glass.

"I'm with Jimmy Buffet," she said, "It must be five o'clock somewhere. What's with the traveling bar and grill, Max?"

"Did I say there was a menu?"

Their eyes were adjusting to the soft light, so they could see to put their drinks down in built-in holders. A small lighted wine cooler and similar refrigerator offered more refreshments and drink.

"How are you?" Max asked.

"Healing," Matt said. "And you?"

"The same."

"Okay," Temple said, "you are two civil guys. I accept that. Why the secret service pickup?"

Max smiled. "It was fun, wasn't it?"

"That's a magician," Temple told Matt, "always goes for the effect."

That didn't fluster Max, who stretched his long legs out between them and drank a savored swallow of Irish whiskey. "I thought," he said, "we needed a consultation somewhere Kathleen was unlikely to be lurking."

Matt nodded. "Meals on wheels for the hard-drinking set."

That merited some laughter to break up the sense of...what? Of divergent paths.

Max nodded at him. "You've spent some crazy nights trying to peel back the layers of Kathleen's brain. Can you predict how she'll react now, having confronted us and done damage?"

"We all took damage from that meeting." Matt glanced at Temple. "Except Temple."

"Damage by proxy," Max said. "I meant physical scars you can point to. You've got to think of Kathleen as a Cold War agent whose day is done. She's lost purpose. The fact that she's a second-generation victim of the Magdalene convents in Europe and the British Isles makes her double trouble."

Temple sipped her drink for the first time. "I got the DVD of *Philomena*, that Oscar-nominated Dame Judi Dench film. And isn't *that* weird?" She smiled.

"What?" Matt asked, wanting to share a rare optimistic moment with her. "The film?"

"No. I mean a 'Dame of the British Empire' named Judy with an *i*. Seems kinda junior high for the high-falutin' Brits. Go, Judi! You're a stand-up dame!"

Max chuckled too. For a moment they were just three friends shaking their heads at the collision of Then and Now.

"Anyway," Temple said, sobering quickly, "the film's a devastating indictment of those convent 'laundries', where they imprisoned 'fallen' girls and women as forced labor. At fifteen, Philomena hardly knew why or how she was pregnant, then her baby boy was taken away at three years old—not at birth, but after *three* years together—to be 'sold' for a thousand dollars to a wealthy American couple. Philomena accepted it as punishment for 'sin', but later married and had a daughter. She never mentioned her 'lost son' to anyone, until she finally told her adult daughter decades later. Even then, the nuns would *not* tell the daughter anything, but the daughter still 'found' Philomena's son in America. He had been a Republican Party bureaucrat in D.C., now dead of AIDS."

"The ironies are brutal," Max said.

"Not only that, the son had asked the convent to give him information on his mother, and they stonewalled him too."

"Beyond tragic." Matt considered what his unwed mother had gone through to give him a "more normal" family life. "Beyond forgiveness."

Temple sighed. "That's not the worst of it. The poor son, dying, requested his ashes be buried at the convent, in case his mother ever came there looking for him. That they permitted, and his grave is marked. The story is…crushing, yet the film celebrates the mother-child connection and faith."

The men remained silent.

"How could your church do that?" Temple asked Matt, her voice trembling with indignation.

"Other denominations did it too. Western as well as Eastern culture demonizes women and girls for being sexual."

"Religions seem to be better at it than anything else." Temple was still raw from immersing herself in so much misery visited upon so many innocents in the film. "Those 'fallen' women were girls kept ignorant, who were taken advantage of, only on *them* it showed."

"It happened to my mother," Matt agreed. "And me by proxy."

"And you're still 'in' the church even though you left the priesthood? I don't think I could get married in a church with that history."

Temple obviously hadn't planned to think, to say that.

The silence was so utter it seemed to be an invisible taut wire between them all.

Max stirred. "Give him a break, Temple. You, being from a family of agnostic Unitarians, don't know what it's like to grow up in a religiously driven environment. I do. There are good and bad elements in every religion."

"That's just it. Religion is supposed to be about being good. I'm just so shocked. I also discovered a devastating song this old folksinger wrote about the 'fallen' Magdalene women."

"Really?" Max was fascinated. "Who's the singer?"

"Funny. It's a first name like Dame Dench's. Joni. Judi. Joni Mitchell."

Max laughed. "She's still very alive and kicking and would be insulted by your description."

"I don't blame you for being angry, Temple." Matt reached to take her hand...fist. "We know Kathleen's mother was in such a place. Kathleen was born there. Since they 'sold' off the toddlers, why did they let the infant Kathleen stay with her mother and the nuns?"

Max drew his legs in and grunted a little at the ache. "They kept her for some reason. Growing up there must have driven her half-mad. Somehow she got pregnant in her teens. So they took her child away."

"And then," Matt said, accused, "she escaped to become an Irish rebel. And you and Sean went to Ireland on a teenage joyride, both went crazy for her, and both abandoned her in one way or another too."

"You've been talking to Kathleen too much," Max said wryly. "When she used threats to Temple to force you into those pre-dawn assignations at a Strip hotel, she tried to seduce you too, didn't she?"

"Maybe. I wasn't having any of it."

"You have some sympathy for her now. That's one result she seduced from you."

Matt shrugged at Max's assertion, but said nothing.

Max pushed himself up as if to argue with his fists. "Sean wanted to be seduced, but missed out. He withdrew from the game Kathleen was playing with us. He stayed an innocent. I had won the competition for her...whatever we hoped we'd get."

"Guys," Temple warned. "We all know what guys that age wanted to get."

"Not me," Matt said, regretting the words the moment they became audible.

"Your problem," Max said with a withering glance. "Some of us have hormones that haven't been hammered out of us by piety and hypocrisy."

"So," Temple said with an arched eyebrow, "you were a just a randy kid, Max?"

"She was...seductive," Max conceded.

"She'd been abused," Temple said. "Victims assume that's the way the game is played."

"How was I to know? She was six years older, a woman."

"That's a lot older," Matt said, "during those teen-to-young-adult years."

"Look," Temple told Max," I don't think either you or Sean meant any harm. You were too dumb."

Max looked down. "Bingo. Absolute jackasses."

"To Kathleen," Matt said, "American boys were probably a breath of fresh air. You'd didn't judge her as a slut, like the nuns and good Catholic boys had been trained to do. You fought for her as a prize. To someone with zilch self-esteem, that was a revelation."

Temple nodded. "Every villain is righteous in his or her own mind. And someone who was manipulated may find manipulating...normal."

Max drove his long, magician's fingers into his hair. "It's clear that Kathleen and I need to reinvent our first, disastrous encounter. That's why every instinct drives me back to Ireland. We've got to fight this out on the old ground, or nobody I care for in the U.S. will be safe."

He glanced at Matt. "I'm not talking about just here in Vegas. I'm talking about Sean and my families, mothers and fathers torn apart by their kids' divided fates. If I could find and bring Sean home to them..."

"*You* could go home again," Temple finished. "And if you go back to Ireland, it's to draw Kitty away from us. That's all you've ever done, Max, is pull the ghosts of your counterterrorism past back from here to the Old World."

"And it's all right to leave," Matt said. "I know somewhere in your mending memory you still care for Temple. It's just that's my job now."

"I'm sorry to say," Max went ahead and said, "that we can't keep meeting like this. We can't keep meeting, at least not as Temple's round card table investigators following her Table of Crime Elements. Here's what I'll be concentrating on: trying to find where Kathleen has gone to ground. She could be going after any one of us. I'm hoping to lure her back to Ireland to give you two some measure of safety, but don't lower your guard for a second until I can assure you she's not a threat."

Matt didn't like the worried look that passed over Temple's emotionally open face. "You don't need to be putting yourself in her path and at risk on account of me," he told Max. "I can take care of myself now, and look out for Temple."

"True, Kathleen was able to knock me out, so you two are the ones who did the most to stop her that night. But I'm the professional here and also have the most in common with her and the most vested interest."

"Did you believe her?" Temple asked. "That your cousin survived the pub bombing seventeen years ago? Isn't that likely a trick to get you to Ireland, where you have enemies and she has allies?"

"Maybe." Max drank again. "Ah, this is good stuff, and there's much more the like of it in Ireland. And," he added, sobering, "I need to find out what disposition was made of Gandolph."

His glance snared Matt's, who nodded. He understood. Max's mentor had been killed before his eyes and he'd had to abandon the body to save his own life.

Temple's eyes grew glossy with unshed tears. She'd known Gandolph. Matt looked away, pained. The emotions she shared with her former love would always remain, not exactly coming between her and Matt, but something he could never share.

As a faithful priest for several years, he also understood loyalty, but would never get how non-celibate men and women could unite so intimately, then separate and move on. Leaving the priesthood had been an agonizing process he still hadn't put behind him. Not unlike the apparent death of Max's boyish cousin.

They said you could never go home again. Matt knew leaving the priesthood had shut several doors of his youth to him. And teenaged Max had run from his own and his cousin's families, their once-close relationship wounded forever by the death of one, yet not the other, young man.

"Max," Matt heard himself saying, "you *can* go home again, if anyone can. You can see Gandolph put to rest, whatever you learn about his grave, or lack of it. Maybe you can find and bring your cousin home, after all. Whatever you find there, you're a fortunate man to have the chance to know the truth. Just don't let Kathleen kill you and undo all this."

Max took a deeply audible breath. "It's now become my theme song to *her,*" he said shakily. "The old ballad, 'I'll Take You Home Again,

Kathleen'. Maybe I can give her some closure too, even if it's only the vengeance and death she's been longing to deal out instead of deal with."

The limo had drawn up three blocks from the Circle Ritz. "You both must be vigilant about Kathleen tracking you," Max said. "I'll do my best to send her a message. It's between me and her now, hand to hand, but she's never predictable."

"Neither," said Temple, bowing out of the car when Ralph opened the door, "are you."

Max nodded shortly. "This is the last you'll see of me for a while then."

Maybe ever, Matt wondered. He nodded and followed Temple out.

19
Excess Baggage

Louie was out when Temple got home, and she was nervous.

Matt had escorted her to her door, kissed her chastely on the forehead, and left her to pack, promising to be back down soon.

She knew he wanted to give her cool-down time from her current disenchantment with nuns, Catholics, and men. Temple knew she'd overreacted, caught up in another woman's tragedy. A woman who could have been Kathleen. Philomena had forgiven the villains of her past. Temple would be damned if she'd forgive the...*witch* in her present. *Would be damned* echoed in her mind.

Not now. Back on track. Her hefty assignment at the Crystal Phoenix would get Max and Kathleen off her mind.

"Louie. Where are you? It's not like you to miss stopping in for a noontime snack," she murmured aloud, stepping out of her high heels to search high and low for him.

Even though the two-bedroom, two-bath condo was 1950s small, especially the two tile-lined guest closets that posed as bathrooms, Midnight Louie could always find a new place to hide his twenty-pound bulk.

So she mussed her hair going on her knees in closets and wrinkled her clothes getting up on the toilet seat to peer out the always-open tiny horizontal window that was Louie's aerial pet door. And she got litter grains pressed into the soles of her bare feet.

She knew Electra would keep Louie's bowls fresh and full, but...not saying goodbye, not seeing him before she left...that made her very nervous.

She returned to the living room, dusted off her feet, fluffed her hair and slipped on her high-heeled sandals again.

She was only nervous because Louie wasn't here to see her off. That was it.

Temple was *not* nervous about moving in with a legendary band. No, of course not.

She'd interviewed and done publicity for world-class stage actors at the Guthrie.

She wasn't feeling guilty about pretending to be with the band for PR purposes only when she was also a snoop, hunting traces of illegal drugs or emotional derangement. No, she was used to consorting with performers and artistic types here in Las Vegas. She was a professional.

Was she some newbie intimidated by maintaining some control over towering rock divas who'd once been mortal enemies? No. That was why she'd packed a lot of leggings that made her look taller, and her most practical high heels, which meant no thick platforms or narrow, teeter-prone wedges.

Still, she sat on the arm of her living room sofa, finally packed with three roller bags by the door, one just for shoes. She would need every inch of those stilettos to command cooperation from what amounted to a dysfunctional family of pampered performers.

A knock on the door had her leaping to her Jimmy Choo-clad feet.

It opened immediately as Matt poked his head around the door, spying the baggage. "Is this an around-the-world cruise or a few nights' stay at the Phoenix?"

"You know how I overpack."

"From one trip to Chicago? No, I don't." He'd reached her then, and kissed the top of her head again. Cautiously. "I'm going to miss you and your picnic hamper."

Temple snuggled into his arms. "Oh, Matt. I'm so worried about leaving you alone here at the Circle Ritz."

"Like *you're* a bodyguard?"

"I'm alert and suspicious and have a loud scream."

"I'll be all right." Matt turned to eye the luggage. "I could almost lift one of those bags now, which means I'll be up to lifting you in no time."

"*Oooh*, visions of thresholds crossed."

"Only if Kinsella finds and disarms Kathleen." Matt didn't sound hopeful.

"Let *them* duke it out. We have more interesting things to do." Temple turned her face up for a more thorough kiss and got it.

She sighed as she laid her head on his shoulder, but not from the kiss. "It's wrong to wish someone dead," she said, "but none of us will have a normal life until that woman is in prison or, you know, gets amnesia. There's an idea. We could just catch her, conk her on the head, and hope for the best. Surely that's not a mortal sin."

"Nor is this." Matt bent his head to meet her lips in their first, leisurely kiss since they'd been lured to a showdown at Max's house.

In the middle of the third marathon kiss somebody gasped.

They jumped apart, and Matt grunted softly at the interruption.

"So sorry, kids!" Electra Lark trilled, not sounding it. "The door was ajar, and I am a nosy landlady, so I just peeked…"

Electra's cobalt-blue-dyed white hair made the blue rinses of "old white-haired ladies" of decades past pale into memory. "I would say 'Get a room,'" she offered coyly, "but you've each got one here. When can I move you two into a bigger unit?"

"Soon, Electra," Matt told her, disengaging from Temple. The ex-priest in him hadn't yet converted to public displays of affection.

"Meanwhile," Electra said, "I rushed up here because we're being invaded."

Temple and Matt exchanged a look. Kitty or an emissary on the hunt? Again, so soon?

Before they could tense for confrontation, a jaunty knock rapped on the door. A tall, dark man in a café-au-lait-colored suit that was a shade or two lighter than his complexion pushed through the door and entered. Behind him came another just like him, and another. And another! All their different, delicately shaded suits could have come in a different cup at a differing price point at Starbucks.

The first man snapped his manicured fingers. "The bags." Two of the men picked up a bag each, as the third rolled in a huge, expensive Louis Vuitton model, at least a three-suiter.

"Oh, my," Electra said, her floral muumuu fluttering with her away from the door. "The Fontana brothers are the most efficient movers I've ever seen," she whispered to Temple. "I wonder if they do windows. These old semicircular frames are quite challenging, one disadvantage of a round building."

The first brother snapped a card from his inside breast pocket. "Call Gangsters and inquire, dear lady. We can provide muscle for almost every occasion."

"I wasn't expecting Fontana, Inc.," Temple said. "I thought Nicky would run over and pick me up."

"Nicky does not 'run over and pick up'. He is an executive now," the second brother said.

"He is our youngest brother, but he does not do luggage anymore," the third added a bit mournfully.

"I see," Temple said. "We have here a Fontana brother for every piece of my luggage, three bags full, but why are *four* of you here, and what's that huge suiter bag doing here?"

"Simple," the first brother said, bowing to them both. "I am Eduardo, in case you were wondering, and I will be living here, which I understand is right beneath Mr. Divine's accommodations." He turned to Temple. "I will also be accompanying him to his nightly radio show and back, in case criminal elements might be inclined to show up."

Temple was astonished. "You're going to stay here, in my condo, alone?"

"Ah, Miss Temple." Another little bow. "I am never alone." He petted one shoulder with the same fondness as someone might stroke a cat. A cat named Beretta. "Armando and I will be attached to Mr. Matt Devine as long as you are a guest at the Crystal Phoenix."

"In a platonic way," Armando said quickly, eyeing Matt.

Temple nodded slowly, then turned to Matt. "I guess you *do* have a bodyguard. Two of 'em. Van promised you'd be all right without me."

Eduardo had strolled to the French doors and onto the tiny triangular terrace. "Which vehicle, Mr. Devine, will I be driving?"

"The silver Jaguar and I'll be driving."

Eduardo shrugged. "Riding shotgun is perhaps the better arrangement for me and my, er, friend."

Temple sniggered to herself at the idea of anyone "riding shotgun" in a Jaguar.

She had joined the men on the balcony and frowned down at two glossy black car trunks she could just glimpse from this angle at her height, or lack of it. "I suppose my chariot awaits below. What make and models are those?"

"Tesla roadsters. Electric. Super fuel-efficient," Armando said from behind them.

Matt frowned. "Aren't they the model that keeps bursting into flames?"

"We drive roadsters, but even if those were the Model S in question, they would not explode when we drive them." Armando shot his cuffs like one to the designer suit born, which he was. "They would not dare."

"Reassuring," Temple said, smiling at Matt.

That flame-out problem had been solved a while back, she knew. Matt, the ex-priest used to modest living, wouldn't know that. He wasn't interested in conspicuous consumption and cars. He regarded the Jaguar bestowed upon him by the courting Chicago TV producers as a possible target and a certain pain in the neck, but recognized the interior creature comforts.

"I'll be fine for the next few days," she whispered to Matt as they shared a goodbye hug, "in the bosom of the Family Fontana."

"Along with all of their Berettas," he whispered back.

"And Eduardo will have your back, so I can rest easy too. Get better, and get ready for a very eager bride-to-be when we reunite again."

"Isn't that sweet," Electra crooned to all and sundry. "I'm going to marry them in my wedding chapel even if that's their second ceremony."

"We'll be there," the four Fontanas promised. "With boutonnières on," Armando added.

"Meanwhile, Miss Electra..." Armando took her arm to escort her to the door. "After Miss Temple is safely seen to the Phoenix, I will return to make for you a divine Bolognese sauce."

"You cook?" Electra eyed the brothers' pale suits, askance at the notion of red sauce in their vicinity.

"But of course. We are Italiano."

"Why are you all not married?" Electra the Justice of the Peace wanted to know.

"Because," Armando said with a wink, "we are Italiano."

20
Cool Hand Louie

If a PR person didn't have chutzpah, she didn't have the right stuff.

A PR person may not be shy about tooting her own horn, but she's got to be passionate about pushing her clients. Temple didn't take on clients she didn't believe in…except now and then when her soft heart did her hard head wrong.

It took a lot of chutzpah—and there was no other word whose very intonation exemplified brass and nerve—to try to mix with a famous group of recording artists a whole generation back in her relatively young timeline.

As a brace of Fontana brothers escorted her to the main Baccarat Suite's double doors, she was thankful for her private lunch with Lionel Bixby. At least one presumably friendly face awaited within.

Emilio and Armando each knocked on a door, then stepped back and swept them both open on Bixby's rumbling invitation to "Come in."

Temple walked through the broad archway, feeling she personified Shakespeare's play title, *Much Ado About Nothing*. Her entrance to the band's main suite, flanked and followed by Fontana brothers toting luggage, hushed the cacophony of instruments and humming and talking musicians.

Van von Rhine appeared from behind the wedge of Fontanas. "Our PR maven, Miss Temple Barr is joining you for a few days, to get ideas for some of the major media promotion we have in mind. Think of her as your group, and personal, publicist. We want every member of

Black & White to be a star in his or her own right. She's the one who can make it happen."

The resulting murmur veered from approving to mildly disinterested...to two wolf whistles from somewhere in the male ranks.

"Thanks for the idea," Temple said, unflustered. The boys in the band will be the boys in the band even when they're *really* sixty-four in another decade or so. "I can see a TV commercial now." She acted it out. "Black & White band guys on the prowl through a black-and-white wood, tracking each of our divas, who are wearing Little Red Riding Hoods. Great trailer, but it would need the right funny-scary music."

Minor guitar chords and an eerily high keyboard sound whined through the musicians lounging on the giant sectional sofa as one after the other picked a note and started embroidering on it.

"Really, Temple?" Van whispered over her shoulder.

Temple answered in a whisper. "I just was throwing popcorn to distract the baboons in the zoo, but if they want to run with it..."

She spotted Lionel Bixby approaching and smiled her recognition.

By now the big man was standing right in front of her and laughing like Santa Claus. "Talk about an entourage, girl, you got us beat."

Temple glanced over her shoulder at the magnificence of the Fontana brothers, who were being ogled by the females in the room—an older blonde woman looking over her shoulder from a small desk along the wall, and an exotically tattooed black woman lounging on the huge sectional sofa snaking through the room. Bixby, on the other hand, or foot, was staring at her feet.

Temple had a world-class shoe collection—new and vintage, true—but owned nothing a rock diva would even glance at through her three pairs of false eyelashes.

She looked down. Oh. A brace of black cats had slipped in with her and were preparing to twine around her ankles.

"Miss Midnight Louise has a boyfriend," Big Bix noted. "He looks mighty gangsta."

Well, at that, Midnight Louie had to do several aggressive ankle rubs and then stop in front of her in guard-dog "gangnam" style. She often found her TV remote was on MTV when she came home after leaving Louie alone.

"These are the hotel's house cats, past and present," Temple said. "If anyone's allergic, we can give them the bum's rush."

At that moment a pair of mobile dust mops ran *arf*ing and growling for Temple's apparently irresistible ankles. Or the cats standing beside them.

Feline backs arched and spat in reply.

Band members sprang up to divert the dogs from the cats. Fontana brothers dropped their cool and scrambled to corral the enemy species. No one could stop the impending face-off and stare-down.

The two dogs, one black, one white, skidded to a stop in front of Louie. Another cat might have gotten huffy. Not Louie.

The big black cat lifted a paw with the solemnity of a conductor commanding silence. The white one rushed him half-heartedly. The black paw brushed its sturdy ruff. The dog reared up and the paw followed. The dog went to its stomach. The paw parried the movement like a fencing blade.

Blackie jumped forward with a lunge. Louie's other paw deployed the *Stop* position. Blackie whimpered confusion. While they all watched, Louie controlled both dogs with the graceful blocking motions of his paws. It reminded Temple of slow-motion shadow boxing.

The dogs, balked, finally surrendered, belly-down in play-bows, their sagacious shaggy faces confused, their hairy eyebrows knitting like a puzzled human's. Louie's right paw remained raised.

In tandem, the dogs sniffed long and deeply at the commanding black cat's paw. Then they put their noses on their own black and white paws, stretched out in surrender, shut up, and sighed.

Released human breaths whispered around the room.

Big Bix broke the silence. "If only we could get along like these dumb beasts, huh, guys and girls? I guess Miz Temple Barr, our personal Crystal Phoenix PR advisor, is a totally a cool customer, for a natural-born redhead."

"Agreed, Mr. Bixby," Van said. "With peace in the animal kingdom achieved, I can leave you to your business."

At that the Fontana boys introduced themselves as on-site hotel security and errand service combined, and promised to keep to the halls and be discreet.

"Discreet," said the buxom black woman Temple would cast as a backup singer, "is not Black & White's style."

"We can go Country or Pop," Emilio assured them, using the music business phrase for versatility, as he and Armando bowed out by drawing the doors closed behind them.

And so Temple was left in the lion's den.

"These dogs are charming," she said to break the ice. "Small but feisty. I get that. What are they, and whose are they?" She trotted over to sit on the huge tufted leather ottoman in the center of the embracing sectional sofa, set her tote bag on it, and brought out her laptop. "They're a great publicity angle."

The black woman moved to join her on the ottoman and suddenly Temple wasn't an isolated stranger impinging on a long-established group, but a reporter doing a group interview, a situation everybody here knew and either loved or loathed. It was Temple's job to make sure they loved it.

"Sessalee," the woman introduced herself.

Temple ogled her muscular, bare, coffee-black arms—de rigueur for fashionistas and even media women reporting from the Red Carpet to the nightly news, now that Michelle Obama had set that style—had numerous lacey tattoos like ink sleeves with Austrian crystals glued on for glitter.

"That look is spectacular, but sure wouldn't work for me." Temple put her pale arm against the gorgeous midnight paisley.

"Don't need to needle it. I've got some killer long fingerless gloves that would rock your red hair color."

"Really?"

Sessalee regarded Temple's equally pale and uninteresting bare legs and the "nude" color heels that were supposed to make short women look taller, as if they were on tippy-toes. Temple was feeling like a Jane Austen heroine at the Rock 'n' Roll Hall of Fame.

"And toe lingerie too," the woman consoled her, "since no one in Vegas can stand to wear hose. Thank God."

Toe lingerie. How exotic. How not Temple. How bonding.

"Great. I'll look into that, Sessalee. Meanwhile—" She looked up to see that the band members had gathered around to see how she'd handle this tiny bit of their exotic lifestyle.

"Meanwhile, I need to do serial interviews with all of you to get ideas for publicity."

A voice broke in. "You don't need to get ideas. Don't worry your little-red-hen-head about it. I already have them all."

Temple looked up to see the woman from the desk was upright and on the move...stalking toward her like a modern-day Medea. Lacquered everything, a bouffant blonde hairdo and hunter-red nails. Eighties chic from the gleaming white silk, figure-hugging suit to the over-tanned, age-spotted hands and face. Heavy jewelry that should have been sold as junk gold when 18-carat gold had topped out at $1700 an ounce. A Rolex watch showing off above a blue-veined hand. One hard-bitten hack flack.

Temple understood the woman in a flash. Widowed or multi-divorced, bi-coastal clientele in her heyday. No kids, maybe, or, if so, long gone. Still needing work in her seventies for money or just for some damn thing to do. Territorial as an old rabid dog. She considered young women in her field an affront, ignorant of the barriers she'd faced and flattened. And now all she had was this resurrected role with Black & White, a precarious enterprise already fraying at the seams.

This woman probably wanted to crush her, but she'd already broken Temple's heart.

"Are you," Temple asked, "Susan Everleigh? *The* Susan Everleigh? You're a national treasure when it comes to Black & White lore. It'd be an honor to work with you from the Crystal Phoenix end. In fact, if you could spare some time for an interview, I'd like to consult with you first. Is there someplace—?" She looked to Big Bix.

He'd already grasped the situation. "This is our central command room, Miz Barr, where we have a five-buffet table and bar." His hand swept to the spread along one wall. "There's a room off this one where you can speak privately with each of us. I'll send in a nice bottle of...I was going to say white wine, but let's call it Zinfandel...for you and Miz Everleigh, our ever-lovin' publicity maven from Day One. Vegas is a new venue for us, and we appreciate the Crystal Phoenix's commitment to our reunion gig. But, first, I'll introduce you and your luggage to your quarters."

Two of the jeans-clad men in the room who might be band members or roadies grabbed her bags. She smiled and addressed the waiting Big Bix. "Show me the way to San Jose."

The men immediately wove through the vast room ahead of her, through a wide archway and down an interior hall. Bixby opened a set of double doors and waved her inside. While her luggage was hoisted onto waiting racks, Bix urged her to "freshen up" and rejoin them when she was ready. He bowed himself out with suave, Fontana-rivaling grace.

Ready? Not really.

She was now a living, breathing "bug" planted in the midst of a bunch of hard-living performers comprised of big and little names, rich and poor bank accounts, and who-knew-what addictions...contradictions...predilections...and vendettas.

Finally, Temple and her luggage were alone at last. She snooped around what would be her quarters for the next week or so, and found she missed seeing...Midnight Louie. Why hadn't he followed her in? Because he was a cat, she told herself, and they go where *they* please, not you.

What a jazzy joint! Jacuzzi and all. No wonder casinos called the big gamblers for whom they comped suites like this...whales. She'd been told it was a bedroom with an ensuite bath. No one had mentioned that the bedroom was as large as her entire condo, sixteen hundred square feet. The bed, like Max's mother-of-pearl-inlaid Chinese opium bed, was an elegant indoor gazebo. This one was enclosed by chrome and mirrored fret-work, and heaped with enough Ralph Lauren linens and pillows to equip a department store.

A huge curved HD TV had its own conversation pit, as did an elaborate mirrored bar stocked with so many top brands that Temple only recognized a quarter of them. Behind stainless steel doors lurked a refrigerator with gourmet stock, and near it stood a fully stocked wine chiller.

If all the band members had this kind of suite, all they had to bring was their drug supply. That was the hardest aspect of Temple's assignment, a drug greenie like her tracking down who was using what and what might be getting to French Vanilla, and into her, in any way, shape or form, to make her go Top-Ten-level crazy. And why.

Temple wandered into the—yes, mirrored—bathroom equipped with a shower for six. It offered three rainfall showerheads and enough handheld sprayers on coiled steel cable to make the user feel the creepy mechanical alien probes from *The War of the Worlds* were visiting from Mars.

Music by Black & White drifted into both rooms.

Temple stood and regarded the six-person jetted tub. It was big enough for her to swim in, and the pattern of jets looked as populous as the rain of bullets that had perforated Bonnie and Clyde's car.

Temple guessed she had a cinematic imagination, and not in a good way.

Gazing back into the bedroom, she reflected that all this glass and mirror and polished chrome and steel might make someone who was a teensy bit drunk, or high, really go zonkers. Especially if that person didn't know she was imbibing something that was literally mind-blowing.

Was Temple at a disadvantage here! Minnesota had its illegal drug problems, but nothing like on the coasts. And Temple's four older brothers had watched her like Prohibition hawks, although she was sure they had tried pot. They all exulted in being on athletic teams, so she was also sure they never erred too much, even with alcohol.

Being Irish, Max's drug of choice was liquid, in warm variations of precious topaz colors. Matt sometimes drank a beer, and the occasional cocktail with dinner, but no Father Whiskey was he. Temple smiled, and then realized he'd be out of reach for a week too. Bummer. She'd never told Matt he was good in bed in case it caused an attack of that Catholic conscience, but he was. Don't mess with a good thing.

Temple sighed. She needed to keep her meddling hands off the delicate process of the Black & White reunion too. Probe, but probe delicately.

Her best strategy was to interview everyone for the forthcoming publicity, all the while turning into her older brothers to watch any and everyone's consumption of alcohol and any addictive or hallucigenic substances.

French Vanilla's erratic behavior might be all in her head, but Temple was hoping it was put there. That was easier to fix.

21
The Flack Pack

"I suppose you consider yourself a corporate spin doctor."

Those were Susan Everleigh's first, bitter words, said before lifting her full goblet of wine and drinking deep.

Lionel Bixby had whisked Temple into his designated interview room, where Susan was already sitting in a black Barcelona chair that made her white suit the embodiment of Black & White.

Being the second to arrive put Temple in a subsidiary position, but she preferred to defer to Susan's bruised ego. More flies with honey, and all that.

A waiter was still fussing over the tray holding yummy canapés, and water goblets for wine. Temple deduced that he had served the suite occupants before and knew squinky wineglasses wouldn't do for this crowd. She accepted a brimming glass.

"I'm not a spin doctor," Temple said. "I'm just a happy flack."

Susan's eyebrows had dwindled to a heavy line of drugstore eyebrow pencil, but she raised them as if exercising a forgotten strength, like doing a long-abandoned ab curl in the gym. "You 'own' that denigrating term, 'flack'?"

"Between us, with tongue in cheek."

"Cheeky. But your generation is snarky. And addicted to social media."

"Not really."

Susan had a desk in the main area, but this was a real office. Its huge desk supported printers, laptops and tablets, a landline and portable phones. Susan headed to the upholstered loveseat with a coffee table before it to hold their glasses.

"Vegas is an old-fashioned venue," Temple explained as they sat. "Image is everything. We're still heavy into TV and cable ads. Print ads. Gotta flash that neon and those showgirl feathers. All that. Also, not a big secret: the major casinos haven't made much off gambling since the Great Recession. So stage shows are of prime importance now. I'm thinking we need to reawaken the Black & White vibe of years ago, the marketing genius that made the time's social concerns interlock with the band's talent and drive. More than music, a whole new cultural demographic."

Susan had crossed her skinny, spray-tanned legs and angled them together to one side, a pose ideal for TV interview shows. She considered Temple's comment, and then nodded with almost painfully slow effort. "I was there for all that…jazz when B&W got going. It just seemed natural at the time. We were teaching the whole world to sing in perfect harmony, and then…the culture crashed."

"How? World peace wasn't a beauty-contest joke then. Having been in the Peace Corps years before was a good thing to put on a résumé."

"How does a young whippersnapper like *you* know that?"

"We whippersnappers use Wikipedia these days, Susan. It's quick. Not necessarily reliable, like a first-person memoir, but a decent place to start."

Susan's arthritis-knuckled fingers armed in crimson false nails turned the goblet stem around and around. "You're a smart young thing. I used to be a smart young thing. We fade. Inevitably, we fade."

"Or we survive and become archivists of our time."

"You're saying this is an opportunity for me."

Temple shrugged. "Somebody's gotta tell this story. A reunion performance run in Las Vegas will attract all the archivists. *Rolling Stone. Variety.* And new kids on the block like *Slate.* Whatever happened to shatter the group can help revive it."

"And you'd share that spotlight with me?"

"I'd give it to you."

"Why, for God's sake?"

"You said it. We fade. The culture shifts and we're out. In my personal life, I'm considering that I might have to change cities, find another job. I love what I do, but will it love me back in the long run?"

"No."

"Here's your chance to prove that conclusion wrong, Susan. Help me figure out what's going bad here with Black & White, and we'll both come out ahead."

"You're saying this…successful reunion might be the last chances for both of us?"

Temple raised her wineglass, still full. "Right. Our job as PR people is basically to fix problems so our little corner of the world runs smoothly. Let's do it."

"Even if it's people who need fixing?"

"*Especially* if it's people who need fixing."

"A toast to crazy-idealistic spin doctors," Susan said with a curled lip, a lifted glass, and cynical tone.

But there were tears in her eyes.

Having established an ally on the inside, Temple invited Susan to send in band members in any order she thought helpful. As Susan had slipped out the closed door, Midnight Louise had slipped in to study the room for a piece of territory to claim.

"What?" Temple asked. "Louie isn't deigning to join us in the wine closet?"

Louise performed the feline equivalent of a shrug. She shook out her ruff, and gave her left shoulder some fast licks.

Then she jumped up atop the desk and sat belly-down on the DVR unit for the sixty-inch flat-screen TV across the room. With her long coat, she resembled a feather-ruffled black hen sitting on a nest.

"I see," Temple said. "You're snubbing the cold couch for some warm electronic equipment."

Louise fluffed her significant tail and curled it around her feet, a signal that she was in no mood for social chit-chat.

Temple shrugged, then heard a knock and rose to welcome the first mystery guest.

He was one of the whites in Black & White, round-shouldered but lean. He covered the path to the loveseat in two motorcycle-booted strides.

"Mickey O'Hara," he said, avoiding shaking hands by waving his spectacularly long and large fingers, the thumbnails filed on an angle like X-Acto knives. "But you can call me 'Spider.'"

Pretty much every visible piece of skin—hands and forearms, neck, temples—was webbed with tattooed spiders. O'Hara was black Irish like Max, with pale white skin, black hair, and blue eyes. That only went to show what counted was on whom the color scheme was executed. What was spectacular on Max was mediocre on Spider. Everything about the man slouched, his eyelids drooping over watery blue pupils, his curled posture. The one exception was his shoulder-length hair, a coarse black mane streaked with lightning strikes of silver, the Bride of Frankenstein look transferred to a guy.

Temple could see why Spider's Frankenstein's monster hands had mastered the keyboards. Band keyboardists, in her experience, wore their hair long because it was what the audience saw as they did their Phantom of the Opera acts over the hot ebony and ivory keys. As a member of Black & White, the hair made Spider O'Hara dramatic and memorable. And Temple bet he could, if motivated, commit murder with those tattooed, tendoned, and powerful hands.

For now, he was sitting on the loveseat beside her, his T-shirted chest concave and one booted foot braced on the coffee table.

"You want my story?" he commented. "I did an autobio in '07 about how I kicked my drug habit. It tanked. Just like Black & White did. That's my story. Period."

"Except for the comeback part."

"*Hah.* This gig's already gone south, thanks to our high and mighty Highnesses."

"You mean the lead singers."

"Call them what you want. I have my own opinion, but it's not printable and sure not promotable."

"What have you been doing since B&W broke up?"

"Time, for one." He pulled out a nail clipper and dug the pointed tool under his nails.

"For drugs," she suggested.

"And assault. But I gave that up after the one arrest. Too hard on my moneymakers." He spread his bony fingers. And laughed. "Last few years? I've been playing piano bar for the tips."

Temple decided not to mention that "Piano Man" had catapulted Billy Joel into the big time. Spider O'Hara was way past catapulting into anything but further downsizing, and knew it.

"This is a huge opportunity for you," Temple told him.

"Oh, yeah?"

"The media coverage will be massive, although I'm starting way too late from a dead stop."

"Dead stop is right. The media coverage won't be about the music. It'll be like it was before. Who really did what to who, and why. And where's Cale Watson."

"There will be money."

"And do you know how many ways it splits, how the percentages fall?"

"No, can you tell me?"

"Let's see." He pocketed the nail clipper with the panache of a Hell's Angel stowing away his switch blade. Then he stretched his fingers on both hands wide. "The two divas." Five fingers went down. "The band members." Three. "The overhead, including freelance backup singers, manager, PR, stage assistants, roadies." Another finger down. Only one finger remained upright. Third finger, right hand. "This is more than I get, after everybody checks out their cash."

"Then why do this?"

"I should be the only member of this ever-lovin', audience-slaying band to hold out? Nah. I don't need the bad publicity. Eats into my tip-jar fund for the rest of my retirement."

He was leaning forward, ending the interview. "You look like a nice, sincere young lady." His grizzled face leered into hers, wafting ciga-rette-smell breath "You are out of your league here in Oz, Munchkin."

Temple stood and extended a hand. "Thank you, Mr. O'Hara, for being so frank. We all are more than we look."

He shook her fingertips—preserving his cuticles, no doubt—and slouched out the door.

"Well." Temple turned to Midnight Louise. "There goes a bitter man."

The cat opened one eye, then shut it, a gesture so slow and bored, there was no way it could be considered a wink.

Temple could hardly wait to see who Susan sent in next.

22
Dysfunction Junction

Of course I had watched my Miss Temple leave the Circle Ritz amid a full court press of Fontana brothers.

I put up with Miss Temple's significant others, but am not about to share my digs with any more eligible males than I have to, even Eduardo Fontana. I had clung to the parking-lot side of the venerable palm tree whose trunk is my ladder, and moved around it to stay hidden as the party left the condo for the automotive flotilla on the asphalt below.

This is getting to be a cast of dozens. Miss Midnight Louise and I will have our mitts full at the Crystal Phoenix.

I may need to call up extra troops from the police substation nearby, where Ma Barker and her minions reside. Meanwhile, I had to race over to the Crystal Phoenix to ingratiate myself with the dramatis personae in the celebrity suites. Luckily, a fellow with the personal attractions of my breed can go anywhere and fit in everywhere.

I make as grand an entrance as my Miss Temple and her dazzling escort of Fontanas by playing Scotch and Soda like a master hypnotist. When it comes to mental command, I am an Old Master. That is the only thing that I am old at, I hasten to add.

So while my roomie settles in by interviewing the scruffier members of the band, I head right for the major leads in this developing drama, the divas.

There is an old adage.

There are a lot of old adages. Many of them are about my kind.

I like the one that goes, "A cat may look at a Queen."

In the old days, that used to be something...one of us literal low-lifes catching a glimpse of a royal personage. Now the paparazzi do it all the time for us.

And, here in Las Vegas, if one wishes to see a queen, you can always visit the proper clubs all over town. I bet you thought you knew where I was going with that observation. I will have you know that a purebred lady cat who is capable of breeding is called a "queen", and many breed organizations can be found in every hamlet and metropolis, even in Vegas.

I cannot understand why a male cat is not called a "king". Gender bias, no doubt.

Anyway, I have let the junior partner of Midnight Investigations, Inc. attend my Miss Temple as she probes the personalities and psyches of the Black & White entourage.

I am used to dealing with my own "entourage" sometimes. I am referring to the elite all-black Ninja Brigade of my dear dam's Cat Pack. Ma Barker runs a tight clowder.

Still, you cannot underestimate the savvy, smarts, and sting of a seasoned alley-cat gang when you need some muscle at your back.

I fear these Black & White music-makers do underestimate such things. Perhaps it comes from cohabiting with Scotch and Soda, who are not only handicapped by being canine, but have an Old World attitude to life.

I have managed to wend my way out of the main room unseen to explore areas that might lead to the higher-end suites. I must be making progress, because Scotch and Soda do an end-around and appear in front of a promising door to bar my passage.

"YeCannaGoHeere. YeCannaGoHeere," they skirl like a pair of Scottish pipes.

You would think a musical group would prefer quieter breeds, such as the barkless Basenji, to save their keen ears from this caterwauling.

I thought I had settled this issue on arrival, but the canine breed is the kind to repeat the same mistake over and over again. That is why they have training classes for them, when no one dares to impose such things on my breed.

"I can go where I please or where my paw pokes a path through," I point out, fanning my shivs. "You do remember who has the upper mitt here?"

"WeCannaAbideYeHeere."

"Weel, I 'canna abide ye' in my way." I get ready to deliver a two-way sucker punch in four-four time—the four and four being my front shivs—when the door opens.

I stare at Jungle-Red lacquered toe shivs perched on a two-inch-thick platform sole of serious South American snakeskin.

My gaze follows the late, lamented snake epidermis winding up in a double helix reminiscent of DNA around a high-arched foot, trim ankle, and slender calf clad in tender milk-chocolate-brown hide.

A female voice commands from on high, "Scotch. Soda. Be quiet! Nilla is trying to sleep. Quiet."

Dark and light shaggy ears and eyebrows lower as the pair performs the cringing ritual it is all too easy for humans to enforce with the canine kind. Granted they needed to shut the Bobbie Burns up.

"Now, that is our good babies." The voice rewards them with such a low, loving tone I am about to join the deceased snakes in winding around her ankles.

"Oh," she says. I spot a fringe of dreadlocks lowering to swing temptingly two feet above my reach. "I have heard about the black hotel cat. This must be little Midnight Louise. We have a feminique moment here."

Jeez. Do I look little? Do I look like a girl? *I* had "heard" one of the two head divas here was delusional, but not to this degree.

Still, the apt operative does not hesitate to take advantage of an opportunity. I contrive to make a little *purrup* in my throat. (This is a gentle version of the human hiccup.) Then I bat my lashes and rub my cheek on her calf so my brushing whiskers provide a delicate after-breeze. She turns into putty in my paws.

"Come on in, sweet kitty. *You* will be quiet. Nilla has heard about you too, and would love to see you. She adores cats."

A double whimper from my rear cuts off after I step through the forbidden door and it is shut behind me.

The first thing I notice is the room is dark for high afternoon in Vegas. My high-tech night-vision apparatus snaps into action. They say soldiers of the future will sport such enhancements, but I am already here, fully loaded and ready to go.

I see a window wall with double curtains drawn across it, the usual sheer inner one under heavy brocade draperies. Against the opposite wall, a king-size bed is heaped with enough throw pillows to cushion a princess from the under-mattress presence of a minute dab of ant poop.

Some potent incense is making my eyes burn along with it. My ears flatten at the New Age music I imagine Miss Electra Lark's psychic Birman cat, Karma, hears jangling in her head day in and day out. Here it tinkles and piddles from a hidden device somewhere.

In the semidark, I feel a catnap coming on, so I shake my head to throw off the hypnotic environment. Spreading my shivs deep into a thick carpet helps me hold on to reality.

Then Red-toes turns on a silk-shaded nightstand lamp with a soft click. I see a figure rising from the pillows.

"Latty," the ghostly dame in white says. "I want to see the famous cat. Get some damn light in here."

"Latty" must be Chocolatte, who strides to the window-wall and pulls the curtains back about four feet. Vegas daylight floods in to show French Vanilla sitting on the edge of the bed in a silky little camisole slip sort of thing my Miss Temple will wear to bed on occasion (usually a sign I am about to be booted off the bedspread by an interloper). The woman's head is bent down, a Cher-huge halo of silver curls framing her white-chocolate-colored face.

I tell you, if I had a sweet tooth, which I do not, these diva-chicks look good enough to eat.

With her dramatic pallor yet fainter, even I can see that this French Vanilla lady is not feeling well. Her stick-thin arms on the mattress seem to be the only things holding her upright. Her drooping spine and head remind me of a leafy plant thirsting for water.

I pad over for a better look. Limp fingers stroke my ears, usually a favorite erogenous zone. I am too concerned about her listless manner to enjoy it.

"So what is happening?" she asks Latty.

The other woman sits beside her. She is awesome in the half-light from the chic little lamp. Her thick black dreadlocks remind me of the wig on an ancient Egyptian queen. This is promising. My breed was worshipped by those sages of the desert. I assume the posture of a statue of their cat goddess, Bast.

This means I must suck in my stomach and sit soldier-at-attention tall, my forelegs pillar-straight, and ears perked like a German shepherd's, my mein noble and impassive.

"She looks like a statue," Latty says with a soft laugh. "How funny."

It is my talent to amuse, even in pursuit of information. The more I look like a statue the more freely they will talk in front of me.

"What is happening out there?" Nilla asks in a weary voice.

Latty pats Nilla's hand. These feuding divas look mighty cozy to me. "We have been assigned a hotel publicist."

"We *have* a publicist, and pay her a fortune, mostly out of pity." For the first time Nilla's voice shows some starch. "I do not want strangers hanging around."

"I am afraid we cannot get rid of her," Latty says. "We asked the hotel to hold off on publicity until we were sure the band could gel for too long. This one is a brisk little redhead. Harmless. She seems able to handle Susan, and Big Bix has cottoned to her. Besides, she has already glimpsed one of your 'spells', and probably is here more to make sure those episodes do not get out to the public, than to publicize us."

"Oh, Latty, I do not know what gets into me. I was fine before we reunited. I just...the tension starts building, like when you have had too much caffeine. The pressure in my head."

She digs her long-nailed hands into the soft silver mass of her hair, which I decide is natural as to mass but artificial as to color. I do not get why human females do so many outré things to their hair when a good tongue-licking is all the beauty ritual the most pedigreed Persian queen needs.

Latty's voice is weary too. "Nilla, you promised when this gig came up you were not usin' anything. Has that changed?"

"No! Not even a toke. I am over all that. Maybe it is the world's worst migraine. Everything zones out and wavers and seems so shrill. And the nightmares. They are horrible. Maddening."

"Could it be return trip on LSD?"

After a silence, Nilla nods. "I did that. We all did that at one time or another. So, why now? Now when we are finally getting together after all those years and that...bitterness...why now do I have to pay for my play and get bad trips?"

Latty pulls Nilla's hands down, gently, and twines fingers. Black and white. I sense genuine affection. "Look, girl. When we were young we slung a lot of ego and temperament at each other. Hell, stuff we did, risks we took, we are lucky to still be alive. Much less still slingin' around onstage in our high heels and ass-short skirts."

Nilla laughed again. "Yeah. Fifty is the new forty, I hear. We once thought forty was the end of all life on Earth. Had to do all our livin' before thirty hit."

"And it did, and we hit it back. Been a lot of sass and sorrow under the bridge," Latty agreed. "We do not smoke nothin' now, but we are still smokin' hot. Right?" She shook Nilla's limp hand and patted Nilla's bony knee. "I will have our Medicine Man look in on you. That is what he is here for."

"I do not need Doc Dryden. I need a friend." The woman on the bed produced a smile as lame as her posture and energy. "Stand by me, Latty. I swear I am not abusing anything. I would not sabotage the whole band like that."

"Sure. Maybe it is just stage fright. You will be fine." Chocolatte patted the other woman's hand.

It struck me as a halfhearted pat, and I know a thing or two about pats.

23
All Made Up

Van von Rhine had used bursts of varying accent colors to enliven all the duotone black-and-white suites…magenta, lime green, cobalt blue, crimson, tangerine, but the pop of color in French Vanilla's suite, a bright lemon yellow, had gone AWOL.

Even the pervasive black and white had been softened to a range of grays.

That was because both sets of curtains on the window-wall were drawn.

It was 11:00 a.m. and Temple had arranged to interview the singer while she was getting made up for the day.

An oversize white satin boxer's robe large enough to have been stripped off the latest heavyweight champion hung from the star's broad but bony shoulders and enhanced her albino look. And, even at this early morning hour, she wore her large, heavy-framed, wrap-around sunglasses. Black on pure white.

The sunglass habit either came from dodging paparazzi cameras or permanently reddened eyes due to another habit, major drug use.

Or both.

Van, what have you got me into? Temple wondered.

Potted and cut flowers lined the back of the desk. A heavy perfume scent made the room seem stuffy, but Temple still detected the acrid undertone of marijuana. Medical marijuana was legal in Nevada, including for nerves and stage fright, she imagined. The bald guy they called Doc was some level of medico in the retinue. He also could be a source of drugs.

Susan Everleigh bustled around Temple to address the star. "Nilla, the waiter will be here with your breakfast soon. And Doc will follow, for your injection."

Temple's mental alarm bells went off.

"Then Sessalee can do your hair and makeup," Susan added.

"Does *she* have to be here?" The sunglasses nodded in Temple's direction.

"I'm afraid so."

Thanks for the enthusiastic recommendations, Susan, Temple thought.

Susan, however, acted as if she were being brave. "She'll be very unobtrusive, Miss French. She'll follow your preparation routine so as not to cut into your rehearsal time. She's a PR person like me, gathering background for promotion angles, getting a sense of what goes into mounting a major Vegas show."

French Vanilla wasn't sure about Temple even now. "What goes in me and on me at this hour of the morning can't be useful, or entertaining."

But it's exactly the point. Temple cleared her throat. "I'll stay out of your way as much as possible," she told the singer. "You can okay or nix any promotion angles I come up with."

French Vanilla's slim white hand made a ridiculously fluid "whatever" gesture. "I don't like people watching me." Dead silence at that extraordinary statement. "I mean, watching me offstage. It makes me nervous."

"Then I'll interview you." Temple decided to breach the Celebrity Wall. She sat on the black leather couch with the woman, at a two-foot distance.

This close, Temple saw the tremor in long fingers tipped with black-and-white nail designs.

A knock on the suite door came before French Vanilla could object to Temple's nearness.

A blinding slice of light from the outer room made the waiter who waltzed in a silhouette in a short white formal jacket and black tux trousers.

"Your private chef has supervised your breakfast, Miss French." A Fontana brother swept a glass-and-metal serving table in front of the star to hold a silver tray.

Susan turned a sofa table light on, permitting the steel dish covers to appear like flying saucers darting out of the gray darkness. With a flourish, Fontana Brother X removed the covers to unveil an array of white serving dishes.

Temple's appetite sat up and begged when she saw three eggs sunny side up presented in cups of curled and crisp maple-scented bacon. Thin slices of pungent gourmet cheese embraced the egg cups. A crepe had been teased into a frill with a dollop of decorative whipped cream and a drizzle of dark chocolate sauce. A creamy heart design topped the latte cup. And a single yellow rose occupied a bud vase. Several crystal shakers with sterling-silver caps guarded the array.

Temple drooled.

"Miss French" pouted at the plate.

Temple saw Fontana X to the door.

"Giuseppe," he whispered, reading her mind. "I watched all ingredients prepared. The crystal shakers are from a locked cedar tea box that travels with Miss French. Those I can't vouch for."

When Temple returned to the sofa, one faintly penciled-in eyebrow had raised above the star's sunglass frame. "You like the handsome waiter, do you? What's your name?"

"Temple."

"I mean your first name. If you're going to be drooling over my breakfast and my waiter, I should know it."

"My first name *is* Temple. Last name Barr."

"How old are you?"

"Almost thirty-one."

Something defrosted in the older woman's pose. "Almost thirty-one. Much better than 'almost fifty-one', believe it, girl."

"Fifty is the new forty, Miss French," Temple said primly. "What may I call *you*?"

French Vanilla laughed. "Just Nilla. And drooling over handsome waiters is healthy, Temple. Only it's very unbecoming once you reach a certain age." She went quiet again.

"Your eggs will get cold, Nilla." Susan had taken Temple's seat beside the woman, and brought a fork toward the elegantly limp hand. Susan was unofficial mother hen, Temple saw.

French Vanilla stuck the tines into the center of an eggy little sun, watching the soft-boiled yolk run in rivulets. That seemed to have released the eating urge. Her fork crumbled the clever cups into bitable pieces.

Susan gave Temple a relieved glance. One thing was already obvious. The whole entourage depended on this one woman keeping herself together. From Temple's observation, Nilla's eating habits wouldn't keep the emperor's nightingale together, or alive.

Susan removed the breakfast tray after putting the rose on a sofa table.

"Now," Nilla told Temple, "Doc comes in to shoot some stainless steel vitamins into my skinny ole veins."

"How do vitamin B12 shots help?"

"Not much that I can figure out, honey, but it's like botox. All the ladies of a certain age get it." She eyed Temple again. "Nobody in Vegas is from Vegas. Where are you from?"

"If I say 'Minnesoda' I'll sound like an escapee from the Coen brothers' film, *Fargo,* so I'll say 'Minneapolis.'"

Nilla actually chuckled. "That movie was a hoot! Did you see it with a guy or your girlfriends?"

"Girlfriends." Temple didn't mention she was in junior high when she'd seen it, given French Vanilla was defensive about her age.

"That's good. Men come and go, but you never lose your girlfriends." She fell silent again.

Temple kept quiet. She wasn't stepping into the ring between French Vanilla and Chocolatte until she knew more about both of them.

Where Nilla's gaze went was impossible to tell. She tilted her head and the unnatural halo of pure-white curls.

She apparently was looking at Temple's hand, specifically third finger left hand. "Looks like you got some high-calorie sugar in your life. Bling, baby, bling."

Temple studied her ruby-and-diamond Art Deco engagement ring with new eyes. Imagine! A rich and famous, even infamous, rock idol was admiring something of hers. Something Matt had selected with her in mind.

"Yup. I'm getting married soon."

"First time?"

"I'm only thirty." Temple had never thought of herself as an older bride. Heck, her aunt Kit had been a first bride at sixty.

"Girl, most women I know have been through two or three divorces by then."

"This is for keeps."

"That's the way to think of it. Positive. What's the guy do?"

Temple wasn't sure where in French Vanilla's personality this nanny side was coming from, but anything to establish a relationship with a possible victim...

"He's a radio counselor and does some occasional guest gigs on *The Amanda Show*."

"Oh-oh-oh. Marry into show biz, you're in for a life of Le Miz."

"You mean misery? Not in this case. Matt's not a show-business person. That stuff just sorta happened."

"Justin Bieber 'just sorta happened', and look how that turned out."

"I know. Rich, spoiled, media-slurping monster. That won't happen to Matt."

French Vanilla rose, towering over a seated Temple. "Fame and dough make monsters of us all. Where's Doc? He insists I need that shot."

"You said the vitamin B12 didn't do anything for you," Temple said, rising.

Nilla wheeled on her, fierce. "It *might* do something. I'm heavy into 'might do' these days." She turned to the door. "Doc," Nilla called in a robust contralto surprisingly like Chocolatte's trademark voice. "Where are you and your magic needle? Bring yourselves on in here."

The bald man bustled in with a rolled-up kit containing hypodermic needles and clear liquids in tiny bottles. Temple itched to get her hands on that emptied bottle, but after injecting Nilla's inner elbow, he rolled the kit and thrust it back into his safari jacket pocket.

Temple wondered what other potions and pills lurked in those many pockets. Maybe some pot too.

"Thanks, Doc." Nilla let the wide satin sleeve fall back over her thin, pasty forearm.

He glanced at the remaining food on the breakfast tray. "Lots left. You really should finish it. That hydrating cup of Zen tea aids memory, mood, and energy. Drink it down, baby."

Nilla shrugged. She'd heard this sales pitch before. Temple wasn't an herbal tea drinker. The brew's pale saffron color didn't encourage her to start now. She abruptly realized that both Doc and Nilla were watching her with questions in their eyes.

"Yes?" Temple asked.

The man answered, suddenly formal. "Lately, I've been prescribing a marijuana cigarette after breakfast."

"He wants me mellow," Nilla told Temple. "They all do. The picky aggravating things we have to discuss when rehearsing for a new venue, especially with all the old band members vying for cameo bits, drive me nuts. You want one?"

With four older brothers riding shotgun on her teen years, Temple's exposure to addictive anything had been limited to one puff, one sip, and no sniffs...anything else was encountered here and there on the fly, and unimpressive.

"Alcohol is my only vice. I never even smoked tobacco."

"Have you never toked?" Nilla's amazement said a lot about the touring musician's lifestyle.

"I'm all for medical marijuana, but I have four older brothers in law enforcement. I was born busted. Go ahead, I'll get a vicarious kick."

Nilla laughed. What Temple said was true, sort of. Her brothers *were* law enforcement on the house rules her parents laid down. By the time she got out and on her own after college, she was too sensible to blow money, time, and jobs she loved on illegal substances.

Doc was already back with a lit roach. The mocking nickname fit. The crumpled brown cigarette made a crude accessory for Nilla's elegant fingers, but if it prevented scary episodes like Temple had glimpsed, thank goodness.

"That's an intriguing scent you wear," Temple said, wondering what was strong enough to overpower marijuana.

"Do you like it?" The woman's energy perked up. "It's an Asian vanilla blend, in my honor, of course. The hotel provided it. I also use it to scent potpourri." She waved at a shallow bowl, and Temple understood why the fragrance was so pervasive. "It's something French called *Datura Noir,* but I call it 'Day and Night' in English. I could have my own signature perfume made and marketed, but until then, this is my new favorite."

Temple marveled at how self-absorbed superstars could be. Of course, "Temple Barr" would never be on a fragrance label.

She could honestly encourage the diva from her PR experience. "'French Vanilla' would be a knock-out marketing success in the fragrance world. Singing superstars seldom have perfume labels, and you're already an icon."

"What a clever young woman. I like you," the star decreed. "Send in Sessalee," she told Doc. "Time to put on my happy face."

"You don't have a personal assistant to do errands?" Temple asked when they were alone.

"I had to fire the last one, so I'm limping along with the boys in the band. They're happy to cater to me because without me and Chocolatte, they wouldn't be working again."

Nilla left her cigarette to burn out in a Baccarat crystal tray, then rose and ambled barefoot down an interior hall. "The hotel has transformed the spa bathrooms here, already quite Luxe, into star-level dressing rooms for Latty and me."

Not kidding!

Temple stood astounded in the doorway long after Nilla had become an elegant figure reflected from every angle in full-length, three-fold mirrors. The effect was a cross between being inside a faceted diamond...and a funhouse attraction. Ego—and every imagined flaw women are prone to—was magnified to the nth degree here.

An endless walk-in closet with its double doors open offered a black-and-white panorama of clothing mixed with silver and gold lamé. Shelves of showgirl-style wigs and headdresses sat on custom head blocks formed to present French Vanilla's face over and over, also reflected over and over.

"This is...stunning," Temple said.

"It's just a fraction of my onstage changes. The largest costume pieces are already stored in the backstage area."

Mine eyes dazzle, Temple thought, but her brain suggested that this magnified world of make-believe surrounding a fragile personality was asking for more trouble.

A knock on one of the ajar doors ended speculation.

A tall and more than pleasantly plump young black woman wearing a long-sleeved white smock and purple tennis shoes advanced a couple shy steps into the dressing room. "Are you ready for me, Miss French?"

This was the tattooed "toe lingerie" woman from the main suite, now in beautician gear.

"Sessalee, we have an observer this morning."

Temple nodded as Nilla went on.

"Sessalee Smith is my irreplaceable magic mirror, Temple. Perhaps, Sessa, you could do a more elaborate daily makeup." Nilla finally doffed the sunglasses and set them aside, revealing blinking blue eyes no more reddened than the tiny eye corner veins Temple saw in her own mirror.

Huh. The chronic druggie theory was looking weaker.

Meanwhile, Temple had to figure out how the makeup artist figured into the personnel under suspicion of providing illegal drugs. Hairdressers, she knew, could fulfill that role, particularly in the lucrative, high-pressure celebrity world.

She watched Nilla sink into the beauty parlor chair provided, eyelids already closed to a mere slit. "Temple Barr. I'm hotel PR, getting a feel for the show."

"Oh, this is the most fun part." Sessalee tied a clear plastic bib around Nilla's long, slender neck, then snapped on latex gloves over her impeccable false fingernails and stood behind the seated star.

The reflection of the women's faces in the mirror presented an enormous contrast. Nilla's had the cadaverous bone structure of a high-fashion model and an almost-albino complexion. Temple couldn't imagine how makeup could enhance the pale eloquence of nature.

Sessalee's rich dark-chocolate face was all perky chubbiness, but her bright green eyeliner and shadow were applied to produce a work of art. Her chin-length green-and-magenta-colored garden of pigtails provided some "pop" in this hothouse, high-style environment as she maneuvered her wheeled stool around her subject. Temple wondered why a woman in her twenties affected a childish look so reminiscent of black stereotypes.

Temple was also surprised when pale foundation and powder were applied to further buff Nilla's pallor. Eyeliner was ancient-Egyptian thick and black. Pastel-tone cream eye shadows with sparkling bits of gold or silver or red made Nilla's pale blue eyes look larger and darker, particularly when a thick, long fringe of black false eyelashes sporting white Austrian crystal accents was glued on.

Delicate raspberry cream rouge highlighted cheekbones, temples, and chin. The slick and shimmering lipstick was an unearthly bright magenta, carefully brushed on with two highlight shades. A final touch was a light tapping with a powder puff to "set" the look.

Temple's beauty routine of lightly tinted foundation to subdue her freckles and brown eyeliner and mascara seemed pathetically grade school.

Nilla slipped out of the chair, tossing aside the plastic protector and redonning her oversize sunglasses. Maybe they were a tribute to Yoko Ono. "I'm dressing now, but, Sessalee, you can stay and do a makeover on Miss Temple."

"Really?" Temple felt like a gratified teenage fan.

Nilla's smile showcased teeth as white and bleached as her hair. She glittered like some gorgeous, sexy, tree-topping angel. "Really."

Sessalee had already donned a fresh pair of gloves and was shaking out the protector. Temple mounted the swivel chair. It required mounting, the height being set for French Vanilla.

Laughing, Sessalee spun Temple around to a lower lever. "First floor coming up. Or down."

"This is so kind of her," Temple said. "And you."

"No problem. I also do Chocolatte now, but I haven't worked on a redhead in ages. This'll be fun."

"How long have you been with French Vanilla?" Temple could

sense Sessalee going quiet behind her as she tied the plastic bib behind Temple's neck. "Oh, it seems like forever. It's been so much fun, and the band has been so accepting, but I was hired just before they all came here."

"How do you get hired as a makeup artist to a star?"

"The woman who'd had the position with French Vanilla fell and broke her ankle. I happened to be a fan backstage at the concert when it happened. I heard all the buzzing about the problem and just volunteered to help. The guy I told happened to be Mr. Bixby."

"A couple 'happened to be's' and a makeup star is born."

"I had to learn a lot fast, but I'd been a makeup freak all my life, since I was a little girl. I love changing people's looks."

"Do you have to act as dresser too?"

"Yes. I'm needed backstage for makeup changes and touch-ups anyway."

"Nilla changes even makeup during the show?" Temple had to keep silent and blind as a foundation sponge swept over her face...lips, lids and all.

"Every look is layered. I add and subtract hues to match the costume changes."

"Poor Nilla must be almost wearing a makeup masque by show's end."

"Chocolatte too," Sessalee said. "Look up and don't blink."

Temple gingerly opened her eyes and did so. "And, going by the clothes in the closet room, the costumes must be showgirl-heavy."

"Not that heavy. Showgirls strut slowly. Nilla and Latty do major singing and dancing. They need all the breath and muscle they have. Their costumes are much lighter than they look. Any major larger-than-life pieces are discarded early in the number."

"I like heels, but I can't imagine how Lady Gaga moves on those pogo-stick-high platform boots and shoes."

"They're small stilts on giant foundations. And she did have hip surgery."

"That's right. I read about that. Do you use latex gloves to keep from contaminating the makeup from person to person?"

"Right. A wrong dab somewhere and you've got a star with pink-eye."

"Am I soup yet?"

"Just your lips left. You'll have to be quiet, not easy for you."

Sessalee had her number—inquiring reporter.

Temple endured several agonizing no-question moments until Sessalee stepped back and said, "There."

"That was fast." Temple gazed at the mirror at some woman with an air-brush job for a magazine cover. "I look like a movie star! I can never leave home without you again."

"Not true." Sessalee pressed some pencils and little pots into her hands. "I used an auburn pencil on your eyes and eyebrows. Liquid-to-powder foundation is best for freckle camouflage. Peach and plum—and maybe teal, for your blue-gray eyes—are your go-to lip and eye shadow shades, also as rouge. For an outstanding occasion, try a bright, true red Revlon lipstick."

"This is great, but how do I get all this guck off?"

Sessaleee produced a clear bottle labeled...Magic Makeup Remover. "Use cotton balls, and *voila!*"

Temple dismounted the chair, examining the decidedly beyond-drugstore brands in her hands. "And, except for the Revlon lipstick, I can never buy makeup without a major credit card balance again."

"You're worth it."

"I can't keep *everything*," Temple said, juggling the loot.

"We don't reuse makeup on anyone else. I'd have to throw these out. You're welcome to anything from your color family in my armament. I rarely need this set of colors." She indicated a tray of luscious hues Monet would envy. "If you want, before the dress rehearsal, when everybody gussies up, I can do a full evening makeup on you too."

"That is so generous, Sessalee. I'd *love* it."

"From that left hand ring, you have someone you'd like to knock off his white horse with amazement."

"You're observant, and right."

Temple followed Sessalee through the empty bedroom and collected her tote bag in the living area, carefully stacking the freebies into its accommodating depths.

Temple was deeply against wolf whistles, but the sounds greeting her in the main band suite were more English bobby-summoning shrieks.

"Thank you, thank you," she said, making a little "curtain call" curt-sy. "Courtesy of Nilla and Sessalee. Now we all need to get back to work."

Still, she kept glimpsing a startling new self in the many suite mir-rors and reflective surfaces, thinking it was a sin no significant others were within miles of her right now. And she wouldn't even be going back to the Circle Ritz tonight to show Matt.

So she snuck back into her mini-suite way at the back and took a couple selfies to e-mail to Matt, with the message, *OK, sooo girly. Star's makeup artist at work.*

24
Deadly Nightshade

In short order, Sessalee's fabulous makeup jobs on French Vanilla, Chocolatte, and Temple left the celebrity suites for the limelight.

After their room service breakfasts, the entire troupe trooped down by the discreet back service elevators to the closed theater.

Temple adored hanging out in the darkened, empty "house" of a theater, where directors and tech folks lounged in the front seats and called instructions to the stage.

The stage lights were dimmed to work level, but French Vanilla still wore her shades. They looked "rock star" with her silver hair. Chocolatte's dreadlocks were festooned with glitter and beads, making Temple look around for Cleopatra's barge.

Temple was relieved to see Max was no longer cavorting like an Olympic gymnast on the towering set pieces and testing the workings until every detail was right and safe for use.

This was Danny Dove's show now, all the way. His angelically curly yellow head seemed to be everywhere…down in the orchestra pit, at the top of the sweeping stairs on the set, onto the highest descending "petal", in the wings to confer with the stagehands on sound and light boards bigger than the *Phantom of the Opera*'s gigantic organ.

His deep, booming voice occasionally peppered the instructions with words much less angelic than his looks.

"Up! No, not that much. Down. Not so much, dammit. Stop. Just stop." Then he'd vault up to the set location where he wanted the lights to focus.

Before Temple could even locate where his voice came from, he was elsewhere. And now he was bounding up the aisle to the seat where Big Bix was holding forth as Black & White's quasi-manager. Nilla and Latty sat beside him, only their wig-enhanced white matte and shiny black hairdos visible to Temple, sitting three rows back.

She had no problem hearing Big Bix's and Danny's "show time" voices, though.

"For the Heaven and Hell entrance," Danny said, "we'll have Miss French descending from the top of the flies, looking like Lady Gaga on stilts even she couldn't wear, in a twenty-foot tall 'skirt' of dazzling white and silver.

"She glides lower and lower, sinking into the clouds of her own gown massing at the top of the white staircase. Chocolatte, in the meantime, is rising from the orchestra pit, singing counterpoint. Her shimmering black skirt ascends up and up, looping up to form a huge train on the dark semicircular stairway down the 'dark' side of our black/white dissected set."

Temple tried to envision the effects, which sounded dazzling.

She saw Nilla's head turn, her striking profile outlined by the soft rehearsal lighting. She would be blinding in performance. Despite some time off in the makeup chair, Nilla was again wearing the wraparound sunglasses that obscured her eye makeup.

"I can't do that descent from heaven thing," Nilla said, her voice flat, and the refusal final.

Danny must have squeezed out a first drop of sweat before he said, "Miss French, the equipment is has been tested several times by unaffiliated inspectors. There will be no such 'fails' as dogged the *Spiderman* production on Broadway a couple years back. You will be riding on a solid platform the audience won't see because your skirt obscures it."

"On a platform that I won't see either," she said. "No. Will someone here listen to me? I can't do this."

Danny and Bixby exchanged a mystified look.

"But," Danny said, "you've done similar stage business before."

"Yes." Nilla made an exasperated sound and shook her snowy head. "I could see better then. I'm older now and so is my night vision. Now... the lights blur, they have halos. I can't distinguish light from dark as I used to. I'd be as good as blind. Would you put a blind woman up on your descending platform, Mr. Dove?"

"Just 'Danny', please. And no I wouldn't." He eyed Bixby. "You didn't say—"

"I didn't know, babe," Bix crooned to the woman. "Nilla, sweet thing, how long have you had this problem? I know you started wearing the sunglasses, but thought..."

"That I was trying to play the camera-shy star? Bix, I can't stand any light in my eyes. Nada. Nil." She laughed, a bit hysterically. "Nil for Nilla. And, it came on...I don't know when. Suddenly, one day...or night...I couldn't stand light."

Temple had quietly come down the aisle. "Were you okay for your last tour?"

"Yes, of course. I do all my own dancing and stage work. I expected to do that here."

"And," Temple asked, "how long have you been on hiatus?"

"A couple months. We were approached on this reunion deal right after the last performance on the road. The hotel people probably hoped to find us more agreeable to a long gig when we were all traveled out," she added with a laugh.

Chocolatte spoke up, "And that worked. We had a lot of 'ifs' about a reunion, but we were ready to settle in one spot. There's a time for Vegas in every career."

"I guess we're...I'm...getting too old," Nilla said with a sigh.

Temple hadn't yet got her answer. "When, though, did you start wearing the sunglasses?"

"Maybe..." Nilla had to think.

Chocolatte didn't. "I know. When we came to Vegas. This is Sun City as well as Sin City. Isn't that when, Nilla?" she asked coaxingly.

Everybody seemed so solicitous when dealing with Nilla. Had it always been like that? Or just now, for this crucial show? And how was Temple going to investigate the distant and immediate past of the entire group?

She met Danny's glance. He was definitely not his usual impish self. He saw the show concept sinking like the Titanic.

"We should get in an eye doctor," Temple said.

"No!" Nilla's voice shook with anger. "My night vision has been weakening for years. I'm perfectly normal. You'll just have to work around me."

"It can be done," Danny said. "The theme is very Aubrey Beardsley."

"Oh, I didn't spot that theme yet," Temple said. "That's brilliant."

"Who is this Beardsley person?" Bix asked.

Temple knew and loved to explain. "Fabulous late nineteenth-century illustrator. Illustrated Oscar Wilde's writing. He used elaborate, dramatic black and white only."

"I don't know about doin' no nineteenth century in the twenty-first," Bix grumble-rumbled.

"I do," Latty said. "I've got Beardsley wallpaper in my powder room at home and it's socko."

"And I don't know about finding set inspiration in Chocolatte's powder room," Nilla said, with a laugh. "I'll have to see it to believe it. If I can."

"Not to worry," Danny told her. "I can fashion a glamorous Beardsley mask that has darkened lenses in them, and mark your stage places with reflective tape. We can always use a dancer double for the high-wire stuff."

"I've always done my own dancing," Nilla said again.

As she and Latty and Big Bix huddled, Temple moved away with Danny.

"You know, my little love," Danny said softly, "aging rock stars need protection from stage lights, so you'll see a lot of them onstage in shades. But. Dilated pupils are a side effect of drug use. I can't risk having a coked-up cookie on my set."

"I know, Danny. I saw her eyes briefly in the spa bathroom, dilated to solid black. That's why Van wanted me on the site. It's funny. The famous feuding divas seem to get along great. Maybe somebody else in the band doesn't like this reunion gig."

"And is playing on French Vanilla as a recovering addict to get her hooked again?"

"That would be rotten."

"No, my dear." Danny stopped and took Temple's shoulders in hand as he looked hard into her eyes. "That would be show business. You watch your high-heeled steps, kiddo. If a saboteur is on board, my killer set could become a literal hit."

25
Casing the Joint

My life is not always lounging at the top of the Vegas hotel heap.

Once I am satisfied that my Miss Temple is safe and sound—maybe not sound of mind after the day's events—I determine drastic steps must be taken to avoid what I smell hanging the air...major crime to come.

I snooze on the roof until dark comes creeping out. Then I rise, shake myself off, and head for level ground.

It is a bit disturbing that I do not encounter my partner during my exit from the Crystal Phoenix, but I am darting under gaming tables and hopping hidden rides on luggage carts so as to make a discreet exit.

Miss Midnight Louise would pooh-pooh any info I got from the purse pooches anyway. In my humble opinion—IMHO, as we say online nowadays when we do not mean to be humble at all, which is no problem for me—Scotch and Soda are too sturdy (and studly in their own feisty terrier minds) to be mistaken for a "toy" breed. So call them tote-bag pooches.

I exit the hotel near the deserted rear pool area, which offers many small, unguarded areas I can slip through. I pay a brief, commemorative visit to my previous home office, the Phoenix chef's sacred koi pond. Hawaiian torch lights are dancing around the large canna lily leaves. You could almost mistake them for eternal flames.

This is a solemn moment in honor of those whom I have battled to the plate. I do miss not having a fast food joint near my new digs at the Circle Ritz, although koi are not the speediest fish in the sea, to their regret.

No time to linger upon days of yore. I have bigger prey to fry.

I am far enough away from tourists now to break into my means-business trot. Once domesticated, my kind can become layabouts who will only walk thirty feet between the refrigerator and the bathroom litter box. Sad. We born to the street know how to foxtrot and Viennese waltz over a lot of terrain in a little time.

Soon the Strip is just a perpetual sunset of blazing red, orange, yellow and purple neon behind me. This is a real neighborhood, quieter, with the cars sparser and the human presence muted.

Beyond some bushes, though, lies my goal, the police substation closest to the Circle Ritz. It might be fun to pop on home and scare the Ermenegildo Zegna designer pants off a Fontana brother by showing up in my condo unannounced.

I have no time for fun, but I am ready to rock and roll. I scent smells much less confusing than the possibly literal potpourri of Black & White Central.

It is the distinct aroma of maybe two dozen calling cards of the feline variety.

Sweet. I slow my pace and wait for what will come next.

When a fringe guard tries to jump me, I duck and dodge so he rolls head over hamstrings into a cactus.

Curses fill the night. Some cop returning from a shift calls out, "The cats are having a rumble tonight" to his brother and sister officers.

The injured party rises up spitting, but I hit him with a right cross to the kisser. My mitt is as thorny as any cactus in the Mojave Desert.

"Settle down, Catso Ratso," I tell him. "I am here on family business."

He sways on his feet, trying to muster some threatening moves. "What family business?"

"I need Ma Barker at the Crystal Phoenix to prevent a crime in progress."

By now Catso Ratso has regrouped and is about to try another fur fandango.

I am ready for him, but a serious growl behind us has the hair standing up on our necks and all the way down our spines.

"Cut it out, boys, or I will have to slap you both into next week with no return ticket," Ma Barker says. "And you, Louie, offspring or not, are not going to get a thing here. I am not about to set one toe-pad across the icy, people-packed threshold of an air-conditioned Las Vegas Strip hotel. I breathe free. I breathe the air as Bast meant it to be inhaled in ancient Egypt, hot and dry. I am a street person and proud of it. Your friends at the Crystal Phoenix? Let them eat crab cake."

"Now, Ma," I plead. And I do mean *plead.* If I were canine (thank Bast I am not) it would be a whine. "Only you have the street smarts and what they call 'the long tail' of experience."

She sniffs. By that, I mean she makes a dismissive noise with her nose, not that she stinks. Although if I had to name her personal perfume, it would be Rodeo Reno rather than Rodeo Drive. What can I say? Ma Barker runs the biggest street gang in Vegas, but she is also the Queen Dumpster diver in town. That is exactly why she is critical personnel for this mission.

Meanwhile, she is trying to palm some inferiors off on me. "If you cannot handle this yourself, I can loan you one of the Black Cat Brigade. Blackula or Pitch or Exxon Valdez."

"No. Those three are still wet behind the ears, literally. Only you will do."

She grudgingly allows herself to sink into a meatloaf position, which means I have two minutes to convince her. "I am not exactly a beauty queen, Louie. I can see how Midnight Louise and even you are presentable enough at these swanky joints, but I do not walk the walk there."

That is an understatement as tall as the Paris Hotel's faux Eiffel Tower. "Snaggle-toothed" could have been invented for Ma, and that was before she tangled with an overweight raccoon to protect her turf and clowder.

One ear is so ragged it is what scientists would call "vestigial". The scar tracks about her face and shoulders would make you think you were looking at Manhattan's hodge-podge streets on Google map's satellite view.

"I need a primo sniff-through of the premises," I say. "I can get you in the back way."

"I thought executive chef Song and his meat cleaver were ever on the watch for your koi-eating self."

"Louise has him wrapped around her forepaw's little shiv. He is her personal 24/7 sushi bar," I say sourly. Maybe I say that sweet and sourly, since we are talking Asian cuisine.

Ma nods and runs a wet pad over one almost hairless eyebrow. "Louise has domestic smarts. She is an outside-inside operator of the new generation. Not you, however. You are hopelessly outdated, cohabitating with a single human."

"My roommate may shortly become a very non-single human," I say unhappily.

Ma misses my nuance. Ma is not a nuance-noticing individual.

"So," she says, "If I go, you just want me to do the usual all-over sniff-through. It sounds like we will have to evade an entire clowder of humans around the place."

"The humans call it 'a band', a singing group and their entourage."

"Hoighty-toighty fussy-wussy."

"Only *you* will have to avoid being seen. I will meet you near the koi pond tomorrow morning. I know the layout and am already familiar to the band members."

"Oh, you are a celebrity hanger-on now, Louie?"

"I hang on to no one unless I sink my teeth in," I growl. "This is a dangerous assignment, Ma. Life and death."

"If you say so. Anything else I need to know?"

I swallow before answering that one. Talk about a deal breaker.

"I hope you are not still eating bugs, as when you were a kit," she says.

"No, I am not. It is just that, well, the hotel's band suites are, uh, infested."

"Bed bugs." She nods sagely. "I hear it happens nowadays in even the swankiest places. No problem for me or my gang. We are used to bugs and *we* bite *them*, but not as snacks."

"No bed bugs," I say, horrified. "The Crystal Phoenix was a top-drawer operation when I landed there as unofficial house detective, and it is even swankier today, now that Louise has inherited my job."

"What else can qualify as an 'infestation'?"

"Ummm..."

"Do not try to distract me with that purring stuff. I am way too old for that ploy."

"You are as young as you feel, Ma." I think of the new guy in the clowder and bite my tongue so I do not say something to put her off. "What I am talking about here are...dogs."

"Dogs! Plural? Deal off. I have put enough in their places for a gal twice my age. I am done interacting personally with the breed. I can give you Blackula and—"

"Ma, only you will do. Only you have the true connoisseur's nose for such a wide range of scents."

"That is true. What breed are these dogs?"

"Not to worry. They are stupid—"

"They are dogs."

"...and I have recruited them as helpers. Their noses, frankly, are a wee tad more sensitive than ours—"

She sniffs again.

"But they are dumb domestic brutes and do not have the street cred you do."

"You are not saying what breed they are."

"A Scottie and a Westie."

"Ach, those Highland mutts are stubborn. At least they are on the small side for keeping in line. All right. If you can smuggle me in without incident, I will do your dirty work for you."

She rises and shakes out her coat, which is a rusty black color with lots of cowlicks. "But you will owe me more of that fast food you leave out for the gang at the Circle Ritz."

"That is a heavy price, Ma. Me giving up so much of my food obtained from the fanciest establishment in town by my Miss Temple." I restrain myself from doing the happy dance. "Yet I will pay it."

Catso Ratso has made progress fanging out cactus thorns and attempts to throw his weight around again. "I do not think you should go, Ma Barker."

"You are eye candy," she growls. "It is not your job to think."

I take a cue and my leave, but I am pretty happy.

Tomorrow me and my mama will have our first joint operation. In fact, I am counting on her sniffing out more than the occasional joint.

26
Rehearsed to Death

Today was off to a good start. Temple awoke with Midnight Louie occupying the adjacent eiderdown pillow pile. It was really sweet how he'd followed her to the Crystal Phoenix to keep her company.

What a promising omen for a move to Chicago...if Louie wasn't holding any grudges after his trip there had put him in jeopardy. Temple was almost beginning to think he was eager for a change of residence.

She scratched his ears. He replied with a deep purr, and then flopped the end of his long, almost prehensile tail over her wrist like a furry bracelet.

"If only Matt were here now, Louie," she mused aloud.

The tail abruptly flopped back onto the pillow. Louie hiked a leg over his back like a rifle and began grooming what Temple called his "underlings".

"I hope Matt enjoys hanging out with Eduardo, and that Eduardo isn't teaching him any bad bachelor habits," she said.

She smiled at the cat. "It's great to have down-home company in this madhouse, but you do groom at the most inopportune times. Ten a.m. Diva wake-up call. Time to don my game face and deal with the morning rehearsal. Let's hope French Vanilla doesn't have another crisis."

A lavish food service table at the back of the theater house was an efficient way to feed the small army of band members and tech people. French Vanilla and Chocolatte had room service for every meal, although they'd graze the common table. Temple gobbled down some scrambled eggs and selected a gloriously caloric pastry to go with the single-serving gourmet coffee machine available.

Then she wandered to the front of the house, where the set was nearing completion.

"Yo," Big Bix called out. "Miz Barr. We are gettin' ready to take off and fly down here."

She followed his booming voice to the front row of seats.

"Well, don't you look pretty since that sweet Sessalee got her talented hands on you," he said.

"Thank you, but not as pretty as this stage is looking. Wow. You guys must be slavering to get up there and bring down the house. I see standing ovations in your future."

"That Danny Dove is a regular reincarnated cross between choreographer Bob Fosse and Sammy Davis, Jr. when it comes to sheer entertainment."

"Those two icons did work together," Temple said, "in the movie musical *Sweet Charity* with Shirley MacLaine, another Vegas Rat Pack veteran like Sammy Davis, Jr."

"Maybe their ghosts will join our act," Bixby said. "The hotel's already got one in residence. Anyway, Danny's got the band on our little glitzy petaled podiums rising up and down and sideways, and the dancers weaving in and out, and even walking on air."

"I know where that 'walking on air' trick came from."

"Yeah, strobe lights."

"And the mind of magician Max Kinsella."

"*Hmm.* Never heard of that cat."

"His new act is next up at this hotel, so you will."

Bix leaned down and close. "Listen. We make it to opening without a crisis, I will be very happy, and surprised."

"What's going on with French Vanilla?"

"Too much."

"And why?"

"I don't know."

Temple sighed. "I don't either. Meanwhile, I'd like to take in this magnificent set while we all hope for only good things happening on it."

"Amen," Bix said, moving to hail Spider as he slouched down an aisle to the stage.

Since Temple had come to Las Vegas a couple years ago, she'd seen dozens of world-class Strip productions, from Bally's *Jubilee!*—that had been running since 1981 and sank the Titanic every night—to Cirque du Soleil's countless and colorful themed extravaganzas of breathtaking acrobatics.

Yet she'd never seen anything like the set taking shape for Black & White. Imagine putting the sets from twenty Busby Berkley thirties black-and-white movie musicals into one big Art Deco mash-up designed by Erté. Now that almost all of its glittering black-and-white glory was revealed, Temple never wanted to leave the theater. Black & White and its divas should be panting to perform in this milieu.

"*Well?*" Danny Dove, grinning, descended on a bungee cord like Peter Pan to alight in front of her. "What's your verdict on what the team of Dove and Kinsella hath wrought?"

Temple could hardly move her agape mouth to comment.

Danny laughed. "It's not quite finished yet, of course. More glitz is coming, you can bet your tiny tush on that. And the mechanisms need fine tuning, but...*well?*"

Danny in full creative mode was a force of nature. He twirled in front of her, ascending again and asking, "*Well? Well? Well?*" all the way up to the distant ceiling that glittered like a geode flashing swaths of black and white crystal.

Applause burst out around Temple and from her own pounding palms, cupped to sound louder, because this set was a show stopper all by itself. Add a legendary crew of singers and musicians, and it would give Cirque a run for the tourist money.

Temple heard laughter amid the clapping, and turned to see the band members behind her, smiling and staring up like kids seeing their first Christmas tree and it was twenty feet tall.

Nicky and Van, halfway down the aisle, had stopped cold to gawk.

Ahead of them, Nilla and Latty on their high-rise heels moved as leisurely as giraffes in a dream. They held hands, like twelve-year-old Best Friends Forever.

Behind it all came Big Bix and his basso Santa Claus laugh, echoing everywhere.

"Black & White," he declared, declaimed, crowed, and chanted, "is gonna rock this Strip from McCarran Airport to the Downtown Experience. That's the whole Miracle Mile, people. Let's tame this monster and hit platinum, baby, plat-i-num."

As the band members slowly moved onto the set with the awe of Dorothy first seeing Oz, Temple saw the black-clad stagehands and roadies moving and shifting equipment like brown ants you only noticed when you looked close.

Danny had swung, this time like Tarzan, to the topmost scaffolding still up, to direct the ongoing projects.

"Where are my stars?" he demanded, stopping the band members from climbing the first three shallow steps. "Safety first, my darlings. Sit in the front row, please, and see how you will be the diamonds in this Tiffany-level setting for your talents and magnificence. Divas, your place marks are taped. And Miss French Vanilla, I'm assigning a set ninja to your moveable unit during the performance so you will always have someone to guide you right. You'll see how that will work during the dress rehearsal tomorrow night. For now, just relax and enjoy your fabulous stage setting."

Danny knew how to whip and flatter performing artists into cooperation. The band members, whispering with excitement among themselves, backed up and sat.

Temple breathed a sigh of relief and climbed the raked aisle to join Van and Nicky.

Nicky gave a triumphant fist-pump as she neared, grinning even more broadly than Danny.

Van had sat on the arm of an aisle seat, too pleasantly shocked to stand.

"Explain this to us, Temple," she asked.

Temple sat in another aisle seat and stretched her legs into the aisle. "First, it's awesome," she said.

"And the band loves it, thank God." Van leaned forward to squeeze Temple's shoulder. "This couldn't have happened without Danny and Max and you. This might work," she finished, looking up at her husband.

"This will set the standard, babe." He bent down to kiss her.

Van's pale face flushed. Like Matt, she wasn't a fan of PDAs.

So Temple segued into her role as guide to all things theatrical and downright marvelous.

"It looks a bit confusing, because portions are still being worked on. Any remaining scaffolding will go down last. It'll stay up until the performers can get properly oriented. They're not spring chickens, and their reflexes will be slower, just as their vision won't adapt as fast to the spotlights."

Van giggled, then covered her mouth like a naughty child.

Van giggled? She was not a giggly person.

"Temple, if those seasoned road warriors in the band heard you were looking out for them like a favorite niece… Don't mind me. I think it's wonderful. There's not a PR person in this town who could think about this enterprise in 3-D like you do."

Now it was Temple's turn to feel a flush in her cheeks. It might seem condescending to some that she would think the band needed looking out for, but the two divas struck her as fragile, and the less famous members of the band showed signs of defensive insecurity. Now that she'd seen what the show *could* be, it was her job to see it went off without a hitch.

"Stage mamas, both of you," Nicky said. "Who knew? Temple, explain how this is gonna look when it's all together."

Temple spread her arms as if to embrace the distant stage. "It's hard even for us thirty-somethings to see the two curving staircases at either side, because they're covered in glossy black on one side and clear Plexiglas on the other, that act like mirrors. Only Danny's dancers will perform on them. They're pros.

"The elevator platforms are for the musicians. They will rise and lower. Then, the ceiling medallions—"

Van looked up, a bit appalled. "They are gorgeous. A Milky Way of glitz, but they…do something too? Isn't that a bit much?"

Temple shook her head. "Cirque du Soleil has raised the stakes in Vegas stage shows. Everything has to be in extreme 3-D. The trouble is that musicians and singers require stability and sound perfection, so these stage elevators have been constructed to be not only silent, but as stable and smooth as…well, French Vanilla ice cream."

Temple glanced at the woman whose larger-than-life everyday look already seemed at home on the gigantic new set. Wait'll she got out her Lady Gaga platform boots and exaggerated costumes. Singing divas nowadays looked like comic-book alien babes. Then Temple frowned and headed for the stage.

Nilla, still wearing her signature sunglasses, was turning in a tight circle, teetering on her already six-inch-high heels, angling her face straight up. "What are those…things on the ceiling?"

"Part of the stage design," Latty told her. "Maybe sound baffles. I don't know."

"They're going to fall down on us."

"No," Latty began, just as Temple got there to do damage control.

"They won't fall," she told Nilla.

"I saw one move." She was so distraught she pushed the sunglasses up like a headband.

Temple noticed Nilla's bloodshot eye whites and irises the swollen black of dilation. Had she been taking something, legal or illegal? Probably.

Temple looked up. The white and black glitter did twinkle like some giant nebula.

"Snakes!" Nilla backed away without setting her foot firmly.

By then Temple was there to help Latty as they each grabbed an arm. Nilla's skin felt moist and clammy.

"Not snakes," Temple said, "swirls of sequins and glitter, like on a gown."

"And they're spinning." Nilla's voice grew sing-song. "The wind is spinning them, the pinwheels. I'm getting dizzy and I like it." She laughed maniacally, making it into a piercing, hysterical aria. Temple heard all motion and buzz hush as everyone stopped to focus on French Vanilla.

"Back to work, minions." Danny's amplified voice drove the crew like Jehovah speaking from on high.

"Nilla!" Latty shook her arm. "What did you take?"

The other woman looked away from the ceiling, her mood suddenly ice-cold. "Chocolatte," she mocked, "like you didn't OD on everything you could scrounge from the alleys behind the dives we played."

"Not for a long time, Nilla, and you know it. We haven't played dives for decades. Where you going, girl? And on what?"

Temple glanced toward Van and Nicky, still sitting along the aisle but looking worried.

"Nothing," Nilla shouted, her shrillness lost in continuing pounding and shouts among the workmen. "I didn't take anything, but I see what I see." She pointed to one of the ceiling medallions. "Those are spiders, black bloated bodies with wriggling white hairy legs and blood drops dripping off them. They're going to poison me. I haven't been feeling right and the spiders are creeping down to get me and swallow me."

"Some questions here?" asked a chipper voice. Danny Dove to the rescue. He eyed French Vanilla. "They aren't spiders, dear one, but beautiful glittering flowers right out of Alice's Wonderland, or Dorothy's Oz. They're elevators. I'll go up and show you. Watch me climb the stairs, something you'll never have to do during the show."

"Show." The word quieted Nilla. "The show, yes. We're doing a show. Altogether. In the altogether again." Her giggle turned into a high keening note. Heads were turning toward her again.

"Ladies and gentlemen!" Danny's voice boomed out over all the noise, covering what were now Nilla's whimpers.

He bounded halfway up the curving black-ice-slick stairway, and had thrust a portable mic pack into his back waist, where a cop would carry a gun.

"Let me demo the workings of this set. The dancers, like me, trip the light fantastic all up and down these stairs." Danny tap-danced as he spoke, riveting every eye on his agile form and the syncopated taps of his flashing feet. "We can tiptoe our way up to the stars..."

He was just under the ceiling. "Tech dudes," he yelled to the men at the sound, light, and set boards with their small blinking lights and octopus tangles of black electrical cords. "Lower this lovely giant petal of an umbrella slowly to the ground."

As his order was obeyed, Danny did a stunning ballet leap across what looked like ten feet of empty space to pose by the central pole lengthening as the nearest medallion slowly lowered.

"*Shazam*," Danny announced. "I am a musician. I am a singer. I'm coming into sight of the audience as my chariot lowers, and, like a flower or a whimsical umbrella, lets down its outer petals."

Danny had mesmerized everyone in the house. Except for Temple, who felt a tremor vibrate French Vanilla's elegant, thin frame.

"Spiders," she screamed at the top of her very developed lungs. "Coming down to devour us, to mince our flesh and snap our bones and run like ants into our eyes. I'll kill them, I must kill them, kill them all."

She twisted free and ran for the stage elevator as it alit, displaying a stunning, glittering interior of illuminated black and white, with Danny standing silent and eerily frozen by the center steel pole, staring at the ground as if he, too, had indeed seen a spider.

"Kill spider," Nilla shouted, hoarse, falling to her knees at the edge of one exquisite petal, pounding on the plush black velvet spangled with silver stars and rhinestones.

Pounding on something that didn't glitter at all.

"Oh, my God," came Danny's shocked baritone. He'd forgotten his voice was amplified.

The words reverberated from every inch of gaudy, sparkling surface before a techie abruptly cut off the mic.

Temple could have used one, but she'd been onstage enough in college to project to the lobby.

"Fontana brothers," she called to the silhouettes guarding the ajar theater doors. "Call an ambulance, close the doors, and call the police. We now have a crime scene."

27
A Mother Nose

The good part is that the Crystal Phoenix celebrity suites are pretty much vacant in the late morning while White & Black are rehearsing.

The bad part of that is Ma Barker is not a morning person and complains about that from the moment I meet her at the hotel's rear pool area, which has lots of shading greenery.

Ma Barker does not have access to time devices, so we meet at one sleeping cat's length of shade thrown by Vegas' most populous flowering plant, the desert-loving oleander. That is around eleven a.m. Bands also do not seem to rise until late morning so we had to wait for them to leave.

The ubiquitous oleander, with its thick pointed leaves and impressive blooms, is used for hedges and screening greenery all over town. We hip cats know, of course, not to even lick a leaf, since it is as poisonous as it is attractive. Ain't that always the case, especially with femme fatales?

I have already checked the rooftop garden, and no oleanders are growing up there, so it is not a suspect in this case. This I tell Ma once I have escorted her inside and into the room maintenance areas, where concealing carts abound.

She sniffs the odor of assorted cleaning potions. "Some of these would be toxic."

"They would have to be ingested in large quantities, Ma. What I am looking for is a lot more subtle."

"I do not do 'subtle'."

"At one time or another, you have dived the most infamous Dumpsters along the Strip," I tell her. "You must have detected substances humans are fond of abusing."

"One does have to be alert for inadvertent pricks from used needles," she says. "Even a bit of leftover crack or coke or whatever would be enough to off those of our size."

I shudder a bit. Ma is truly an urban survivor. I have always been able to con a bed or a meal out of a human, but Ma does not trust a one of them.

"Where is the clowder you call a band?" she asks.

"They are rehearsing a show in the main floor theater. That did not go so well yesterday. If we discover a seriously bad drug, we can save the show!"

"What is this 'we', black cat?"

"You, Ma. Of course."

I study the carts for the signature Black & White logo on the water glasses and bed linens Miss Van von Rhine custom ordered.

"Here is our ride." I hop aboard the bottom level where we can hide behind plastic packs of toilet tissue. Yes, even that bears a ritzy B&W monogram.

I know we will be twelfth-floor bound soon. The hotel staff can only clean the suites when they are vacant during rehearsal time.

"So," Ma says, curling up on the stainless steel, "we are visiting the territory of a bunch of caterwauling hopheads and faded celebs."

"Recreational drugs are an accessory of the touring band lifestyle," I admit. "I am looking for something more exotic, something that would make the taker go crazy."

Ma nods. "Loco Charlie, the yellow tabby, was never the same after getting into something bad. He kept thinking his stripes were living pit vipers trying to bite him."

"What happened to him?"

"Besides chewing his coat into a terrific mess? He got hit by a Fed Ex truck one day trying to outrun his imaginary tormenters."

I wince. "That is what we are looking for here. Something that would drive a body mad."

Rubber-soled black mules approach our cart and push it into motion. We keep still both ways during the elevator interlude and while rolling into the suites.

Ma shuts her eyes as a scrabbling sound and Scottish-accented arfs attack our cart. Big black and white and hairy snouts thrust into our hiding place.

I slam a four-sharp combo on Scotch. *"Hsst.* We are undercover, laddies, here to sniff out a bad guy. Or gal. Put a plaid sock in it and I will fill you in on the mission once we all ditch the hotel maid."

"Are we off tae be detectives?" Soda asks, panting. "Like Burke 'n' Hare?"

"They wur corpse snatchers," Scotch says scathingly.

The maid is also urging quiet, so the pair back off. The minute she goes into a suite bathroom, I nudge Ma to hop off.

Then it is only a matter of herding my unlikely trio, with many hisses for silence, to the French Vanilla suite. Luckily, that is opposite the area where the maid is toiling.

"Some plush place," Ma Barker observes, sinking dew-claw deep in the thick white carpeting of French Vanilla's living room. "I detect something sweet and cloying."

"Like…decay?" I wonder in alarm.

Speaking of alarm, the two resident canines descend on Ma in a show of hysteria. *"Whooourrrrryoooo?"* Scotch and Soda croon.

Ma Barker arches her back and stiffens every hair. *"Seee my fissst in your kisssers!"* she hisses in reply.

"Stay back!" I warn. "My mama is an expert in street fighting and street drugs. Between what you two have been exposed to here all along, and her experience of Vegas drug dealers, we should find out what is making Miss French Vanilla so loco."

"Loco?" Two puzzled and tilted heads regard us, cute as a postcard.

Ma Barker smacks down cute.

I search for an Old World word. "Daft," I say.

Soda's black eyes in his shaggy white head focus harder as he consults with Scotch. "I think he means 'doolally'."

"Doolally," Scotch finally croons, "the verrry word. 'Tis how oor mistress has been acting."

"Mair sniffing 'n' less talkin'," Ma Barker, er, barks. She has done a passable job of speaking their language. I am impressed.

"All right, team," I tell them all. "Scotch and Soda, you know all the familiar scents associated with Miss French Vanilla. Ma, you know every blend of narcotic, opiate, and hallucinogen to hit Vegas. I want a total forensic sniff-down here."

The dogs move out, snouts to floor like Roomba vacuum cleaners, snuffling with gusto. Ma and me jump up to take the overland route, with the silent but deeply considered sniffs of our kind. The terriers use the slapdash Google search approach, while we employ the finely tuned nose-touch of a Rembrandt of scents.

We turn up two marijuana roaches in a tray in no time flat and call the dogs over.

"Ach," says Soda. "That is Miss Chocolatte's brand. 'Chocolate Chunk', she calls it, and then laughs."

"This other one is just Juicy Fruit," Scotch says.

"The chewing gum?" I ask.

"Nae, nae for chewing. For smokin'. They make jokes aboot it bein' a gum, though."

So it goes, with Scotch and Soda taking the low road, and Ma and me taking the high road. That is always the way it is with dogs and cats. We cats are the more elevated species in every way.

After half an hour on the LED bedside clock, we meet in the bedroom to compare observations.

We agree that the overbearing smell of cosmetics and marijuana complicates the search. Even the dogs are bathed in a scented preparation.

"Such a shame." Ma Barker shakes her head. "If you were not half-drowned and dried out like a human head of hair, if you bathed yourselves, your natural scent would not hamper your investigation. So despite having the superior nose for news, you are worthless."

That sets the pair growling.

"Are there any new scents?" I ask them.

"There is a perfume I canna place," Soda says. "Miss French Vanilla is partial to me because my coat matches her silvery hair color."

"That is not so!" Scotch is most indignant.

"She always has herself pictured with me on her lap," Soda says. "Your black coat would just blend into her clothing. Whereas my striking white coat is always eye-catching, like the late Miss Elizabeth Taylor's white Maltese, Sugar."

"'Eye-catching?'" Scotch is having none of this. "Like a stye in the corner of an elephant's eye, you are catching!"

Mention of the Maltese breed puts me in mind of Nose E., the Maltese bomb and drug-sniffing dog employed at celebrity events. He would be far more professional than these two Highland ninnies.

Ma Barker takes them in hand with a quick cuff to each one's ears. "Pipe down, Highland laddies. There is an exotic drug scent I have sniffed a time or two, once when we were hitting on a high school lunch crowd for snacks."

"That is not good," I say.

"Aye," says a grumpy Scotch. "Takin' advantage of the young ones is a low, sneaky act."

"I *meant,*" I say before Ma Barker can skin a canine nose or two, "that it is not good for youthful humans to be preyed upon by drug dealers."

"What I sniffed that day, I have encountered again here, in these rooms." Ma furrows her scanty brow hairs. "Not long after, the students no longer made a clowder outside the school for lunch. I believe they had been forbidden."

"Probably," Scotch mutters, "because the authorities feared yur scurvy clowder would give the puir children fleas, or worse."

"No." I nod at Ma. "They wanted to stop the drug deals. Where did you smell that scent here, Ma?"

Ma leads us into French Vanilla's bedroom, to a bedside table covered with human litter. I spot a black satin sleep mask. Pill bottles. Lotion bottles. All bottles with writing on them the size of a pinpoint. Only one is decorative. I recognize the word "Noir" on it, which is French for black. I recognize the word because my lost love, the shaded silver Persian I call the Divine Yvette, discovered she was French (with my encouragement) and would sometimes call me "Louie Noir".

We are somewhat estranged now, however, by miles and career changes. So goes modern love. I am now seeing the black Oasis Hotel house mascot. Come to think of it, my love life is Black & White, like the band name. You could also call me Rainbow Louie, but I do not like to boast.

A blood-drawing tap on the sensitive, less-furred skin near my ear halts my fond reminiscences and brings me back to the current problem.

Ma has stretched her rangy frame up to run her nose over the tabletop array and has something to tell me. "That exotic street drug scent clings to one of these bottles. I recall one dealer, an Asian woman, who was busted for selling something deadly. She was known as Yellow Oleander."

So maybe oleander *is* the poison French Vanilla is getting, if not an illegal drug in the usual sense. *Grrreat!* I do not doubt the average troubled rock star has access to all the prescription drugs street users would kill to get, and here in Vegas the band members would find it easy to expand their repertoire.

I can only conclude that I should pay immediate attention to the many pockets in Doc's safari jacket and the contents of *his* suite.

A drug bust was not what I was looking for here anyway, but a mind-altering substance that is *not* taken recreationally. Hard to find, I know, but I am optimistic.

"Are we done?" Ma Barker is in the doorway, ready to abandon civilization and all its comforts for a speedy return to her Street, Sweet Street.

At this point, bracketed by a panting Scotch and Soda eager to nose down every room in this maze of suites, I envy her.

28
Spider Web

Lieutenant Molina stood alone on the stage, facing a rapt audience. "Who found the body?" she asked.

Temple raised a tentative hand Molina spotted immediately.

The lieutenant did not look pleased. "'The sky is falling,' said the Little Red Hen," she quoted. "Or is that Chicken Little?"

"Either way I find it insulting," said Temple, the petite redhead.

"It's Chicken Little," Danny said, "and Temple wasn't the first to see the body."

"I was the first to know it *was* a body," Temple said.

Molina narrowed her piercing eyes, which were cop-car headache-rack blue, come to think of it. "There's a distinction here, and it's important to you," she told Temple.

Danny lowered his voice. "Someone in the room got a bit hysterical when the descending mini-stage came down from the ceiling."

"'Descending mini-stage.'" Molina eyed the grounded unit. "More like a stalled UFO fit for Elvis, and we've had enough of that in Vegas lately." She eyed Danny. "You're Danny Dove, the choreographer, aren't you?"

"Yes, Detective."

"Lieutenant. Molina. And you designed this set?"

"Yes."

"I hear a certain hesitancy there."

Temple closed her eyes, knowing what was coming. Molina's ear for nuance was as fine-tuned as a priceless Stradivarius violin.

"I had a consultant give me some help," Danny admitted. "He's not here today, though."

Wait for it, Temple thought.

"Who is he?" asked Molina.

"A magician named Max Kinsella. He played the Goliath. You must have heard of him. Really a class act. Terrific at moving vertically and unconventionally onstage."

"So I've heard." Molina smiled lazily, slightly swaying like a hooded cobra sizing up a victim. "I've heard of the unconventional Mystifying Max. So he knows the setup as well as you do?"

"Better, Lieutenant."

Temple cringed as Danny went on, innocent of Molina's long-standing suspicion of Max.

"You see," Danny said, "these descending units give us so much versatility."

"They even double as a body bag," Molina pointed out. "Clever."

Danny now got it. "Oh, no, Lieutenant. That's not what I meant, not what was intended."

Molina, uninterested in back-peddling, glanced at the unit parked on the stage now. A forensics team was using a huge digital camera to film the body, the vehicle, and every point of interest on the static stage set and among the onlookers as if making a *Nova* documentary.

Lionel Bixby slumped on the stage steps, listless with shock. When Temple had sat by him as they waited for the police, Big Bix had whispered in a raw, disbelieving voice, over and over. "My God. Dead. After all this time. Really dead? Now? Why? How?"

Bixby seemed to think the dead man might be Cale Watson. Temple didn't know why, except Watson's disappearance had always haunted the band. If so, now all the original members of Black & White were here and accounted for.

Could it be? No onlooker had really seen the body, obscured first by guarding Fontana brothers, then EMTs, and now CSI people.

Temple wasn't sure Big Bix was fit to answer questions just now. She was sure Molina was sure ready to ask them.

"How long could the body have been there?" Molina asked Danny Dove.

Danny thought hard. "I was the last to leave last night and the first to arrive today."

"Really?" Molina was racking up careless admissions like an usher at a movie theater.

"So…I left at eight p.m. last night and returned at nine a.m. this morning." Danny waited for the next question.

"Who was the first to detect the body?"

Danny frowned. "That's the thing. She didn't detect the body. She… imagined the body was something else."

"What?" Molina's tone was sharp.

This sounded like shilly-shallying to her, when Temple knew Danny was only struggling to be truthful about Nilla's behavior, which amounted to corpse abuse.

Danny tried again. "She thought the unit was some kind of giant spider that had swung down on its web-line. She attacked it."

"The unit or the body?"

"That's just it, Lieutenant. If your people weren't swarming all over the unit, you'd see the unit was lined in plush black and the body was facedown, dressed all in black. You could look right at it and not discern what or who it was."

"Okay, Mr. Dove. I get that, but who *could* it be? My people found no ID."

Danny didn't know about Cale Watson. His supple features grimaced in worry. "Our scene-change people dress all in black. I haven't had time to do a head count yet."

"Then get on it. First, though, show me who was seeing spiders."

Reluctantly, Danny nodded toward French Vanilla sitting on the shallow stage steps not far from Big Bix, her long legs splayed, huddled over a cup of something. Chocolatte curved around her in support. A flash winked to capture the dramatic shot.

"Omigod," Temple said. "I've got a freelancer covering the rehearsal, but that photo must not get out anywhere."

"It won't," Molina assured her. "Alch," she called.

The veteran detective, who had that ageing Scottie dog look down pat, lifted his shaggy gray head.

"Get all the memory cards that photographer has taken in this hotel for the last—" She consulted Temple with a Look.

"Two days," Temple said, "but that's all property of the Crystal Phoenix."

"Not if it's evidence."

Temple groaned. There went her online podcast and print material.

"Meanwhile," Molina said, "who *is* this kook who was seeing spiders?" She glanced up at the décor. "Although this set is pretty creepy."

"It's not finished. You just wait." Temple said.

"It is finished for now, until I release the premises. Now, who is that woman?"

Temple had no choice. "French Vanilla of the Black & White rock group. Her legal name is Selma Sue French."

But Temple had Molina at the words, "French Vanilla".

"French Vanilla?" Temple had never heard Molina sounding this uncertain. "What's she doing here?" She looked around. "What's going on here?"

"It's a super-secret runup to a major stage show reuniting Black & White," Temple said, "the band from the—"

"I know who and what they are and when they were. All of them?"

"All of them. At least the core members from the original union. Some backup singers floated in and out."

"French Vanilla and Chocolatte successfully went solo for decades after the breakup. They're reuniting?"

"They were, until this dead body hit the stage. You've got to solve this fast, or it'll be an entertainment world disaster."

Molina wasn't listening. She was circling around to get to Nilla and Latty. Doc Dryden tried to intercept her. Molina eyed his pleading figure and jerked her head. Alch's partner, tiny Merry Su, moved him out of the way with one hand on his fingers in some magical, mystery hold.

Molina, in her usual pants suit and loafers, put a foot up on the third shallow step and bent down to talk to the two women.

Temple was not about to miss this. They shouldn't speak without a lawyer, one each in fact.

"She's in shock," Chocolatte was telling Molina. "I won't have her interrogated without her attorney present."

Temple was in shock when Molina deferred and nodded, all the while studying French Vanilla with the eye of a botanist probing a plant structure under a microscope.

The fascination was mutual. Nilla straightened up, her muddied vision seeming to clear. "Latty brought me hot chocolate," she said, lifting the mug. "Chocolate from Chocolatte," she said, smiling.

Molina glanced at the food service cart for the performers and technicians against the wall.

"Who are you?" Nilla asked, like a child.

"Carmen Molina."

Temple nearly swallowed her tongue. C.R. Molina, career woman in the overbearingly male law enforcement field, *never* used her first name on the job.

Nilla didn't know that. "Carmen," she repeated "Pretty. It's almost like Caramel. You could join Chocolatte and me. Do you sing?"

Did Molina sing? Temple wanted to say. *Like a fallen angel. Stop by the Blue Dahlia club and catch "Carmen" doing her torch singer act with the three-guy band, only she's avoided her surprise appearances there lately...*

"A little. In the shower," Molina said.

Nilla reached a hand tipped with that exotic custom fingernail job to pinch Molina's khaki blazer sleeve, then shook it a little. "Carmen. I think I might have known you once, Carmen. You must forgive me. I've grown older. Grown old. I forget so much, and lately, even much more."

Molina stepped back from the stairs. She spoke to Latty. "Get her out of here. I'll need you both, with whatever team of lawyers you deem necessary, to make statements at police headquarters tomorrow."

Molina turned away and almost stepped into the natty Zegna-suited arms of a Fontana brother. Molina was about five-foot-ten and wore low-heeled loafers to lessen being intimidating to men. It didn't work.

"You're in my way," Molina said, looking him up and down.

On the other hand, nothing female could intimidate a Fontana brother, or escape his gallant attention. He looked Molina up and down in a way she probably hadn't experienced since the Ice Age.

"Yes. Pardon. I am Julio Fontana. My assignment here is to facilitate. I will escort the lady stars to their suites, as you indicated." He bowed and did just that.

Molina swiveled to regard Temple, frowned like Zeus getting a headache and giving birth to Athena, the goddess of war, and stalked offstage to confer with her troops.

Temple saluted the disappearing Fontana brother and his super-star charges

Then she went to console, and grill, Danny Dove.

29
Catastrophy

"**What a disaster** for my esteemed bosses, Nicky and Van," Miss Midnight Louise moans from the sidelines. "We must save the show and the day, Louie."

"Hey. We are not Judy Garland and Mickey Rooney in a nineteen-forties movie musical, putting on a show. We must be the sophisticats here, to match the mood of the times and the situation."

"At least," Louise says, slinking along the black-painted walls of the theater perimeter, "we match half of the décor. One of us should interrogate the annoying Scotch and Soda in the suites later. Sad to say, in view of what has happened here, they might have seen or heard something they did not know was vital. So like dogs, good at noise and sniff, but lousy at stealth and smarts."

"What we need here is ears around the whole Cinemascope panorama, or a skateboard each."

"Fret not, senior partner. I anticipated dirty work at the rehearsal and took the liberty of importing the Black Cat Brigade from Ma Barker's street gang."

"You mean the ninja unit I founded? That is as sneaky and underhanded as a human, Louise." I do not mention that Ma refused my request for reinforcements. Dames! Always in it together, just like French Vanilla and Chocolatte these days.

"Thank you. I will give the crew the silent meow."

At that her lips sync a mew heard around the world, or at least our current corner of it. I spy sets of black ears popping up all over Mr. Danny Dove's black shiny staircase and the edges of the black-bottomed ceiling mini-stages. If I did not know better, I would suspect a

Disney-Mickey Mouse conspiracy. The ears are everywhere!

With Louise having already set up the ninja crew here at the rehearsal hall, I have no alternative but to go into the doghouse upstairs. At least I have accustomed Scotch and Soda to reporting to the superior species, and will get to see what is going on with French Vanilla and Chocolatte.

It is too bad our breed does not have a sweet tooth, so we would appreciate the divas' stage names more. I know that canines, especially, are as averse to chocolate as one of the divas is to some unknown substance.

Before this is over, I will know the name of the nose candy so disrupting to humans.

30
Double Trouble

Surprisingly, when Temple turned from Danny with no new insight, she saw that Molina had allowed the band medic, Doc Dryden, to return to the suites, as well as the two divas.

Had Las Vegas' finest female homicide officer gone soft? Temple eyed the vast theater. It was far too big for something in the air to make everyone present a little loony.

She didn't trust anyone around Nilla at the moment, so she joined the party Julio was escorting up the aisle.

"Hold it, Shorty." Doc Dryden stopped and turned to look down his long nose at her. "I need to tend my patients in private."

By then the group was opposite a sober Nicky and Van.

"The hotel needs a representative in the celebrity suites," Temple said, catching the couple's attention, "in case of a lawsuit."

Van's pale skin got ashier, but Nicky nodded his agreement immediately. "And of course I'll have a brother or five at various entrances to the suites, so you're not disturbed."

"Me, disturbed?" A visible pulsing in Dryden's right jaw indicated he was furious.

Temple smiled. "I'm sure you could use an aspirin right now too." She whisked around to Nilla's other side and let him trail them to the private elevator.

Nilla needed the extra support to board the elevator on her elevated heels. Now that her panic attack had passed, she was oddly giddy. Temple wondered if she even realized someone had lain beneath her demented blows. Dead, true, and unable to feel, but…

"Oh, maresy doats and doesy goats and little kits eat ivory," Nilla sang under her breath.

Temple recognized a garbled gimmick song from the forties, hardly Nilla's era. She met Latty's eyes. The woman's shrug sent her black dreadlocks into a Medusa-like shimmer. "She's like this elevator, goes up and down," Latty leaned down to whisper to Temple as Doc put his passkey into the elevator slot.

The party made it into the main living room suite, where Scotch and Soda came ankle-crowding around. That perked up Nilla.

"Pretty boys," she crooned, "you know I like my pretty boys."

Temple considered the terriers, with their contrasting black and white bow-tie collars, more dapper than pretty.

"Calm down, pups," she urged the dogs, wondering what "pretty boys" French Vanilla might have had back in the day. Dryden helped her and Latty maneuver Nilla onto the couch. There she slouched, long legs akimbo, sunglasses askew, and her eyes clearly inebriated now.

Susan Everleigh abandoned her small desk and rushed to help transfer Nilla to her bedroom.

"What's she on?" Temple asked Doc Dryden. "You're here to prevent such lapses."

He was digging in his camouflage-patterned knapsack of supplies, so cool and counterculture.

Temple wanted answers. "And what's in those hypos you give her at every little burp? We have a house doctor. I'll call her in unless you tell me what you think you're doing?"

Dryden threw himself into the nearby Barcelona chair. "You do it, then. You handle this loony. I don't know what gets into her." He scowled at Chocolatte. "Ask her best friend, if you believe these two jealous witches ever really made up, or just share money fever."

Chocolatte straightened to her full imposing height. There was nothing slack about *her* face. "We brought you aboard, Medicine Man, because you were working in some low-end clinic in Cleveland. You know Nilla was fine, just fine, when we all got together to plan this gig."

"You must have known something could happen." He hunched his knees up on the five-thousand-dollar chair, sullen as a twelve-year-old.

"It's when we hit this hotel. Maybe when this gig became the real thing she started snapping. Started using something."

He eyed Temple. "I give her vitamin B shots and when she's…irrational, a sedative. Ask any shrink. Very low dose. You all aren't getting *me* on a Michael Jackson charge."

Now that they were back on the twelfth floor, and Latty and Nilla had retreated to their suites, the rest of Black & White assembled to kick back in the common area with its refreshments table. Given the size of the guys' motorcycle boots, "kick" was the word for it.

Temple watched them stock up on food and drink—mostly junk food and hard drink—and scatter to their suites. Any drugs of choice were kept there, or discreetly concealed on their persons.

Sally Everleigh sat at the computer desk along one wall, probably toying with how to slant press releases for when news of a dead body on the set came out. Temple could hear the computer keys clucking as sporadically as a hen sitting on one stinking big egg. Finding a good "angle" to cover an anonymous death and a hyped entertainment event was not a PR assignment that tripped off the keyboard in four-four time.

Bixby slumped on the deserted sectional sofa, an unopened can of beer in his loose grip. He looked ten years older.

Temple poured some wine and joined him, kicking off her shoes and curling up her feet.

Bix's gold tooth flashed for a millisecond. "Hey, Ms. Miz. Bet this is a bummer day for you and your PR work too."

"Yeah. Do you think Nilla will come around?"

"She has before."

"Are you all right?" Temple asked. Did he even know what he'd muttered to her?

"My band and our big reunion date are looking to be shut down before they start up again. So I'm not all right."

"I mean, after seeing the dead man."

He frowned at her. "What you gettin' at?"

"You seemed really shocked."

"Shocked? This crazy-assed, floating, flower-thing comes crashing down with a beat-up dead dude as a centerpiece? I was surprised, all right."

"Somebody suspicious could have been hanging around," Temple pointed out. "Fans today are busting into stars' homes, stealing their belongings, sleeping in their beds. Some fans, or even paparazzi, could slip in backstage and come to a bad end by hiding someplace dangerous, like this jungle gym of a set. The police will be checking out that option."

"Yeah," Bixby said. "That's right! Security staff are always hustling some fool of a fan guy or girl, or a photographer, away from backstage. I didn't think of that."

Big Bix was looking more focused, so Temple tried another possibility. "Some fans have made stars' private texts and photos go viral. Was anybody bothering the divas that way? Though their phone numbers must be as secret as a Swiss bank account numbers."

"Well, yeah," he said, "half the fans nowadays seem to be hackers."

"What about fans from the old days?"

"They are all probably using those simple Jitterbug phones for oldsters." Bix pulled an Android smart phone from his pants. "I mostly play tic-tac-toe with the buttons on this monsta and hope to get somewhere, it's so complicated. Our hardcore fans are too old for cyber stalking."

"What was the real story on the divas' breakup years ago?"

"Can't you read the Internet? Everything since Adam had indigestion and coughed up a rib is on there now."

"The printed 'facts', are plain and simple," Temple said. "First it was Cale Watson and Velveedah Hooker. I can sure see why she was eventually renamed Chocolatte. Like Ike and Tina Turner before them, they were burning up the rhythm and blues charts, but only so many black-couple acts were going to break out to the big time."

"Yup. Selma Alabama was struggling, Selma Sue French sang like an angel doing guard duty at the heavenly gates, a white soprano the likes of Whitney Houston." Bix bowed his head in tribute. "But talent don't always out. Then Cale caught our act at a chain hotel when we were a three-man band. Cale, wanted to blend the bands right away. Wanted to call it Ebony and Ivory. I told him he couldn't take that Paul McCartney song title. Tacky, you know. So one thing led to another and he came up with Chocolatte."

"You coined the French Vanilla name for Selma Sue, didn't you?"

"Yeah. How'd you know?"

"You liked that it was subtle, that you were secretly playing tribute to the black musicians who migrated to France."

"Black & White. That was the answer. Something a bit different at the time, and, you know, young lady, there were still many clubs that wouldn't book Cale and Chocolatte, and that even later wouldn't book Black & White. The group was in your face for the times."

"These times seem to be harking back that way."

"I gotta agree with you. The freaky mail just for Chocolatte has turned virulent in the past five years."

"You went with the French Vanilla side of the break?"

"No, I stayed with Chocolatte. When the girls began talks about re-uniting their bands for this gig, I became Big Bix again, sorta manager." He gave his solid-gold grin. "They both trusted me. We're all too old now to remember back when we got frisky with each other."

"So you get to see French Vanilla's fan mail too now?"

"For the past couple months."

"Letters, e-mails, texts?"

"All of the above. You want to see the latest batch?"

"Ye-es! The police will be getting around to this pronto anyway."

Bixby got his big frame moving and was back in five minutes with a portable file box that locked. He pulled out file folders. One black, one white. And shrugged when Temple's face registered the apropos system at work.

He set the box on his lap, and paged through the files.

"You need to turn that stuff over to Lieutenant Molina ASAP," Temple told him. "I'm texting you the phone number."

Bixby started to close the file box.

"But...not until I get a rundown on the contents."

Bixby's eyes narrowed. "I don't think you're a need-to-know person on this stuff."

"For anticipating possible publicity issues," Temple said. "And in thanks for the great lunch I treated you to in the Ghost Suite. That huge chocolate sundae was worth your fudging a bit on who gets the scoop on your Freak File."

He chuckled. "I'm lucky you're not a lawyer. Okay. Over the years we got a lot of adulation, and a lot of trash talking. We had lost cousins crawling out of the woodwork like roaches at a comedy club. Obsessive fans that were really creepy, asking for nail clippings and such. Hopeful kids wanting auditions. Sometimes we'd give them and their parents a backstage pass."

"That could be dangerous now."

"Nobody knows yet what we'll draw fanwise until the opening, but, yeah, we'll get all of what's in this box and more."

He pulled out a clipped set of typed letters and envelopes. "Here's another 'lost child' claiming to be Chocolatte's daughter."

"What about French Vanilla?"

"She got and gets the same crazy range of claims. Ex-husbands, kids. I wouldn't be surprised if an ex-pet wrote in."

Temple laughed. "Maybe Scotch and Soda have had some extra-domestic romps."

"That black cat of yours who regards our suites as some new stomping ground...wouldn't surprise me if he wrote a blackmail letter after some of the stuff he's seen here."

"Has either diva had to get a restraining order?"

"Tons in the old days, but where are those folks now?"

"That's the crazy thing. Where is Watson now? You're afraid the corpse is Cale, aren't you?" She caught him by surprise, as she'd wanted to.

"I thought—" Bixby swallowed hard. "It was natural to think..." He shook his head.

"So you don't think some of those nutsy fans could have been stalking either diva, and maybe spotted Cale Watson hanging around here, also drawn by the reunion news? Maybe a possessive fan wanted to kill him as a rival."

"Nah. That's crazy now. Most of that serious stalking stuff was years ago, when both girls were in their prime. Those nut cases end up incarcerated or commit suicide or just disappear. Sometimes we alert the police in the cities where the sickest letters are postmarked, but e-mail or texting is hard to trace and stop."

"I don't get how Cale Watson could disappear for decades like that."

"Black folks have known how to be on the down-low for a long time."

"But why?"

Bixby held up his hands as if Temple held a gun on him. "I give up, Miz Barr. I couldn't even speculate years ago, when both Nilla and Latty went missing for almost a year. For a while we thought Cale had run off with one of 'em, but they showed up in fringe clubs and he didn't. And both ladies were singing the blues, but neither of them was doing the talking blues. After a while, Cale Watson became a forgotten man, like Judge Crater or something. Why are you wearin' my old brain out when folks younger and maybe even wiser, or more suspicious, than you couldn't come up with anything?"

"Tomorrow those divas are going to be interviewed by the toughest homicide detective in town. It's my job to make sure this whole house of cards doesn't come tumbling down."

Bixby chuckled. "That woman cop is one long drink of law enforcement. She'll handle our divas better'n we could ever do it."

"You don't sound worried that one of the divas could have met with Watson and killed him."

"With the kind of dives Cale had to lose himself in to stay out of sight, he'd be a mighty hard man to kill. Anyway, those divas wouldn't want to dirty their fancy nail jobs on him, for sure, at this point."

31
A Darker Shade of Cale

After Bixby left for his suite, Temple remained in the deserted main area, thinking. Actually, she was in a blue funk. Van and Nicky, although gracious and understanding at the scene of the crime discovered, were probably panicking and huddling with Danny Dove right now.

She should be there, but her energy seemed to have left itself on the stage set.

Temple only became aware of a shuffling figure raiding the food and drink tables when a Baccarat glass shattered on the marble floor, accompanied by a curse.

She jumped up to clean up the mess, the only one she could handle now at least.

"We got maids for that," the man said. He was already pouring Johnny Walker Black into another glass, four fingers full.

"You're Beau Weevil, aren't you?" Temple realized she hadn't interviewed this guy, and a whiff of his bad breath may have been why. He took scruffy to new lows.

"No."

Temple was stumped.

"Wilson is the name. Bowman is my first name."

His jeans with holes in the knees were the real thing, not fashionable impersonators, and his *Black & White Rocks* T-shirt was more of a menu sample than respectable casual wear.

"I'm sorry I missed interviewing you," Temple said, descending into insincerity.

"That's me, at the back of the band, watching all their asses. Not that's it's a burden with the girls. The drummer is the Lost Man."

"But you're an original B&W member?"

"Yeah." He collapsed onto the sectional, sloshing scotch over his leg and the cushion. "I been here before there was a Black & White."

"Which band did you start out with?" Temple sat a careful foot and a half away from his flailing drinking arm. She realized the scotch whiskey wasn't only thing sloshed in the room. Wilson's eyes were bloodshot and his scraggly white stubble showed his age.

"I was with Selma Alabama, when we was already black and white. More raw rock than rhythm and blues. Me on drums, Mickey O'Hara on piano and Beau on guitar, all backing up Selma Sue French."

"So 'Spider' O'Hara was also in French Vanilla's original band?"

"I mean *Mickey,* Miss. Those were our names until Cale Watson came along with a plan to merge us with him and Chocolatte."

"That worked out, didn't it?"

"You call a bust-up lasting almost twenty-four years working out? Now it looks like another bust-up, thanks to Cale Watson."

"What do you mean?"

"I don't know. I guess I mean, that's gotta be the dead guy Nilla was hammering on. Cale Watson. Wouldn't you know he'd come back from the dead…dead, and ruin the band all over again?"

"But he created Black & White."

"He created a vehicle for Cale Watson. He created a playground for his ego to cut loose in, and that ego soon tore what he had created apart. With our bad luck, I don't doubt he's back, in the same role."

"Does everyone in the original bands feel this way about Watson? I thought it was a love triangle with the divas that did in B&W. That the threesome all left in a huff, abandoned the band?"

"*You* thought? The press thought. The critics thought. The fans thought. Nobody got it right. You wanta know who named me 'Beau Weevil'? It was Cale. He made Mickey into 'Spider' too. Named us after insects. Yeah, Cale was good about coming up with names. Chocolatte was first. It was short for 'Hot Chocolate'. He did not treat that woman good even before Selma Sue and our band came along. When we did join up, we found out he liked to slap Chocolatte around."

"And French Vanilla ran off with him?" Temple was shocked by the band's tawdry roots compared to the unified front they represented.

"Cale Watson put on a good show when you first got to know him. Latty was in a jealous funk, maybe because he wasn't hittin' Nilla…yet. Women in the music business back then weren't surprised to be used and abused. Now they run the show, kids your age or less, like Katy Perry or Taylor Swift. *American Idol,* where you been all my life?"

"You make me sorry I can't carry a tune."

"That's all right, girl." He leaned precariously over to pat her knee. "You got a good job here with people you like."

"With people I need to get out of hot water."

Wilson laughed wearily and caressed his glass of Johnny Walker. "We woulda been back in the sweet life, and now our divas are in double trouble again. All because of Cale. Again."

"He sounds like a candidate for murder, all right. Where was Lionel Bixby in all this? He strikes me as the leader type."

"Lionel Bixby. Cool cat. He'd been with Selma first, in every way, then hooked up with Chocolatte right after the meld. That was over fast once Cale took over us all. You know how Lionel is called 'Big Bix'?"

Temple nodded.

"That's not what Cale called him." Beau Weevil Wilson leaned in again and whispered, nearly asphyxiating Temple with expensive scotch fumes. "Cale called him 'Little Dicksie'. That hadta rankle, but ole Lionel knew B&W could go places and he just faded into the background, like we all did when Cale started propelling us into an up-and-coming concept."

"And nobody, not even the paparazzi, figured out why or where the two divas and Cale Watson went when they disappeared?"

"Rehab is the usual suspect in my line of work, and everybody was gettin' so intent they were doin' a bunch of stuff."

"Apparently both women broke with Watson during the year they were missing. You could almost suspect they did him in together."

"That was one rumor. I just know that after the press found them singing incognito there was a big fuss about it. Old band guys had scattered. Only Big Bix, as he renamed himself after Cale was gone and not missed, went back to the music business, with the old lead girl, Chocolatte, to run her band and career. Then he got a college teaching job offer, a big deal for an old sideman and band manager, and he retired to be an instant prof, imagine that."

Bixby, Temple thought. Acting like he'd been out of the game on both the pleasure and business sides, when he was clearly allied with one diva and not the other. And now acting as bipolar as French Vanilla, pretending Cale Watson hadn't ever crossed his mind as the dead man.

"Why did the women keep the names Cale Watson had given them after he was out of the picture?"

"Nilla was using the name 'Snow', but the money was in being 'French Vanilla'. Heck. She even mighta done it for sentimental reasons. She wasn't around long enough to see Cale's worst side. Latty might have done it out of revenge, because she'd been through all his badassery and now she saw a way to take his career plan for her own."

"And now," Temple said, "they're both prime suspects in Cale Watson's murder, if that's really his corpse. Why did anyone wait so long?"

"Cale was a big, bad man. I don't think no diva could have done him in."

"Especially not French Vanilla, being such a drugged-out mess all these years."

"What you talkin' about?" Beau had relaxed enough to be rolling a joint as he talked. "She just did a little weed now and then, like me. She's the one who was all cleaned up and anti-drug when she showed up again. Hell, she's done 'don't drink and drug' public service ads. She's been lecturing the band since we reassembled here. She's the one with big recording contract. Chocolatte's ridin' on her skinny coattails now. Vanilla French was flying high without artificial help. Guess we all were a bad example. Guess gettin' together again pushed her off the wagon." Weevil shrugged. "That's what happened to Philip Seymour Hoffman, after twenty clean years. That's life."

It was also death, and now it was time for Temple to confront someone who had loved and hated Cale Watson with some pointed questions.

Before Lieutenant Molina did tomorrow.

32
Diva Direct

When Temple knocked at French Vanilla's door she was surprised by a velvet breeze on her bare calves. Midnight Louie announcing his presence.

After a while, the diva cracked open the door. Temple could sense her eyes wincing at the hall light behind the sunglasses. Her shimmering black-and-white-painted nails grasped the door edge for dear life.

"I came to see how you're doing," Temple said, "and offer any help I can to prepare you for the police statement tomorrow. I know the law enforcement people involved pretty well."

"That's generous of you, but hardly part of your job."

"Actually, I think it is." Temple smiled. "And…you've been very sweet and helpful to me."

Nilla's brows lifted over her heavy sunglass frames in a polite frown. "Why shouldn't I be?"

"You're a diva, and you know the rep divas have."

"I've never traded on that. What did I do for you?"

"You loaned Sessalee to me for a fabulous makeover…"

Nilla nodded, bewildered. "That was just girl playtime."

"You were even nice to Lieutenant Molina, who you'll learn tomorrow is one hard-boiled cop, and which I have a hard time doing."

"So I'm a saint? This saint has had a terrible day, as you know. Miss Barr, why are you here?"

"Temple, remember? I'm here to try to help you have a less terrible day tomorrow."

Nilla looked down. Through her sunglasses, Louie must look like a shapeless black blot. "And why is the cat here?"

Temple watched him brush by Nilla's legs and pause to sniff the air. "Cats like to explore."

"So do you, I guess." Nilla left the door open to totter into the dressing room.

Temple shut the door behind her, and found Nilla sitting at her fancy dressing table, her face reflected in the mirror above it. "Nobody can help me."

"Now, that's the self-absorbed diva coming out," Temple said. "And that's not the 'Nilla' I've seen over the past couple of days."

"Who is she?" the star asked. "That 'Nilla' you like?"

"She's thoughtful. Kind. Considerate to younger women like me and Sessalee and, God forbid, Carmen Molina. You know her from somewhere, don't you?"

Nilla laughed. "Why don't you two don't get along?"

"She thinks my ex is a criminal."

"Is he?"

"No." Temple smiled. "But sometimes he skirts the law."

"What does she think about Mr. Diamond-and-Ruby Ring?" The sunglasses nodded at Temple's hand.

"Probably that he's too good for me." Temple grinned. "Look I'm a PR person. My job is to tidy up awkward, and maybe even lethal, situations like this one. Molina's a cop. It annoys her when I know more than she does sometimes."

"Do you?"

Temple shrugged. "I might now, if you'll talk to me honestly."

"And why should I?"

"Because I'm a young career woman and you could be my mentor. Because you like to mentor young women. Because you have a mother gene."

Nilla slammed a silver-backed brush down to the dressing table's mirrored surface, which cracked. Temple knew Van wouldn't mind that happening in a good cause, and saving the Black & White reunion was a good cause.

"Carmen Molina." Nilla seemed to be staring at her image in the mirror. "You do notice the little things, Miss Temple. Yes, I did recognize her. She auditioned as a backup singer for one my tours, maybe seventeen years ago. She was a kid. Young, raw talent. She had those gutsy low notes I so envied and need filled in. My…'people'…felt she was too tall for backup. That she'd overwhelm my stage presence. We passed. Later, I got gutsier in my business dealings, but it was too late for her."

"She sings," Temple said, amazed that Molina had lost a big chance because of the height Temple envied her. "At a local club, sometimes. When she isn't handling murder cases and grilling rock divas. You could still help out young Carmen."

"How?"

"If I understood what happened between you and Cale and Chocolatte thirty years ago, I know I could…help Molina solve this case."

"Or—" Nilla raised the brush toward her airy aureole of silver curls. "You could have just told the murderer you're a nosy young woman who knows or wants to know too much, that you have police connections, and are dangerous."

"Oh, please." Temple pointed to Midnight Louie lashing his tail against the carpeting. "You have a witness. Besides, I don't think you're a perp. You're a victim. And you always have been."

Nilla's bleached upper teeth bit her lower lip until it was corpse white.

"You're getting angry now," Temple said, "but when your head clears, which isn't often lately, you'll know what I'm talking about."

"You don't know anything!" Nilla pushed the brush away across the desk mirror and put her face in her hand, shoving the ever-present celebrity sunglasses up like a headband. "I'm going blind."

"Oh, no." Temple knelt beside her.

"You saw it. Everyone did. My vision comes and goes. I can't predict it. One instant a stairway is a step. Then it's a black nothing. The only things I see vividly are nightmares. Sometimes they're enchanting, like a drug high…then they become a horror movie in my brain that never ends. I want to tear the images out." Her pale fingers and long nails drove into the thistle of her hair like combs.

"I'm so sorry," Temple said, understanding much now. "It's not anything you're taking?"

"Ibuprofen and a statin med? I looked up medication side effects on the Internet right away."

"You're getting vitamin B injections."

"Those have no effect."

"But Doc's also been sedating you. I can understand the panic attacks, given your sight issues. I've heard of people going completely blind from a medication, and recovering."

"That's a relief. I suppose." Nilla sighed. "Now that you know my darkest secret of the moment, I suppose I can tell you all the dead and gone secrets."

"You didn't run away together, did you?" Temple asked.

She was now sitting at Nilla's feet, like a child awaiting a story. Midnight Louie crowded closer, as if to hear. Nilla's hand reached down, felt his furry head, and stayed there.

She smiled. "At least the cat knows how to keep a secret. We didn't 'run away together'. I ran and Cale followed."

"You were leaving Black & White."

"Yes."

"Why?"

"You're right. I was a victim. Latty tried to tell me he was controlling and that the more I got involved with him the more he'd force his will on me. I thought she was just jealous. Jealous that Cale had brought me and my band into their act. Angry that she didn't make it until I came and Black & White took off. Jealous of me for my romance with Cale. I didn't believe what she said about Cale, because why would she still want him, if he was such a bad dude?"

"But he had been *her* bad dude. So you two did feud?"

"She did. I was more naïve, and really not up to defending myself. Cale was my White Knight, I thought. My black White Knight. He was so sophisticated, crooning about the huge success we'd have, seducing me. He used drugs to bring me up, and down."

Nilla sighed. "He enjoyed our cat fights over him, said negative publicity was better than positive. Is that true, Temple?"

"Pretty much, but the price of performing badly in public eventually turns back on a performer's sense of self-esteem. How did you get the nerve to break the hold of drugs and break with Watson and B&W? That took enormous grit."

"I had no choice. I knew I had to rehab myself and I'd never do it around Cale and B&W. Something more important than me and my singing came up. Oh, my dear, can't you guess why I had to run away and get clean?" Nilla reached down blindly to grab Temple's hands.

Temple talked it out. "Only rehab would break Cale's hold on you… otherwise you'd do just what he said. And he wanted total control, of the money too, I bet, of what you sang. They used to call that keeping woman barefoot and pregnant. You weren't out of sight in just rehab for a year…"

Temple really heard what she'd just said.

"You were *pregnant*. Why run? If you didn't want to marry Cale, the times they were a-changing, and celebrity women were becoming single mothers with no career fall-out."

Nilla pulled her hands away to cover the sides of her face. "It wasn't the public. It was Cale. He insisted that I have an abortion. He didn't want a 'ball and chain' and said a baby would destroy my sexy lady image."

"Can we say Beyoncé? Even back then he was wrong."

"Cale had 'discovered' me. I was so young in 1980, still a teenager. I never grew up. Lotta band members are like that. They do adult stuff like sex and drugs, but never…mature. So who could I go to? Choco-latte was the woman scorned, and hated me. Bixby didn't like Cale, but he couldn't deny that Cale had built the band as he'd never been able to do. And Black & White had to have Chocolatte and French Vanilla. I ran. And Cale followed."

"I've heard he could be abusive."

"That too. The other thing was Cale liked his ladies needing drugs. I'd seen crack babies and no way was I going to drink or drug while pregnant, once I knew. Cale would keep me on the stuff if he had to inject me himself. I knew he would. So I ran."

"You keep saying that, like it was literal."

Nilla's face sank deeper into her hands, until her voice was muffled. "He caught up with me outside a Planned Parenthood office in down-town Detroit. They'll refer you to places where you can have your baby too.

"Cale grabbed me by the arm coming out the door in the early evening. Rush hour. Scared the shinola out of me. Callin' me 'baby this' and 'baby that', but not wanting any baby out of me. Calling me stupid white bitch not havin' any baby, and he knew a place close by that could take care of it right now."

"So I ran. I ran out into traffic. And he followed."

Temple could guess the next revelation.

"He got hit. Hard. By a big delivery van. Ironic, huh? No delivery for me, one special delivery for him. I did not slow down. I did not look back. I went to the place I had written down on a notepad and I had my baby. No one knew. I used my mother's cousin's name. I had gotten sober and I was sober while I was there. I left there sober and I have been sober until this last week or two, when I started having shadow LSD trips and my sight started going in and out all at once."

"You gave up your baby for adoption? What was it?"

"I don't know."

"You don't know?

"The only way I could do it was never to see or hold the baby, never know anything about it. They gave me a lot of heat about my decision, but I was not moved. Heart of Stone. How did you suspect so fast I'd had a baby?"

"For a temperamental diva, you have a mothering way with younger people around you, now that I think about it. With anyone young enough to be your child."

Nilla was quiet for a bit. "After a time like I went through, I think that anyone out there could be my child, grown up, that I could pass him or her on the street or at a local TV station show. You are always haunted."

"You might be able to trace your child. There's a great book and movie you should look into, *Philomena*."

Nilla's head turned away. "I've heard of it. I'm afraid to see it, read it. It's too late."

Temple knew better than to argue. Maybe later, when this mess was solved. Molina would find the murderer and it wasn't French Vanilla, Temple felt with all her heart. Unless…it *was* French Vanilla. She certainly would have panicked if Cale had approached her again after all these years.

"Were you afraid all this time of Cale coming after you again?"

"At first. That's why I performed under a false name. When the tabloids found out where I was and who I was, I hired a detective and a bodyguard. Cale never showed up. The detective couldn't find him. Not even among traffic fatalities. I figured he staggered off somewhere alone, and died. He was that…stubborn. If he'd had a breath or a bit of brain left in him, he'd have come after me. You do not walk away from Cale Watson."

"Apparently you did." Temple grabbed the dresser edge to hoist herself up from the floor.

Nilla laughed. "Getting too old to sit on the floor. Don't you know your knees are the first to go?"

"I'm not that old," Temple said, "although I know I look about twelve."

"Don't you worry. You talk like about forty-five. I don't know how my past miseries are gonna help you discomfort Miss Carmen Molina, but I'm going to feel a bit better when I go to the police station tomorrow morning, knowing you and Mr. Cat are on the case."

"His name is Louie, Midnight Louie," Temple introduced him. "He's a very good listener."

"How did you come up with the name?"

"I didn't. It was what people around this hotel who saw him as a stray called him. Some cats are like that. They know their name and figure out some way to get you to use it."

Louie, knowing himself to be under discussion, preened a bit, and then, of course, did something disgraceful. He lofted atop the dressing table, startling poor blind Nilla, and started to stalk along the many beauty products. At home he could do what Temple called a "perp walk" along her kitchen counter or bathroom cosmetics shelf and leave not a breakable touched.

This time his tail flicked a taller bottle.

"Oh," Temple called out to warn Nilla. "Louie! That bottle's going over."

Somewhere during her speech, it did indeed fall flat on the mirrored service. Another little crack. More damage control for Van to fix.

"I'm so sorry." Temple picked up the bottle. "Just when we praise him we goes postal. So like a cat." She righted the bottle and sniffed her fingers. "*Hmm.* Lovely scent. I could use a signature perfume," Temple said, thinking of going one-up on the impossible to compete with Revienne. "What is this?"

"I don't know," Nilla said. "It has that strong vanilla scent, so it's something the hotel made or found and furnished as a perk, I suppose."

"This is a deep, dark secret," Temple told her, "but Van's first name is short for Vanilla."

"Really?" French Vanilla whispered like a girlfriend.

"Van *hates* the long form, so it's extra thoughtful of her to have provided a perfume tailored to *your* name."

"This hotel's service is fabulous. I even have a bottle on my nightstand too."

"You don't mind if I get some? If I can afford it?"

"Darling girl, you can have that bottle the cat laid claim to, in his own feline way."

"Really? See, you're way too nice to be a diva, much less a murderer, and I'm going to make sure you don't get railroaded. I'll keep your secret too, as long as I can," Temple promised.

And, she was going to look into the causes of sudden vision loss, too.

Nilla stretched out her pale fingers. "Thank you."

Temple clasped hands, avoiding tangling with the long false fingernails painted with a black-and-white Art Deco pattern.

She enameled her naturally long and strong fingernails, but she'd never understood how even women whose jobs involved punching cell phone and keyboard buttons could function with those mandarin-talon things. Even Sessalee wore false fingernails under her latex gloves.

Must be some latent desire to be a cat.

Later, in her suite, she made a call that would unleash havoc and the dogs of war on Black & White and everyone involved with this deadly reunion.

"Molina," came the answer after one ring.

"I have something big and bad for you."

"Midnight Louie?"

"Some band members think they can ID the body."

"Nice of them to promptly let the authorities know, like good little citizens. Why would they tell you? And my own suspicions on that possibility are being checked out right now."

"So you suspected it's Cale Watson?"

"At first sight. I know the Black & White backstory. Since you're such a successful little snoop, I'll let you accompany the divas to head-quarters tomorrow. Their statements should be a wonder to behold." She cut off the call.

Temple was relieved not to have squealing on the band on her conscience. And that she'd have a front row seat for Black & White: The Interrogation.

33
Black & White Lies

"**You can't go** in there," Molina said, neatly cutting Temple out of the pack of divas, diva lawyers, and Detective Alch as they assembled in a crowded corner of the Crimes against Persons unit the next morning. Temple joined Molina in watching body language as French Vanilla and her attorney were ushered through an unmarked door into a nondescript room beyond.

"*You're* not doing the interrogation?" Temple was astounded. She always pictured Molina leaning over some poor cowering soul in an airier police version of an old-fashioned Catholic Church confessional booth.

Without answering, the lieutenant herded Temple through a nearby door. "We're going in here."

The door closed, isolating Temple with Molina in a dim, small room smelling of stale smoke with a giant, horizontal mirror-size window on one wall right out of a TV cop show. The clichéd surveillance room looked a lot better than it smelled in person.

Mid-century modern aficionados would recognize the wide, horizontal, blackboard proportions that killed narrow, high, pre-WWII windows for good. From then on, everybody looking out on everybody outside, and everybody inside, was in danger of being on display.

Of course the display was never more dramatic than the interrogation "spy window" seen on endless cop shows on TV.

"I can't believe I'm here," Temple said.

"You're lucky you're not on the other side of that window." Molina folded her arms, not a good sign. Temple knew body language too and relied on it. In a way, a public relations professional had to be a good detective too.

"I understand," Molina said, again keeping her eyes on the other side of the glass, "you've actually moved in with that mob from Black & White. Must annoy the fiancée."

"Matt is not an interfering sort of person."

"Maybe he's more interested in not being interfered *with* these days?"

"Huh?" Temple frowned at Molina's profile. What was she implying? Something mean, no doubt.

Temple had expected—hoped—to be peering at one of the two divas in an interrogation room. "Which side of the two-way glass am I on?"

"What the side you're on means is that you don't get to sit. You get to stand and watch."

Oh, goody, Temple thought, *I'm a real girl detective now.*

Molina had put up with her on crime scenes before, but had never invited her to a police interrogation. She almost pressed her nose against the window and panted, she was so excited. And such famous suspects too.

Then a man was escorted in and left sitting at a table bolted to the floor.

She turned on Molina. "Danny Dove? Vegas' premier choreographer is under suspicion?"

Molina was pacing, head down. She looked up. "Last to leave, first to show up the next morning."

"That's what choreographers do."

"If he's so prestigious, why does he keep janitor's hours?"

"That's a big, dangerous set. He'd want to make sure the all the mechanical boards were off at night. And he'd come in early to try some leaps and dance steps on the set parts that had just been installed. That's what Fred Astaire would do, work alone on a movie set."

"Fred Astaire didn't have any corpses pop up on his set overnight. That I know of."

"It might not have happened overnight. Gosh, the guy could have been up there for…a couple days."

"Not according to the coroner."

"What killed him?"

"OD on drugs, but his face was scratched and his trunk and arms were badly bruised."

"So he was in a fight."

"Or flailed around under the influence. We seem to be dealing with a hallucigenic here. He might have been clawing at his own face. Some of his own DNA was found under a couple fingernails, but no other."

Molina stared into the other room. "I'm betting the women know a lot I could use about Cale Watson, but will be uncooperative. At best, or worst, either could be an accessory, and maybe the cause. If Cale came back to take a piece of Black & White, anybody in the band could have wanted him dead."

"What's the point? They'd be sabotaging his or her own comeback."

"You of all people know that bad publicity reaps big rewards. The Miley Cyrus and Justin Bieber Principle. One thing's certain…the body was moved to the airborne stage unit, so it took someone who knew the way around a tech board, and a stage set. And Dove does. Somebody wanted to delay discovery of the body."

"Or…someone wanted to announce in a spectacular fashion that Cale Watson had really left the planet at last. Sure sounds like revenge."

Temple heard a low-level tapping sound. She eyed Danny sitting alone at the table, looking like a twenty-four-year-old choir boy with his mop of curly blond hair. His fingers were drumming the tabletop, but not from nervousness.

"Look," Temple said, "he's working out a production number while he waits."

"Little Drummer Boy had better pound out a convincing alibi."

"Watson was a big man, and Danny is…"

"Stronger than he looks. Choreographers are. They sling bodies around all the time."

With a clicking sound, the interrogation room door opened and Detective Su entered. She was wearing cowboy-boot-style mules with steel toes, which added to her height and fiercely tough persona. Temple understood that a petite Asian woman would want to pump up her presence and authority. Especially if her name was Merry Su.

Su seemed reluctant to sit and lose her advantage, but did. "Mr. Dove, you understand you're being questioned about the person found dead in one of your production's mobile set pieces?"

He nodded.

"Say 'yes' or 'no', please."

Danny looked around, now aware of the recording system. "Yes."

"Do you have any idea who he was?"

"No, I don't. He was attired in black, so when I was over the shock of the discovery, it occurred to me it might be one of my 'invisible' set movers."

"They wear black?"

"Yes, down to more comfortable versions of hockey masks. Spandex. All of them showed up when I did a roll call as soon as the officer suggested it."

"How many were there?"

"Four."

"So you had four masked ninjas at the rehearsal."

"I've worked this way for years. Every magic act on the Strip uses 'invisible' assistants. Houdini did it, for God's sake."

Temple felt her spine stiffen. The next second she heard Molina's pleasant contralto wafting inside the interrogation room.

"A word, please, Detective Su."

Su excused herself and left as Molina also slipped out of the observation room.

Temple was left behind like an inconvenient chair, gazing at Danny's puzzled face. She wished she knew Morse code and could tap out a reassuring message on the glass. But then there'd be two of them in the interrogation room.

Just as Su stepped back into that room like an actor reentering a scene, Temple felt a waft of air at her back.

Su took her time sitting down again and rearranging her file folder. That would not fool Danny. He knew theatrical business when he saw it.

He gave a quick grin that warmed Temple's heart. It was hard to see a friend in this position, where his hard-won reputation meant nothing and he might by accused of anything.

"So," Detective Su said, "you did employ a magician to help with the set design and staging?"

"Yes."

"Who was—?"

"The best in business, as I am at my profession."

"Quit dodging. Do you want me to say it, or you?"

"The Mystifying Max."

"Whose real name is?"

"Max Kinsella."

Temple turned to give Molina a glare. "Lame, Lieutenant. Max just did Danny a favor. What on Earth would he have to do with a Black & White reunion show otherwise?"

Glares bounced off Molina. "What if one of the set 'ninjas' was Kathleen O'Connor in disguise?"

Temple gasped at the crazy logic of that leap.

"She has to be somewhere," Molina went on, "and she's stalking Kinsella. Whither he goest…"

"Kitty the Cutter goes." Temple bit her lip. "Max wouldn't kill some innocent bystander."

"She would. She's masqueraded as the airborne magician, Shangri-La. I saw that woman perform once myself. Maybe this dead guy got caught in the middle and she killed him."

"What does Grizzly Bahr say about his condition?" Temple asked, just to remind Molina that the friendly neighborhood coroner was a friend of hers.

A PR woman can never have too many friends in the right places, and Grizzly shared her love of exotic footwear, only his were size twelve cowboy boots. That element had even come into solving a bizarre murder not long ago.

Molina made a face. "The dead man was out of shape."

Temple knew there had to be more she wasn't hearing. "Not a good candidate for leaping around stage sets like a ninja," she said.

"No," Molina admitted, "but he was black, so the link to Black & White is…too intriguing to ignore."

Temple frowned. "How old was he?"

Molina laughed under her breath. "Fifty-four."

"Ten years shy of a Beatles song kind of age," Temple said. And around the age of many in the band.

"Not a common age for being murdered," Molina noted, "unless it's in a family dispute or a bar or a street crime…robbery, assault."

"What killed him?"

Danny's rising voice from the other room over-rode Temple's question. "It was very confusing, Detective Su. Miss…Vanilla was somewhat distraught, and the mobile unit, as you call it, is designed to descend either slowly or swiftly without apparent human agency."

"Can you talk English, Mr. Dove? How was this 'Vanilla' person distraught? Are you saying this flying object fell, and wasn't lowered?"

Danny squirmed. He knew his testimony was damaging to French Vanilla. "I had ordered the tech staff to set the mobile stage in motion, but I was startled when Miss French reacted with so much fear. Everyone was. Perhaps she hadn't been paying attention, and it seemed like a rogue piece of stage equipment coming right down on her. Understandably, she was a bit disturbed."

"Mobile stage. What is it and how does it operate?"

"Imagine a giant mechanical tulip, Detective."

"That's a tough assignment."

"It's not red or yellow, it's black and white. Imagine a round ministage that can spin and move from side to side, as well as rise up and down on a hydraulic central post in the ceiling. The decorative outer ring of 'petals' are in the folded up position as the unit rests under the ceiling and also as it descends. The petals slowly lower with the unit, unfolding. By the time the unit rests on the stage floor, the petals are ramps the musicians, singers, and dancers can use to move onto the main set."

"So this French Vanilla was the only one to see the unit was descending. Why?" Su asked.

"She and Miss Chocolatte had come in for the first time to see where they'd be performing."

"You were planning to lower a mini unit as part of that tour?"

Danny nodded. "First, I wanted them to see the impact of the set as the audience would, before the moving parts became involved."

"Musicians and singers and dancers being the moving parts?"

"Yes. Miss French Vanilla was looking up, of course."

"And when did you notice her reaction?"

"When she…became agitated. Said giant spiders were coming down from the ceiling."

"Is there any sense in that?"

"The units' design is organic," Danny said. "They were meant to be seen as big gorgeous black-and-white Dahlias or peonies maybe, also as unnatural objects of nature…mechanical flowers."

"But not giant spiders?"

Danny paused. "No. We didn't think they'd frighten the audience. Thrill, yes."

Detective Su sat back as if satisfied and about to dismiss Danny. Then she leaned rapidly forward.

"Spiders? Does that sound like delirium tremens to you, Mr. Dove? Was Miss French Vanilla drunk? Was she on something?"

"I couldn't say."

"Witnesses say she was kneeling on the floor, pounding on one low-ered 'petal' ramp of the unit. That she was pounding on the revealed body that rested upon it."

"The unit's interior was black upholstery. I didn't see that a body was there until she had been…removed and everybody crowding around backed off. She was disturbed by the descending unit, as would anybody be who didn't know it was there. I was damn shocked myself when I saw it almost ready to touch the stage."

"You didn't hear it."

"The mechanism is silent. With a heavily wired music performance going on, nothing can creak. Not the set, not the left knee of a dancer. Not on my stage."

Su frowned, then snapped, "You can go. For now." She stood and left the room, while Danny tried not to look toward the window.

The door opened and a uniformed officer gestured him out.

Temple found her neck and shoulders were as tense as if she'd been pounding out press releases on her laptop for hours.

"He's not a serious suspect," Molina said.

Temple jumped. She'd been so concentrated on Danny's

interrogation she'd forgotten she wasn't alone in the room.

"Your ex might be, though."

"You never give up," Temple said.

"Thank you. That rogue IRA operative you three tangled with, who put two of you in the hospital, you're not safe from her. Kinsella is her primary target, and he was working on this set with Danny Dove. The dead man might have been a confederate and tried to kill Kinsella."

"Max wouldn't leave a body behind to mess up Danny's and my lives."

"So you say he would be capable of killing."

"Someone who was trying to kill him? He'd do what he'd have to do, same as you and I."

"Kinsella and I would have a better chance of succeeding than you."

"Probably, but he would have warned Matt and me if he'd tangled with anyone connected to Kathleen O'Connor."

She digested that. "And he didn't."

Temple nodded.

"You care to check that with him?"

"Max thinks we should stay separated to avoid attracting Kathleen. So...I have no idea where he is."

"The idea for this assignment was that you'd be living at the Crystal Phoenix with all that high-level security."

"And the Fontana brothers."

"And the Fontana brothers. Why are women so endlessly fascinated by that Gang of Ten?"

"Are you kidding?" Temple wondered.

Molina waited as impassively as Mr. Spock could on *Star Trek*.

"Guess you're not kidding," Temple concluded. "They're handsome, respectful and gallant, a wee bit dangerous. They savor living La Vida Fontana, and every last one of them is a candidate for *The Bachelor* reality TV show. Of course, with the youngest and eldest married now..."

"To your boss and your aunt. Isn't that a bit incestuous?"

"Naw. I can handle it. Besides, I grew up with four older brothers who were rowdy, crude and rude, always trying to either ditch me or ambush me. The Fontana brothers treat me like a princess, but one who knows her own mind, and they're happy to help rather than hinder."

"I was the eldest in my family," Molina said, surprising Temple with the personal information. "I had all the responsibility. I made sure the boys didn't ride roughshod over the girls. They can do that."

"Yeah. It's kinda sad girls get dumped on in their own families." Temple smiled. "But my brothers grew up semi-civilized, I guess, and I ended up tougher than I look."

"Yes, you did," Molina said, stunning Temple again. She turned to the window. "Here come the main attractions. Pay attention here," she added. "You were on the scene when the body was discovered and you've been living with these people in the Crystal Phoenix celebrity suites. At the moment it suits me more to consider you a valuable witness rather than the usual…usual suspect."

Then she grinned and became totally focused on the room and the two people sitting at the table. "Since you've been in the lap of the whole outfit, I want you to let me know if anything French Vanilla and her lawyer say, or do *not* say, is untrue or suspicious. I am not happy that every possible suspect here has been living like one big family all together. Really confuses the issues. I can't imagine they'd want to be in each others' pockets like that, especially a group that busted apart decades ago."

"That's not unusual in the music world these days," Temple said. "Beyoncé and her team rented a big, big house and lived together for weeks to come up with the music she released on her *Surprise* album via WalMart. I've been semi-living with these people for a couple of days, yes, but I can't guarantee that my observations will be useful."

"Unfortunately, you have the gift of being on the wrong scene at the right time. I can guarantee that I can tell if you know, or think you know, anything useful."

Temple shifted her weight for another long standing and watching session, already sorry she'd worn her working heels, and not some flashy little flats. Still, being three inches *less* short around the tall lieutenant was a psychological advantage.

Nilla's lawyer was not what she had expected—a middle-aged man with a smarmy edge. The young woman wore narrow, navy-framed designer glasses and a charcoal-gray suit so plain and simple you knew it had to be costly. Her briefcase was high-fashion black neoprene with steel hardware, a bow to animal causes. The warm, tanned tone of her complexion looked like cold cocoa next to French Vanilla's pallid skin color framed by airy white curls like a blown-dandelion head. Temple would bet that Ms. Mousy's work-nerd impression would serve her well in court. Nilla was still wearing sunglasses, but the lawyer nudged her and she took them off. Her eyes seemed weak and blinking, but the pupils looked normal now.

Thinking of misleading impressions, just then Detective Alch shuffled in, shuffling papers. He looked so amiable and comfortably past his prime that you'd assume he was a pussycat.

As he sat at the table and took his time donning half-glasses. Nilla started drumming her inch-long nails on the use-scuffed tabletop. She seemed nervous, twitching to a playlist unrolling in her head alone.

Beside Temple, Molina gave an appreciative chuckle.

"Ms. French," Alch began, looking up at last.

The attorney looked up from the laptop she had produced to intervene at first word. "That is my client's legal surname, yes."

"I was sorta hoping it wasn't 'Vanilla,'" Alch said, turning his attention on Nilla. "Otherwise I'd have to be looking for her in the Spice Girls aisle at the grocery store."

The joke was feeble and meant to be. Nilla stirred at the mention of another vocal group, now long blasted apart like Black & White had been.

"You, Miss French," Alch stated, "were the first to realize that there was a body on the stage."

Nilla shook her exotic head. "No."

"My client had never seen the set before," lawyer lady said. "The stage scene was almost in a complete blackout. Visibility was minimal, and all that excess of glitter was obscuring."

Alch shuffled papers, then said, "Ms. Schultz, I am not addressing you." He drilled Nilla with sudden gruffness. "We have witnesses that you were bent over the victim, on the floor, pummeling his lifeless body."

"It was a spider." Nilla's nails prevented her from making fists, but she struck the flats of her palms on the table, over and over. "The ceiling was full of webs, glittering with dew, but they didn't fool me. There were giant spiders hiding up there, in the darkness."

"Giant spiders." Alch sat back. "I guess to you the victim was a giant spider from a dark past, all right. I guess you were beating the tar out of a corpse because you knew it was your runaway missing lover from twenty-some years ago. Are you going to claim you didn't know he'd made a return engagement just yesterday?"

"Cale." Nilla gasped more than spoke. She'd been the only one not to suspect that. "Cale? He'd been dead to me for so long. I never expected to see him again, and didn't."

"He wasn't dead two nights ago when the hotel security cameras caught him on the twelfth floor service hallway," Alch thundered, as much as Alch could thunder. It was more of an ominous distant rumble. "Are you going to tell me the love and mystery man of your life got all the way up there and then failed to contact you?"

Nilla still had not grasped it. "Cale was on the suites' floor with us?"

Temple, on the other side of the window wall, gasped too. "Cale Watson was captured live on camera?"

Molina ignored her, leaning forward to watch French Vanilla.

Nilla was numb to everything around her. "No. I never saw Cale up there. I never dreamed he could be there. I would have freaked if I'd seen him. He was a bad man. I wanted nothing to do with him. No. What came down from that ceiling wasn't Cale. I saw a spider. A giant spider with a big bloated body, and hairy black legs, and eyes like lasers."

Ms. Schultz slammed her laptop shut and leaned in front of her client. "She denies seeing the man. She's not saying another word. Nor am I." She stood and took Nilla's thin upper arm in one forceful hand, jerking the superstar upright.

Nilla teetered out as obediently as a child.

"She's worse than a day ago," Temple said, moving up against the window to watch their exit. "It's like she's turned to jelly."

"Being involved in a murder can do that," Molina observed. "There's obviously some mental derangement there, and, if she's guilty, that will be for the courts to decide."

"Do you really think this woman is capable of climbing a sky-high set and killing someone forty feet up?"

"No, but an accomplice could, and a good candidate for that role is up next."

Temple was not surprised to see Chocolatte ushered in. Her attorney was male, Latino, and almost smooth enough to give the Fontana brothers some competition. Almost.

He pulled out the chair for his client, bent solicitously to consult with her, then sat back in a "show me" position.

Latty was alert and poised.

"Miss Velveedah Hooker," was all Alch said, with a nod. "You and your one-time performing partner, Miss French, have been estranged for almost twenty-four years. Why did you both commit to a reunion show?"

"Because we'd been estranged for almost twenty-four years. Girlfriend feuds seem a bit silly at an older age." Latty eyed the empty ashtray and arched her delicately plucked eyebrows.

Alch nodded, and Latty made riveting stage business out of lighting up. Unlike poor Nilla, she retained all of her diva ways.

Temple was surprised to see the singer smoke. She had smelled that rank wardrobe-saturating odor in the main suite, and seen used ashtrays, but had assumed the men were the culprits. Maybe tobacco explained Latty's raw, driving contralto.

Alch pursed his lips, but took an aggravatingly long time to come out with a question. Latty's heels tapped out her impatience on the concrete floor, while she tapped ash from her cigarette up above.

"You pulled Miss French off the corpse."

"I pulled Miss French to her feet after she tripped from looking up for so long. That mix of darkness and the reflective swaths of brilliants made it hard to tell one level of the set from another. Mr. Dove didn't expect us to try any performance turns on that introductory visit, but no reflective tape had yet been set down, and we women in our high heels…it's a wonder we didn't break our ankles."

Temple got tense all over, and Molina noticed instantly. *"Hmm. Is* someone here setting up grounds for a lawsuit? Or an alibi for someone else," she asked.

"It's true the set was overwhelming at first, but *I* had no trouble in high heels."

"Those singers have two inches of heel and a couple inches of platform even on you. She has a point. Was it possible Miss French tripped and then berated the surface she fell upon?"

Temple thought back. "She was mesmerized by the ceiling. We all were. She went down fast. Could have tripped."

"Or tripped out?" Molina was honing in on her real question. "Was she high on something?"

"Hard to tell. She was emotionally unstable. Maybe the reunion brought back all the ugliness of the breakup. Latty seemed to be shepherding her, though. And they'd broken up over both women being involved with Cale Watson. Are you sure it's really him who's showed up after all these years?"

"The telltale whorls say yes. Like many musicians, he'd been arrested for drug possession and left fingerprints. There's still no trace of where he's been or what he's done. The man dropped off the pop personage meter and stayed underground all this time. You'd think he was a domestic terrorist from the Sixties."

"Why would he have come back now?" Temple fussed. "Could he have wanted to revive his career and rejoin Black & White? PRESUMED MURDER VICTIM RESURFACES TO SING MALE LEAD. That would be headline news, but it might have destroyed the reunion gig for the two divas and the entire band."

Molina tented her fingers with their short, unvarnished nails under her chin. For a torch singer, in her everyday guise she was plain vanilla. "Obviously, somebody else thought so too."

34
Go Ask Alice

"**I'm late, I'm** late," Temple murmured as she changed into her dress rehearsal duds that early evening. "For a very important date."

Even Molina couldn't stop the music.

The band had been rehearsing for the show for a couple months before descending on Vegas. Nicky, Van, and Danny were determined that getting the performers through a run-through dress rehearsal as scheduled would improve morale.

Matt had been invited, and Temple was so anxious for him to see the show. And she was anxious to see him. Her few days with the band had been so surreal she felt like she'd be returning from a different planet when she sat with Matt in the theater tonight.

She didn't want to disturb the divas, but she hung about the common hall to their suites, hoping to catch Sessalee coming or going. The makeup artist had promised Temple a high-impact evening makeover, and time was getting short.

French Vanilla slipped out of her suite with full wig and makeup on, and her satin boxer's robe over her first costume.

"Have you seen Sessalee?" Temple asked as she swept by, sans sunglasses, for a change.

"She did me over an hour ago," Nilla said. "You always lurk around the halls like a crazed fan."

Temple was speechless at the sudden mood change, even though she knew French Vanilla suspected her of being…a snoop. Temple eyed her glittery watch face and heaved a sigh. She couldn't wait for much longer.

"Temple, girl," a voice boomed behind her, making her jump. "You look like you lost your BFF."

"And you look amazing," she told Latty, whose face was a dark rainbow of glitter makeup and applied crystals. "I know *you've* seen Sessalee."

"She's not around?" Latty examined the hall. "She disappeared a few minutes ago, muttering about more glue. She's probably backstage already."

"Oh."

"Oh? That is the most pathetic 'Oh' I've ever heard."

"It's just that Sessalee said she'd do a special evening makeup on me tonight."

"She did have a separate kit with her. She got a cell phone call and put it down on my dressing table, I think. Maybe she got upset about the glue, or something was wrong backstage, and…forgot. Let me check."

"Oh, I can't make you late. It's nothing. Nude is still a very popular shade this season."

"Poor bunny." Latty's rich chuckle was as soothing as milk chocolate. "If the kit is there, I can do you myself in five minutes flat."

"But—" Temple was alone in the hall again, feeling like the world's biggest nuisance.

A minute or two later, Latty reappeared, flashing a small box. "Right where she laid it. Your colors are auburn, teal, and plum, right?"

"Yes, but I can't let the star do my makeup."

"Who'd be better at it, Miss Temple?" Latty winked an eyelid holding so many false eyelashes it was amazing her eyes could stay open.

In a minute, Temple was in the diva's makeup chair, spun around to a scary height, and "holding still" and "closing your eyes" and "looking up". In the advertised five minutes, Temple was gazing into the mirror's softer version of Latty's look.

"It's perfect."

"Yes, it is." Divas were not shy about their skills. "Now let's hustle our bustles down to the theater and knock 'em dead."

Temple gasped at the old show biz expression, under the

circumstances, but Chocolatte hadn't noticed and was hurrying away like a glitzy black version of the White Rabbit.

35
Tripping the Dark Fantastic

A makeover by a rock star can do wonders for a girl's ego. So she had Face by Chocolatte and had added French Vanilla's Datura Noir scent at her wrists and the pulse points on her neck.

The pleasant culinary effect of vanilla and almond aromas reminded Temple of "bitter almond" scent of Strychnine poison. Showed where her mind was at. This scent was fit for a Film Noir femme fatale, if she couldn't use the more modern, heady Dior perfume actually called Poison.

Going to the dress rehearsal of a fabulous new Strip show was exhilarating, even with a murder case waiting to be solved in the wings. The show must go on. Temple had sent a Fontana brother for her short, glittery vintage '60s dress and the prize Stuart Weitzman heels covered in Austrian crystals with the image of a black cat on the heels.

She had to suppress a vision of a Fontana brother on his knees digging in her overstuffed closet, but she was sure Electra had known what he should bring back. She took the empty elevator down to the theater.

"Temple!" Van never spoke in exclamation marks, but she did now when Temple arrived and found a small crowd in the aisle. "You look like a movie star."

Nicky, beside her, spread his hands to shape an imaginary marquee: "'The face that launched a thousand shows.'"

"Thanks, guys. You look pretty natty yourselves. Oh." Temple had just realized that every Fontana Brother in the house wore black tie and white dinner jacket, including Nicky.

"I guess I'm black and silver," she added, looking from her silver dress and black evening bag to her Midnight Louie shoes.

"You match the stairs," Van said, nodding at the stage. She looked stunning in a slim black suit with a wide collar of shoulder-framing white satin. "And we have a not-so-surprise package for you."

The gathered Fontana brothers split to admit someone to their ranks…Matt, also in black tie and white dinner jacket and totally toothsome blond.

"Matt!" Temple held out her arms. "I feel like I haven't seen you in weeks."

Everybody else vanished. Metaphorically and actually.

"Missing you too. Temple, you look so gorgeous, I'm afraid to touch you."

"I feel the same way, but that's not the point."

So they crushed each other's fancy dress while everyone searched for seats around them. Temple wasn't worried. Danny would put them in the front row.

"You look so well," Temple whispered. "Better than ever."

"The photos you sent really warmed up my lonely sickroom."

"*Oooh.*"

"And…are you wearing perfume? That's new."

"Eau de Rock Star. French Vanilla's signature vanilla fragrance, Datura Noir."

"Vanilla. No wonder you smell good enough to eat."

"Move along, folks," a deep authoritarian voice demanded. "No lingering or longing in the aisles. Move along."

Danny Dove laughed and clapped Matt on the shoulder. "Good to see you again, bro."

Matt turned to do the handshake, one-shoulder hug guy pals did these days. Matt had been there for Danny at a bad time, as he had for a lot of people. Temple was so proud of him there were tears in her eyes.

Or maybe she was allergic to the glitter-laden rock-star makeup. *Shoot!* She finally finds her perfect vamp look and has an allergic reaction.

Meanwhile Danny was ushering them down the aisle to the front row.

He seated them and finally took in Temple's new look. "Temple, darling, delightful, de-lovely girl, you should be up there on that stage. *Mwmmph.*" He kissed his palm and sent the smooch her way before racing off to supervise the backstage area.

Temple and Matt settled into their seats, holding hands over the common armrest. Matt lifted their twined hands to kiss Temple's ring finger. She nearly swooned. He looked like Prince Charming out of a Disney movie. She was Cinderella. They would live happily ever after.

She was so happy. *Zip-A-Dee-Doo-Dah, Zip-A-Dee-A.* She felt like a dancing hippo from Disney's *Fantasia.* Well, something much more attractive than a hippo in a tutu. Say Tinker Bell. *"I'm flying,"* from the *Peter Pan* stage show.

"Temple," Matt said, shaking her hand a bit.

"Isn't the set beautiful? Perfect. Black and white and all glossy and shining like an ice rink, all those stairs. I love the suspended petal-things. Danny is brilliant. Black & White—the band—is lucky to have him. And Max. I mean, not really Max, but he did contribute.

"And Midnight Louie. He found the body. Well, he was up with the body. We found him and it together. Wasn't he? Or was that another time? It's lucky that Molina, the dumb flatfoot cop, didn't arrest Midnight Louie. I'm glad she's not here tonight."

"Temple."

"Are you saying something? You'll have to speak up. All the music is just too overwhelming. I hope the sound system isn't malfunctioning. Oh, look, Midnight Louie is doing a soft shoe down the white mirrored staircase. He was so cute in a similar scene during those cat-food those commercials he did. A natural.

"Goodness, they're playing 'Good Morning,'" from *Singing in the Rain.* I love that musical."

"Temple!"

"Stop shaking my hand, Matt! We *are* more than friends. I can't see very well. All those lights, everything is black and white. Well, it's supposed to be, isn't it?

"Let go of my hand! Are you trying to steal my ring? You can't have it, Shangri-La. Besides, you're dead and you don't need it.

"Let go, I love that music. 'Gotta Dance...'"

"Temple, Temple…"

"Wow, Matt. I can't hear you, or see you. The lights are so bright. I'm facing a Stairway to Heaven…or Hell.

"Oh. Which stair do I take? The black on the left, the sinister side? Or the white, bright side? I'm wearing silver, like a knight, so I would look best on the black. Bet nobody knew I could tippety-tap up a staircase like Ginger Rogers. I need a feather skirt, though.

"Here I am, at the top of the world. Which, peering into the darkness, seems to be empty.

"Just me and my shadow, all alone and feeling blue."

36
Blinded by the Bright

I am as flabbergasted as the next guy, who is the guy sitting next to my Miss Temple (who happens to be Mr. Matt Devine), when she leaps up from her aisle seat and goes scampering up the three steps to the stage and then across the empty stage apron.

I know for a fact the entire onstage cast of Black & White with its backup dancers and singers are poised backstage at various levels to make their spectacular entrance on the opening song.

I know this because I made it my business to examine the set and its official occupants both before and during the band's arrival. And I have the Cat Pack ninja brigade stationed at all the operative points.

If anyone tries to sabotage this act, or if Miss French Vanilla is off her rocker again, I and my underlings are placed to move swiftly to block, stall, or report any outrages.

I had not counted on my own roomie throwing all her inhibitions to the wind and waltzing onstage like she should be there.

Holy Hathor! (She is the ancient Egyptian cow goddess.) "By Great Bast's chin whiskers!" I mutter.

"I am not sure Great Bast has chin whiskers," a low voice murmurs beside me.

"Well, Great Bast is an older lady, going on five thousand," I tell Miss Midnight Louise, "and ancient Egyptian lady pharaohs did wear ceremonial beards. I thought you were watching things at the celebrity suites while I was looking for dirty work on the stage set?"

"I was. I saw Miss Sessalee sneaking out by the service elevator, but lost her on this tourist level."

"Forget that! My Miss Temple is doing a 'French Vanilla'. There she is, teetering on my signature shoes. She could tumble down that wicked staircase any minute."

"Your shoes? They are hers. And I watched her every second upstairs," Louise spits back. "She was fine."

"Not now. Look at her holding her arm up against the bright stage lights. She could fall twenty feet. We must get her safely offstage. I never thought you would doze off on the job."

"Somehow she consumed an unauthorized substance," Louise says.

"What did she eat and drink upstairs?"

"A room-service chili and taco plate with a diet cola."

"*Arghh.* That is such an unhealthful diet! I need to be putting her on Free-to-Be-Feline at home."

While we dither, some of the dress-rehearsal audience has rushed the stage, a throng of men wearing formal black and white. Fontana Inc. mills around on the black stage apron, seeing, as we do, that startling Miss Temple with sudden moves could cause one Humpty Dumpty of a great fall.

"Think, Louise! We do not have much time. An illicit drug would be expanding throughout her system now, and she is such a tiny thing for a human..."

"Do not lose your cool, Pops. The taco makings could have included marijuana plant, the kind they use for cigarette filling. I sniffed tons of that stuff around the place. And any liquid or powder could be concealed in chili... Then there is the matter of her light-blindness. I wonder...I must inspect the scene of the crime."

With that, Miss Midnight Louise gambols up the steps to the stage and then races up the black staircase.

I see the ceiling units slowly lowering. The stage crew is trying to get Miss Temple on the equivalent of a down elevator, without startling her.

Louise's flat-out run has the crowd holding its breath, but my partner takes a detour about six feet away from Miss Temple, and leaps to the edge of a descending petal behind her. I want to shut my eyes. Louise is hanging on by her eight front shivs. Thank Bast the petal interiors are upholstered.

A noose of perked ears is tightening on the dark fringes of the set. The Black Ninja Brigade is readying to pounce if needed. Below, the stage crew stops the unit's descent, conferring in whispers in the wings. Louise, now on all four feet at the unit's rim, leans her face toward Miss Temple's.

"Here is a black bunny," my usually rational roommate announces loudly to one and all. "Pretty bunny. Do you want to sit on my shoulder?" The alert crew recognizes a cue when it hears one. The unit silently slides closer and lower, so that Louise's questing muzzle nears Miss Temple's face.

Really, this is a scene one should put on a Valentine candy box, or on a liquor bottle, to reference the current milieu. Louise's delicate whiskers and awesome olfactory skills have her "kissing" Miss Temple's face to detect what substance is on her breath.

Miss Louise recoils as if shocked. Then she jumps six feet back down to the black staircase, races through the milling human feet onstage, up the aisle, and through the unguarded theater lobby doors.

"Louise," I yowl. "Do not desert us now!"

Too late. I sigh. If I have to be called a "pretty bunny", I will just have to put up with the public humiliation. I weave through the crowd scene and prepare to make my live stage debut. I am the only one left here who can distract Miss Temple without spooking her. Pretty funny that a black cat should play that role.

I do a soft-paw shuffle in a zigzag pattern up the mirrored white stairs like an old vaudeville hand, or foot, rather. Miss Temple loves that vintage stuff.

I have cut a caper or two in my younger days, so switch to a four-foot double-limp intro, and then the crossed-ankle scissors kick. The ladies always went for that one.

Meanwhile my terminal member is doing the charmed snake sway with a question mark end. I then leap into the unit Miss Midnight Louise has deserted.

"You are easy on the eyes," Miss Temple remarks.

I look into her eyes, and freeze with shock.

Her baby blues are as black as those of a demon in a horror movie. That means they are as good as blind. No wonder she is tottering like a spinning saucer. When my pupils are that wide open, I am blinded by the light.

Black & White had done a cover of that very song, but I realize it might become Miss Temple's swan song. Never have I felt the disadvantage of "just being the little guy" before. My mitts are tied, while Miss Temple is raving and roaming ever nearer the edge of the stairs.

Wait, Temple hears herself think. Wait. This can't be right.

It's like she's in a dream where the viewpoint is hers and also not hers. When some other first-person version of herself is in the driver's seat and Temple can eavesdrop on her own thoughts as they occur.

Something on the white staircase is coming after me. Maybe it's Nilla's big, bad black spider.

It is black. It's tap-dancing too. Oh. It's my partner in the dance routine. I see a dazzlingly white-fanged smile. Only the smile. Then, no. Now I see a cat, a black cat. It's pulling an old-fashioned pocket watch out of its black leather waistcoat and muttering, "Get me to the church on time."

What would a cat being doing at a church? Getting married, of course. Like me.

My, this black ice mountain is high. I see a unicorn at the top of the neighboring white ice mountain. Maybe I can catch a ride on it. Or just catch it. And then there are those magic upside-down mushrooms going up and down all around.

That one has a passenger. I lean across...something...to see into it. Oh. The giant flower is smoky and filled with...pot. Naughty, naughty. I know that smell, and there sits a tall lean fellow in a coat of many colors wreathed in pipe smoke like Santa on a jag.

"Little girl," the Caterpillar says, "I can make you small and I can make you tall, but most of all, I will take you on a Technicolor trip away from this black-and-white world."

And he changes into the Knave of Hearts, nibbling at a platter of decorated tarts, which all have playing card faces.

The Cowardly Lion jumps out of nowhere and chases the Knave away.

I do not believe anyone who calls me "little girl" and look down.

My goodness, I am high. High up.

Everyone below is small and...agitated, like ants with their house of sand falling in on them.

Some are white-chocolate-covered ants, ten of them. No, twelve. That twelfth is trying to climb my mountain, but the other ants are stopped from doing it. Good.

I hear more gasps from the people below and turn to look. Something is streaking down the aisle toward the stage. Something black with white feet.

The crowd parts out of simple shock. You do not often see one of my breed hell-bent on a mission like Rin-Tin-Tin. I am expecting Miss Midnight Louise, but a stranger with two white forefeet blows by me, using my studly shoulder as a first step for a flying leap into the ceiling unit hovering like a UFO just above Miss Temple's shoulder.

I begin to think I have overdone the nip myself. This interloper repeats the kissy-kissy face act. My poor Miss Temple is so far gone that she falls for the smoochy stuff again but I must admit it stops her dangerous rambling about the set. A foreign white mitt rises to Miss Temple's face for a gentle, calming pat.

None of the Black Ninja Brigade has a white mitt. Yet this touchy-feely stranger pets Miss Temple's lips and cheek and even her closing eyelids. Then it brings up the white left mitt and repeats the process.

I scratch my head. Literally. I sense photos being taken of these Hallmark moments from far below, where people are holding their breaths. I see one of the Men in Black and White has broken from the pack and is climbing the stairs silent as a mouse while these Hallmark moments are going on.

Mr. Matt! He is eyeing a ceiling unit that is being lowered behind and to the right of Miss Temple.

I glance to my Miss Temple is who muttering, "A black bunnie and a White Knight. I never believed there was a White Knight, but here he is."

Temple is still watching herself think and act, playing both actor and audience. She's never been so disoriented. Her Other Self grabs the spotlight and the monologue back from a brief moment of clarity.

The black bunny that leapt into my flying gondola has turned into a white rabbit with long, floppy ears and big feet. And pointed sharp teeth.

Meanwhile, I am a princess at the top of an ice mountain and one of the milling ants below has turned into a White Knight and is charging up the mountain on a unicorn to save me!

But two queens have appeared on the plain below, a Black Queen and a White Queen, and they are both shouting, "Off with her head!"

I am very attached to my head, and I shout, "No, never."

The Black and White Queens pelt me with black and white roses that are dripping red blood, until the Duchess mounts the White Stairs and gets close enough to throw her baby at me. Horrified, I catch it. When I look into the swaddling, I see a baby...pig face, which is when I know the Duchess is someone I know and is on...the police force...and I am about to be arrested, for murder.

Or murdered, whichever comes first.

Black & White land is no longer so sweet and musical and happy, and the moving magic mushrooms bring Caterpillar and the Black and White Queens and the Duchess all closer to me.

What shall I do?

The black rabbit—yes, he has changed color—stands waving his tail toward the white stairs. Yes, he has lost his white mittens.

The White Knight is still charging up those stairs on his white unicorn, which he seems to have been doing for a very long time.

When the cabbit leaps to the back of the knight's charger, I think, oh, well, and jump too, just as the White Knight vaults into thin, unsupported air to catch me.

Falling, falling into the knight's firm grasp, and all the while someone is shrieking endlessly in the black night sky.

I think it's the two queens.

And I think I want to go back through the looking glass.

With every eye riveted on the precarious couple, Miss Midnight Louise and I make a subtle getaway against the camouflaging cover of the black staircase.

Just as we weave through the stage crowd, a huge sigh of relief signals me to turn to view a heroic leap by Mr. Matt. He has swept Miss Temple off her feet and my signature shoes...and into the safe haven of an adjoining ceiling unit.

Mr. Matt and the stage crew are applauded as Louise and I duck into a row to avoid an emergency crew rolling a gurney toward the stage.

"Relax. She will be all right, Pop," Louise says. "I have cracked the case."

Oh, really, and that bold claim is supposed to relax me?

37
Black on Her Feet

Temple felt the terrible bright lights burning through her eyelids like lasers.

Blind? Was she blind? She turned her head aside to escape the painful glare.

Then someone propped her eyelids open and aimed a tiny spotlight straight into her left pupil.

No!

"She's waking up," said a distant, foggy voice.

"Thank God," said another voice, somehow familiar from a dream.

"The retinas are returning to normal," the first voice said. "She needs dark glasses. This young lady has been on quite a trip. I'll have to notify the police."

"I *am* the police," said a voice that jerked Temple out of her nice, floaty state. Molina was here. *Uh-oh.*

Someone slipped a glasses frame onto her nose. She blinked to see people's faces all around her, through a yellow haze.

"My White Knight," she murmured into Matt's worried face, the closest to hers. "What a dream I had, like Alice in Wonderland. And you were there. You saved me."

"I'll be your White Knight any day." He squeezed her hand.

"And the caterpillar was there, smoking his hookah pipe. And Nilla and Latty were the White Queen and the Black Queen."

"Is this behavior normal?" Molina asked.

"All this was real to her, at the time." The other woman's voice has a gentle Indian lilt. *She is the doctor,* Temple deduced. At least she could still deduce.

"And Midnight Louie was the White Rabbit," she recalled, "only he was black and he had a shadow. Maybe *that* was the Cheshire Cat."

Temple saw a blond curly head at the back of the crowd. "And you, Danny. You were the Cowardly Lion with a huge mane…"

"Wrong book and film, Munchkin," Danny said with a wink.

Temple blinked and saw a bit better. "Oh, and are my Midnight Louie shoes all right?"

"Don't worry, Dorothy," came Molina's wry tone, "they're in my personal custody and just fine."

"And *you* were there, too, as the Duchess and you had a ba—" Temple's wits were reassembling fast. She suddenly knew better than to tell Molina she had been carrying a baby. A baby pig. Too insulting to teenage daughter, Mariah, and Molina's profession. "A badge."

"Thank goodness," Molina said. "I assure you I still have it and hope to use it on whoever did this to you. Do you know who?"

Temple blinked. She saw a shadow with a shadow, like the two Midnight Louies. "I can't say I know that," she said slowly, "but I know I must know something someone doesn't like me knowing."

The doctor asked, "Is her logical process normally this circuitous?"

"What a lovely, musical voice you have, Doctor," Temple said dreamily.

"Yes to the circuitous logic," Molina said. "Normal, but a bit exaggerated at the moment. Doctor, do you have any idea what the substance is and how it was administered?"

"Recreational drugs that aren't injected can be given to unknowing subjects," the doctor said. "And even forced injections. That doesn't seem to be the case here. This young woman was dressed for a formal event. One assumes she was capable at that point of dressing herself. It must have happened shortly after that."

Temple looked down at a horrible flower-figured hospital gown. "Oh, my vintage '60s dress! It's gone." She patted her cheeks. "My hair, my face. I must be a mess."

"Perhaps," the doctor said, "but you are recovering without having your stomach pumped. I don't know what substance has proved so unhappy for you, but I am not sure it went through the digestive system, so I took the conservative approach of letting you simply sober up." She looked over her shoulder. "Are you aware of any new exotic drugs on the street, Lieutenant?"

"Nothing that would produce a high like this. We'd have the addicts boogying down the Strip."

"I ruined the dress rehearsal," Temple moaned. "I remember I just…danced up on the stage. I'm so humiliated."

"Actually," Danny said, "you were highly entertaining, especially when your cat joined you in a soft shoe routine."

"Louie! Is he all right. I always assume he can take care of himself…"

"He took care of you this time," Matt said. "He ran to you and distracted you until I could get up to the ceiling units and get you into one."

"Midnight Louise ran to your rescue too," Van said." She climbed all the way up into a ceiling unit to get close enough to lick your face. It was so sweet. Her affection froze you in place so Matt and Danny could manipulate the units close enough for Matt to grab you and land you both in one."

"Wow, Matt," Temple told him. "That must have been a Nureyev-level leap. I hope you didn't hurt yourself. And you did it all from horseback."

"Horseback?" he said.

"In my dreams. Was there a White Knight in *Alice in Wonderland?*" she wondered.

"There was in *Through the Looking Glass,*" Van assured her. "You accessed all of Lewis Carroll on that drug."

"Say," Temple said. "I wish we had footage of that whole thing. Parts might make a crazy-good trailer."

"She's getting better," Molina decreed, heading for the door. "And, that freelance photog you hired did record the whole thing, which I will shortly be reviewing."

"You're not going back to those Crystal Phoenix suites," Matt told Temple.

"But I have to," Temple said. "I'm the only one who knows that whole crew."

Matt folded his arms. "Not alone."

"The Fontana brothers are all over the place."

"Not in your bedroom, I hope."

"Of course not, Matt. Unless one is delivering the breakfast tray."

"You need a roommate."

"You?"

"You need a roommate who isn't going off to a job between eleven p.m. and three a.m." He sounded all firm and manly, and, sadly, right.

Temple unleashed a huge sigh. "I've built rapport with the band members. I know the personalities and the layout. I'm invaluable."

"Sadly true." Molina had remained by the door during the discussion and now looked at Temple long and hard. "You do need a roommate. I've got one. Detective Su."

Temple's heart sank. Alch's partner was even tinier than she was, but terse and impersonal. She could not see them sitting crossed-legged on the bed lacquering each other's toenails.

"It's a suite," Molina said. "There must be a foldaway bed or three somewhere."

"Probably," Temple said as Van nodded, "but how'd I explain a police officer roommate showing up?"

"PR assistant. Su's gone undercover as a hooker; she can certainly disguise herself as a career woman. That's the only way you're going back into that mess of celebrity suites and old wounds and overweight egos. Someone tried to seriously undermine you, if not kill you."

"Someone sure helped me embarrass myself. How will I explain it?"

"Overwork." Molina narrowed her eyes to steel-blue slits. "Meanwhile, I'll have your blood work analyzed. I want the name of this drug as much as I want the person who's using it to sabotage Black & White's reunion debut."

38
Je Reviens

Max is both *Perseus following the thread to the central answer to the puzzle, and the Minotaur at the center of the maze,* Max read, *not a hero or a monster, but puzzle and solution in one package. If I can untangle the threads that tie Max to Ireland and Las Vegas, to Kathleen O'Connor and IRA plots and money, to past and future, he'll be safe. We all will be.*

The words were Garry Randolph's last, written on his laptop computer before he had saved Max's life by spiriting him out of Switzerland to Northern Ireland with a brilliant, spur-of-the moment plan.

That had been Gandolph the Great's last, best illusion.

Who will be his Adriadne? Gandolph had mused onscreen. *The indefatigable puzzle-solver and his only love...*

Max looked away from the screen. He didn't want to read Gandolph's next words, or his mentor's opinion on relationships that were no more, along with most memories of the past few years blotted out by traumatic amnesia.

He had to glance past the next typed words to arrive at...

Will it be the relentless homicide Lieutenant Carmen Molina, who knows that a Max with a memory might be able to help her close some local cold cases?

"*Hah!*" Max burst out, as Sherlock Holmes was wont to do. It would be a cold day in the Treasure Island Hotel's erupting volcano before he'd share info with a copper.

Will it possibly be his stalker, Kathleen O'Connor herself?

Max shook his head. Gandolph must have been nearing his dotage.

Or will it be some other person entirely? The ex-priest Matt Devine, perhaps. He was successful in tracking down his wicked stepfather.

Max smiled at the last phrase. Garry…Gandolph had a wry sense of humor.

"What about *me* solving my own mess, Garry?" he asked the computer. "I'm a DIY guy."

Garry would never answer, but Max still could. He heard the keening chords of an Irish ballad and picked up the cell phone lying like a TV remote control on the arm of one of the big leather chairs he and Garry had used for media watching when they'd shared the house.

"Max." Her voice was ever sweet and low. Shakespeare's King Lear considered that "an excellent thing in a woman", but this commercially plugged-in world would think of an artificial sweetener.

He answered in kind. "Revienne." And in no way was she saccharine. Artificial…a little, like most French women.

"How is your head going?" she asked.

He smiled. She was so European. All charm, especially when her English revealed a second-language twist.

"It's going fine."

"Do you want me to come over?"

Pause. What for? "The place is a mess, as you can imagine."

"I would like to see your mess."

"Any special reason?"

"I have a gift for you."

"Is it a surprise?"

"Yes, I suppose. Liquid gold."

"Hmm." Max enjoyed playing cat and mouse with Revienne…he enjoyed playing with her, period. Maybe it was time to quit games. "This a social or a professional visit?"

"You mean in my capacity as a psychiatrist or a…former traveling companion."

"Yes."

"Why don't we try it and find out?"

"Good idea. We can order pizza in."

Her laughter was lovely. "What a wonderful thing to do. So American."

A half hour later, Max had run the dishwasher and dusted the kitchen counters and the main room furniture with an old knit turtleneck. He hadn't bothered renewing the cleaning service when he'd gotten back from Europe. A house without Garry seemed not worth keeping up.

He'd also sat in his big leather chair and opened the hidden arm compartment to check the security systems. Kathleen had already been here and done her worst. He didn't expect an encore, but you never know...

Most people heard a doorbell and went to answer it, maybe with a check of a front-door peephole.

Since his living room had been the scene of a shooting, Max checked the security camera view of his front door on the computer. The location of the modest house that had belonged to three men more or less of magic—Orson Welles, Max's mentor Garry Randolph, and himself—had been a best-kept secret known only to his ex, Temple Barr.

Now Matt Devine and the police and Kitty the Cutter knew the address. And one more person, who'd driven him home from the hospital. Revienne Schneider, shrink.

When the doorbell rang and he went to greet her, he saw she wore designer Bermuda shorts and blouse of ivory silk. Her skillfully highlighted blonde hair was pulled into a ponytail low on her nape. Not that the word "ponytail" nearly conveyed the deceptively simple, elegant style Revienne favored.

He opened the door with a smile. "When a cell phone won't do—?"

She smiled back. "I know. I'm so rude. So what if the place is a mess? That's why you didn't invite me in before."

He stepped back and opened the door wide for her to enter.

Max watched her "ankle" into the living room like a Mike Hammer dame, only with class. She was willowy and blonde and brilliant.

"You can come in now. It isn't the mess I thought," she called back at him. "Is this where whatever happened…happened?"

"I didn't know it was a place of pilgrimage," he said, entering and gesturing her to a seat. "My hospitality is spare at best."

"Bachelors," she said, settling into a club chair and crossing smooth, bare legs. "That's why you Americans have a TV show dedicated to them."

"And don't forget bachelorettes."

"It's so absurd to be discussing these trivialities, Mr. Randolph."

"Why not? We have no secrets now."

"That's even more absurd," she said, settling her designer tote bag beside her bare legs. "I came because I've picked up what you call, I think, in your Film Noir movies, 'a tail.'"

"And so you headed right here."

"No. You underestimate me, Mr. Randolph."

"Hardly, Dr. Schneider."

It was a game they had played, when he abducted her or she attached herself to him, when he was on the run from a Swiss sanitarium-turned-killing-ground. He had used his mentor's last name with her, and she in turn used it now as a prod, a goad, a reminder of their haphazard intimacy, now that Garry was dead.

She tilted her head to an especially flattering angle. "You had me investigated through Interpol, careful man. Or onetime careful man." She looked around. "When you have less left to protect, one becomes careless."

"How careless are you?"

"Not at all. My rented vehicle is parked nowhere near here."

"You walked all that way, in those?" He nodded to her lavender spike heels.

"Your former fiancé manages that, and more, from what I hear from Van von Rhine."

"You actually went to Swiss finishing school with her?"

"Everything about me is actual, as you found when Interpol reported back. And," she added, "in a hotel room or two."

"Life on the road is so revealing," he said. "Your 'tail' is female?"

"Yes. Why am I not surprised? You seem as popular among that set as any one of the amazing Fontana brothers."

"They are incredible, aren't they?"

"And all over the residents of the Circle Ritz wherever they may go right now, as you know."

He shrugged.

"It's hard being a lone operative," she said.

"That from experience?"

She shrugged. "You should leave this house."

"I have a sentimental attachment."

"Or a death wish."

"You could say that about Houdini, Madam Shrink."

"Absolutely. Magic acts are death-defying, death-denying and wish-fulfillment all in one. I find it interesting that your acts are all about flying."

"My acts?"

"Performed by you, or in another persona. I investigated you as well, dear Mr. Randolph."

"I was noted for walking on air. That's not quite flying."

"That only proves you're a realist. You need to take that woman who's following me seriously."

"I take all women seriously."

"That is the problem. Your attitude is likely to be reciprocated."

"I won't be driven out of where I want to be."

"You mean 'need' to be. I know. I love that expression, 'shrink'. So American, gruesome and direct. A head-shrinker." Her smile faded. "I know from experience, you can't protect everyone you love. You can't even protect *anyone* you love."

"You've gone beyond helping anorexic and suicidal girls, Revienne." He caught her gaze, and abandoned the game of cat and mouse. "Look. We share similar personal tragedies. Your dead sister, my dead cousin. You've been driven to trying to make a difference on an international stage. That doesn't translate to what's been going on here in Vegas, or even my own international…ties. Don't underestimate your 'tail', she has psychoses even you haven't heard of."

"I doubt that. Do you know what 'Revienne' translates to?"

"'Return', roughly speaking," he said quickly.

She nodded. "I brought something to christen your homecoming," she said while pulling a bottle-top over the tote bag's gold leather rim.

"Jameson's." He was impressed. "Much appreciated. I'll put it in the kitchen. No living room bar."

"Casual. I like that." She followed him into the kitchen, then stopped. *"C'est magnifique!"*

"Garry was a bit of a gourmet." Max was pleased to share his mentor's enthusiasms. "Killer refrigerator, built-in wine cellar, appliance garage." Max put the whiskey bottle on the granite countertop, then flourished open stainless steel doors as if demonstrating the emptiness of a trick cabinet onstage. Only these doors opened on fully occupied shelves and racks.

"You cook?" she asked.

"I eat."

"When is the pizza coming?"

Max hefted his cell phone. "Speed dial. I want to know your preferences. Gourmet or junk food?"

"Whatever you wish."

"Combo," he decreed, and gave instructions to the waiter, er, order taker on the other end.

"Combo. I still do not know all the slang."

"Short for combination. Don't you want to go back in the living room to sit down? We can have Jameson's, or you could select an appropriate wine far better than I."

"Max Kinsella, deferring a choice to me. I want to stay here." She looked around at the hanging copper cookware over the island. "It resonates with your friend's passion for food and wine. For life. That is a precious legacy. *L'Chaim.*" She lifted an invisible glass.

The tribute touched Max. He lifted her up atop the island countertop to sit, and…*flashback.* The same motion, almost the same mood with another woman: red hair, sharp and good-humored, oozing intimacy. Or was that vibe coming from Revienne?

"Now that madam is seated," Max said quickly in headwaiter tones, "what may I pour? Perrier? A red or white wine? Whiskey?"

"First the pizza, then the taste buds decide. Perhaps even beer."

Max lowered his head. He was still averse to that idea. He seemed to have awakened from his recent coma with an odd distaste for beer and ales, maybe dating to his cousin's apparent death during an IRA pub bombing in Belfast years earlier. And now Gandolph, dead in Belfast only weeks ago.

"Or not," Revienne said swiftly, palming the side of his face as smoothly as he would palm a card. "I wish I had met Garry Randolph. He is legendary."

He looked up, shocked. Their game was over, and not because of anything he'd intended. She had read his mind...because she knew every bit of his history, and Garry's.

"You came up clean as a Christmas angel in Interpol," he said. Objected.

"I'm so flattered you checked. I'm not a field agent. I am, yes, a 'company shrink'. I need deep cover."

"Or deep covers," he said. Bitterly.

She sighed. "Don't be dramatic. That was not part of my assignment, which was to assess your mental deficits and get your mind and body working again."

"That you did, lady."

"You are welcome, Mr. Randolph. Perhaps we should forget the Randolph surname you told me on the road from the Swiss clinic to hide your identity. It doesn't seem right, though, to call you Max."

"Why should you be around to call me anything? Or is your 'assignment' still live?"

"Yes, and I want to be around and call you whatever you want to be called." She drew his face closer and kissed him. It was nice, dammit.

"This is all off," he said. "I never mix business and pleasure."

"Right," she said, sounding like a skeptical American woman. "Meanwhile, let me do my job. You are obviously the key to an international conspiracy that involves money and weapons. In these post-terrorist days, that is vital to many agencies and interests, here and abroad."

"I'm working on it."

"Fine. My job is to learn anything about you and the real Mr. Randolph that would help get the people who needed to kill you."

"That's been *my* job for almost fifteen years."

"Is it going to be so hard, Max? To talk to me, honestly? You know my...what did you call it? Rain and pain. Let me be your partner. I won't betray you or what you hold dear. I'll help keep all that safe, even from my allies. You have to understand now that whatever forces are trying to destroy you, you have counterforces determined to stop them, because they will harm far many more than you and Garry Randolph."

Maybe so, he thought, but it's all over between us from this moment on.

The pizza was going to taste like cardboard.

And she wouldn't be staying around as a charming take-out dining partner.

"I need to think about it," he said, handing her the chic bag, heading for the hallway and ending the pleasantries.

When they got there, he was strangely reluctant to shut the door on Revienne.

She paused on the threshold. "I don't think this is goodbye, but merely *au revoir.*" She leaned close on a wave of perfume to whisper, "Mr. Randolph."

When the door closed, he pressed his back against it and laughed at himself.

Whew, Kinsella, get a grip.

Revienne was French. She was entirely too hot to be good for him.

39
A Merry Ménage

The war council was held late the next morning in Temple's hospital room. It was now crowded with Matt, Nicky and Van, some Fontana brothers, Detective Su, and most of all, Lieutenant Molina. Merry Su had been transformed by a short bobbed brunette wig with bangs, tortoiseshell glasses, a linen suit and, gasp, high heels.

Matt had arrived earlier with Electra's choice of hospital-checking-out clothes, a salmon-pink palazzo pant outfit Temple would ditch the instant she got back to her Crystal Phoenix suite. She had been adamant about "going back in" the murder zone.

First, Temple had to swear she felt fine after her night in the hospital for observation.

"No flashback delusions?" Molina asked.

"No."

"No…cravings?"

"I never did drugs, which probably is why I went way off the chart when I was given something, and I sure don't have an itch to do it again."

"You'd feel bad. Edgy. Out of control," Molina told her. "Addicts need more drugs to stop the ugly feeling of coming down. Normal feels like hell."

"I feel a little tired and a lot embarrassed, but I've been both of those before and lived."

"Is there anything, *anything* you partook of in common with French Vanilla? Food? Drink?" Molina's questions now were intense.

"No, just what was set out for everyone."

"That's unfortunate," Molina said, trying to pace and coming up close on a broad-shouldered Fontana brother. "And you bozos," Molina snapped at him and all his ilk, her vivid eyes in blue lightning mode. "You were supposed to be watching the food and drink for possible tampering. You saw nothing?"

"We not only watched, Lieutenant," said the Fontana whose face Molina was getting into, "we tasted." Julio, Temple thought.

"Everything?"

"Everything."

Molina raised an eyebrow, Mr. Spock style. Julio raised his own eyebrow to match.

"Impressive," she muttered, eying the entire pack. "Then whatever was administered was individual." She turned to Van. "You weren't charging Black & White for consumables, Miss von Rhine, but you must have recorded the items and costs for tax purposes."

"Of course." Van nodded at Nicky. "Figure that out with your brothers."

"All right." Molina instinctively tried to pace again, but was baffled by a wall of Ermenegildo Zegna suits in all directions. "The executive chef had assigned a long-employed and trusted under-chef to exclusively prepare everything for the celebrity suites. The Fontana brothers will continue supervising preparation and delivery, and will now note who eats and drinks what."

Temple nodded, trying not to smile. Every time Molina in marshaling-the-troops mode came up against a Fontana brother, she stepped back in a huff. For some reason, Fontanas en masse unnerved her. Temple wondered what Molina had heard about them. And from whom.

She exchanged smiles with Matt, and realized from his amused expression that he might have the answer.

The Fontanas, of course, regarded Molina's orders with the highest degree of attention, courtesy, and an air of male interest and assessment so subtle that she had probably never encountered it before in her law-enforcement life.

When Temple had first met Fontana Inc., she'd found it helpful to regard them as a pack of showy and elegant Afghan hounds who had excellent manners and could be taught to heel. Maybe Molina had finally become aware of their attractions.

Temple and the Fontana brother on kitchen duty, Ralph, had listed every bit of food she had eaten yesterday. With so many avowed drug users on the premises, anything could be doctored. Accidentally or not.

Molina had also slow-cooked Temple's recovering brain by grilling her for possible clues that might betray who had killed Cale Watson or had threatened the divas or anyone in Black & White.

Zero.

Matt continued to question sending Temple back into "that pit of vipers".

"She has a bodyguard," Molina pointed out. "Night and day."

Matt sized up the ultra-feminine new Su, openly dubious.

"I have black belts in three martial arts forms." The pint-size detective looked ready to demonstrate on Matt.

"Other than employing royal tasters," Temple said, "I'm confident we have enough safeguards in place. French Vanilla is off my suspect list, simply because she's unable to see well enough, as well as being the victim of a gas-lighting."

"'Gas-lighting?'" Su asked suspiciously.

"There was a 1938 Broadway play," Temple explained, "called *Gas Light,* about a Victorian husband trying to drive his rich wife crazy by pretending only she sees the new-fangled gaslights turning up and down. Ingrid Bergman was wonderful as the film version's self-doubting wife. I checked online, and from then on tricking somebody to doubt their own senses has been a recognized form of abuse called 'gas-lighting'. So sayeth Wikipedia."

"Thanks for the info download," Molina said, sending Matt, Nicky and Van and the Fontana brothers on their way. Only Temple and Detective Su remained for Molina's final instructions.

"The drug-tampering is pretty much done," she said. "The perp will now be concentrating on keeping the method from coming to light. Obviously, someone either thought Miss Barr knew something, or Miss Barr inadvertently got into something meant for French Vanilla. This 'gas-lighting' business is taking attention from investigating the Cale Watson murder. That is the prime crime here. Stay safe," she added, nodding at Detective Merry Su and Temple in turn.

Matt was waiting in the hospital's drive-up area. He got out of the purring Jaguar to seat them, Temple in front. Once he returned to the driver's seat, he looked back at Detective Merry Su. "You get to initiate the backseats. Let me know if you have any complaints."

"Cool wheels," Su said. "I should drive."

40
The Color Yellow

"**I have done** my best," I tell Miss Midnight Louise, "to alert my Miss Temple to the lethal substances abounding here. She is due back soon, and not getting the message could prove fatal this time."

We are meeting in the rooftop garden to avoid eavesdroppers, but the doggie droppings on the putting green have not been picked up yet and are confusing my sense of smell.

Louise is as frustrated as I am. "I was sure this was the place to find a solid clue. Here we get Ma Barker's clue about a drug dealer named Yellow Oleander, and we are surrounded out here by oleanders of every color *but* yellow."

Not only that, but our color perception is our one attribute not quite up to human levels. We see blue, green and purple quite well, and, luckily, yellow. Red and other warm colors gray out.

"We know oleander is lethal," I say, "but I have never heard of it being imbibed by humans as a recreational drug."

"No," Louise says definitely. (Everything Miss Midnight Louise says is definite.) "Miss Temple's reaction onstage certainly resembled that of a kitten who had gotten an overdose of catnip. She was not as violent as Miss French Vanilla, pummeling the dead guy."

"Was the poison meant to kill, or disable? Anyone near that multi-level set without all of her senses operational could fall to her death."

"Or could get into that condition Miss Temple was in afterwards, which I do not understand at all," Louise says.

"There is something you do not understand? Pray tell me, and I will be able to rise from the turf where I have fallen in shock."

"Sarcasm does not become you. I do not understand the state humans call 'embarrassment'."

"That is a mystery to me also." I think for a moment. "I bet that a dog might know. It could be that is what they are feeling when they lower their ears and look away."

"That is guilt, and equally to be avoided at all costs. I am glad our kind is never reduced to such subservient behaviors, guilt or this embarrassment. I sincerely hope your Miss Temple got over that lapse right away."

"I believe she was talked out of it."

Louise is ready to desert the rooftop. "If we cannot find the right evidence out here, we must try another tack."

"Wait! We have not been using our unique advantage, honed by thousands of years of natural selection."

"And that is...?"

My answer is to run at the chain link fence near the stairs leading to the hotel's service area. Heedless of manicure damage, I hurl myself almost to the top of the six-foot barrier of twisted steel, wrapping my tender toes around the brutal diamond-patterned links.

I crane as much neck as I have. Being an owl or an ostrich would come in handy now. If I was hoping for that field of golden daffodils from the poem, I am out of luck. Gray, aka red or pink, and white oleanders extend from precipitous roof edge to precipitous roof edge.

My weight is pulling my shivs loose, so I only dare take one last look around...and spy a bald spot in the greenery.

"There," I tell Miss Midnight Louise, "on a straight line between the freshest dog doo-doo and the Paris' Eiffel Tower."

"Stop with the crow's nest histrionics," Louise says. "I am not going to catch you if you fall."

By then I have loosened my death grip shiv by shiv and break free of the fence...to land hard on sun-hot asphalt roofing material. With a screech, I make like a pogo stick to get my abused toe pads back to cool green grass.

Louise is waiting for me by the brown signposts. Perhaps stink-posts is the more accurate description.

"Ouch," I say as I rejoin her, but get no sympathy there. She is a hard-case dame.

Gingerly, I lead the way through the maze of potted plants and at last spot some leaves different from the oleander's spiky dark green variety. These leaves are pointed, but broad at the base, and cluster in a star-shape. From their midst rise stately blooms of the color yellow. "Here," I say, and stay.

Louise joins me to examine one bush. "I have seen blue blossoms this large, on the clinging vine called morning glory."

"These are a similar trumpet shape," I explain to Louise, "much admired by humans. This plant matches nothing else here."

"Not exactly accurate, Pops. I ran across a couple pots of cannabis en route."

"Hmm. The marijuana must have been imported, too. The hotel would not allow this. Both came here with the band as a private patch of...recreational drugs...or a murder weapon."

"You are saying this evidence was planted, Pops?"

"And someone may now be wanting to get rid of it ASAP."

"You do not even know what 'it' is." She reaches a dainty toenail to a leaf, but I bat it away.

"Get your mitts off me, Daddy-o."

"No touching! If this is the source of toxic and mentally confusing drugs, we dare not touch it with mouths or mitts. We cannot tote even a single bloom or leaf into the suites area as a clue."

"I hate to admit this," Louise growls softly, "but we need a human to investigate this evil growth."

"First, we need a couple of the Ninja Brigade from the stage area up here to watch this rogue plant. Anyone who comes near it is a pretty solid suspect for something bad—malicious mischief or murder."

Her eyes blink in agreement.

"And," I add, "we must bring the evidence I found discarded in the suites and that you collected to Miss Temple the minute she returns. At least that is mostly safe to handle now, and it will mean more to my roommate than a vegetable clue."

"Even then, she will have to be pretty smart for a human to put our two-and-two together."

"Not to worry. I have been training her for some time. Although the breed is generally not the brightest, rather like the canine, she is a notable exception."

41
"You Naughty Kittens..."

"You have it made," Detective Merry Su declared to Temple, looking around the suite she occupied. "Cool guy with a cool car, cool PR job, cool digs at the classiest hotel in town."

Su turned from examining the room to examining Temple. "Why the hell do you have to trespass on my job?"

"I'm not."

"Not once, but twice."

"What are you talking about?"

"Your going undercover as a teen at the reality TV show where Lieutenant Molina's daughter was a cast member. For the first time in my career, my slight stature was an advantage instead of a joke, and some amateur waltzes in and gets to be Joanie-on-the-spot at a serial murder scene."

Temple took a new look at Detective Su and recalled her usual garb: a plain pantsuit that was a mini-version of Molina's style, only darker and in a size 0. She wore boots like Molina too, only hers had chunky two-inch heels. Her shiny blue-black hair was always pulled into a severe bun at her nape. Despite her small size, Su's all-business attitude would have made her a totally unconvincing teenager, Temple had thought. Now, with Su got up as Suzy Secretary, Temple wasn't so sure.

"I'm sorry about that," Temple said, "and Zoe Chloe Ozone is too."

Su almost stamped a spike heel. *"Argh."*

Temple blinked. It sounded like the preface of a martial arts attack.

"Zoe Chloe Ozone. That airhead false identity of yours," Su said with disgust. "I have no idea how you got away with it."

"Because I did," Temple said gently. "Why don't we move on?"

She eyed the room, hoping any additional bed was in the dressing room area because Su and the chip on her slightly padded shoulder would make an awkward roommate. Temple needed to find something that would solve this case faster than fast.

"There's a huge closet," she told Su. "You can put your things there."

Su hefted her tote bag. "This is it."

"I love tote bags too." Temple smiled, hoping for something in common.

"Alch gave me this. It was left behind at the police station a few years ago."

"Oh. I'll call the maid to make up a bed." *In Outer Mongolia.*

Temple sensed a slight noise at the door to the suite and turned.

Su was in attack stance, legs braced, arms extended, firearm aimed.

"Wait," Temple shouted as the door swung inward…and Midnight Louie dropped his forepaws to the carpeting.

"I shut that door," Su said, not moving an inch.

"It must not have quite snapped closed. Louie instantly detects any door he can get through, and goes there."

Su holstered the big semi-automatic pistol at her tiny back and stalked to the door, examining it and Louie like crime scene evidence.

Then Su addressed Temple. "I'm not waiting here for domestic arrangements to be made or any more twelfth-story cats to break in. I'm going to the common area to get some insight on the members of this murderous has-been band."

She marched out.

Temple phoned Van and begged that a bed be set up for Su…anywhere but in her bedroom. It didn't help that Van agreed, yet signed off with a chuckling remark about "odd bedfellows".

"Louie," Temple told the cat, "I need to solve this murder pronto and get us back to the Circle Ritz."

She'd no sooner spoken than another black cat violated the ajar door. Midnight Louise rocketed inside. She was in flat-out play mode, batting something small around the room like a hockey player punishing a puck, only she'd kill and eat her prey before Bobby Orr ever would.

Louie tore over the main room sofa to jump down and bat the item away from Louise and…under the sofa.

"Oh no, guys. I don't need to chase hockey-playing cats at the moment. Dangerous drugs could by lying around this place, you know."

By now Scotch and Soda had heard the action and had raced in to join the game, growling and snapping in play.

Midnight Louise ran around to the sofa side to paw for the prize, and fight off Soda. Louie was patting under the sofa's rear, using one long black foreleg, then the other…while Scotch sniffed thoroughly at his unguarded rear. Louie turned with a hiss and growl.

"Darn, I don't need this now." Temple got on her knees beside Louie and reached her fingers and forearm under the sofa, patting around for what might be…a dead cockroach shell. That was what it had looked like in motion.

Scotch and Soda transferred their curiosity to Temple's odd actions, sitting behind her, heads and ears cocked. If one of them tried to sniff her raised behind, a major slap-down was in store.

"I swear…" Temple wasn't feeling anything but carpeting, so she got up and grabbed one of the slick magazines set out on the sofa tables. *Hmm. Architectural Digest,* French edition. La-ti-da.

She straightened to call off the dogs. Such orders would do no good with cats.

Scotch and Soda whimpered and backed away. About three inches.

She knelt again and swept the magazine spine in an arc that ended back at her knees. Good thing she didn't wear hose. They'd be shredded by now. Even so, her knees were getting a mild rug burn… *Aha!*

Temple had pushed out into view not one, but two dead bug carapaces. She'd had no idea cockroaches came in décor-matching shells these days. Maybe something Van had arranged in honor of Black & White…

"Huh." Temple examined the parti-colored items in her palm. Nothing to get squeamish about, but strange nevertheless. They were false fingernails. Diva nails. She put them in an ashtray atop the sofa table, and then divan-dived again, moving the magazine's arc farther afield.

She didn't stop until she had ten false fingernails, all found under one large corner of the sectional sofa.

By now Louie and Louise were also sitting back with doglike interest. The cross-species quartet made a snazzy photo op. Too bad. All Temple had now were two handfuls of diva nails in an ashtray.

She struggled up for the last time, and lifted the magazine back to the table, a gesture that had Scotch and Soda backing up, growling. Apparently, they'd had newspaper training. Sitting on the couch, she examined the ashtray stash in her lap.

Yup, an entire set of custom diva nails, which both Nilla and Latty wore. And Sessalee. Temple saw why they'd been tossed. Some of the narrow lengths were twisted. Others were bent and distorted at the tips, and chipped. Some had hairs or fibers clinging to them...

She eyed the cats and dogs, who eyed her back. A huge source of hair, if not fibers. She examined the discarded fingernails again. None had fang marks.

Hairs and fibers, oh my. Hot evidence! Did she have a little something for Detective Su to trot back to Molina for forensic examination. Actually, Temple could use a vacation from Su already.

"This is a ridiculous idea," Su said when Temple presented her with a plastic bag of hard-used false fingernails. "These items have been contaminated by animal saliva anyway, if your theory that the cats or dogs hoarded the disgusting things is correct."

"Dogs excel at collecting disgusting things," Temple said. "And the fibers might be more useful than any DNA-bearing material, and faster to test."

Su's face was stony.

"I'm just guessing about that," Temple added humbly.

"At least it's a fresh plastic baggie. I shouldn't leave you alone."

"I'm surrounded by ankle-biters. You can post a Fontana brother at the door."

Su actually looked interested. "Which one do you prefer?"

"You pick." Temple grinned.

"Fine." Su stowed the baggie in her suit coat side pocket, exactly where Molina carried things. God forbid a female officer should tote a wrist-wallet, much less a purse. "I'll be back."

Temple nodded. Even the dogs may have nodded.

"*Phew,*" Temple said aloud, when the door had shut on Su. "I can enjoy being a girl again for a while."

She left the animals in the living area, and went into the adjoining spa bathroom and dressing room. Last night's hallucigenic antics had fatigued her. Maybe she could manage a long whirlpool bath before Su got back. Things still felt a tad dreamlike.

She sat at the dressing table and looked in the mirror. Mashed red hair. Pale and naked face with her freckles standing out like a rash. *Ouch.* No makeup at the hospital, of course, and the EMTs had wiped off any remainders while treating and transporting her, except for faint eyeliner smudges under her eyes. Great look for a zombie movie.

She reached for the brandy snifter holding the cotton balls and saw the cover was knocked off. Funny, she usually replaced things. She reached for Sessalee's "magic" makeup remover and found her hand in something damp and sticky. *Like blood!* But her palm came away clean.

Temple blinked. The large bottle holding Magic Makeup Remover had been overturned, its clear contents had leaked onto the glass-topped table.

"Louie, have you been rambling up here again while I was gone?" she yelled into the other room, just on principle.

He dashed in and leaped up on her left side, just as Midnight Louise leaped up on Temple's right, bending to sniff at the spilled makeup remover.

Temple's hand with its longish real fingernails pushed Louise away. "That stuff could be bad for you. Did you knock that container over, like Louie did my perfume yesterday?"

Cats! Curiosity wasn't going to kill any cat on *her* watch.

She looked left fast to make sure Louie wasn't into anything he shouldn't be... Darn! He was nosing her perfume bottle again. It was about to fall...! She caught it, and caught a whiff of the strong scent that drew Louie. Kinda luscious, and certainly potent. Matt had sure noticed it.

Scent.

She never wore it.

She'd worn it lavishly last night, as a last, festive touch to an expected evening of watching a dazzling show. French Vanilla used the fragrance regularly. Both women had showed symptoms of LSD-like states. Could a mere perfume cause that?

Temple raised her hands to halo the simple, vertical glass bottle. It wasn't showy like the latest designer fragrance bottles today, which could easily replace one of Elvis' oversized glitzy belt buckles.

Even the label was restrained. "Datura Noir."

Never heard of it.

She bet Google had.

Where was her cell phone when she needed it? Oh, yeah. On the bench at the foot of her bed. Wouldn't fit in her evening bag last night.

She eyed both cats. "Don't move a whisker, don't sniff, and most of all, *don't touch.* I'll be back in the shake of a lion's tail."

She dashed for the bench, happy to see and seize the phone that still lay there, and raced back to the dressing table. The cats had remained statue-still. Sets of green and gold eyes watched her sit and manically punch cell phone buttons with interest.

Datura Noir led her to Fragrantica.com, where she read avidly. *"Datura Noir by Serge Lutens. An Oriental Vanilla fragrance for women launched in 2001. Features coconut, tuberose, tonka bean"*—not sounding so great…ah, better—*"almond, lemon blossom, mandarin orange, musk, Chinese osmanthus, heliotrope, myrrh, vanilla and apricot."*

The foreign words whirled senselessly in Temple's mind. What was a Serge Lutens? Search. Okay, the man who'd invented the Datura Noir scent. Fab site, lots of…black and white…very Art Deco-Asian. Maybe that was why Van had chosen it for French Vanilla's room beside the vanilla scent. Available at high-end retailer Barneys. Temple read through user reviews ranging from rapturous to "meh". Then one review flooded her mind with a more sinister set of words.

Desert flower…large trumpet-shaped blossoms…intoxicating scent… euphoric and hallucinogenic…will draw you in and mess with your head like no other…

Temple switched to searching just for "Datura".

Witches weeds...Deadly Nightshade...Belladonna...Datura, aka Jimsonweed or Stinkweed! Atropine, scopolamine, and hyoscyamine... every part toxic... Causes amnesia...delirium...photophobia...pupil dilation... Shiva...Aztecs...shamans... U.S. young adults...recreational high...deaths.

When Temple looked up from the phone, she saw Midnight Louie watching Midnight Louise, who was daintily patting some cotton balls that had fallen from the container. No. The cover had been off, but she'd seen no loose cotton balls...

"Hey," she told Louise. "Those are used." She picked them up. Sure enough, smudged with her new makeup color palette—purple, teal, and auburn. Temple knew she'd thrown away the cotton balls she'd used with the makeup remover the other day.

These cats must have been raiding the wastepaper baskets in the women's suites for days, hunting toys to bat around. Louie had rounded up some discarded diva nails. Maybe Midnight Louise had snagged something interesting too.

Temple looked more closely at the cotton. Every smidge of color, and there were plenty, shimmered in the daylight...but not nearly as much as the original makeup had *sparkled* in the lamplight of evening.

She gazed at Midnight Louise, who'd settled into licking a paw and running it over her eyes and face again and again and again...washing it.

"You naughty kitten," Temple said. "You lost your mittens. Your new white mittens. And I begin to guess why."

She speed-dialed Molina, eager to reach her before Su got back to headquarters.

"You again," Molina answered.

"Do you have a consulting expert in botany?"

"No."

"What about abnormal psychology?"

"That's the DA's department."

"How about an exotic drug expert?"

"Again, for trials, not investigation."

"A good narc!"

"Not since Dirty Larry, but I can dig up an undercover officer if I have to. Why do I have to? What's this about?"

"Lock down the celebrity suites immediately and get the forensic team in. The entire place is contaminated with a deadly toxin called Datura. It's what got to French Vanilla and me, and enough of it can kill. Su's on her way over with some evidence, so I'm alone here."

"Where are you?"

"In my suite."

"You are not alone with Fontana brothers on the perimeter. I'll text Julio to do the lockdown immediately and send you a bodyguard. Stay put. I mean it."

Temple was staring at her phone's wallpaper. Her heart was beating hard. She shouldn't touch anything. All those scary exotic words still circled in her head.

She finally found a few familiar ones that shocked her even more.

Molina had *Julio* on *text message?* Wasn't he the Fontana brother who'd dared do the lifted-eyebrow duel with her?

O my-oh, me-oh, on the bayou at the Hotel Rio! Some crazy jambalaya was going on in the consenting adults department.

42
Stoli Moments

The Fontana Brothers' takeover had been swift, casual, and creative.

By the time Emilio had extracted Temple and her new baggie of evidence from her suite, the divas had been lured out from their retreats into the common area, where Aldo—suit jacket off, silky designer shirt sleeves rolled up—was making a cocktail shaker with ice chips sound like a maraca.

A new cart had rolled into place next to the regular food and drink buffet. This setup featured exotic bottles of name-brand liquor, manned by brothers at each end.

The excitement had brought Scotch and Soda bounding around, shuffling along the food table for dropped bits.

What a diversion! Viva Fontana Inc. Temple was tickled P.i.n.k. vodka pink.

"The management," Aldo announced, "is debuting Black & White cocktails in honor of you all in the original Black & White. Everyone residing here is present?"

He glanced at Temple for an answer as she did a head count, or a pothead count. Beau Weevil, Spider O'Hara, Lionel Bixby, Doc Dryden. Oh, and Susan Everleigh in her effacing desk corner.

Nilla had her dark sunglasses on, and clung to Latty on the sofa. She was crooning softly to herself, her posture slack again. Her ankles turned out over her platform spikes like those of a preteen girl who'd never worn heels before.

"Sessalee?" Temple asked.

"She doesn't have a bedroom here, but she's in my dressing area," Latty said. "She's moving extra cosmetics to the backstage stand for the show."

Temple eyed Aldo, who eyed Armando, who vanished down the hall to collect the makeup artist.

"This is really clever cross-promo work, Ms. Miz," Big Bix said with a wink at Temple. He leaned over on the sofa to pat Nilla's nearest hand. She jumped with a tiny shriek.

"Spider," she murmured under her breath, shrinking away from Bixby toward Latty.

Where was Molina? Temple thought. *Come on!* Nilla was not going to last much longer. On the other hand, had the doped-up diva unconsciously noticed something off about Bixby? Everyone here was a suspect for something.

Aldo produced a martini glass decorated with embossed black lettering of B&W in an elaborate design, like a crest. Applause came from the boys in the band. Emilio lifted a martini glass with the same design in white. This time the applause was more prolonged.

Then Giuseppe presented a tall glass wider at the mouth with the black and white crests intertwined on both sides.

"For the boyos in the band," Aldo announced, pulling a full glass from the under-cart shelf. "A Guinness Irish stout and French Vanilla ice cream float."

His elevated potion brought hoots of appreciation. The near-black color of the full-bodied, bittersweet iconic British ale provided a black bottom topped by a foamy froth of vanilla ice cream sprinkled with chocolate shavings. This was a manly bar drink with a wink at the soda fountain that women would love.

The brothers busily passed out the glasses to the men of Black & White, who were all muttering "Cheers" at each other.

Temple supposed that getting suspects tipsy might be a whole new trend in crime-solving.

"But," Aldo said, his voice sinking low with drama. "What of the ladies? Have we neglected the Beauty over the Beast?"

Emilio shook his head. "No, we have not. I present the…Chocolatte."

He lifted a filled martini glass from the shelf, a glass layered with shades from bitter dark to sweet milk chocolate to the blackened sugar crystals sparkling around the rim. He moved to Latty, and bowed his brunet head to present the drink.

"The Black Queen," Temple murmured to herself as Latty's black-and-white nails wrapped around the stem.

"And," Armando announced, flourishing another prepared drink from the shelf, "the French Vanilla."

This one was Snow Queen white with a rim of icy, sparkling sugar crystals. Armando noted Nilla's out-of-it state and looked around the room. "Which cocktail would the other ladies prefer?"

Silence could be deadly, but this one emphasized Nilla's eerie cooing.

Susan Everleigh broke the spell, striding forward. "Your brilliant idea, Wondergirl?" she said to Temple. "That's fine. I've had my time. Give me the white one, honey boy. It matches the real color of my hair."

She patted her bottle-blonde hairdo, then wafted the glass out of Armando's hand and bowed to the room before retreating to her desk along the wall. She was done clinging to faux youth.

Denying credit would be too public, Temple realized. So… "What's in the diva cocktails?" she asked Aldo.

"For Chocolatte… Kahlúa, Stolichnaya chocolate vodka, and Bailey's Irish Cream."

"*Hmm.* And the French Vanilla?"

"Vanilla Stolichnaya vodka, Lady Godiva white chocolate liqueur, and white crème de cocoa."

Temple turned to the last woman to arrive in the room. "Sessalee, which are you having?"

Sessalee seemed startled to have been singled out, or even noticed. Her ebony face shone with some suppressed emotion. She hesitated for a too-long time.

"Chocolatte," she said suddenly, as if making a statement, not merely expressing a preference. "The Chocolatte is the one for me." She shot the two divas a glance Temple couldn't read.

Emilio was already holding two other black and white cocktails. Aldo quietly bowed low to put Nilla's drink on the sofa table in front of her. She'd already had too much of something. She wound a fingernail into a coiled silvery curl at her temple and cocked her head at some unseen something.

Temple remembered that feeling all too clearly. *Where was Molina?* she wondered, when a sharp knock on the door was followed by someone entering.

Several someones. Molina, Alch, Su, and more Fontana brothers.

"Stay seated," Molina ordered, "and if you're standing, find a place to sit. We are here to conduct an autopsy on Black & White—the band, the singers, the whole enchilada—and, most of all, the late Cale Watson."

"Can we still drink?" Beau Weevil called out. His Guinness float already had him up in the air.

Molina ignored him and captured Temple's elbow.

With Scotch and Soda milling around their ankles, Molina and company escorted Temple through the nearest door.

It happened to be the hall to the diva bedrooms.

"You have more evidence. Where to now?" Molina asked.

Scotch and Soda schooled around their feet like fuzzy Zebrafish, growling under their breaths.

"To the scene of my crime," Temple said, leading the way to Latty's dressing room, which was, now that Sessalee had been extracted, empty.

Oh, wait. Temple groaned to herself as she took a quick glance around.

Midnight Louie and Midnight Louise were waiting for them.

43
Face Value

"Su," Molina ordered when Temple showed the crowd into Latty's living area.

Detective Merry Su gave Temple a smoldering look and reached into the tote bag over her shoulder. She pulled out one of those magnetic mitts you use to dust furniture. All white and fluffy and fresh now.

And put it on the floor.

It started moving.

Like a Roomba self-automated vacuum cleaner.

The Midnight feline duo immediately swarmed the intruder, which started wagging its tail.

Molina shrugged at Temple's stunned look. "Drug and bomb-sniffing dog. Name of Nose E. Swear to God it's a real dog, trained to be acceptable as a purse pooch at celebrity events. It has stopped would-be terrorists. Do you think it can handle some drugged-out musicians?"

"That would seem to be the skill called for," Temple said.

"Okay." Molina pursed her lips. "Looked up Datura. It's all that you promised it was, and more. I apologize for sending you into this death trap, and your unauthorized 'trip' at my expense. I'm ready to take this place and every Black & White member and associate apart. Why did you want to divert us into this private area?"

"For privacy. I've collected more evidence since, uh, Su rushed back to you with the first batch."

Temple had tried hard to word this so it didn't sound like *she* had *sent* Su back with evidence. Do *not* alienate your LVMPD partner, no matter how reluctant. Susan Everleigh had shown her how to accept unwanted but useful help.

"Let's see it," Molina said.

Temple pulled out the baggie holding the multicolored cotton balls and waved it.

Molina squinted at the item, then asked, "Cotton balls?"

"With my makeup on them."

"Pardon me. I don't think your makeup is a collectible item."

"Well, somebody did. None of you police folk were there to see my big debut on the Black & White stage, just the results, but send in a Fontana brother, if you don't believe me. A couple of black cats were up on the precarious staircase top with me, and one of them had little white paws."

"So? I've read bedtime stories featuring critters like that."

It was disturbing to think of Molina reading bedtime stories to Mariah.

"I know 'skeptical' is your credo," Temple said, "but, remember, I was drugged out of my gourd."

"There *is* recorded evidence of that."

"Why did that happen? How? Why would my black-cat version of the Cheshire Cat—"

"You were hallucinating, seeing these two cats here in the windmill of your mind at the time..."

"No. Everyone said they saw them. Why would one of them pat my face, *one little white paw* after the other?"

"Mariah's cats do that sometimes. When she's been eating tuna fish. Your Midnight Louie here has performed in TV commercials. You should know food scents get cats to perform. You hallucinated the white paws on your black cat."

"I had *not* been eating tuna fish. I *had* recently had my makeup done by an expert, my eyes, my cheeks, all over. In these colors."

Molina opened the baggie.

Nose E erupted in crazed, high-pitched barks, leaping twice his height to reach the bag.

"He's been given the Datura scent?" Temple asked Molina.

"God, yes." The homicide lieutenant stared down at the hysterical dog trying to scale her pant leg and own significant height to reach the baggie now in her custody.

"That proves my makeup was tainted with Datura," Temple said.

"Dogs and cats may be more hypersensitive to smells," Molina turned to tell Temple, "but no way am I accepting at face value any version of events based on what your cats did or you saw or did in your... altered state last night."

She looked around Chocolatte's dressing area. "I assume French Vanilla's area mirrors this layout?"

"Yes. Van would assign them identical quarters, given their feuding pasts."

"Given the feuds in their pasts," Alch said, speaking for the first time and to the point, "a wide-spread toxic attack would disguise a lot of rancor...and maybe a major plot to commit mayhem and murder."

"Exactly," Temple said. "Once I'd realized today how the drug had gotten into my system, I realized only two people could have done it easily, Sessalee Smith and Chocolatte."

"Why them?" Molina asked.

"Sessalee had gone out of her way to promise me a custom evening makeup for the dress rehearsal. I couldn't find her when everyone was preparing for that, but the divas had already been made up. I was near Chocolatte's suite searching for Sessalee when Latty came out. She said Sessalee had mentioned the custom kit for me. She went back to check her spa area and returned a couple of minutes later, saying she'd found the kit. She then applied my makeup herself."

"So, either Sessalee had pre-doctored your makeup or Chocolatte doctored some makeup for you on the spot," Molina said.

"Yes, but why—"

"'Yes, but...' Mariah's favorite opening line." Molina sighed. "Try using something more original."

Temple fell silent. "There's no substitute for 'Yes, but'. I don't know *why* anybody would do that to me."

"To discredit you maybe," Alch said. "Or, someone knew you were snooping around and hoped you'd tumble off that dangerous set and break your neck. One man, Cale Watson, is already dead and was found on that set. And one diva has been on very thin ice on the same set twice already, thanks to her own drugs, or one slipped into her food or makeup."

"Yet," Temple said, "Chocolatte would have no good reason to apply French Vanilla's makeup if she was the one using drugged cosmetics."

"Yes, but..." Molina sighed when she realized she'd fallen into the same trap she'd knocked Temple for using. "Anybody could have prepared Datura-contaminated makeup and planted it on either diva's table. From what you say, the black and white diva makeup palettes were worlds apart."

"French Vanilla wasn't overdosed by accident...unless she's the poisoner and absorbed too much of the Datura by mistake. Apparently not that much of it can do harm."

"The skin and eyes have been used for medication delivery for a couple decades now," Molina said. "Datura is a deadly intoxicant as well a toxin. That the doses used here haven't killed somebody yet means more is going on than the murder."

"Sabotage," Alch said.

Temple was still fixated on the Who over the Why. "Sessalee toted the cosmetics she was using from suite to suite, although the divas had plenty there to use themselves on a daily basis. She wore latex gloves and threw away applicators each time."

"Highly suspicious," said Detective Su, "if she was handling a substance that was toxic on contact."

"Or...good professional hygiene." Temple frowned. "If *Chocolatte* was dosing the creams and powders with Datura, though, she knew Sessalee would never react while applying them."

Su glowered at hearing an alternate theory.

"She'd need a setup for creating powders," Molina said.

"With all the powdered mineral cosmetics today," Temple pointed out, "a WalMart pestle and mortar for cooking could be on any woman's dressing table for blending."

"Powdered mineral makeup?" the lieutenant asked, looking as confused as Alch.

Molina and her daily low-tint lip gloss did not have a clue, Temple thought. Even her Carmen persona only wore dark-red lipstick for gigs.

"After this is over, and if Sessalee *isn't* the culprit," Temple said, "I'm sure Sessa would offer Carmen a makeover, for educational purposes."

Su swallowed a giggle at the look on Molina's face.

"Can we please get back to the poisoner," Molina ordered, no question mark in her tone. "What was the point?"

"To destroy the reunion, or French Vanilla," Temple said.

"Or the Crystal Phoenix," Alch added.

"But why?" Su asked. "Everybody benefited."

"True," Temple said. Su practically glowed to have her rival back up her remark.

"Chocolatte benefited even more than French Vanilla," Temple went on. "I heard Nilla was commercially more successful. She's the one who least needed this reunion."

"So much more reason," Molina said, "for Chocolatte going along and playing nice."

"Unless," Temple said, "Chocolatte had never forgiven Nilla for taking Cale Watson away from her."

"All this is speculation," Molina said. "We need evidence. Detective Su. Put that dog on a leash and take him through every room and up to every person on the twelfth floor, and down to the service and kitchen areas too. Confiscate any targeted substances in any form. Take some Fontana brothers if you need assistance. Do this suite once we've left."

Temple smiled at Detective Su. When she was assigned to Temple as a roommate? *Horrid.* When she was sent off with a hyperactive toy dog and a posse of Fontana brothers to follow up on Temple's clues and deductions? *Sweet.*

Detective Merry Su's parting look at Temple was as poisonous as... well, Datura.

"I hate to say it," Molina told Alch, "but we need to confront the members of this zoo en masse and start chipping away at motives, whereabouts, and alibis. Drug charges are a pretty big club, and we'll have those at least by the bagful."

"Oh, goody," Temple said. "An Agatha Christie-Hercule Poirot suspect smackdown. What a classic way to expose a baddie."

44
In High Cotton

I grab my partner by the scruff of her ruff and yank her into the adjoining walk-in closet for a private chat.

"I must admit that stunt of yours with the cotton balls was pretty, well, ballsy, Louise. They cannot be evidence because they were literally underfoot collecting dirt and maybe even random DNA, but they did help convince Miss Lieutenant C. R. Molina that my Miss Temple was under the influence of some tampered-with topical products."

I examine my partner's petite feet. "You were indeed a 'black bunny' with white forefeet. You buried your fore-shivs in cotton balls."

"Cotton balls that were soaked in Magic Makeup Remover and then covered with Miss Temple's tainted makeup. I was both removing the bad substance and preserving the evidence."

"You put your faith in a mere cosmetic product?"

"Why not? A mere cosmetic product was used as a weapon. Besides every bad deed has a good fairy somewhere with an antidote, Daddy-o."

"I am never going to consider you to be a good fairy."

"*Phfft.* Your Miss Temple must have convinced someone she harbored some clue or evidence about the crimes involving Black & White then and now. I am glad her recent mental 'trip' has not knocked that knowledge clean out of her head."

"During that episode I recalled Mr. Max's amnesia problems and instant messaged an urgent plea to Bast."

"We need to get to the main suite to catch all the fireworks."

"Just a minute. I have been wanting to ask. How did you tumble to my Miss Temple's face paint being doctored?"

"It was after you knocked over Miss French Vanilla's perfume bottle. The scent lingered. When I got close to Miss Temple to try to lure her down from the stage set, I realized her face had the same smell. All of that silly makeup stuff is scented, but not with the trademark perfume from someone else who went catnip-crazy onstage also."

"So you went for the makeup-removing elixir."

"And I had to mimic your 'clumsiness' in knocking over a dressing table bottle."

"It is too bad we had to take a bum rap, but it is not the first time. So how did you manage to navigate all way back from Miss Temple's suite in record time, with the makeup remover-soaked cotton balls curled in your front mitts, and keep them pristine enough to retain their usefulness?"

"First, the hotel maids clean the celebrity suites any time the occupants are away for any length of time. I knew the service elevator would be going up and down like a yoyo when I needed to use it.

"Second, I knew I had to break the Fourth Commandment of our kind's Code of Courtesy and knock over a container or two as if I were a clumsy oaf dog. Getting two cotton balls soaked with spilled remover was easy. Not destroying them on the trip back was hard."

"That would be the rub, yes."

"So I did the Kangaroo Lope with my rear legs and supplemented it with Chimpanzee Run from time to time. I was at full-bore Chimpanzee Run when you saw me coming up the aisle onto the stage."

I know just the moves Miss Midnight Louise employed, relying on her powerful thigh muscles to burn up the distance, like a human runner, but then using her curled fore-mitts to touch ground now and then like springs to move fast, but keep the precious cotton balls as uncontaminated as possible. The Chimp Run is sometimes known among us as the Homo sapiens Knuckle-dragger.

"Then," Louise purrs, "I just had to get Miss Temple to play kissy face with me. Since she was looped out of her mind, she cooperated, even though I was not you, condo gigolo. *Voila,* as they say in the show-cat circles."

"Well done," I must admit. "Every witness took you for a white-mittened interloper at the time. Luckily, Miss Lieutenant Molina was not present and has assumed Miss Temple found the makeup-saturated cotton balls in the normal process of washing her face after she got back from the hospital."

"Now," Louise says, shaking out her ruff. "We must get to the main room to help our allies take Black & White apart to find the killer of Cale Watson."

I must admit she is right.

I am doing way too much mandatory admitting right now, but I have my own bright idea of how we can confront a crook with some irrefutable evidence.

For a happy ending, you cannot touch that.

When Miss Midnight Louise and I return to the main room, we corner the fluffy white canine dust bunny under the buffet tablecloth.

Off duty for now, he is attempting crimes of nasal impairment with some tortilla chips and a rather disgusting vintage of spilled rum and Coke, the drinkable kind.

"Nose E," I say.

"It has been a tense day," he says. "I have been handed over to the Dragon Lady and forced to sniff for pot and related leafy substances until I have developed a condition that requires self-medicating."

"We need one last sniff job done."

"Here. Try my collar. It is inundated with leafy green mayhem."

"Poor boy," Louise coos. "You have been overworked. We need a seasoned nose that only a canine can provide."

"That is suspicious. Your kind claims to despise my native talent."

"Not at all," I say. "Only you can lure these jaded law enforcement types to a seriously illegal and destructive, undercover, mind-bending, paw-corroding, carnivorous vegetable piece of produce called Datura."

"My goodness. That is nasty stuff. I have detected it contaminating a whole range of things today."

"We are talking the actual plant," I say.

Shortly after, we have accessed the sliding glass doors by having Scotch and Soda yammer at them to be opened by human hands hoping to shut them up.

Now we have sprung Nose E on the vegetation without.

Like a bee for a hive, like a hipster for some jive, he is heading for the site Miss Midnight Louise and I identified beforehand.

Of course, our human masters are hot-footing it behind us.

Lo, Nose E heads for and marks, in disgusting doggie fashion, the humble Datura plant, full of trumpet-shaped blooms. All yellow. The dye is cast. The wolf in the sheep flock has been found.

The source is identified and only the Why and the Who remain to be seen.

The Who, of course, is a famous rock band.

45
Planted Evidence

Temple surveyed all of Black & White sitting glumly in the main lounge area.

She had come to know these people, a little, and had some sympathy in her heart for all of them. They had been "huge", and then not. They had endured obscurity, fame, new obscurity, and then being hunted down in humbling circumstances and brought back from the dead.

Her mixed emotions were a consequence of being an undercover agent, aka "rat", she hadn't expected.

Molina's forensic people had bagged and tagged a lot of leafy substances, a bunch of hypodermic needles, and strange little bottles.

The Fontana brothers still guarded the perimeter, but the Party Hearty atmosphere of earlier had left for the coast with Procul Harum. That was an obscure musical reference, Temple knew, but she was channeling eerie, sad songs right now.

French Vanilla, for all her fading lily looks, and Chocolatte, with all her robust diva dignity, still seemed awesome, like the icons they were.

Everybody else looked like a bedraggled bird on a wire.

Temple's gaze passed over the scruffy—Beau Weevil Wilson, Spider O'Hara, Doc Dryden—to the solemn—Big Bix Bixby, Susan Everleigh, said divas, and Sessalee Smith.

Most solemn of all? Molina, Alch, and Su.

Temple? She was the woman in the middle, part nemesis, part victim.

"Look," said Doc Dryden. "You cops don't have warrants to search our premises for drugs."

"We have something better," Alch answered. "We have permission from the hotel owners."

"Still…" Spider O'Hara tossed his dramatic long hair. "We have civil rights."

Molina stepped ahead of her colleagues to take the floor. "We aren't interested in your personal supplies of recreational drugs. In fact, on the whole, your stockpiles are exceedingly bland."

"Bland?" Beau Weevil objected. "Black & White is not a bland band."

"Look, Lieutenant." Grizzled Lionel Bixby leaned forward, elbows on his knees. "We're not kids anymore. We know this is a second chance. The hotel rules were no hard-core illegal drugs. That wasn't difficult to abide by. We're just a bunch of mellow fellows heading toward golden oldies. Our divas may still look like foxes, but women know how to fake it until they make it. Us band guys are too old to blow our last chance on blow."

"I agree, Mr. Bixby," Molina said. "You band guys are all pretty toothless when it comes to possession charges. So, relax. And cooperate. I'm only looking for, and found, one substance, that's not specifically illegal, but if it's used for recreation, it'll kill you before the law can get you anyway."

She glanced at French Vanilla. "You've all seen evidence of its use in your disintegrating diva, and a replay of its lesser effects in the actions of your house PR person, Miss Temple Barr."

"What is this shit?" Beau Weevil muttered to Spider O'Hara, oblivious to being overheard. "Those girls were tripping out on some stuff we never heard of?"

Temple smothered a smile. The band's good ole boys were so jaded they were like newborn infants.

"I'm not here for drugs," Molina said. "I'm here for Keyser Söze."

The weird name and change of topic made for a long silence.

Molina went on. "That was the name of the mysterious master criminal in a film called *The Usual Suspects.*"

O'Hara's arm pumped high. "*Kevin Spacey rocks!*"

"Yes, Mr. O'Hara," Molina said. "You've got it. Keyser Söze was the *most unusual* suspect. Here we have a *most unusual* victim. Cale Watson. A supposed dead man. You all knew him. Some of you may have loved him. Many of you evidently loathed him."

The room remained silent. No denials came, except that French Vanilla started softly singing "Runnin' through the Rain, Gettin' past the pain".

Temple understood why she sang the word "running" instead of "walking". She'd last seen Cale Watson running after her, before she escaped into a world that had found him dead only after more than twenty years.

"And," Molina said, pacing now and coming up short on a perimeter Fontana brother.

Only Temple could see her wink. *Wow.* Which Fontana was that? Julio?

"One of you…" Molina paused, seasoned sadist that she was. "One of you is not who you pretend to be."

The band exchanged glances, having known each other since they used Clearasil acne control. Ultimately, the glances focused in one direction, on one person.

"Su," Molina said, letting her detective step into the limelight.

"My task was to investigate backgrounds."

Temple spotted a lot of shifty eyes among the guys, but one woman held still, like a rabbit in the short grass. Temple winced for the one who'd been caught.

"You." Su marched up to Sessalee Jones. "You are adopted." Su's lack of emotion made it sound like a crime. Maybe in this case it was. "Your true adopted last name is Conover. Your adopted parents think you are working toward a master's degree in Theater Arts in California, but you left UCLA six months ago to follow French Vanilla's and Chocolatte's bands and become a recognizable fan. We checked your tablet computer. You had used the website, OutYourIllegitimateParent.com to trace the woman who had given you up at birth in Detroit."

"That was a dead end. My mother saw to that. She refused to reveal her name so no one could trace her. I had the right to search, but I could never reach her. My adoptive parents had the facility's name and location. The counselors were sympathetic, but could do nothing."

Sessalee smiled. "That's where my deadbeat dad came in handy. He wouldn't stop looking for my mother. He visited the place after my birth, demanded to know if my mother had been there, described her, threw his weight around. Said *Cade Walston* was somebody. He had rights. He looked like a street junkie. They didn't believe him. They said he was mentally off, with a head twitch and garbled words. And anger management issues."

"So how did you know the incident happened?"

"They put a note about it in my file, to warn my adoptive parents. And that information they *would* share."

"We can subpoena records, Miss Conover," Molina said.

"And that garbled name led to Black & White," Detective Su suggested, "which had played Detroit months before your birth, so one of the two divas had to be your..."

Temple was ready for the term "parental unit".

"...birth mother. Did you choose which one as an arbitrary decision, or on evidence, Miss Conover?"

Sessalee was shaking with anger, and something else. "I don't know. What do you think?" she demanded. "Look at my skin color." She doffed her smock sleeve to show a chubby but toned black arm, glitzy and tattooed. "You know something about that, Detective Su. You decide."

Sessalee pointed to the embracing divas. One was so much an absence of everything, color, posture, attention, mind. The other was dark, concentrated, intense. "Did the white woman abandon me to save face for having a black baby, or did the black woman sacrifice me to her career? One of them has been denying it for almost twenty-five years. Who'll ever claim me now? Only someone I'll reject as totally as she did me."

Molina stepped back. Sessalee's righteous passion had every breath in the room held. What had someone in Black & White done?

"Ba-by?" came a wistful voice. "Is that my baby?"

French Vanilla extended a questing, trembling hand. "I've been dreaming of you for so long."

"Oh, shoot," someone else muttered from the background, all choked up.

Probably Beau Weevil, bless his muddled slacker heart.

46
The Mothers of Invention

Molina looked accusingly at Temple, who just shook her head. She'd known and kept Nilla's secret, though she shouldn't have, and now that didn't matter.

It came down to the fact that one of these women was the mother who'd abandoned Sessalee, and either of them could be a murderer.

Nilla lifted an arm to brush off the sunglasses like an annoying lock of hair. Her pupils weren't pinpricks but they were still narrowed. "Reject you for your color? Oh, no, baby," Nilla crooned more than said. "Oh, no. Not you. Never you. *Ihadto. Ihadto.* He was going to make sure you never…were. *Never were.* I had to run, run. He ran. Ran. After me. Ran. Into cars. I ran. No, no. I couldn't keep you. *See you/see you.* Just had to make sure you were there. Hard, they called me. Yes, hard. Very hard. I knew he would never stop running after me. Even if he ran into cars. He would never let me go. *I would never let you go.* But I would have to. I *never* saw you. I couldn't see you and let you go. I never knew your color, baby. And now. No, no. Don't think it for a moment. You are beautiful, perfect…what you should be. You are my baby."

Temple couldn't see, and it wasn't a lingering effect of Datura on her vision. There wasn't the proverbial dry eye in the house. Yet one of those weepy eyes looked through the cold, defensive gaze of a murderer.

"Really?" Sessalee was asking. "You never even saw me? Gave me up unseen? Really? It wasn't how I looked?"

"No, never. Beautiful, you are beautiful. Oh, I'm not myself lately,"

Nilla keened, looking wildly around. "I need to be myself now. Who did this to me? Help me."

Everyone was still shocked into place, and silent.

A sudden motion. Sessalee moved to take Nilla's outstretched hand and sat on her free side, this pairing of black and white together for the first time, after all these years.

Nilla straightened away from Latty to curl herself around Sessalee as silent tears burnished mother's and daughter's faces.

Terrific reunion, Temple thought. Heartbreaking. And yet…neither of this pair was free of suspicion. Both had even *more* motive to kill Cale Watson if he'd suddenly appeared, threatening to ruin lives all over again.

Temple knew Molina would be even more intent on forcing the whole truth to the surface, here and now, when emotions had been ambushed and defenses might be surprised into weakness.

"Sessalee." Molina stepped forward. "When and how did you discover that Cale Watson was probably your father."

She sniffled and collected herself, wiping her wet cheeks. "I listen to oldie rock stations." She gave her mother a wry smile. "Maybe music is in the blood. 'Walkin' in the Rain, Talkin' through the Pain' was one of my favorites. You know how those DJ's on those stations announce biographical tidbits about the singer or the band? I'd looked but never found any Walston. One day I heard Cale Watson mentioned and I heard it like the DJ had said *Cade Walston.* Then he said how Cale Watson had disappeared so long ago. I knew about Chocolatte and French Vanilla being in the same band years ago. Yawn, everybody knew that. I knew about Black & White, but I wasn't a fanatic. That's when I realized that Cale might be my father. I looked up B&W on Wikipedia and found the band split-up was all about the two divas and Cale."

"So," said Su. "You started following Black & White performances, becoming a familiar backstage fan."

Nilla smiled and stroked Sessalee's hand. "One night I pulled off a false nail. I was panicked in the wings, but Sessalee was right there with a little zip bag of cosmetics and eyelash and nail glue. "That's when I noticed her. She was so cute and professional at the same time. I said I owed her for the free nail repair and gave her a dressing room pass."

Temple couldn't help thinking of that Bette Davis film, *All About Eve*, where a clever and ambitious fan worms her way into the Broadway diva's life and takes her friends, her lover, and her role. Was Sessalee faking all this emotion? Had she been gas-lighting Nilla?

"If you felt that rejected by your mother," Molina asked, "didn't you also despise your father?"

"No. I didn't care about my father. I knew it was 'natural' for men like Cale Watson back then in the music business to abandon inconvenient children. I've seen *Dream Girls*. But for mothers to abandon their kids… And I didn't feel rejected until I knew either French Vanilla or Chocolatte was my mother. If it was French Vanilla, I'd know it had to be because I was so very black, like my father. That was why she jettisoned my father and me. My adopted family was black, and beautiful, but an adopted kid always feels rejected from the start."

"What was the point of stalking Black & White?"

"To figure it out. Actually…" Sessalee turned to Latty. "Once I started working for the group, I wanted it to be her, because French Vanilla was so…sweet at first, but then we moved to the hotel and she got moody and screwed up with the constant diva sunglasses and her panic attacks."

Nilla just lowered her eyes and said nothing. Temple couldn't let that go. *I'm not myself. Someone help me.*

"Sessalee, the same thing happened to me dress rehearsal night, for the same reason," Temple said.

If Molina could have kicked her in the shin, she would have. Temple felt a firm grip on her upper arm as she was bodily and not gently moved back.

"I'm asking the questions here, and making any comments," Molina said.

"I gather that Watson's pursuit of his pregnant girlfriend got him nailed in traffic. Su, have Alch check on any traffic accidents seven months before Miss Conover's birth date. He was apparently permanently impaired, or he wouldn't have dropped off the map."

Nilla shuddered. "I didn't mean…"

"Something came together when the media rumors of a Black & White reunion started getting around," Molina said. "The same rumors that attracted Miss Conover dredged up Cale Watson. He came here, to Vegas and this hotel to meet some member of Black & White he'd managed to contact. Was he back to claim a place in the revival? It certainly wasn't to find a child he didn't care about except as a way to manipulate Miss French. Someone here agreed to meet Cale Watson. Any volunteers?"

Molina was pacing again along the row of Black & White members, nailing them all with a fierce glance. "Anyone here who wanted Cale Watson dead more than he or she wanted the Black & White reunion to succeed? Or did that person think that he or she could have it both ways?"

Temple was still wrapping her Datura-swathed head around the on-site vengeful daughter scenario.

"Wait a minute," she said. "If Sessalee was presenting herself as a major fan, wouldn't she maybe be in the Freak Fan file kept on Black & White? Why didn't you cop folk figure that out when you got the suspicious letters and e-mail files to check?"

Molina cocked an eyebrow at Alch, who cocked an eyebrow at Su, who turned on Temple with a glare.

Temple eyed the group in turn. "Didn't," she asked, "you get the Freak Fan file copies from Big Bix?"

"No," they all said. Slowly.

For a big man, he'd been blending into the background with the guys in the band.

"I forgot. Really." Bixby's shrug was sheepish "It's been one crazy crisis after another."

"You're the group historian. You shouldn't have forgotten," Temple said.

"I can tell you that no 'Sessalee Smith' was in there," he said. "I'd remember that first name."

"I wrote fan letters," Sessalee said. "I wanted somebody to notice my name. And you did, Big Bix. You're the one who let me start standing around backstage. You were really cool about it."

Alch had come quietly to stand by Bixby. Everybody stared at the genial band manager, a big man with a lot of weight to throw around. The band people and Temple were looking sad. Everybody liked Big

Bix. Except maybe Cale Watson.

Molina was looking happy. "Watson found more of a welcoming committee here than he wanted. There had been a fist-to-body fight, but Watson's face was also scratched. Scratches like that imply a female. Punches a male. Was it a three-way brawl? We have a set of mangled false fingernails that may not provide usable DNA, and three suspects to match them with, the divas or the angry and abandoned daughter. Or they might simply be routine castaways."

Temple, the professional event manager, was seeing it all now, unfolding like a musical theater's murderous ballet sequence.

"Cale," Temple said, ignoring Molina's rule of silence. "He'd showed up uninvited, visible only to the hall security camera. He came to check out the old cast, the new show, the set. He had bullied someone into meeting with him, but instead encountered someone already there, someone who knew him and didn't want him coming back from the dead to grab a piece of the pie. A band member on the deserted set who saw what damage Watson could do.

"There was a fight, a rough, crude struggle. No one was young anymore. Watson was like a punch-drunk boxer. He'd been on a twenty-some-year concussion jag, not quite tracking. But…the idea of Black & White being hot again sang to his busted synapses.

"They duked it out, like in the old movies. Watson was knocked out. The winner knew he had to get the guy away from there. Maybe find a stage dolly and roll him out the back service area. Pay him off to disappear when he came to, give him drug money. Or…kill him if necessary.

"But…Watson's real contact came along, to find a nice present. The blackmailer laid out cold like the corpse he was supposed to be. A second of improvisation, a fatal needle in the arm—maybe the blackmail victim had brought a fatal heroin dose as a weapon. Then the body was wrestled onto a lowered ceiling unit and hoisted up to be discovered later. Dead guy in the flies. Besides, whoever punched out Watson would take the rap.

"Anyone in Black & White could manage that, through years of backstage tech savvy and drug ingestion. The body, discovered later, would have injuries that could be linked to someone else, bear no trace of the murderer, and boost public interest in the new show. A win-win.

"You like?" Temple asked Molina.

"Excellent supposition, with a few loose ends. The second person on scene has all the hallmarks of being a woman." she said. "Clearly, a PR person had the most at stake in the murder."

Molina was looking at Temple, but every eye in the room slowly fixed on Susan Everleigh. She shook her peroxided hair and started to rise and issue firm denials.

"Easy, Susan," Temple said. "The lieutenant is just kidding."

"No, I am not. The key question is was Cale killed to prevent a ruinous meltdown of the reunited band? Or because somebody hated his guts, and practically everybody did? Was it for love-hate or money? Or both? And what would the person who'd KO'd Watson do when the body was found to be gone?"

"Nibble his or her nails and roll with whatever went down?" Temple suggested.

"You seem to be fixated on fingernails, Miss Barr." Molina turned away from her.

"Lionel Bixby, stand and put your hands behind your back. I'm arresting you for battery on Cale Watson. Alch, take him in and read him his rights."

"Big Bix beat up Cale Watson?" Temple asked, horrified.

"Motive. He was the closest thing to a manager Black & White has," Molina told her. "Opportunity. He was in charge of the show, and had reason to be babysitting that set when Cale showed up. And we never got that box of Freak Fan mail, because it held communications that would lead to Sessalee Conover. Bixby had become as fond of her as his divas and he always kept his divas' secrets. Right?"

Temple and the man himself nodded as Alch snapped the cuffs on him.

"Wait," Temple said, grasping at a striped soda-fountain straw of hope for Big Bix. "You said battery."

Molina nodded.

Then the murderer was still at large.

47
The Uneasy Suspects

"Oh, hell," Beau Weevil said. "There's a second act to this story."

"The first act," Molina said, "was money. Now comes love and hate, and everybody in this room had reason to hate Cale Watson, if only for messing with a good band and career by dropping one diva as a romantic partner for another."

"Now that Miss Barr has laid out her story, I'll unveil mine.

"The most exotic element in this case is the use of Datura." Molina looked around the B&W crew. "Datura is a plant that is totally toxic in every leaf and blossom and seed pod. Some ill-advised druggies have tried to use it recreationally"—here she looked into every evasive male eye—"but it's too unpleasant to be reliable. At the least it can cause nightmares. At the worst hallucinations and death. It has one useful medical application. When you get your eyes dilated at the eye doctor's, a yellow stain is applied. That is a non-toxic derivative of Datura."

"My sight loss!" Nilla said, sitting up. "My confusion. My awful daydreams and worse nightmares. And wait—! Those lovely scent bottles in my rooms…I gave one to…dear little Temple. Oh, my God."

Molina shook her head. "Every possible item in these suites that might conceal Datura has been sampled. It's all over the place, but the perfume is harmless, or it couldn't be marketed. Any consumable—from food to drink—that you could doctor with marijuana, you could lace with Datura. In tea leaves, cigarettes, breakfast, lunch or dinner. Also, it could be ground as fine as cinnamon and added to any topical cream or powder. The skin is a particularly good conductor and so is the eye.

"It can kill, and maybe eventually it would have, but it was intended to kill someone softly, with a song, the siren song of madness. With false accusations of drug use."

Molina stopped in front of the two divas, still sitting with Nilla separating Sessalee and Latty. "Three women, each with a powerful secret. No one but Cale knew French Vanilla had borne a child. No one but Sessalee knew she had a mother in Black & White. No one but Chocolatte knew…what was Chocolatte's secret?"

"I did not have one, ma'am." Latty stood and stretched her arms wide.

"But you have a mortar and pestle hidden in your dressing table. And it's Lieutenant."

"I don't even know what a mortar and pestle is."

"But you do." Sessalee looked up at her. "You nearly bit my head off when I found it and was going to mash up the Shimmer Sienna Seduction powdered eye shadow with the Limelight Green shadow."

"Before the dress rehearsal," Temple asked Sessalee, "I was looking for the special makeup kit you made for me."

"I had it, but Latty needed me to get some new colors she'd found to the backstage makeup area, so I left it with her."

"So what was the point of dosing me?" Temple asked Latty.

Molina knew. "By then Watson was dead and Miss Hooker was interested in making the Datura poisoning a general phenomenon. I notice that Miss French's symptoms have tapered off."

"And my motive?" Latty asked.

"A poisonous, undying hatred of your rival and the man who abandoned you all those years ago," Molina said. "You didn't want Black & White to rise again, you wanted to take French Vanilla down in the most humiliating and public and unrecoverable way."

"I'm not a murderer."

"No, not until Cale Watson became both a danger and a deliciously helpless subject of revenge."

Temple had an objection. "She couldn't have gotten away with one or the other crime very much longer."

"No," Molina agreed. "The means was fiendish, but the method was clumsy. And you don't need to absorb Datura to be mad."

"I *am* mad!" Latty said, her face a ferocious mask. "I've been mad all these decades. And I *did* care about Black & White once, before Cale's lust and Nilla's naïve stupidity ruined all our careers. It was wonderful, delicious to see Nilla tripping out like some second-rate Ophelia. And Cale, he looked like a wasted bum lying there. He was a nothing already. I just finished the job."

"And now," Molina said, "I'll finish mine. Su."

Su marched behind Chocolatte and cuffed her with zest, savoring the exotic names. "I arrest you, Velveedah Hooker, aka Chocolatte, for the murder of Cale Watson."

Molina took over. "You killed him with a fatal injection of heroin while unconscious, and hoisted his body on the mobile unit to be discovered. Wrestling the body into position destroyed your false fingernails, which contain fibers from Watson's clothes. You filched the heroin from Doc Dryden. Nose E found it in his camo bag. That's another arrest attributed to that too cute to be so effective dog." She eyed Temple on the "too cute" phrase. "Mirandize her, Su."

"You didn't tell me half this stuff," Temple hissed at Molina as petite Su marched out the tall diva, and loose lips all over the room started buzzing.

"Neither did you." Molina quirked a Mr. Spock-style interrogatory eyebrow. "So, Temple Barr, PR. How are you going to get this show out of hot water and headlines and en route to Vegas glory, with only one diva left standing?"

"It looks impossible," Temple said, "but I'll think of something."

Molina sighed. "I'm afraid you will."

48
Black and Blue Dahlia

Miss Midnight Louise and I have never formally attended a soirée together.

We both wear formal white tie, despite deep inner objections.

We are both getting our pictures taken with Scotch and Soda in their respective black and white formal ties. Despite deep inner objections.

"We must think of this as good publicity for the firm," I tell Louise, as we perk our ears to match the Scottish lads and the points of our silly ties.

"Maybe we will end up on a carton of cream," she suggests. "That is far tastier and more healthful than the hard liquor the terriers shill for."

"Gourmet cream, I hope. At least we have all ended up alive and kicking at the launch party for Black & White: The Smash."

"You look ridiculous in that white tie, and it is crooked."

"I know! But how can I resist Miss Temple when she is cooing about how handsome I am in formal attire, and I almost lost her the other night."

I give Miss Midnight Louise a sideways glance. "Who sweet-talked you into looking like Ellen DeGeneres hosting the Oscars?"

The hairs along her spine twitch twice. "The Fontana brothers ambushed me on orders from Miss Van von Rhine. It is hard to refuse a Fontana in flattering mode."

"It appears that our festive homicide dick feels the same way."

She glances at Miss Lieutenant Molina. "A female cannot be a 'dick'."

"Oh, I do not know about that," I reply mysteriously, channeling my inner Karma.

In fact, this afternoon the resident, self-proclaimed psychic Birman summoned me to her fifth- floor penthouse suite to inform me there will soon be a radical change in my lifestyle. For this, I risked dulling my manicure climbing the old palm tree? I will believe it when I see it.

"I must admit I am a bit excited," Louise says. "I have never ridden in a Gangsters stretch limo before. They served vanilla ice cream with Kahlúa and white chocolate. And Albino Vampire and Black Russian cocktails, as well as Black & White scotch on the rocks. I and the dogs, of course, had plain cream. Nor have I ever been to the famous Blue Dahlia. The only thing missing is Mr. Max. He did contribute a lot to the stage set."

"Right, he designed those cursed descending Cupcakes of Death that nearly did in my Miss Temple and made a great movable bier for Mr. Cale Watson. Do not let your head be turned by soda fountain treats from the hands of Fontana, Inc., my dear girl."

"And what mind-altering aperitif did your Miss Temple give you, that you would call me 'your dear girl'? That sounds like an admission of paternity, Pater dear."

"It is merely a common expression, not a confession."

I eye the club environment, which I will not admit I am also thrilled to see. When that magenta-and-turquoise neon Blue Dahlia sign reflected in my eyes I felt transported to another, more classy yet primitive time, when my name would have been Spade, Sam Spade.

And Miss Midnight Louise would have been my leggy Gal Friday. Black Friday, get it? A guy can dream.

"Let us," Louise suggests, "tour the premises and eavesdrop on our nearest and dearest humans. They are so amusing to watch when the whole clowder congregates to socialize. They can be surprising, and sometimes surprisingly catty."

I could not agree more, so strike out on my own to supervise my charges at play. Mr. Nicky Fontana and Miss Van von Rhine have rented the entire place for the night. The occasion is the imminent opening of Black & White with French Vanilla: The Smash Hit. We also celebrate Miss Lieutenant C. R. Molina resuming her undercover role as the chanteuse "Carmen", at the special behest of Miss French Vanilla.

I do believe Miss Sessalee has been working her wiles on Miss Carmen, as she so masterfully—mistressfully? I am nothing if I am not politically correct—transformed my Miss Temple. It is a pleasure to see this young lady come into her own as the stage artist she is in her own way, like her mother.

Anyway, Miss Carmen wears a purple silk-velvet gown that once clung to some film femme fatale in the forties. I know, because my Miss Temple had an ever so amusing short silk-velvet frock from the twenties, which I accidentally jumped up on in a playful moment. My shivs made a perfect right-angle tear about the size of a pair of dice, and I heard the lecture of my life on all things silk-velvet and vintage. Which means that I will take out any entity—animal, vegetable or mineral—that should ever threaten said fabric again. And that includes moths, which were already on my hit list anyway.

So, Miss Carmen's gown has me for an anonymous bodyguard tonight.

Anyway, on her silver-sequined platform forties shoes (another no-no for me after I…well, I digress again), and with her diva makeup job etc., Miss Carmen is a knockout.

The Fontana brothers are voting on that with their feet, having brought her an orchid wrist corsage presented with suitable ceremony. Miss Carmen appears to be enjoying their attention as they each visit the small tables of both sitting and standing height that bedeck the room, including hers, with admirable frequency.

Far be it from me to point out that the pattern of tables mimics the arrangement of the Black & White set ceiling units. I attribute this subtle effect to the presence of…Mr. Danny Dove, who looks splendid in a black dinner jacket so becoming to men of a blond coat, although he is not so splendid as Mr. Matt Devine, who is even more becoming in his white dinner jacket, giving the Fontana brothers a run for their reputations.

My Miss Temple has chosen to wear black in my honor. This is not a color I associate with her and it might perhaps be too funereal, given the danger she faced lately. However, she lives up to my native hue, and how!

Even I know this is an adult-rated, sequin-and-bead number from the fifties, strapless, as they say, and body-hugging until the bottom flares out below the knees in a froth of tulle and sequins known as a mermaid skirt.

I happen to know this outfit cost a mint at Leopard Lady vintage re-sale and has been hiding its light, its black light, in the deepest darkest corner of her closet ever since I have known her.

Of course she accessorizes it with my signature black-and-white Stuart Weitzman pavé Austrian crystal shoes.

She is now chatting with her aunt, the former Kit Carlson and current Mrs. Aldo Fontana. Yes, the eldest and youngest of the Fontana clan are now wed and who knows what men in the middle may crumble next?

I am placing my bet on Julio, who has asked a stunned Miss Carmen to dance. The small stage is crowded with the B&W musicians joining the usual three-man band. And the tiny dance floor is open.

Fontana brothers, like a flock of very suave doves in their white dinner jackets, descend on all available females. One snags French Vanilla, who looks happily flattered. I can tell she is telling her partner he is too young for her. Another brother steers a giggling Miss Sessalee French Conover around the tiny space. Aldo sweeps Miss Kit Carlson into a dramatic tango with dips.

It looks like Mr. Matt is the next to dance, as Miss Mariah has cornered him by announcing, "We need to practice for the Dad-Daughter dance at school. I don't know how to do this walking around stuff."

Gracious as always, Mr. Matt casts a look over his shoulder at Miss Temple, but gamely guides the teen menace around the floor, exchanging nods with her mother.

Mr. Rafi Nadir, standing at the sidelines, watches with what Miss Midnight Louise would call a "grumpy" expression. Mr. Matt does not know who Rafi really is, so my Miss Temple sidles up to Mariah's unacknowledged father to comfort him.

"Matt and I will probably be married and moved to Chicago before the Dad-Daughter dance comes up."

"Mariah will expect him to fly back for it," Rafi says with a grim smile.

"You seem to have real rapport with her now."

"I have been locked out of her life for too long. A teenager does not look at a father as anything but someone to rebel against."

"You are helping her live her dream of being a singer. Look at Sessalee, she has finally found her birth mother in her twenties. It is never too late."

"You are an eternal optimist," Mr. Rafi says, smiling down at her. "My life is good now. I guess I can humor my daughter's crush on your fiancé. I do not know if I can take her mama and a Fontana brother hookup. What do you make of that?"

"I love it," Miss Temple says with a Cheshire cat grin. "Beauty and the Beast. The Fontana brother is the Beauty, of course."

Rafi chuckles. "Molina may be hard on you, but she is hard on everyone, herself most of all. I cannot blame the guy. I always knew she cleaned up well out of uniform."

"You are not—?"

"Nah," he says quickly. "That is done. The most important relationship in my future is with my daughter."

I back away, unseen. That is true, what Rafi said, of me too.

This is a sobering thought, so a couple minutes later I sneak up on Miss Temple and Mr. Matt tripping the light fantastic, now that Mariah has become unglued to dance with her father. Very Sweet. You will never see me dancing with my maybe daughter.

Miss Temple and Mr. Matt are doing a sort of waltz two-step that allows not a centimeter of space between them, and I have to move fast and watch my tail because they could tread over a crocodile in their current mushy state, and not even notice it.

"Now I know what 'cloud nine' means," Mr. Matt says, "And you expect me to leave you alone here in that dress to go to my *Midnight Hour* gig?" he is asking. "Are you crazy? What kind of an effective PR arrangement is this?"

"It is very effective if you are panting to come home for three hours," she says. Demurely. Yeah, right.

At this point he presses his cheek to hers to whisper into her ear, so I am once again ignored and kept ignorant. Well, I can see where this scenario is headed. I plan to be faithfully by my Miss Temple's side (and bed) along about three a.m. this morning to gather any headline news.

This romance stuff is a yawner for my kind, though, which handles such matters in a quick and dirty mode that is much less time-consuming, so I slip over to where Mr. Danny Dove is talking with his bosses, Miss Van and Mr. Nicky.

"So," Mr. Nicky says. "You expect a smooth opening."

"Smooth as French Vanilla," Mr. Danny answers. "You know the tabloid and national news on Chocolatte are going to make your show the hottest ticket on the Strip? Nilla had been mentoring an American Idol runner-up, a black woman about Sessalee's age. Pipes like a church organ. We still have our 'Black & White' divas and Sessa's found a soul sister."

"Sounds ideal, but it is *your* show," Miss Van von Rhine tells him. "You are deservedly tops in your field, but we are happy that our little hotel will make you even 'toppier'."

Danny bows and kisses her hand. "Your little hotel is the best place to work in Vegas."

Van smiles at her husband. "I can hardly wait to see what Max Kinsella will do with his own magic show for us."

"I will be there to help him out," Danny vows.

I cannot help but think Mr. Danny Dove might be needed. All right. I will admit it. Like Miss Midnight Louise, I am worried about the absent Mr. Max. He is the odd man out now. I have always sympathized with such fellows, having been one. I wonder where he is tonight. Somewhere warm and comfy, I hope, which is what I would wish for myself.

Still, there is so much juicy eavesdropping to do here...except the seven musicians crowding the stage strike a chord and stop the music.

Mickey "Spider" O'Hara at the mic quiets the wild applause to announce, "Here, in her return engagement at last, is the incomparable... Carmen."

I station myself beside Miss Mariah Molina, a daughter who has been acknowledged by her mother her entire life. Unbeknown to her, her father Rafi Nadir sits beside her, the trusted singing coach whose sudden appearance in her life she is too young and self-absorbed to question.

I know what it is not to know your father's identity. I did not meet Three O'Clock Louie until he retired to Las Vegas. I had encountered my maternal unit, Ma Barker, first. Suddenly, I am struck by comparing Miss Mariah Molina to...Miss Midnight Louise.

This is a bummer of a bad trip. Am I a deadbeat dad? Am I a senior delinquent? Do I have to cozy up to Midnight Louise with apologies and obeisance? I will wait and see how Mr. Rafi Nadir handles it.

Now, I must pay attention to what is going on here and sort out the guilty parties later, even if one of them is...me.

"Mom looks...hot," mini-Molina says. And makes a face. "She is too old for that. What happened to her?"

"She is doing what she was born to do," Rafi says. "We all need to use the left and right sides of our brains."

"You mean she is a mix like Black & White, half cop and half crooner?"

"Yup. I was too," says Rafi, who used to be Blue in the L.A. cop world, and now is in private security.

"You were a cop?" Mariah turns to look at him. This is news to her, and her tone has been denigrating.

She is pushing fourteen and thinks she is a hot number who knows everything, but even I could tell her a thing or two, did I deign to speak to humans, or to youthful humans in the process of becoming human.

"Rafi, did you know Mom? From before?"

"A little." He is watching Miss Carmen take the mic and quiet the crowd with a couple of commanding looks. "I did not really know her before. My loss...and yours, kid. Shut up and listen, for a change."

Mariah looks a bit hurt and maybe she needs to.

Mariah mama's voice comes out over the mic, a Capella at first. I am something of a midnight crooner myself and settle back to listen.

Okay. You are going to have to put your paws on a keyboard and Google "Begin the Beguine", like I did when I heard this was to be the song of the evening. I am talking an iconic Cole Porter song, and this Porter guy was Mr. Piano Man before Billy Joel was even born.

This is a long, complex, soulful song, folks, with a Latin beat and a lot of drama. It is about a love that might have been, and I see a lot of folks here who can relate to that, although most are pretty in sync now.

Miss Ella Fitzgerald did a championship version, and Mr. Frank Sinatra and even Elvis the King sang the song.

Miss Carmen has the low, strong voice to make the song gutsy, not whiny. We are all sitting back, lost in the music, when a crystal-clear soprano joins in and interlaces with the melody and lyrics. French Vanilla, a vision in sequined black and white, moves from the back of the intimate area, serenading the audience as she threads through them to the stage. She even bends to direct a phrase at Miss Midnight Louise and me in our lowly position as "groundlings".

Then she joins Miss Carmen at the mic for a repeat of the last refrain that sets the Blue Dahlia's walls shaking.

There they are a new edition of musical "memories evergreen", as the song says. They are diva and devotee, suspect and cop, mother and mother, and each is singer and song.

One would think this a hard act to follow, but Miss French Vanilla takes the mic.

"I understand that a young singer is in the audience. Maybe she would care to join us for a song. Come on up." She is looking at Molina Jr., who is unmistakably her mother's daughter, not unlike the situation between Miss Midnight Louise and myself.

Miss Mariah Molina throttles an escaping *"Squeee"* to death and accepts Mr. Rafi Nadir's prodding to rise to the occasion.

Breathless, she mounts the stage steps.

"What name will you perform under," Miss French Vanilla asks, making room between herself and Miss Carmen.

I know this is a trick question. I have overhead Miss Temple saying that Miss Mariah was going through the usual "name hate" stage and using "Mari", despite having a nice song about the wind using her name in the title, which was even sung by Mr. Clint Eastwood in an old movie.

So Miss Mariah digs the toe of her peep-toe, baby-pink pump into the black stage floor. "I think I will use one name, like you do," she says, looking from Miss French Vanilla to her mother. "So...just Mariah."

"Mariah Carey will be shakin' in her Jimmy Choos," Miss French Vanilla says. "And what will you sing?"

"Golly. Ah..." She searches out Mr. Rafi Nadir in the audience. He makes a circling motion with his forefinger and puts his hand to his ear. "How about...'Call Me Maybe'."

The band gets going and in no time you have Miss Carmen and Miss French Vanilla jiving like teen queens to back up Miss Maria on a bouncy Bubble Gum hit from a couple years ago.

The audience is jumping and singing along, and even Miss Midnight Louise is tapping her tail, although she denies it afterward.

When all the fence serenading is over and the trio is back in the audience, Miss French Vanilla says, "You have got your mama's music genes, Mariah. How would you like to join my backup singers on weekends?"

Molina Junior's mouth is a maw of amazement. "Can I, can I?" she asks everyone in sight...her mother, her singing coach, my Miss Temple, Mr. Nicky and Miss Van, me... *Me?*

Of course Miss Lieutenant C. R. Molina has suddenly taken over the body of torch singer Carmen and is looking dubious.

"Let her," Mr. Rafi urges.

A Fontana brother steps up beside the now forbidding-looking cop mama. "Of course Gangsters will provide transportation and escort portal to portal, and backstage presence."

Miss Lieutenant Molina turns to go eye-to-eye with him. "I cannot have stretch limos showing up at my door in my neighborhood, Julio."

"We have a *muy bueno* low-rider edition."

"Or stretch anything."

"A pity. Perhaps there is a vehicle readily available that it would be amusing to stretch later, then, like a...Mini Cooper."

"Beyond cool," Mariah shouts then.

I believe what we have here is a done deal. And I am most interested to see that Miss Lieutenant C. R. Molina is perceptive enough to tell one Fontana brother from another and even address one by name.

In fact, Julio is escorting her and Mariah back to their table and doing the chair pulling and pushing routine with both.

Hmm.

I also see that my Miss Temple and Mr. Matt are practically sitting in the same chair, red-gold and yellow heads together, and exchanging confidences that likely have nothing to do with crime or me.

Time to bow out and get home to the king-size bed first.

On my way, I collect Miss Midnight Louise to check out the restaurant's rear, where Ma Barker and the gang are having a catered Midnight Leftovers party arranged by Fontana Inc.

They are feasting on blackened catfish and smoked oysters.

"A decent spread, Louie," Ma Barker says, "with a savory aroma and piquant seasonings, but it does not compare with the crunchy, full-bodied golden nuggets you leave us outside your condo. Keep them coming."

"No sacrifice is too large for you, Ma." I try not to choke on the idea that tasteless army-green kibble is culinary gold to a relative of mine.

Miss Midnight Louise only shakes her head and palms an oyster tidbit before we leave. She has the most versatile mitts in the business, I do believe.

49
First Step: Shoe Up

It was almost three o'clock in the morning. Matt had barely arrived at his Circle Ritz unit when his phone vibrated. Temple texting him to come down to her condo.

She had "a new little something in black and white" to show him.

That was an offer he couldn't refuse, so he took the service stairs at a gallop instead of the slow, and noisy, elevator. No point advertising his night moves to the neighbors.

Temple was waiting in the ajar doorway, wearing one of her fluffy fifties peignoir sets, nightgown and robe, both see-through nylon, but so much of it gathered that the effect was G-rated. At least while it went unexplored.

"This gown is red, not black and white," he said, gathering her and her airy pleats into an embrace, "not that I'm complaining."

"No, you're just being literal. Come into my parlor."

Matt was already there, and looking toward the bedroom.

"Here." Temple almost skipped away to pose like Vanna White by the living room sofa, which was oatmeal beige.

Something black-and-white was perched there, but Midnight Louie was all-black, and the item, while the size of a Scottie dog, was zebra-striped.

"Louie's new carrier." Temple was triumphant. "I went to All-Mart after you left the party for work and bought it."

"That's nice." Matt always got blandly polite when he was puzzled, a habit he was trying to break.

"It's to replace the leopard-pattern one that was destroyed when Louie had his little gangland adventure in Chicago."

"Oh."

"Do you think he'll like it?"

"No more than he liked the last one."

Temple's happy face turned to a frown. "You think so?"

"I mean," Matt said, revised, "this one is the color and pattern of prey, not a competing predator, like the first one. I predict Louie will love it."

"Well, he'll have to, because this is his carrier for our next trip."

"Our next trip? Chicago again?"

"No." Temple tucked the empty carrier over her shoulder, where it looked ridiculous. "Minneapolis, to meet my parents."

"That's thinking ahead."

"Not really, Matt. I want to go as soon as possible, because then we can get married as soon as possible."

"I'd been feeling lately that you weren't in any hurry."

"I'd been feeling the same way about you." Temple dropped the garish carrier onto the sofa seat. "What we have here is a failure to communicate."

"Me. I'm the failure. I let Kathleen blackmail me into playing her mind games, thinking I could humanize her."

"If *you* couldn't humanize her, nobody could." Temple took his hand and led him through one of French doors to the tiny triangular patio that formed a "corner" for the round building.

It had a few potted plants Temple sometimes forgot to water, but mostly it was used for checking out if anyone was in the pool or what cars were in the parking lot.

Tonight Matt's silver Jaguar kept side-by-side company with Temple's red Miata.

Temple leaned her back into him so they could look out together. "I never come out here to see the glow of the Strip," she said, "but there it is. All that neon makes it look like Las Vegas is on fire."

"Beautiful, but the city's magic is tarnished for me. I never dreamed Kathleen O'Connor would turn up at Max's house and lure us there. Some counselor I am. I never dreamed she'd attack us personally."

"She liked to keep a distance between herself and her prey, but she changed that with you. Maybe you changed her."

"For the worse."

"Maybe not." Temple nodded at the farther eave of the balcony's small overhang. Something dangling there caught the light like a miniature mirrored ball. Shiny white surface, soft black sole. Black and white.

Matt bounded to get it down. "Dear God. This is the shoe you wanted to wear to my mother's wedding, that Kathleen stole the mate of and dangled from my balcony roof precisely there, just one floor above, to tell me she was threatening you."

He wanted to climb up to his balcony right now, to see if she'd left any surprise for him. Temple's firm hand on his forearm stopped him.

"Returning that shoe is her signal that she's taken me off her 'endangered species' list."

"She's taunting you."

"No. She's bidding me an unfond farewell. It says 'Bye, girlfriend, I'm done with you.' I've been snubbed as a worthy target."

"It's like she lives to shatter other people's history." Matt shuddered.

"And their futures. Which is why we should fly up to Minnesota ASAP. Decide where and how to get married just as fast—to satisfy us, not various relatives—and move to Chicago."

"I like your thinking, but…I may have blown the Chicago talk show deal. I kept putting them off because of my devil's deal with Kathleen. Everybody and his or her cousin want to host a talk show nowadays."

Temple smiled her inscrutable PR woman smile. "Maybe you just made them more eager." She studied the halo of Strip lights festooning the horizon. "Max must be tempting Kathleen to follow him to Ireland, but I don't want to wait around here to make sure. If the producers no longer want you, we can find other jobs in Chicago…or Minneapolis."

"Start over, you mean." Matt looked around. "I'm still fond of this place and the people in it—despite a few bad memories of Kitty the Cutter."

"We could keep one unit as a vacation place," she said. "You gotta love the Fontana brothers, but I don't need them as neighbors."

Matt started laughing. "You're saying we could just take off and do anything."

"You're still syndicated on the radio. You can do that from anywhere. PR never goes out of fashion. And," Temple said, her voice going tight, "I've given you a 'trial run' long enough when it's against your conscience. Time to make an honest Catholic of you."

"Temple, I don't regret a moment—"

"I do." She really heard herself and laughed. "I regret that I didn't say 'I do' to you a lotta months back. Let's go to Minnesota, do the engaged couple do-si-do with the family, and have a ton of fun finding out what we want to be when we act like eloping teenagers instead of way-too-responsible adults."

Matt picked her up and spun her around. She seemed as light as her filmy attire. "I love it, and I love you, more than I've even dared to let myself feel."

50
Burnt Out

Max awoke at dawn, his legs aching like hell.

He tried to sit up, but his long limbs were all at angles, jammed into something resembling an illusionist's claustrophobic box.

Memory returned in an unpleasant rush. He wasn't crammed into any device of his trade...he was only encased by his Volkswagen Beetle. The small car boasted generous headroom for tall drivers, but it was lousy for sex or sleeping.

Max would be doing neither anymore in the house on Mojave Lane.

He pushed himself into a semblance of sitting, inhaling the stench of smoke before he saw what was left of his house during daylight. It was in worse shape than he was. Collapsed roof, gaping and battered front door barring entrance to a blackened forest of framework.

Kathleen O'Connor's reaction to seeing Revienne visit his house.

He'd arrived home yesterday evening to find five or six neighbors in the front yard trying to dowse the blaze with garden hoses. Water was scarce in the current Vegas drought. The hoses were about as effective as pissing on the house.

Oncoming wails had promised swift professional help, but the structure was already too far gone. Fighting off restraining neighbors who meant well, Max knew he needed and wanted only one thing from that house if he could get it.

He pulled the neck of his knit turtleneck sweater up around his mouth and nose as a mask, took a diver's deep breath, and barged up the walk into the smoke-filled house.

He was lost instantly in smothering heat that sucked the air from his lungs. He only needed to get down the hall to the main room on the right. Thirty feet to go. The upright walls of the maze collapsed as he elbowed them aside. Tangible waves of heat seemed to singe him inside and out. Flames snapped forward to greet him.

In another instant, a bulky helmeted figure the size of Hulk Hogan was wrestling him back the way he'd come and cussing him out.

Outside, Max bent over double, coughing up phlegm and smoke, while EMTs guided him to their truck. But the arms that crossed his assaulted chest also hugged to his body a shield, the smooth metallic case of Gandolph's laptop.

"Man, you're crazy." A fireman shook his helmeted head "I hope what you got out of there was worth the risk."

Max held the computer closer. "Latest important info," he was able to rasp. But the firefighter had turned back to the flames.

His neighbors surrounded him as he was ministered to on the rear bumper of the ambulance. They assured him they had called the fire in as soon as they saw and smelled or heard it. They'd tried to save the house, but couldn't. They were sorry.

Max nodded and expressed thanks over and over. He'd been keeping a low profile here and had never seen most of them, and vice versa. That wasn't unusual in Sunbelt states where dawdling in the hot sun wasn't a daily habit. Max forgot about coping for a few blessed moments and let their sympathy wash over him. He told them he had somewhere to sleep that night.

His ten-yard dash had done no damage. He was free to be…homeless. Later, he watched the ambulance and fire crews leave, after giving the necessary information and no more. Finally alone, he surveyed the smoking ruin from the curb. A total loss. It was insured, of course, but the structure had also housed all his known and not-yet resurfaced memories of his second father, Garry Randolph. Of Garry's magician persona, Gandolph, of the ghost of Orson Welles, himself a magician in more than one way. Max saluted them both.

Then he had curled up as much as six feet four could in the Beetle and waited for morning, trying to sleep. Apparently he had, because his damn cell phone woke him at six a.m. Who the hell—?

Oh. Lieutenant Molina.

"Waking you up from a night of carousing?" her alto voice asked. She didn't apologize.

"Something like that. What's up?"

"I have a report on that party you were interested in, but I don't want to hand it over publicly. Meet you in Sunset Park in twenty minutes?"

"All right…picnic table near the parking lot?"

"Right." She was gone without any wasted words.

Distracted, Max combed a hand through his thick black hair. The silly gelled haircut he'd affected to look different while he went around Vegas was history. His fingers came free, covered with dried goop and ashes.

Great timing, Molina, he thought. Before he found food and a shower, he would find and confront Kathleen O'Connor. He'd been planning on it, and now he might be getting a lead on locating her. And one more reason to do it.

The irony of meeting someone in Sunset Park at dawn wasn't lost to him, numb as he still felt.

Molina was sitting on a picnic table in her summer khaki pants suit, a couple Starbucks takeout cups beside her.

"Thank God," he said, coming up behind her and swooping a cup into his hand.

Her hand had automatically jerked toward the gun at her back waist. "Jeez, Kinsella. Don't do that. Don't sneak up on me."

She turned around to see him fully. "Why do you look like something dragged out of Dumpster?"

Max was pouring the coffee down his throat, rather than drinking it. "House burned down last night," he said, the roof of his mouth already paying for his haste.

He sighed, almost contented.

"The nutcase did that?"

"Most likely. Watcha got?"

She handed over a manila folder that was lying beside her. Inside was a typed form. Max left ash-smudge fingerprints on the folder as he opened it to scan the report.

He mumbled his reactions. "Officer Richardson, bike patrol. Great way to monitor the Strip. Spotted near Paradise numerous times. Interesting. Nothing on last night."

"Officer Richardson turned that in when the day shift ended yesterday. Your house? Burned down last night? Total loss?"

"Total, everything tangible in it and not tangible."

"My God. The moment she found where you lived she breaks in, lures your associates there and Matt Devine ends up shot. Now, she's burned that house down. Arson is a major crime. My people have spotted her, and this latest vendetta makes her even more official police business. We're going to bust her."

She snatched the folder back. "Don't even think of getting there before us. The best thing that could happen for you and yours is to get her into the system, charged and convicted, and doing time."

"Yeah," he said, "but I may not be your most credible witness."

"You agree to let me handle her?" Molina sounded dubious, although that was her default.

"I was planning to leave the country in a day or two anyway."

"Northern Ireland?"

He nodded. "I…had to leave Garry's body behind. I tried to leave it where people who might give him a decent burial would find it. I need to go back and find his final resting place."

Max ran a hand through his hair again, as if hoping his fingers would come out clean this time and this was all a bad dream. They remained gummy.

"You're walking into a nest of old enemies in Northern Ireland," she said. "Don't throw your life away on some sentimental quest."

"Me, sentimental?" Max laughed. "I'm glad we met here. Before and after you catch Kitty the Cutter, maybe you can keep an eye on the Circle Ritz folks."

"I am not your private security company, Kinsella."

"Kathleen may be planning to use them for her next target."

"True. But my actions have to be professionally justified, and… your ex is too damn good at figuring out when something bad is going down."

"Temple up to anything I should know about?"

Molina hesitated. "*Nooo*, only that I'll breathe one giant sigh of relief when's she's married and moved to Chicago. And takes that damn cat with her."

"Me too," Max said cheerfully. That coffee had been super strong. "There is one item that might be left among the ashes of my house. If so, I give you permission to claim it. Actually them."

He loved the look of mystification on her face. When a magician could get a hard case like Molina panting for the final reveal, the payout was sweet. "Garry had a superb wine collection in a stainless steel kitchen vault. It might be safe."

"What would I do with all that wine?"

"Drink it. Or save it until I come back."

"I know why you're going to Ireland. You're hoping to lure Kathleen there after you and away from your Circle Ritz friends. Or should I say, 'charges.'"

"Maybe." He shrugged and jumped down to put the empty coffee cup in a trash bin. "Thanks for breakfast."

Molina got off the picnic table. She took a firm, law enforcement stance, giving him a hard look.

"Kinsella. Are you all right? You're reeling from a lot of losses on every front. Now's not the time to go haring off anywhere. One thing. Revenge always has unforeseen consequences. Can I give you some…" She was momentarily lost for words. "Well, motherly advice?"

Max was stunned. He'd just lost a second father, but he'd never faced what his leaving his family at seventeen might have done to his mother. Molina was right. He was reeling. But he couldn't go home again until he had put "period" to his stalker's obsession and, maybe, life. And, if that last option was necessary, then he'd be a murderer and couldn't go home again anyway.

He shut his eyes on the impossibility of any path he might choose, the risks of the one he had fixed on.

He felt her hand on his shoulder. "Max. When you leave people for their own good, or because your own obsessions have gotten the better of you, they don't always take it as a noble and necessary act. Be careful. You owe it to people you know and love now to come back alive."

He opened his eyes and removed her hand. "Under advisement. And my advice to you? Get your groove back. Knock 'em dead at the

Blue Dahlia. Or knock yourself out with a bottle of Garry Randolph's finest. All work and no play makes a life of regret."

He kissed the top of her hand. "Thanks for the tip and the advice. Ye'll take the high road and I'll take the low road, and I'll get to Kathleen afore ye."

He was striding across the parking lot when she yelled after him.

"That's a damn dumb move, and you're quoting a *Scottish* song, not Irish, Kinsella."

Max chuckled. Trust a singer to know the difference.

51
Black Velvet Band

Max sat at the bar of the Neon Nightmare club, Garry Randolph's laptop beside him. The building was deserted, its entrances and exits boarded up. Some unopened bottles of liquor still stood on the mirrored shelves. Bankruptcy meant dead, and commercially dead in Las Vegas meant totally abandoned.

Luckily, that had not been the case with him. He'd had friends here, from the late Gandolph to Temple Barr and Electra Lark, the Cloaked Conjuror and, oddly, Rafi Nadir. Now, Nicky and Van at the Phoenix. Maybe, on a good day, Lieutenant Molina.

He'd come in through the roof, using the equipment of a magician turned second-story man on a much bigger scale.

He hadn't stopped by the club-like headquarters of the consortium of magicians who called themselves the Synth, but had rappelled straight down to the bar. The last time he'd done a trick like that, the cord had been tampered with and he had slammed into his own image in the black Plexiglas walls.

Max and his reflection were the only residents now. This club's consortium of magicians had slunk to ground somewhere else in Vegas, dodging debt.

Yet he wasn't surprised to hear measured footsteps approaching behind him.

"You stink," a voice said.

"I suppose I do," Max said, turning. "Did you torch the place personally, or hire it out?"

Kathleen O'Conner shrugged. "Maybe. Unlike good Catholics such as you and ex-Father Fabulous, I don't do confession anymore."

"He used to annoy me too," Max said.

She was wearing all black like him. Her clothing wasn't accessorized by the ashes and char he wore from face to foot. He hadn't stopped to look in a mirror, to change clothes, to do anything but dart into the burning house and rescue the one thing most important to him, and meet Molina to confirm Kathleen had gone to ground where he thought she had. The cops wouldn't know about Neon Nightmare.

"Have you been to church?" she mocked.

He was momentarily puzzled, then touched fingertips to his forehead, the first move in making the sign of the cross. They came away gray. "Ah. Ash Wednesday, you mean."

Ash Wednesday preceded Lent, which commemorated Jesus' forty days of prayer and abstinence in the desert, where Satan came to tempt him. Catholics went to church the morning of that Wednesday to wear forehead ashes for all to see until they wore off by evening.

Max rubbed his fingers together. "Just dust and ashes from the fire, Kathleen. We don't need to get grandiose and dogmatic about it."

He tried not to gloat. Molina and the sketch of Kathleen had confirmed she'd been seen in this area. Max merely had to make a show of showing up to draw her out of hiding.

She circled him at a distance, her motorcycle boots echoing on the nightclub's reflective black floor. "I suppose you lost everything. All your magical illusions, all your furniture—that exotic opium bed—and clothes, everything belonging to Garry Randolph."

"You ripped your way through my closet weeks ago. Thanks to my concussion on this very site, and the resulting coma, I had very few memories left of the place. The house had a certain historical interest, having been owned by Orson Welles in his later years, but few people remembered that."

"Orson Welles. Another phony prestidigitator."

"Welles did dabble in magic." Max flourished his fingers and presented a black paper rose. "He had a magic touch with film for quite a while."

"You're suspiciously calm."

"Hysteria won't bring anything back." He set the rose on the bar.

"Are you armed?" she asked.

"You don't want to kill me, Kathleen. That would spoil your fun. Then again, I don't really know how many people you have killed. If any."

She stopped at once, that sinister, stalking beat of steps silenced. "What are you going to do? Buy a new house? You have plenty of money. You'll have more once you start performing at the Crystal Phoenix again."

"Glad to know my fans are following me." He got up and went behind the bar to scrounge a couple of dusty glasses and a bottle of house Irish whiskey.

She moved to the bar, curious. "I'm surprised you stayed in that house once I'd been there. You'd been hiding out in plain sight all these years. Max Kinsella living in a suburb, an aging suburb."

He shrugged. "I knew you'd come calling again." He poured whiskey into the tumblers. "A little dust won't hurt either of us."

Max studied her face for the first time. Transparent tape secured a square of slightly rusty gauze to her left cheek. "A plastic surgeon could erase those nasty cat scratch scars. You need to make sure the wounds don't get infected."

"I didn't know you had an animal act going, like the late, unlamented Shangri-La and her crazy Siamese cat, Hyacinth."

"Shangri-La *is* lamented." Max's voice grew stern despite his wish to keep low-key with her. A man like the Cloaked Conjuror had only one chance of finding a woman who could work with him and live his isolated, guarded life, as Shangri-La had. "She was more than a convenient body double for you. She is deeply mourned. Will you be?"

"Do I care?"

"I'm guessing not." Max sipped the restorative whiskey, surprised this rotgut could take the raw, smoky taste out of his mouth. "It's time we talked. Sit down at the bar, take the weight off your feet."

She did as he said, pulling the second glass close. "Like we did in that park in Belfast."

"Sir Thomas and Lady Dixon Park."

"You remember that?"

"Things are coming back. Roses and camellias and woodland."

She looked at the liquor, but didn't drink.

"I wanted beer, but we drank ale in Belfast," he said.

"Another found, fond memory?"

"It's pretty likely. I remember older and newer bits, not the stuff in the middle. Did you try to kill me here at Neon Nightmare? Did you mess up my bungee cord so I'd crash?"

"No." She smiled. "I didn't have to. I have…have had associates that consider you a danger. Did you kill Santiago?"

Santiago had been her South American partner in amassing cash and guns for the IRA, and probably scammed the cabal of magicians who called themselves the Synth into helping them.

"No." Max considered who really had, a name he'd never give up to anyone, unless he had to. He suddenly understood the attack at the Jailhouse Rock Café. Good thing he was leaving the country.

He'd only turned on the lights over the bar, partly to lure Kathleen out of the darkness, partly because the light board was a mess. Now he could really study her.

He tapped his oldest memories. Lush was the only word for the image of Kathleen that came to mind, waves of thick black hair, skin as smooth as heavy cream, lips full and red. That look might be irresistible, but was fleeting.

Kathleen wore aquamarine-tinted contact lenses now. They didn't distract from the fine lines at her mouth and eyes, the dead-black hair color, maybe colored to cover early gray. She was pushing forty, and had been downsized. The IRA no longer needed a seductress to tease hundreds of thousands out of rich Irishmen in North and South America. Only remnants of the official and unofficial IRA remained, despite pockets of unrest still kicking up in Northern Ireland.

Her day was done.

Max stirred to shift the weight on his legs before he spoke. "I have some ideas about your 'associates', but you've seen to it that I'll be occupied now with other matters than plots in Las Vegas."

"Sean," she said. The satisfaction in her voice made him want to slap her right across that damaged left cheek. Matching her venom would never work. "Sean Kelly." She savored the name to torture him further.

"He was so…Irish. Copper-red curls. Freckles. Hazel-green eyes. So American and openly dazzled. I could have fallen for him if you hadn't been there, if you hadn't seduced me."

"Kathleen. I didn't seduce you. Sean and I were seventeen."

"In Ireland you were men at that age."

"In America, especially in good Catholic America, we were boys, young and stupid and abashed teenage virgins hoping for a make-out session with a pretty girl."

"'Make-out session.'"

"An American expression for kisses and clutches, but nothing more."

"You did more!"

Max looked down into his drink. "I remember the park, so green and leafy and private it seemed like a leprechaun would drop by. Enchanted. I remember leaving it in a daze, all thought of competition blotted out, wanting to see Sean, to apologize…but I knew I couldn't share.

"The pub where we had left him was in ruins, shattered limbs and wood lying about, and the police pushed me away with the crowd. I knew I'd have to tell Sean's parents, and I knew a fury I never guessed could exist.

"And that's all I remember. Now. And maybe then. Until I met up with Garry Randolph and he took me under his wing."

After a silence, she said, "You don't know what it could mean to be Catholic on the Auld Sod."

"I'm afraid I've been told. I know now what you'd been through."

"Do you? That was nothing compared to what you did to me."

"Tell me. Tell me my sins, Kathleen, because I certainly don't remember them."

"First, there was the mortal sin of lying with me."

"I probably confessed that one when I got home with Sean's body, in the parish church, before the funeral was held."

"I confess nothing, not since I escaped those bloody nuns and priests at the Magdalene laundries. Then, after your precious cousin died, you had no time for me. It was 'Who did it', and 'Why did they do it' and 'If I hadn't left him, maybe Sean would still be alive'. Maybe you'd have been dead too, but that never occurred to you."

"That's normal behavior, Kathleen. Sean was like a brother. I was slightly older. I felt responsible. His parents had told me to watch out for him. I said, 'Yeah, sure,' and then I went off and left him alone in place where he'd die, alone. Only…"

"That's why you're here now," she said bitterly, "looking for me. Where's Sean? Where's precious Sean? That ex-priest said you'd thought you might have cared about me, might have…loved me, but you had not a moment for me after that bombing."

Max sipped whiskey. Nobody normal would consider his concentration on the bombing and getting Sean home for burial, and running wild with guilt and thoughts of revenge to the exclusion of all else, abandonment.

He told her all that now, what he remembered, what he pieced together, what Temple had told him, as he must have told her then. He left his family because his aunt and uncle couldn't help thinking it was unfair Michael had survived and not Sean, and wonder why they weren't together.

And Max couldn't, wouldn't say. He'd come back to Ireland to identify the bombers. Instead, he'd attracted too much dangerous attention. That counterterrorism group pulled him into its orbit, first for protection. Then, after he'd IDed the IRA men who'd set the bomb on his own, they'd recruited him to subvert terrorism in Europe.

Michael Aloysius Xavier Kinsella had become the Mystifying Max and, after years of undercover European action, had a chance to "retire" to performing in the U.S. Except the IRA men who craved revenge would never retire.

"I think, Kathleen," he told her, "that you were far more effective at extracting revenge on me than the entire slew of IRA groups put together."

"Thanks."

"You never feel guilt, do you?"

"No. They tried to beat it into me, and into my mother before me, but they never did."

"Why did they keep you as a child, why didn't they send you to an American home for a few thousand dollars?"

"Because my mother resisted them, no matter what they did. I was the spawn of Satan as far as they were concerned. We were too pretty, too much made to lure men into sin, all we girls and women in the laundries. We were worked to early deaths and thrown into unmarked graves. I helped dig some of them."

"How could you escape the breaking of your health, even if they couldn't break your will?"

"Because bloody"—she paused to scream the obscenity that exactly described the indecent act—"Father Donovan didn't want me marked for my penance sessions with him."

Max leaned back as if he'd been slapped. Such hypocrisy was epic, the brutality incomprehensible. "Until you got pregnant."

"Then the nuns were at me, how did that happen, you sinful girl? You must have sneaked out. We can't trust you alone for a moment."

"Your mother?"

"In the ground of the back garden, feeding the nuns who killed her."

"And you escaped. How?"

"I pretended to be sick of childbed fever and begged for Father Donovan to come and hear my confession. Then I hit him on the head with a bedpan and snuck out because the nuns were accustomed to leaving us alone together and not watching."

"They couldn't have been that naïve."

"There was God and there was Father and there were the nuns, and nobody could disobey all down the line."

"You took your child with you?"

"I'd leave no girl infant in that hellhole. By then there was a group against the laundries. They promised to find her a decent home and watch her through the years."

"So, child-free, you joined the IRA because you had a taste for manipulating men in your own turn, specializing in seduction for gun money. Victims of abuse crave control."

"Here's the truth of it, Max Kinsella. I've slept with enough gullible and despicable men to earn millions for the IRA, but I wouldn't sleep with you again to damn my soul."

"You hated that I felt guilty about Sean's death."

"I was sick of your bloody guilt over your cousin. I hated that you ruined a time when I thought…well, it was all blarney, you just a boy or not. A girl is there only to be used. And now you'll be hurrying back to Ireland to look for sainted Sean, and you'll have a devil's time of finding Fact One about that bombing or any trace of him. I know. He may not have died, but he disappeared. So good luck to you. You'll be sleeping with guilt for the rest of your life."

"You know a person who feels nothing ordinary people do…guilt, sorrow, empathy…is a psychopath, don't you, Kathleen?"

"And proud of it."

Max slid the slim silver-cased laptop in front of him and opened it. All he had left of Gandolph was on this hard drive.

"You can't use that in here," she said. "No wifi."

"Luckily, ye old Neon Nightmare was not only a hot spot for night-clubbing, but I can create a hot spot here. I was able to save Gandolph's computer. It contains photos of our last visit to Northern Ireland, where he was murdered."

"And now his house is dead too."

He ignored her hateful jibe and turned the screen so she could see the green, green grass of her homeland. Of his ancestors' homeland, from which they had been driven like starved, abandoned beasts.

"Very pretty," Kathleen said in an ugly tone.

He showed her the narrow cobble-stoned streets of Belfast, the fiery red facade of the Temple Bar pub. That photo caused a tic in her left cheek.

Next came shots inside and outside the pub. Irish folk in tweed caps, then outside, children with red cheeks, a closeup of a lovely colleen with black hair and rosy lips.

Kathleen's face twisted to see that fresh, unmarked face. "You've lost the redhead to a bloody holy eunuch," she told him, "and the blonde looks to be a loss, so now you've got your eye on a brunette half your age?"

He turned the image around and smiled at it. "Oh, I don't think I've got quite that many years on her. Actually, I've never met the lady, but I thought that you might like to. She's your daughter."

"My daughter? You're lying. She can't be found, ever. I saw to that, and I don't ever want to see her."

"Too late." He flourished the image again.

It was striking how alike they were. Like sisters, almost twins. Kathleen must have been obscenely young when the priest impregnated her, probably as soon as it was physically possible. How to make a monster: be a monster. And no birth control allowed, no, that would have been a sin...

Her cheek was twitching again. "What do you want?"

"Will you join me in a road trip back to Ireland, back to Belfast, on a quest to recover old memories?"

"You just want to lure me away from your friends here in Vegas."

"Maybe, but they aren't easy pickings now, with all those Fontana brothers hanging out at the Circle Ritz, cluttering up the place. Along with a lot of black cats."

She touched her cheek. "You want to look for your bloody cousin Sean."

"To find my cousin Sean. That too."

"Again, it's all about Sean."

"Not totally. I saw an abandoned Magdalene laundry. It will take guts to go home again, Kathleen."

"That sodding old song again! 'I'll Take You Home Again, Kathleen'. Do you know how many years ago I got sick of hearing that from the boyos in the IRA?"

"No, but you can tell me on our jaunt to Northern Ireland."

"I can slip a knife between your ribs as sweet as through butter on our jaunt to Ireland too."

"Braggart."

"You could kill me over there and end it."

"I don't kill people. I protect people from getting killed."

"Your problem."

She pouted those once-rosy lips, now pinched and bloodless with bitterness. "You think I'd follow you anywhere."

"You already have." He raised his eyebrows and produced an inquiring look, realizing only then that was the Tom Selleck *Magnum, PI* shtick that made the actor famous long, long ago.

She laughed despite herself.

A bit of the brogue salted her voice. "You have a nerve on you, Max

Kinsella."

She sounded like his Kinsella grandmother, spry at ninety and with many memories of the Auld Country.

He remembered another of the old songs his granny used to sing under her breath while embroidering pillowcases, those old songs of sorrow and struggle that had made him love Ireland and fight for her unseen until he could get himself there at seventeen.

> *Well, in a neat little town they call Belfast,*
> *apprentice to trade I was bound.*
> *Many an hour's sweet happiness,*
> *have I spent in that neat little town.*
>
> *A sad misfortune came over me,*
> *which caused me to stray from the land,*
> *Far away from my friends and relations,*
> *betrayed by the black velvet band.*
>
> *Her eyes they shone like diamonds.*
> *I thought her the queen of the land.*
> *And her hair, it hung over her shoulder,*
> *Tied up with a black velvet band.*

52
La Vida Louie

Some people have sit-ins when they want to protest some appalling situation.

Some of my breed have sit-outs.

That is how I happen to be concealed in the dark of night behind a large pot holding a more than somewhat stringy Desert Marigold plant. Given the major role plant life played in my latest case, this is appropriate.

What is not appropriate is what I overhear.

I do not refer to all the mushy stuff that makes me flatten my ears in an attempt to block it. There should be a v-chip so four-footed domestic cohabitators are not exposed to such human sentiments and resulting activities, which render the community bedroom useless for far too long.

I notice that, aside from the hideous zebra-striped carrier I would not allow even a hairball of mine to enter, no mention is made of how *I* would like to get a fresh start, and where.

Frankly, it takes a lot of city to hold Midnight Louie. I have only deigned to visit the Big Apple and Chi-town earlier because of their suitably sophisticated and global rep as happening places.

Minneapolis will not cut it.

For the first time, it occurs to me that my happy domestic scene is in danger. They do not even consider that I could hold down the home place here at the Circle Ritz on my own while they seek a happy ever after in some mild (as opposed to wild like Vegas), cold, and boring clime.

I will lose some of my reason-deux-etre if I do not have my little doll to look after, but she appears to plan return visits, at least.

I tell you, it had never occurred to me, during all the dangers we have been through, that she would find a human forever-housemate. That is just not my lifestyle. Mr. Max was more my speed, with his come-and-go ways and habit of totally disappearing for months. I was always there to comfort my Miss Temple when his fate was unknown. Mr. Matt will not be providing me that opportunity now, being the settle-down type.

I remain on the balcony lamenting the changes being foisted upon me by something as unimportant as human hormones when the fronds of the big palm tree in the parking lot tremble.

I look up with distaste. I am not in the mood for words of wisdom from the resident New Ager, Karma the Sacred Cat of Burma, and probably Bermuda, for all I know.

I discover no higher plane is speaking to me, thank Bast!

However, I also discover I am not alone.

Miss Midnight Louise has taken my private path up the palm tree trunk to *thunk* down onto the balcony beside me.

Ordinarily, I would take umbrage at trespassers, but my umbrage has picked up and gone for the moment.

"There is still a Fontana brother or two around the place," she notes, "according to the wheels parked outside. Miss Electra Lark seems to have taken a shine to Italian cuisine. Do not worry, Pop. I am sure you will be happy living La Vida Fontana."

Tailpiece: Midnight Louie Has The Last Word

Now that we are past the Y word, I know all of my faithful readers are a-Twitter over the looming end of my alphabetical adventures, the Z book.

Me too.

Rest assured that I will do my best to ensure that the dreadful zebra-print carrier plays no role at all in my further adventures.

I myself am not a-Twitter because I leave tweeting to my feathered friends and onetime meal partners before I had access to a refrigerator. Also, I have inside information and can assure you all that Z will not be the last book in the series.

I insisted on this personally, because there are loose ends to tie up and I do not trust the human cast to behave well enough to do so on their own.

They have shown no signs of doing that previously.

So the last installment will be *Cat in an Alphabet Endgame,* definitely an ending title and a nice "bookend" for the renamed first book, *Cat in an Alphabet Soup* (formerly *Catnap*).

As for the title sequence of my next series, several of you have offered darned good suggestions. One was that the titles work their way through the alphabet again with double A, B, C words etc. That has already been blown by Miss Carole when she did the Diamond Dazzle, Emerald Eye, Flamingo Fedora, Golden Garland, Hyacinth Hunt sequence.

And, truth to tell, my Miss Carole blew it from the first. After writing *Catnap* and seeing the Jim Dandy detective I was, she decided my exploits needed to continue. Determined to be original, she had planned the rest of my titles to avoid copycatting the titles of any other feline mysteries out there. So she titled the second book *Pussyfoot*.

The publisher's sales force squealed like a little mouse that roared and said only "Cat" in the title would sell well. (I could have told them and Miss Carole that.)

Then came the search for a non-imitative title format. Fatigued, Miss Carole submitted endless variations on dramatist Tennessee Williams' *Cat on a Hot Tin Roof* pattern. *Cat up a Tree, Cat down a Well,* etc.

Cat on a Blue Tuesday caught the top editor's eye, and he made it the more predictable Blue Monday.

Miss Carole also noticed that Blue was only two letters along in the alphabet and, now clued in that I was not a one-book wonder, decided to continue the alphabet on the titles' "color" words.

She also really wanted readers to know how to read the series in order, since it was forbidden to number books in mystery series, as fantasy series do. When readers caught on to the interior title alphabet, she figured that would be another little "mystery" they solved.

Miss Carole is all about big mysteries and little mysteries in her books. Since I am all about solving them, we make a good team and plan to continue to the last word.

Very Best Fishes,

Midnight Louie, Esq.

If you'd like get Midnight Louie's *Scratching Post-Intelligencer* newsletter or information on his custom T-shirt, contact Louie and Carole Nelson Douglas at PO BOX 33155, Fort Worth, TX, 76163-1555 or sign up at the website, www.carolenelsondouglas.com. E-mail: cdouglas@catwriter.com

Tailpiece: Carole Nelson Douglas Muses on This and Cat

Growing up in Minnesota, with its three percent minority population at the time, I knew the mixed-race couple on our block was a rarity. For years, I watched the little boy, who looked white, walk to the nearby well-regarded public grade school. And I watched his older sister, who looked black, wait on a nearby corner for a bus to take her to some other school who-knows-where. And I wondered what that does to a family. And a block.

On a lighter note, it's all in the details. Scotch and Soda entered the fictional scene when I thought Louie could use some animal assistance in the band's celebrity suites. The canine mascots of Black & White scotch were obvious candidates for the job. That brand is no longer sold in the U.S., but is available in Britain. Even the Scottish terrier breed is not as popular as the Westie now. Times and fashions change, but I hope the doughty black "Scottie" sees a resurgence.

Revienne Schneider's distinctive name was inspired by a fragrance, although I'm allergic to scent and never use it. During a group college trip to Europe, we visited a Paris perfumery. I tried everything. One fragrance outshone the rest. Oddly, Je Reviens was invented by the House of Worth, founded in the nineteenth century by the first French couturier. English-born Charles Frederick Worth's amazing rise from stock boy to pioneering Paris couturier (with the help of his wife) figures in my fourth Irene Adler novel, *Another Scandal in Bohemia*.

Since Art Nouveau and Art Deco are my favorite decorative art periods, I was delighted to learn that the House of Worth created the Je Reviens scent in 1932 and sold it in a blue crystal bottle designed by René Lalique. If you simply must have Datura Noir—and there are rumors it may be discontinued—you can buy it online, and can also visit the SergeLutens.com site.

I invented the protagonist's first name in my first novel, *One Faithful Harp*, set in, yes, 1893 Ireland. I'm not Irish, but I've always been drawn to Ireland. The publisher liked her name so much they changed my title, *Amberleigh*. (And they liked the name-turned-title so much they soon after named someone else's historical novel *Camberleigh*, after a manor house.) I was still working as a journalist when *Amberleigh* came out, and heard a new mother in another newspaper department named her baby Amberleigh. (That baby may have cursed my invention later and now goes by plain "Amber", which wasn't the popular name then that it is today.)

Perhaps someone will have the first name of Revienne someday, and enjoy being unique.

Speaking of unique, our eldest cat, a Tortie found on a neighbor's roof fourteen years ago, is named…Amberleigh.

Midnight Louie Mysteries

The Bestselling MIDNIGHT LOUIE Feline PI series

"just about everything you might want in a mystery; among other things, glitzy Las Vegas…real characters, suspense, a tough puzzle… On top of it all, a fine sense of humor and some illuminating social commentary." —*The Prime Suspect*

"Las Vegas' feline detective extraordinary returns…an excellent follow-up…and Louie is an irresistible combination of Nathan Detroit and Sam Spade. There is plenty of interest here for a lengthy, fun-filled series." —*Mostly Murder*

Cat in an Alphabet Soup [formerly Catnap]…Cat in an Aqua Storm [formerly Pussyfoot]…Cat on a Blue Monday…Cat in a Crimson Haze…Cat in a Diamond Dazzle…Cat with an Emerald Eye…Cat in a Flamingo Fedora…Cat in a Golden Garland…Cat on a Hyacinth Hunt…Cat in an Indigo Mood…Cat in a Jeweled Jumpsuit…Cat in a Kiwi Con…Cat in a Leopard Spot…Cat in a Midnight Choir…Cat in a Neon Nightmare…Cat in an Orange Twist…Cat in a Hot Pink Pursuit…Cat in a Quicksilver Caper…Cat in a Red Hot Rage…Cat in a Sapphire Slipper…Cat in a Topaz Tango…Cat in an Ultramarine Scheme… Cat in a Vegas Gold Vendetta…Cat in a White Tie and Tails…Cat in an Alien X-Ray…Cat in a Yellow Spotlight…(forthcoming) *Cat in a Zebra Zoot Suit…Cat in an Alphabet Endgame*

ABOUT THE AUTHOR

www.carolenelsondouglas.com
www.wishlistpublishing.com

CAROLE NELSON DOUGLAS is the award-winning author of sixty novels in the science fiction/fantasy, mystery/thriller, and women's fiction genres.

She currently writes the long-running Midnight Louie feline PI, cozy-noir mystery series (*Cat in an Alphabet Soup, Cat in an Aqua Storm, Cat on a Blue Monday,* etc.) and the Delilah Street, Paranormal Investigator, noir urban fantasy series (*Dancing with Werewolves,* etc.). Both series are set in imaginative variations of Las Vegas. Midnight Louie is a "Sam Spade with hairballs" who prowls the "slightly surreal" Vegas of today, narrating his own interlarded chapters in his alley-cat noir voice. Delilah walks the mean streets of a paranormally post-apocalyptic Sin City, fighting supernatural mobsters with wile, wit and grit.

Douglas was the first author to make a Sherlockian female character, Irene Adler, a series protagonist, with the *New York Times* Notable Book of the Year, *Good Night, Mr. Holmes.* Her award nominations run from the Agatha to the Nebula. She has won Lifetime Achievement

Awards from *RT Book Reviews* for Mystery, Suspense and Versatility, and was named a Pioneer of Publishing. Her Midnight Louie novels and stories have also won multiple Cat Writers' Association first-place Muse Medallions.

An award-winning daily newspaper reporter, feature writer and editor in Minnesota, she moved to the Sunbelt to write fiction fulltime and was recently inducted into the Texas Literary Hall of Fame.

35831004R00195

Made in the USA
Lexington, KY
25 September 2014